NEBULA AWARDS SHOWCASE 57

NEBULA AWARDS SHOWCASE 57

The Year's Best Science Fiction and Fantasy

EDITED BY

STEPHEN KOTOWYCH

2021 NEBULA AWARDS®

Presented online on May 21, 2022

Best Novel

The Unbroken by C. L. Clark, published by *Orbit US* and *Orbit UK*

★ **Winner:** *A Master of Djinn* by P. Djèlí Clark, published by *Tordotcom* and *Orbit UK*

Machinehood by S.B. Divya, published by *Saga*

Plague Birds by Jason Sanford, published by *Apex*

A Desolation Called Peace by Arkady Martine, published by *Tor* and *Tor UK*

Best Novella

Fireheart Tiger by Aliette de Bodard, published by *Tordotcom*

A Psalm for the Wild-Built by Becky Chambers, published by *Tordotcom*

★ **Winner:** *And What Can We Offer You Tonight* by Premee Mohamed, published by *Neon Hemlock*

Sun-Daughters, Sea-Daughters by Aimee Ogden, published by *Tordotcom*

Flowers for the Sea by Zin E. Rocklyn, published by *Tordotcom*

The Necessity of Stars by E. Catherine Tobler, published by *Neon Hemlock*

"The Giants of the Violet Sea" by Eugenia Triantafyllou, published by *Uncanny*

Best Novelette

"Just Enough Rain" by P.H. Lee, published by *GigaNotoSaurus*

★ **Winner:** "O2 Arena" by Oghenechovwe Donald Ekpeki, published by *Galaxy's Edge*

"(emet)" by Lauren Ring, published by *Fantasy & Science Fiction*

"That Story Isn't the Story" by John Wiswell, published by *Uncanny Magazine*

"Colors of the Immortal Palette" by Caroline M. Yoachim, published by *Uncanny Magazine*

Best Short Story

"Mr. Death" by Alix E. Harrow, published by *Apex Magazine*

"Proof by Induction" by José Pablo Iriarte, published by *Uncanny Magazine*

"Let All the Children Boogie" by Sam J. Miller, published by *Tor.com*

"Laughter Among the Trees" by Suzan Palumbo, published by *The Dark*

★ **Winner:** "Where Oaken Hearts Do Gather" by Sarah Pinsker, published by *Uncanny Magazine*

"For Lack of a Bed" by John Wiswell, published by *Diabolical Plots*

Andre Norton Nebula Award for Middle Grade and Young Adult Fiction

Victories Greater Than Death by Charlie Jane Anders, published by *Tor Teen* and *Titan*

Thornwood by Leah Cypess, published by *Delacorte*

Redemptor by Jordan Ifueko, published by *Amulet* and *Hot Key*

★ **Winner:** *A Snake Falls to Earth* by Darcie Little Badger, published by *Levine Querido*

Iron Widow by Greg van Eekhout by Xiran Jay Zhao, published by *Penguin Teen* and *Rock the Boat*

Ray Bradbury Nebula Award for Outstanding Dramatic Presentation

Loki: Season 1 written by Bisha K. Ali, Elissa Karasik, Eric Martin, Michael Waldron, Tom Kauffman, and Jess Dweck (Marvel Studios)

What We Do in the Shadows: Season 3 written by Jake Bender, Zach Dunn, Shana Gohd, Sam Johnson, Chris Marcil, William Meny, Sarah Naftalis, Stefani Robinson, Marika Sawyer, Paul Simms, and Lauren Wells (FX Productions, Two Canoes Pictures, 343 Incorporated, and FX Network)

Shang-Chi and the Legend of the Ten Rings written by Dave Callaham, Destin Daniel Cretton, and Andrew Lanham (Walt Disney Pictures and Marvel Studios)

★ **Winner:** *WandaVision: Season 1* written by by Peter Cameron, Mackenzie Dohr, Laura Donney, Bobak Esfarjani, Megan McDonnell, Jac Schaeffer, Cameron Squires, Gretchen Enders, and Chuck Hayward (Marvel Studios)

Encanto written by Charise Castro Smith, Jared Bush, Byron Howard, Jason Hand, Nancy Kruse, and Lin-Manuel Miranda (Walt Disney Animation Studios and Walt Disney Pictures)

Space Sweepers written by Jo Sung-hee 조성희
(Bidangil Pictures)

The Green Knight written by David Lowery
(Sailor Bear, BRON Studios, and A24)

Best Game Writing

Coyote & Crow by William McKay, Weyodi Oldbear, Derek Pounds, Nico Albert, Riana Elliott, Diogo Nogueira, and William Thompson, published by *Coyote & Crow, LLC*

Wildermyth by Nate Austin, Anne Austin, and Douglas Austin, published by *Worldwalker Games, LLC*

Wanderhome by Jay Dragon, published by *Possum Creek Games*

Granma's Hand by Balogun Ojetade, published by *Balogun Ojetade* and *Roaring Lion Productions*

★ **Winner:** *Thirsty Sword Lesbians* by April Kit Walsh, Dominique Dickey, Jonaya Kemper, Alexis Sara, Rae Nedjadi, and Whitney Delaglio, published by *Evil Hat Productions*

Other Awards

Damon Knight Grand Master Award
Mercedes Lackey

Kate Wilhelm Solstice Award
Petra Mayer
Troy L. Wiggins
Arley Sorg

Kevin O'Donnell, Jr. Service to SFWA Award
Colin Coyle

TABLE OF CONTENTS

SHORT STORIES

WHERE OAKEN HEARTS DO GATHER

Sarah Pinsker

About "Where Oaken Hearts Do Gather" (5 contributors, 5 notes, 7 comments)

▶ "Where Oaken Hearts Do Gather" (Roud 423, Child 313) is a traditional English folk ballad. Like many traditional songs, the lyrics are unattributed. Child transcribed twenty verses, and a twenty-first got added later (and is included here for some unknown reason—I keep writing to the Lyricsplainer mods to get someone to delete it or include it as a separate entry, but nobody responds, and all they've done is put brackets around it. Sometimes I hate this site.) Most modern recordings pick and choose verses and include far fewer than the full twenty. There are several variant titles, and the characters' names shift through the various broadsides and folk and rock versions. –*BonnieLass67* (<u>11 upvotes</u>)

▶ The song has also been passed down as "Fair Ellen," "Ellen and William," and "Sweet William's Heart." There's a distant cousin in the ballad "Robin Hood and the Waking Wood," which changes William to Robin Hood and gives him a revenge arc; that one has always struck me as a derivative corruption, though it wasn't the first to steal someone else's narrative and give it to Robin Hood. –*BonnieLass67* (<u>7 upvotes</u>)

▶ It was documented in John and Alan Lomax's 1934 book American Ballads and Folk Songs as "While Oaken Sisters Watched," with a number of changes and Americanizations. In modern times, the ballad (or its variants) has been recorded or played live by artists as varied as Joan Baez, the Grateful Dead, the Kingston Trio, Windhollow Faire, Dolly Parton, Jack White, and Metallica. The verses each chose, and the order they chose to sing them, change the meaning of the song. –*BonnieLass67* (<u>6 upvotes</u>)
> Have you heard the abomination that was on Idol? Some finalist butchered it as "Where Broken Hearts Do Gather." –*HolyGreil*
> If we don't speak of that I can pretend it doesn't exist. –*BonnieLass67*

▶ This song, included among the famous ballads documented by Francis James Child, is an allegorical tale of a tryst between two lovers and its aftermath. –*Dynamum* (2 upvotes, 1 downvote)

> That's awfully reductive, and I'm not sure what allegory you're seeing. There's a murder and a hanging and something monstrous in the woods. Sets it apart from the average lovers' tryst. –*BarrowBoy*

> Fine. I just thought somebody should summarize it here a little, since "about the song" means more than just how many verses it has. Most people come here to discuss how to interpret a song, not where to find it in the Child Ballads' table of contents. –*Dynamum*

▶ Dr. Mark Rydell's 2002 article "A Forensic Analysis of 'Where Oaken Hearts Do Gather'", published in *Folklore*, explored the major differences and commonalities and their implications. In *The Rose and the Briar*, Wendy Lesser writes about how if a trad song leaves gaps in its story, it's because the audience was expected to know what information filled those gaps. The audience that knew this song is gone, and took the gap information with them. Rydell attempted to fill in the blanks. –*HolyGreil* (1 upvote)

> I've found my people! That's the first time somebody has ever beaten me to mentioning Rydell's work in a conversation before. I got a state grant this year to make a documentary about him and his work and his disappearance. It's going to be called *Looking for Love in All the Lost Places*. I named it after his blog. Have you read his blog? It's a deeper dive into the stuff in his article. More personal, in the way an academic article isn't supposed to be. –*HenryMartyn*

> No, only the article. Didn't know he disappeared either. I'll check it out! –*HolyGreil*

> @HenryMartyn it's been two years since your last post on this tune. I keep hoping to get news about your documentary. –*HolyGreil*

Listen to the Kingston Trio: "Where Oaken Hearts Do Gather"
Listen to Joan Baez: "Where Oaken Hearts Do Gather"
Listen to Windhollow Faire: "Where Oaken Hearts Do Gather"
Listen to Steeleye Span: "Where Oaken Hearts Do Gather"
Listen to the Grateful Dead: "Where Oaken Hearts Do Gather"
Listen to Metallica: "Where Oaken Hearts Do Gather"
Listen to Moby K. Dick: "Where Oaken Hearts Do Gather"
Listen to Jack White: "Where Oaken Hearts Do Gather"
Listen to the Decemberists: "Where Oaken Hearts Do Gather"
Listen to Cyrus Matheson: "Where Broken Hearts Do Gather" [FLAGGED by BonnieLass67] [UNFLAGGED by LyricSplainer ModeratorBot]
Full Lyrics for "Where Oaken Hearts Do Gather" (traditional) (7 contributors, 95 notes, 68 comments, 19 reactions)
(see disambiguation for other versions)
(see related songs)

One[1] autumn[2,3] as the wind blew cold
and stripped red leaves[4] from branches
Fair[5] Ellen[6] ran to meet her love
Where oaken hearts do gather[7,8]

[1] Some versions begin "In autumn…" One early broadside notably began with "each autumn." –*BonnieLass67*

[2] Like the more famous "Barbara Allen," this ballad begins by setting the season. In "Barbara Allen," of course, the season is spring, the season of new love. –*HolyGreil*

[3] "Barbara Allen's" "merry month of May/when green buds all were swelling" is also echoed in the 1880 hit "The Fountain in the Park," also known as "While Strolling in the Park": "I was strolling in the park one day/in the merry merry month of May/I was taken by surprise by a pair of roguish eyes/in a moment my poor heart was stole away." I wouldn't mention that except for the literal heart getting stolen away Temple-of-Doom-style in this song. –*Dynamum*

[4] trees that have red leaves in autumn include black cherry, flowering dogwood, hornbeam, sourwood, red oak, white oak, winged sumac, sweet gum, and red maple. it's reasonable to assume this is referring to red or white oak trees given the title. –*HangThaDJ*

> *White and red oak aren't native to Britain. –BarrowBoy*

>> *What if it was originally "rowan hearts" not oaken hearts? Rowan berries could leave a red carpet, plus there's all that great mythology around rowan trees. –Dynamum*

>>> *A) there's no record of a rowan version (check me if I'm wrong, @BonnieLass67, you seem to be the version expert) B) rowan leaves turn more yellow than red, C) the line says red leaves, not berries. –BarrowBoy*

[5] It's interesting that the woman in the song is referred to in almost all versions as "fair," despite her actions. –*Rhiannononymous*

> *She could just be fair as in blond? –Dynamum*

> –*BarrowBoy marked this as a stretch–*

[6] Alternate versions feature the usual gang of "Maggie," "Polly," "Molly," "Jenny," and "Peggy," etc. as seen in countless other songs, and also "Elswyth," which I haven't seen in other ballads. I've looked to see if there's a version of the song with willow trees, given the derivation of that name, but haven't found one. –*BonnieLass67*

[7] the woods, presumably. –*HangThaDJ*

[8] In his 2002 paper, "A Forensic Analysis of 'Where Oaken Hearts Do Gather'," and subsequently in his blog, the University of Pennsylvania professor Dr. Mark

Rydell attempted to track down the exact provenance of the ballad. He said that not every ballad can be traced to a specific incident or location, but this one had a couple of markers that made him think it was possible. He pointed out that of the two common British species, English oak tree leaves turn coppery brown, not red, in autumn, and sessile oak leaves turn yellow. While it's true that the song doesn't specifically say the red leaves are from oaks, it's the only tree mentioned specifically, and it's right in the oldest known name of the song, so presumably it means oak trees when it says oak trees. North American oaks might more specifically meet the red leaf missive, Rydell pointed out. In that case, the song would have had to make its way to British lore from America, when songs moved more commonly in the other direction, or else somebody would have to have brought North American trees to Britain early enough that they'd be mature for this song. (Why mature? Nobody pictures skinny little saplings when they're talking about oak trees. And there's a "gnarled and knotted ancient" in a later verse.) In his initial research, Rydell attempted unsuccessfully to locate a village with a bridge and a steep embankment and a stand of imported oak trees somewhere nearby. Later, after consultation with a botanist, Rydell came to understand that American oaks planted in Britain don't necessarily have the same bright color there that they have in their native country; anthocyanin, the main red pigment, needs bright, crisp autumn days to kick into high gear. It just isn't the same in overcast, damp climates. He concluded that he would not be able to use tree species alone to trace the ballad, but he still had other clues to pursue. *–HenryMartyn*
–BonnieLass67 marked this as cool stuff–

Sweet William robbed the butcher's son[9, 10, 11, 12]
He turned her heart to fancy
And bade her meet him 'neath the[13,14] bridge[15,16]
Where oaken hearts do gather

[9] This line sets William up as a robber, thus deserving of his fate, and the next line makes you think that Ellen is as fair and innocent as the first stanza implies. *–Rhiannononymous*
[10] The Kingston Trio's version changes this to "Sweet William WAS the butcher's son/ WHO turned her heart to fancy." *–BonnieLass67*
[11] Sweet William was supporters' nickname for Prince William, Duke of Cumberland, known as Butcher Cumberland to his Tory enemies! He died relatively young, with no children. Possible link? *–Dynamum*
–BonnieLass67 marked this as a stretch–
–BarrowBoy marked this as a stretch–
> *There's absolutely nothing to connect this with Prince William, Duke of Cumberland. You're barking up the wrong oak tree. –BarrowBoy*

[12] Dr. Mark Rydell, in attempting to pinpoint the origin of the song, posited a theory that the line should actually read "Sweet William, Robert Butcher's son." –HenryMartyn

> *there was a robert butcher born in liverpool who became an australian politician! he had three sons and five daughters, but he was probably born too late to be referenced in this ballad. –HangThaDJ*

>> *Yeah, Rydell dismissed him. There's nothing connecting this song's path with Australia. It didn't need to be a famous Robert Butcher, just one who was locally famous enough to be worth putting in the song, so Rydell tried looking for any Robert Butcher whose son named William might have died under unusual circumstances. Rydell found what he was looking for: an aging solicitor named Robert Butcher, living in a village called Gall, had written a strangely passionate pro-hanging letter in the 1770s, right around the time that its prohibition became a popular cause, saying "there are circumstances for which, tragically, hanging is the only proportionate response." Not "crimes" but "circumstances." Rydell said in his blog that he was going to England to check Gall out for himself. He made one more post from something called an internet café–this was pre-smartphone, so I guess that was the only place he could get online?–anyway, one more short update and then he never posted again. (Did I mention I'm making a documentary about him? I'm planning on visiting Gall this October. I've got an appointment lined up with the woman who runs their town historical society too. Hopefully I can get some answers.) –HenryMartyn*

>> *What a fascinating story! Your documentary should be really interesting. –HolyGreil*

>>> *You should check out Rydell's blog Looking For Love in All the Lost Places too–it's like a folksier, less academic version of his research. You can still find it on the wayback machine even though he and his host site are both long gone. –HenryMartyn*

>>>> *did this robt butcher have a son who was hanged? what was he hanged for? –HangThaDJ*

>>>> *I've messaged with the town historian, like I said, Jenny Kirk. She said Butcher's letter is in their museum. She warned me that it's just a one-room museum-and-gift-shop, because nothing much ever happened there, but because of that, its publication in London was one of the bigger things that happened to anyone from Gall. He had four sons, one of whom*

> *was named William. His William did die by hanging, but there's no mention anywhere of a crime or a trial. I can see why Rydell thought this was a good lead. –HenryMartyn*
>> *Did you ask her if Rydell ever got there? –HolyGreil*
>>> *First thing I asked! She said that would've been back when she was a kid, and they don't keep a visitor log. –HenryMartyn*
>> *i always think of historical society ladies as old biddies. –HangThaDJ*
>>> *Can confirm she is definitely not an old biddy. –HenryMartyn*

[13] Variously, "the bridge," and "Toll Bridge," in the British versions. "Tall Bridge" in one early American version, "Fall's Bridge" in Dolly Parton's. Unclear whether "Fall's Bridge" means a bridge belonging to someone named Falls, or a more poetic version involving autumn. *–BonnieLass67*

[14] If it's a toll bridge, maybe the toll is what William pays in the end. *–Rhiannononymous*
–BarrowBoy marked this as a stretch–

[15] The fact that William asked her to meet him under the bridge goes well with the robber line, since we're told he's sweet but then immediately told that he's both a robber and someone who would lure a young woman under a bridge. Maybe it's an ironic sweet, like an ugly mobster called Prettyboy or something. *–Rhiannononymous*

[16] Guys! I'm here! In Gall! It has almost everything mentioned in the song: a village, a woods, a stone bridge with a steep embankment. No red carpet of leaves, even though it's October, but everything else seems to check out. *–HenryMartyn*
–HolyGreil marked this as cool stuff–

"Don't go," said Ellen's sisters two[17,18,19,20]
"There's no good that can follow
A man met moonlit 'neath the bridge[21]
Where oaken hearts do gather"[22]

[17] the sisters function as a sort of greek chorus here. *–HangThaDJ*
–BonnieLass67 marked this as a stretch–
[18] Ellen and her sisters represent the three Fates. *–Dynamum*
–BarrowBoy marked this as a stretch–

[19] I've always thought the sisters were just sisters, trying to warn Ellen, like a good sister would. There are lots of songs where family tries to warn a woman that her man is no good. *–Rhiannononymous*

[20] It's worth noting again that the American version documented by the Lomaxes was "While Oaken Sisters Watched." *–BonnieLass67*

[21] Okay, but if you take the whole verse as the warning, "There's no good that can follow a man met moonlit 'neath the bridge," it can either be a warning telling Ellen not to go because there's danger for her, or it could be a warning that there's going to be trouble for him, in which case they might also be saying Ellen herself is no good for William. They seem to know an awful lot about this very specific thing – not just that no good can follow meeting a man at night under a bridge, but also specifically meeting a man at night under that particular bridge, where oaken hearts do gather. *–Rhiannononymous*

> *Or oaken sisters watch –BonnieLass67*

[22] The quotation marks are obviously not part of the song as passed down orally, but they're in all the sheet music and broadsides I've ever seen. In this stanza the chorus really does sound like it's part of a quote from the sisters, like they know this place by its reputation. *–BonnieLass67*

Fair Ellen turned her eyes from them
For she had long decided[23]
To meet him while the village slept[24,25]
Where oaken hearts do gather

[23] This plays like you would expect in this kind of song. Young woman rejects advice from her wise elders and chooses love, and then discovers too late that her family was right and she's set herself up for tragedy. This ballad later twists that expectation. (Though that leads to the question of why her sisters don't want this, if they don't mean the usual 'it will lead you astray.') *–Rhiannononymous*

[24] I used to think this meant that the village itself slept where oaken hearts do gather. *–Dynamum*

> *That's just stupid. –BarrowBoy*

> *Hey! I said 'used to.' And anyway, there were trees there before people, prob-ably, so technically I'm right either way. –Dynamum*

[25] The village that Rydell located, Gall, was adjacent to a small, dense woodland that would have been larger back then. The main road went north/south, with south heading through the woods and over an old stone bridge. *–HenryMartyn*

> *I'm here now! Bus took ages. Gall was bypassed by the major motorways, so the village is pretty isolated. But that means the woods are still woods! It's a bit of a walk to the bridge, and very dark at night, but doable. I'll admit I was*

hoping there'd be graffiti carved into the bridge saying "William was here" or "El and Will" or something. –HenryMartyn

Fair Ellen's steps did lightly fall
On autumn's red-stained blanket[26,27,28]
As off she ran to meet her love[29]
Where oaken hearts do gather

[26] Could be blood! *–Dynamum*
[27] This brings us around to what was previewed at the beginning– there the leaves were being stripped by autumn wind, here they're already on the ground, but she's off to meet her guy. *–Rhiannononymous*
[28] Hear me out: if you go with the "in autumn" opening variant that the Dead used instead of "one autumn," this is something that happens every year. The leaves turn red, and off sweet Ellen goes again. That would explain the different-but-repeated nature of the opening and this stanza. That's what always happens; what happens to William specifically is what happens **this** time. *–HolyGreil*
–HenryMartyn marked this as cool stuff–
[29] Her light steps and "her love" here tell us that from the narrator's perspective she is in love and has no intent to deceive. That makes what happens all the more surprising to the listener. *–Rhiannononymous*

Young William stood in moonlight's glow
When Ellen came[30] upon him
And kissed him as she stole his heart[31]
Where oaken hearts do gather

[30] Some versions use "fell upon him" instead of "came upon him" but that definitely changes the nature of the meeting. *–BonnieLass67*
[31] Still playing with expectations here. We expect "stole his heart" as in fell in love, but the next stanzas makes it grossly literal. *–Rhiannononymous*

She begged sweet Will to show her how[32]
He differed from the others[33]
And prove to her his love was true[34]
Where oaken hearts do gather

[32] This verse is placed interestingly since if the previous one is to be believed, she's already fallen on him/come to him and stolen his heart, literally or figuratively. Why this demand? –*Rhiannononymous*

>*Some versions do move this verse earlier. Some move it to before the previous verse (usually matched with "fell upon him" instead of "came upon him" since in that case they've already arrived at the same place.) The other variant places it third, just after the invitation to the bridge, as if it's her response. –BonnieLass67*

> *Huh! Either of those would make more sense, since it seems like otherwise this verse interrupts action with a plea. She's making the demand after she's already set things in motion. Unless they had already talked it over, and this is her hoping that he does what he's promised. –Rhiannononymous*

[33] This implies that this has happened before. It's sort of melancholy. Men... –*Dynamum*

[34] There's no answer given to her request that he prove himself, or else the verse that follows is the test where he's supposed to prove himself. –*Rhiannononymous*

His beating heart[35] she placed inside[36]
A[37] gnarled and knotted ancient[38]
to quicken[39] come the springtime thaw[40]
Where oaken hearts do gather

[35] There's really no figurative way to take this. And ew, why is it still beating? –*Dynamum*

[36] ironic that she places the heart so delicately after ripping it out of his chest. –*HangThaDJ*

[37] Some early variants say "*her* gnarled and knotted ancient." –*BonnieLass67*

[38] Gnarled and knotted ancient what? That's a weird description. –*Dynamum*

> *"A gnarled and knotted ancient" = presumably a very old tree. –Rhiannononymous*

> *Hey @HenryMartyn, did you or Rydell find a tree like this? –HolyGreil*

> *All the trees I've seen are new growth. –HenryMartyn*

[39] Maybe she thinks his heart in the tree will beat faster when she visits –*Dynamum*

–BarrowBoy marked this as a stretch–

[40] I think this is the other meaning of "quicken," like "to enter into a phase of active growth and development" per dictionary (example is seeds quickening in soil). –*BarrowBoy*

> *But then why place it in an old tree instead of in the ground? –Dynamum*

> *How would I know? –BarrowBoy*

And in his chest she built with care[41]
A nest of twigs and leaf-fall[42]
An acorn[43,44] cushioned there to grow
Where oaken hearts do gather

[41] Again, it goes out of its way to say how much care she took with this part of the operation. –*Dynamum*
[42] In his blog, Dr. Rydell said "The true nature of the exchange made by Ellen and seemingly agreed to by William is perhaps the greatest mystery remaining in this ballad." Jenny Kirk is helping me do research into Gall's local folklore. She was telling the truth that their museum is crap, but she's great. –*HenryMartyn*
[43] Maybe this acorn becomes the sapling at his grave? –*Dynamum*
[44] fun fact: only one in ten thousand acorns becomes an oak tree. –*HangThaDJ*

And turned he then to look at her
With eyes still seeking answers[45,46]
She kissed him twice[47] and left him there[48]
Where oaken hearts do gather

[45] I think this line goes out of its way to make clear that he's not vegetative at this point, pardon the pun. He's aware enough to ask questions, though you'd think he would have looked at her before now, and asked questions before now, like "Hey, do you mind putting my heart back? I'm using that." –*Rhiannononymous*
[46] Maybe he was under some kind of spell? –*Dynamum*
–*BarrowBoy marked this as a stretch–*

> *Stop marking me down! A few lines later he has literally no voice, so a spell isn't unreasonable. He's trying to use his eyes to ask questions. –Dynamum*
> *@BarrowBoy all you ever do is mark stretches and shoot down other peoples' theories without ever offering any yourself. Do you care about this ballad at all? –Dynamum*

>> *I don't even like this song. The melody's okay, but it needs a bridge. –BarrowBoy*

>>> *technically it has a bridge. old, made of stone... –HangThaDJ*
>>> *Argh. If you don't like the song, why are you here? –Dynamum*

>>>> *For those sweet sweet LyricSplainer level badges. U? –BarrowBoy*

> I love the song, but also it's fascinating! A lot of songs are straightforward, but I love the ones like this that develop a sort of detective team. We've got BonnieLass with all the background/history stuff, and Henry the dashing young field work expert, and DJ with random facts and Greil with musicology and Rhiannononymous on language details. –Dynamum

> > What does that make you? Comic relief? –BarrowBoy

> > > Better than you, the one everyone hates but has to put up with. –Dynamum

> > If @HenryMartyn's our field researcher, can I point out that he's stopped responding? His last response here was on the last verse, over a year ago, and he hasn't posted on any other songs either. I keep checking in hoping he'll tell us more about his film. I wish I knew his real name. –HolyGreil

> > > Hmm. I searched "state arts grant" and "Mark Rydell" and "Looking For Love in All the Lost Places" and got a hit in Pennsylvania. Looks like he's a Henry from a city called Williamsport (William's Port? coincidence?) who was a senior at the University of Pennsylvania when he got the grant. I'm not going to post his actual surname here. It seems rude. –Dynamum

> > > Look at you with the real detective work!

Thanks for the lead.
Hmm. He was part of
the grant announce-
ment, but not the end
of year presentation.
–HolyGreil

[47] Is twice significant? She'd already kissed him once (as she stole his heart) but it's unclear if this is a second kiss, or two more kisses. *–Rhiannononymous*

> *Maybe the second kiss takes his voice. –Dynamum*

> *It's true that he's already using his eyes to ask. –HolyGreil*

> *I said he was under a spell and got mocked for it! It's not like this all has to have exact basis in truth. Maybe they just like kissing. –Dynamum*

[48] Where did she go? This song never quite makes her and her sisters seem like part of the village. *–Rhiannononymous*

Young William to the village went
His feet still knew the pathways[49]
He knew he'd left his years[50,51] behind[52]
Where oaken hearts do gather

[49] He'd made this trip so many times he knew it automatically. (I almost said "by heart") *–Dynamum*

[50] "His years" = the rest of his days? Living on borrowed time now? *–Rhiannononymous*

[51] Some variants say "his fears" instead of his years; others say he left "something." *–BonnieLass67*

[52] this does make it seem like some kind of spell, like he's stumbling back without knowing what he's doing or what has happened. *–HangThaDJ*

> *THANK YOU. I TOLD YOU. –Dynamum*

["Wake up," he cried, though no one heard[53,54,55]
"And find the wicked woman[56,57]
Who stole my life and voice away
Where oaken hearts do gather"]

[53] It doesn't say anything about her taking his voice before this. *–BarrowBoy*

54 @Moderator can we delete this verse or add it at the bottom? It's only in a handful of the twentieth century versions and nothing earlier. Not part of the original ballad. –*BonnieLass67*

–*Lyricsplainer ModeratorBot has received this comment and will bring it to a moderator's attention–*

55 It changes a lot, doesn't it? "Wicked woman" sounds like it was written by someone else entirely. Without this verse, William just goes along with what's happening. –*Rhiannononymous*

56 Interesting that he doesn't know where to find her. There's no verse where the villagers show up at her house, either, even when they spring into action. –*Rhiannononymous*

57 i feel bad for him, but he's kind of a jerk here, trying to shout in the town square in the middle of the night or whatever for everyone to come listen to his problems. i mean, not that any of this is his fault, except he did tell a woman to meet him under the bridge without any regard for the trouble he could get her in. and it does seem like he consented to her test? –*HangThaDJ*

And when the village came to him[58]
He could[59] not tell his story
Or say what fate befell their son[60]
Where oaken hearts do gather

58 Does anyone else think it's strange that "the village came to him"? Where was he? I mean, I guess it means the villagers, not the village, and they came to him at his house? –*Dynamum*

59 "Would not" instead of "could not" in some early variations. –*BonnieLass67*

> *Ha! Would not = wood knot! Get it? –Dynamum*

–*BarrowBoy marked this as a stretch–*

> *@Dynamum I like that pun no matter if it's a stretch. Don't let him get you down. –Rhiannononymous*

60 This collective "their son" is fascinating considering what they do next. This song has some messed up families, y'all. –*Rhiannononymous*

>*Wait, it's collective? Like "the son of the village?" I thought it meant "their son" like William and Ellen's son! –Dynamum*

> *I never thought of that, but that works too! Especially with the whole quickening thing! We talked about quickening a seed, but not quickening a womb. –Rhiannononymous*

–*Rhiannonymous marked this as cool stuff–*

–*BonnieLass67 marked this as cool stuff–*

–*HangThaDJ marked this as cool stuff–*

They looked at him with mournful eyes[61]
Then listened for his heartbeat[62,63,64]
Then hung him from the gallows pole[65]
Where oaken hearts do gather[66]

[61] The mournful eyes have always made me think they've seen this before. *–Dynamum*

[62] It's unclear whether they listened for his heartbeat because they'd seen something like this before that his tale reminded them of, or because he looks unwell. *–Rhiannononymous*

[63] And, y'know, he wasn't speaking *–BarrowBoy*

[64] Did people know about heartbeats by the time this song was written? *–Dynamum*
> OMG *have you heard of Wikipedia? –BarrowBoy*

[65] This has always horrified me, that they just went and hung him. I guess it's understandable if they were freaked out that he didn't have a heartbeat, but still... *–Dynamum*

[66] Out of all the stanzas, this is the one that makes the least sense with "where oaken hearts do gather" as opposed to "while oaken sisters watch." *–BonnieLass67*
> *Yeah, the town gallows pole was likely not in the same place where oaken hearts do gather, unless you count that a gallows made of oak might contain oaken hearts, whatever they are. –Rhiannononymous*
> > *As you might guess, Gall took down their gallows pole like two hundred years ago. –HenryMartyn*

And in the woods[67] fair Ellen wept[68]
For she had truly loved him[69]
And tried to claim[70] him in her way[71,72]
Where oaken hearts do gather

[67] It's interesting that she's in the woods again here, since she had left him there? Didn't she go home? *–Dynamum*

[68] How is she still being called fair? *–BarrowBoy*

[69] It's interesting that the song tells us this, since otherwise you'd think she's monstrous. I mean, her actions are still monstrous, but somehow it's better if they're done out of love? *–Rhiannononymous*

[70] Some versions say "keep" instead of claim. *–BonnieLass67*

[71] This "in her way" does a lot of work. *–Rhiannononymous*

[72] Some versions say "and hoped he'd prove his love to her," which would harken back to whatever proof she was demanding of him earlier. –*BonnieLass67*

And Ellen's sisters bowed their heads[73]
"There's no good that can follow
A man met moonlight 'neath the bridge
Where oaken hearts do gather"

[73] greek chorus back for an encore of their greatest hit, "i told you so." –*HangThaDJ*

The villagers with torches went[74,75]
To rid their woods of danger[76,77]
There to avenge the boy they'd hung[78]
Where oaken hearts do gather

[74] This verse and the two above it and one below it are often sung in a different order. –*BonnieLass67*
[75] i'm anti-villagers with torches and pitchforks generally. –*HangThaDJ*
[76] They're going to burn the oak trees. William must have given good directions before they hung him, if they think they know which specific trees to burn. –*Rhiannononymous*
> *Spoiler: for real, they chopped and burned ALL the oak trees they could find. Jenny's older sisters say it was barbarous, and I've seen the result myself. Everything is new growth from the past forty years since they stopped that practice, but you can see the damage done. –HenryMartyn*
[77] I wonder what the actual danger is that they think they're protecting against. Have they had other men stolen this way? I guess if you let it happen once, it could happen more... –*Dynamum*
–*BarrowBoy marked this as a stretch*–
> *Argh. Go stretch someone else. I'm just saying we've all got our eyes on Ellen, but what do her sisters do all day other than watch? And @HenryMartyn, what do their town records say about stolen people? –Dynamum*
> *Jenny says they lost all their old birth and death records in a fire they lost control of. –HenryMartyn*
[78] so they felt like they had to hang poor william, but then they go out and avenge him for the wrong ellen did him? there's some misdirected anger here. –*HangThaDJ*

But neath the bridge they saw no trace[79]
Nor down the steep embankment[80]
And none could ever find the place[81]
Where oaken hearts do gather[82]

[79] Beneath the bridge they saw no trees or they couldn't find Ellen? It's unclear. *–Rhiannononymous*

[80] The steep embankment was another specific geographic clue that Dr. Rydell had hoped to find. *–HenryMartyn*

> *Can confirm: it's here! The bridge goes over what's now a sort of dry gully, but the banks are steep. And, cool thing! I don't know whether it's the stone or the moss or some mineral or what, but I guess something's leaching into the ground here that's tinting the leaves red near the bridge. I wonder if Dr. Rydell ever got to see this. –HenryMartyn*

[81] The only rhyme in the whole ballad, for what it's worth. *–Rhiannononymous*

> *Some early variants have the third line as "and none could find poor William's heart." It's possible that the line was original and this change came later, since it's odd to have a single rhyming line. –BonnieLass67*

>> *If they couldn't find William's heart, does that mean there was one old tree that the villagers didn't manage to find? –Dynamum*

>>> *I don't think @HenryMartyn can search the whole forest. –BarrowBoy*

>>> *fun fact! a forest has a traditional legal definition as land owned by the sovereign and set aside as a hunting ground. –HangThaDJ*

>>>> *He can't search the whole woods, then. –BarrowBoy*

[82] I don't know why I'm only thinking of this like fifteen verses in, but if you frame a song around oaks gathering, isn't the opposite of that to disperse? Maybe they couldn't find them because they sometimes go elsewhere. Maybe this whole song exists to tell you what to do if this particular thing starts happening to the oaks near you. That could be why it's tall bridge and fall's bridge etc too, and different names=different aliases. Maybe there's a rotation and this town tried harder to get the warning out and protect themselves. *–Dynamum*
–BarrowBoy marked this as a stretch–

Long winter passed then came the thaw[83,84]
That set springtime a-budding
A sapling grew from William's grave[85]
Where oaken hearts do gather

[83] The Dead turned this verse to major instead of minor. *–HolyGreil*
[84] The Kingston Trio ended with this verse. *–BonnieLass67*
[85] Are we not even going to talk about this sapling thing? *–Dynamum*

> *I found a grave that I think is William Butcher's, though the stone is very worn and it's hard to tell. There's no tree, but I took the next verse to mean that the sapling that grew at the grave was cut down too. –HenryMartyn*

And every spring[86] the villagers
To the woods bring torch and axe
To cut short every sapling grown[87,88]
Where oaken hearts do gather

[86] And this verse holds Dr. Rydell's last two big clues! "Every spring" suggested that they might have some sort of village tradition that was still passed down, even if they didn't know why anymore. On his blog he said the village he found, Gall, had an annual spring festival with a parade and bonfire. *–HenryMartyn*
[87] Rydell had speculated that the village he was looking for would be near a woods full of mature oaks (keeping in mind that there are plenty of places where woods have been cut back over the centuries, so it wasn't necessarily there to find at all; he looked at places that had been forested in earlier times as well). Then he realized what this verse implied. Instead of looking for a woods full of oaks, he wanted to go looking for a woods that was, unusually, missing its oaks, under the assumption that the village had kept cutting them down. So now I can personally confirm the woods near Gall is full of old hornbeams and ash trees and the like, but almost no oaks at all. The oaks that are here are younger, which matches up with recent changes to the village's festival. It used to involve cutting down all the oaks at the end of the summer and burning them in a bonfire, but conservationists argued that was wasteful and poor management, and they stopped doing it in the 1970s. I got here too late for this year's fest, but apparently now they just do a symbolic burning of a single tree they've chopped down for the purpose. *–HenryMartyn*
–BonnieLass67 marked this as cool stuff–
[88] Interesting that this accounts for the saplings in the woods, but not the one at William's grave. Did they cut that one down or leave it? *–Rhiannononymous*

> *I was asking about that sapling too! –Dynamum*
> *There's one broadside that includes a verse that may answer your question. "And when that day the villagers/uprooted William's sapling/a keening cry was heard by all/where oaken hearts do gather" –BonnieLass67*
>> *Why wasn't that one generally included? That's great. –Rhiannononymous*

> *Child may not have liked the sourcing. In that one version, it replaced the big Revenge On the Trees verse, which was definitely original. –BonnieLass67*

Still sometimes[89] when the wind blow cold
And strips red leaves[90] from branches
Fair Ellen takes[91] another love[92]
Where oaken hearts do gather[93]

[89] Some early versions say "somewhere" instead of "sometimes." Somewhere doesn't make as much sense, since presumably the where is known, even if the trees weren't found. –*BonnieLass67*

> *That "somewhere" was something Dr. Rydell speculated about in his final blog post. That post was published widely after his disappearance and derided as sentimental and unmoored from fact by many of the same people who had praised his original forensic work. He had worked so hard to find this village, only to start musing about whether a stray "somewhere" might mean this had happened in more than one place. It undercut everything except the song's extensive travels. –HenryMartyn*

> *You haven't told us anything about his disappearance! What's up with that? –HolyGreil*

> *After that last post saying he'd landed in London and was heading to Gall, he stopped posting and all his known emails bounced. He never returned to his professorship. Nobody here rememb ers him, and there's nothing in the police records (I was trying to be thorough.) Unsolved mystery. –HenryMartyn*

[90] I'd just like to point out you've discussed stealing voices and oaken hearts but you'll only accept accurate botanical explanations for the red leaves. Not every line has to be perfectly based in truth. Magic? A portent? Some weather pattern that changes the amount of anthocyanin in certain years? A poetically resonant image? (@BarrowBoy, I'm going to beat you to the punch.) –*Dynamum*
–*Dynamum marked this as a stretch–*

[91] I love the present tense in this verse, like it's still going on. And the multiple meanings of "take" here: take a lover, take a life, or the whole sentence "takes another love where oaken hearts do gather" like she's bringing him home to meet the family. –*Rhiannononymous*

[92] And this reminder again from a narrator that we have no reason to disbelieve, saying that it's a love she takes, not a victim. –*Rhiannononymous*

[93] In his last blog post, Rydell wrote "One of the strange things about this ballad is that we're never quite sure what kind of story it is. Is it a warning about monstrous

trees or monstrous lovers? A cautionary tale about forest management? Are we meant to laud the villagers as heroic for their actions? The Gall festival would suggest so, but then why is Ellen portrayed so ambiguously? Maybe we are meant to sing it as the love story of sweet William and fair Ellen. If you ignore the incongruous "wicked woman" verse, neither lover betrays the other's expectations, and it's only because of the villagers that their story turns tragic." –*HenryMartyn*

> Having been here a while and listened to Jenny and her sisters, I've come to think it's a little of all the above. Maybe Rydell is right that it's a love story with a message that love involves give and take, and some ask for more than others. That's not always such a bad thing, if you're willing to give. –*HenryMartyn*

> *@HenryMartyn can you ask your friend Jenny if there are any old oaks that escaped the festival? Like in the "none could ever find the place/none could find poor William's heart" verse? –Dynamum*

>*Thanks for that suggestion! Jenny says she thinks she knows of one. We're taking another walk in the woods tonight. I'm still looking for the right ending for my film, but I think I'm close. It feels funny to be searching for traces of Rydell where he was searching for traces of truth in this ballad, like we're all chasing each other. Anyway, thanks for your continued help on this, friends. If nothing else, maybe we're part of the cycle, bringing an old song to new listeners. –HenryMartyn*

. . . .

Sarah Pinsker is the Hugo, Nebula, and Philip K Dick Award winning author of *A Song For A New Day*, *We Are Satellites*, *Sooner or Later Everything Falls Into the Sea*, *Lost Places*, *Haunt Sweet Home*, and over sixty works of short fiction. She is also a singer/songwriter with four albums on various independent labels. She is the writer in residence at the Kratz Center for Creative Writing at Goucher College, and lives in Baltimore with her wife and two weird dogs. Find her online at sarahpinsker.com.

FOR LACK OF A BED

John Wiswell

Noémi tried to focus on the mermaids and ignore the floor. She lay in the middle of her living room, upon a nest of laundry bags and blankets, hoping for just a couple hours of sleep before she had to open the shop tomorrow. The new pain pills did as little as the old ones, and so she pulled the covers over herself at sundown and tried to use the internet as medication.

Chronic pain and Mermaid Tumblr. It was a normal night in her world. Videos and GIFs of those fish-tailed people swimming, their fins swirling through water currents, sometimes lulled Noémi into distraction. She needed those distractions tonight.

Her phone buzzed with a text from Tariq. He was working late.

TARIQ
u want a bed, but would u sleep on a sofa?

NOEMI
I'd sell a kidney for a sofa.

TARIQ
what if some1 died on it? but u keep ur kidneys

Okay, it was a weird offer. But was this that much weirder than the selkies down the hall who kept offering her herbal remedies? You knew you were pathetic when selkies pitied you.

You also knew you were pathetic when your roommate offered you dead people's furniture. But her mother had worked with estate auctions, so Noémi had grown up with plenty of grim hand-me-downs. A bed was out of her price range. She knew what her mother would've said.

NOEMI
Is it clean?

TARIQ

clean as a disney movie

She sat up and her entire spinal column rioted. She felt vertebrae kicking over trash cans and lighting cars ablaze in her lower back.

NOEMI

Dying on a sofa would be the highlight of my year.

"Good!" Tariq yelled from the hall outside their apartment. She didn't register it was him until their door swung open and he shimmied in butt-first, dragging a bulky sofa behind him. "Because I am not carrying this back to Apartment 3A."

It was sand-colored with brown freckles, a fashion risk even for a freebie. At least it wasn't splattered in gore.

She meant to run a hand over its arm rest, but immediately found herself sitting on it. Sinking into the cushions felt like a hug from a friendly giant. The honking and crying and thrumming of the city outside their apartment seemed to calm down.

Forget sleeping on the floor; she never wanted to touch the floor again.

"Hey," she said, "try sitting on this."

Tariq asked, "Did you take your meds tonight?"

She asked, "Someone died on this?"

She couldn't hear his answer over the sensation of touch not hurting for the first time in hours. The leather was so warm, so welcoming, just like skin.

Tariq shook Noémi's foot, and she pulled her blanket over her face. She mumbled, "I don't need dinner. I'm turning into a human ramen."

He said, "It's eleven."

Sunlight blurred her vision and she rubbed the grime from her eyes. "Eleven? Then how is it light out?"

"They invented this thing called 'A.M.' You slept through your alarm."

"No..." She didn't know what she was denying. She stretched out on the sofa. For the first time in weeks, her back didn't feel like it was on fire. The pain had calmed to a dull throb—an annoying pain rather than an intense one. If she'd overslept, her body obviously needed it. She almost felt more tired than yesterday.

Tariq pried the fleece from her hands. "I made you a couple waffles. Please, please eat them."

Her appetite was a magician; it had one hell of a disappearing act. Pain made it easy for Noémi to skip meals. Still, with bleary eyes, she read the concern in her friend's face. It was the same concern she'd felt on so many nights when she helped him through his anxiety attacks.

She smiled up at him and said, "You know something? I slept."

He offered her a hand up. "That's pretty awesome. We should party tonight."

There was no party that night. The food truck broke down and Tariq texted that he was stuck helping his uncle fix it.

Noémi felt for him and was relieved at the same time; she could barely move her fingers by the end of her shift at the pet store. Gryphon chicks were adorable, but insisted on being hand-fed, and the basilisks had broken out of their blackout cage and were looking at customers again.

The pain ground her brains into powder. What people didn't understand about chronic pain was that it wasn't about your legs going weak – it was about getting mentally exhausted managing the assaults. All day, she fantasized about sitting down.

Once home, she barely opened her string cheese before plopping onto her freckled sofa. Lying on it was like her entire body was biting into a marshmallow. This she had an appetite for. The cushions slid apart, enveloping her in the leather, like it wanted to swallow her.

In her dreams, it did.

Her phone vibrated on her chest. It was work. It was also noon, and she didn't know what day.

She answered, and picked her string cheese off the carpet. She must have sleep-punted it.

She said, "Hey Lili. Sorry. I must have—"

Lili cut her off, "I think the mogwai are picking the locks on all the cages after hours."

Lili was a succubus and normally had everything together. If she was as nervous as she sounded, then this was dire.

Noémi forced herself to stand free of the sofa's wonderful grip and walked to the center of the room to wake up. Her spine popped and she shuddered. She asked, "Did they eat after midnight?"

"Not this time, but I found one molesting the breakroom pantry."

Noémi was sitting on the edge of the sofa. She didn't remember sitting down. "I found the nicest furniture. You've got to come over and try it."

"You know that when I say 'the monsters are picking their locks,' I mean 'get your butt over here immediately,' right?"

Noémi said, "Got it."

She hung up, and had the funny desire to kiss the sofa goodbye. And why not? Nobody was watching.

She leaned in and smooched a cushion. It smelled like a perfume that Noémi had only ever encountered in dreams.

Then it was 6:24 PM. Her phone had eight messages.

She thought the knocking was Tariq having lost his key, but it was Lili at the door. All six feet and two inches of her. Lili's normally lustrous golden hair frizzled out like copper wire. She had gory paw prints on her skirt which hopefully weren't her own blood.

Noémi said, "Oh my gosh, Lili, never in a million years..."

Then Lili was inside her apartment, stooping to go nose to nose with her. She thought the succubus was going to bite her head off. "Where were you?"

"I've almost never missed work like that, and it won't happen again, I promise."

"I thought your new meds killed you or something. Your landlord said you wouldn't answer the door."

Noémi bit the inside of her cheek. "I may have slept through her knocking."

Lili gripped onto Noémi's shoulders. "So you're okay?"

"I'm awesome. You know I wanted a bed, but we found a sofa and it's the best thing in the world. My body must still be catching up on sleep."

Noémi backed into the apartment. The sofa was tucked into the far wall of their combo kitchen/living room. She fought the urge to curl up on it right now.

Lili looked like she'd bitten into an extremely ripe lime. "When did you invite her?"

"Her? Are you gendering my furniture?"

Lili pointed a sangria red fingernail at the sofa. "That's not furniture. That's a succubus."

Noémi tilted her head. Giving it a few seconds didn't make it make any more sense. "I know you're the expert, but I'm pretty sure succubi don't have armrests."

"Come on. You know my mom is a used bookstore, right?"

"I thought she owned a used bookstore."

"The sex economy sucks. With all the hook-up apps and free porn out there, a succubus starves. My mom turned into a bookstore so people would take bits of her home and hold them in bed. It's why I work at the pet store and cuddle the hell hound puppies before we open."

Noémi asked, "Is that why they never bite you?"

"What do you think? Everybody else gets puppy bites, except me. I get fuzzy, affectionate joy-energy. Gets me through the day, like a cruelty-free smoothie." Lili blew a frizzy strand of gold from her face. "But this sofa has devolved really far into this form. I know succubi that went out like her—she's just a pit of hunger shaped to look enticing. No mind. Just murder. Where'd you even find her?"

"It was a freebie. I mean, maybe somebody died while sleeping on it, but that doesn't mean anything."

"And you're sleeping all the time now? Always on it? She's totally eating you."

"My sofa is not a murderer."

Tariq walked in through the front door, and they both looked up at him. He said, "Hey ladies. Breaking it in?"

That's when Noémi realized both she and Lili were sitting on the sofa.

They shrieked, and ran from the apartment, dragging Tariq with them.

Noémi and Tariq slept in the stairwell that night, each careful to jab each other in the ribs if they started inching back towards the apartment. Lili tore across the city in search of anyone who doubled as a furniture mover and an exorcist.

Noémi didn't sleep a minute for the rest of the week. The pain that had dwindled during her affair with the sofa now returned with the cruelty of a direct-to-video sequel. For most of the day, she could barely think. Through the nights, crashing in the back room of the monster pet store, she could barely sleep. Everything was a fog of social auto-pilot.

She had to bribe Lili to come back, promising to scrub the hell hound cages. The puppies had eaten a mogwai and their bowel movements had turned into some horrible form of post-modern art.

Lili arrived at the apartment wearing a bright yellow hazmat suit. Tariq donned six pairs of plastic gloves before deigning to touch the succubus-turned-sofa. He and Lili had to do the lifting.

Noémi could scarcely stand up straight, let alone carry furniture. Instead she stuffed the remaining sofa cushions into a trash bag. She hesitated over the last one, on which she'd laid her head for the easiest nights of her year. She held it, thinking about how people got lost.

When Noémi came into the alley, Lili was dousing the sofa with equal parts holy water and kerosene.

Tariq reached for the garbage bag, but Noémi clutched it to her chest. Noémi asked, "Do you really think the sofa is that bad?"

"Yes," Tariq said. "Pure evil. She haunted our apartment without paying rent."

"She was probably lonely. She couldn't find a companion she could keep. But now she's found a new identity, and someone who appreciated her..."

"She was eating you."

"Could we ask her to, you know, stop eating me?"

Lili emptied the last liquids over the sofa and said, "There's no consciousness left in her. She's just hungry furniture now. And you're just loose change about to get stuck between her cushions."

"I didn't feel like loose change. I felt different. Everybody gives you magnetic bracelets, and pot brownies, and tells you to sleep with your legs over your head. It all did jack for me. But the sofa was helping."

Muttering something in Latin, Lili tossed a lighter and torched the sofa. The backrest went up first, in a brilliant blue flame with silver smoke that climbed the alley's brick walls. They needed to make this fast or their landlord would catch them in the act.

Tariq said, "I'm not going to tell you how to feel." He stretched out his hand, offering to take the bag. "You want me to do the honors? Technically I was the one who brought her home and started all this."

"Nah," Noémi said, avoiding eye contact and tossing the bag of cushions onto the pyre. It went up in even more lustrous smoke, so thin it could've been vapor. It smelled like tears. "Let's get out of here."

Tariq said, "Look, take my bed until we find you something, okay?"

Noémi put a fist over her mouth. "Are you sure?"

"The surest. I've got a lead on some money."

She hugged her friend for a fierce moment in time.

Then they ran before someone called the cops.

Noémi knew she'd woken at 5:32 because that's when the text came in. It'd taken her forever to wind down, but she'd guess she'd slept four and a half hours. That was a record since the bonfire, and this was her first night trying out the secret weapon.

The incoming text read:

TARIQ

got a pair!!!!

Limited edition sneakers. You downloaded an app that pinged you at a random time and if your GPS reported you were in a certain radius of a certain boutique, you got a crack at one pair of obscenely expensive shoes. Tariq had basically haunted that neighborhood for days waiting for his phone to vibrate. With the magic of economics, he could flip the shoes to a trust fund kid and turn them into a new bed.

Or he could turn it into rent.

Or, as Noémi expected, he could sink all of those dollars into his uncle's food truck. It was family and livelihood. And you couldn't carry a treasure chest to the surface when you were fighting to tread water.

She texted him back:

NOEMI

You woke me up. Jerk.

He'd get a good laugh, never believing she'd really slept this late. She wouldn't have believed it either, if she only had his bed.

She scooted to the far edge of the mattress, leaving her pillow behind, letting her feet scuff across the carpet. Impact sent sharp tingles up her calves, sparks of pain where yesterday there had been an inferno. When she stretched, the sparks sprang up at her spine, and then down her arms.

These were aches. They were not agonies. They were things she could live with, if it didn't mean getting swallowed up by a spell from the other side of the bed.

One minute passed. She timed it on her phone.

Two minutes.

Three minutes.

The oblong lump lay in its pillowcase on the other side of the bed. Sofa cushions weren't supposed to be pillows, although this one was changing Noémi's mind. Neither Lili nor Tariq had noticed that the bonfire had been one cushion short.

Noémi asked, "And you're not trying to kill me?"

She leaned in and hugged the cushion to her chest, in the way she liked to be held. It squished so perfectly that she wondered if there was a metric scale for comfort. She was able to put it down easily; no succubus mind control was at work. If this thing was self-aware, it wasn't manipulating her anymore.

"A lower dosage of you is helping," she said. "This way we can stay together. You won't hurt me. You'll eat me, but on my terms."

The succubus-turned-sofa-turned-pillow said nothing in return. It was as good as inanimate. Lili was probably right that it was mindless, save its hunger. But it had a home now, and someone who consented to having her pain eaten. Noémi hoped her pain was delicious.

Idly, she petted the pillow's seams, wondering when Tariq would figure it all out. They needed to talk before his bedroom turned host to a witch trial.

Two more texts came in: one of Tariq kissing a shoebox, and a second asking about her.

TARIQ

u get any z's?

NOEMI

Only because I had company.

TARIQ

lol you better buy me new sheets

A moment later, he texted again.

TARIQ

some1 i shld meet?

She hesitated with her thumbs on the screen, creating an accidental string of N's. Lying to him now would be a mistake. God, she'd be dead without her friends.

NOEMI

Yeah. I'll introduce you tonight.

He texted another picture of himself holding the shoebox up like it was the Infinity Gauntlet. She snorted so hard her eyes crossed, then reclined against the succubus pillow. So this was what relief felt like.

. . . .

John Wiswell is a disabled writer who lives where New York keeps all its trees. He is a Nebula and Locus Award winner, and has been short-listed for the Hugo, World Fantasy, and British Fantasy Awards. He is the author of two novels: *Someone You Can Build A Nest In* and *Wearing The Lion*.

LET ALL THE CHILDREN BOOGIE

Sam J. Miller

Radio was where we met. Our bodies first occupied the same space on a Friday afternoon, but our minds had already connected Thursday night. Coming up on twelve o'clock, awake when we shouldn't be, both of us in our separate narrow beds, miles and miles apart, tuning in to Ms. Jackson's Graveyard Shift, spirits linked up in the gruff cigarette-damaged sound of her voice.

She'd played "The Passenger," by Iggy Pop. I'd never heard it before, and it changed my life.

Understand: there was no internet then. No way to look up the lyrics online. No way to snap my fingers and find the song on YouTube or iTunes. I was crying by the time it was over, knowing it might be months or years before I found it again. Maybe I never would. Strawberries, Hudson's only record store, almost certainly wouldn't have it. Those four guitar chords were seared indelibly into my mind, the lonesome sound of Iggy's voice certain to linger there for as long as I lived, but the song itself was already out of my reach as it faded down to nothing.

And then: a squall of distortion interrupted, stuttering into staticky words, saying what might have been *"Are you out there?"* before vanishing again.

Eerie, but no more eerie than the tingly feeling I still had from Iggy Pop's voice. And the sadness of losing the song forever.

But then, the next day, at the Salvation Army, thumbing through hundreds of dresses I hated, what did I hear but—

"I am the passenger...and I ride and I ride—"

Not from the shitty in-store speakers, which blasted Fly-92 pop drivel all the time. Someone was singing. Someone magnificent. Like pawn-shop royalty, in an indigo velvet blazer with three handkerchiefs tied around one forearm, and brown corduroy bell-bottoms.

"I see things from under glass—"

The singer must have sensed me staring, because they turned to look in my direction. Shorter than me, hair buzzed to the scalp except for a spiked stripe down the center.

"The Graveyard Shift," I said, trembling. "You were listening last night?"

"Yeah," they said, and their smile was summer, was weekends, was Ms. Jackson's raspy-sweet voice. The whole place smelled like mothballs, and the scent had never been so wonderful. "You too?"

My mind had no need for pronouns. Or words at all for that matter. This person filled me up from the very first moment.

I said: "What a great song, right? I never heard it before. Do you have it?"

"No," they said, "but I was gonna drive down to Woodstock this weekend to see if I could find it there. Wanna come?"

Just like that. *Wanna come?* Everything I did was a long and agonizing decision, and every human on the planet terrified me, and this person had invited me on a private day trip on a moment's impulse. What epic intimacy to offer a total stranger—hours in a car together, a journey to a strange and distant town. What if I was a psychopath, or a die-hard Christian evangelist bent on saving their soul? The only thing more surprising to me than this easy offer was how swiftly and happily my mouth made the words: *That sounds amazing.*

"Great! I'm Fell."

"Laurie," I said. We shook. Fell's hand was smaller than mine, and a thousand times stronger.

Only then did I realize: I didn't know what gender they were. And, just like that, with the silent effortless clarity of every life-changing epiphany, I saw that gender was just a set of clothes we put on when we went out into the world.

And even though I hated myself for it, I couldn't help but look around. To see if anybody else had seen. If word might spread, about me and this magnificently unsettling oddball.

Numbers were exchanged. Addresses. A pick-up time was set. Everything was so easy. Fell's smile held a whole world inside it, a way of life I never thought I could live. A world where I wasn't afraid.

I wanted to believe in it. I really did. But I didn't.

"What did you think that was?" Fell asked, in the parking lot, parting. "That weird voice, at the end of the song?"

I shrugged. I hadn't thought much about it.

"At first I thought it was part of the song," Fell said. "But then the DJ was freaked out."

"Figured it was just...interference, like from another station."

"It's a big deal," Fell said. "To interrupt a commercial radio broadcast like that. You need some crazy hardware."

"Must be the Russians," I said solemnly, and Fell laughed, and I felt the world lighten.

And that night, tuning in to Ms. Jackson, "This song goes out to Fell, my number one fan. Wouldn't be a weeknight if Fell didn't call asking for some Bowie. So here's 'Life on Mars?' which goes out to Laurie, the girl with the mousy hair."

More evidence of Fell's miraculous gift. A thousand times I'd wanted to call Ms. Jackson, and each time I'd been too intimidated to pick up the phone. What if she was mean to me? What if I had to speak to a station producer first, who decided I wasn't worthy of talking to their resident empress? And who was I to ask for a song?

Also, I loved "Life on Mars?" I wondered if Fell knew it, had read it on my face or smelled it on my clothes with another of their superhuman abilities, or if they had just been hoping.

I shut my eyes. I had never been so conscious of my body before. David Bowie's voice rippled through it, making me shiver, sounding like Fell's fingertips must feel.

I wondered how many times I'd been touched by Fell, listening late at night, trembling at the songs they requested.

I remembered Fell's smile, and stars bloomed in the darkness.

But before the song was over, a sound like something sizzling rose up in my headphones, and the music faded, and a kind of high distortion bubbled up, and then began to stutter—and then become words. Unintelligible at first, like they'd been sped up, and then:

"...*mission is so unclear. I could warn about that plane crash, try to stop the spider-webbing epidemic. But how much difference would those things make? I'm only here for a short—*"

Then the mechanical voice was gone. David Bowie came back. And just as swiftly was switched out.

"Sorry about that, children," Ms. Jackson said, chuckling. An old sound. How long had she been doing this show? She always called her listeners children, like she was older than absolutely everyone in earshot. I heard a cigarette snuffed out in the background. "Getting some interference, sounds like. Maybe from the Air Force base. They're forever messing with my signals. Some lost pilot, maybe, circling up in the clouds. Looking for the light. Good time to cut to a commercial, I'd say."

Someone sang *Friendly Honda, we're not on Route Nine*, the inane omnipresent jingle that seemed to support every television and radio program in the Hudson Valley. I thought of Fell, somewhere in the dark. Our bodies separate. Our minds united.

"Welcome back to the Graveyard Shift," she said. "This is Ms. Jackson, playing music for freaks and oddballs, redheaded stepchildren and ugly ducklings—songs by us and for us, suicide queens and flaming fireflies—"

Fell's car smelled like apples. Like spilled cider, and cinnamon. Twine held one rear headlight in place. When we went past fifty miles an hour, it shook so hard my teeth chattered together. Tractor trailers screamed past like missiles. It was autumn, 1991. We were sixteen. We could die at any moment.

The way to Woodstock was long and complicated. Taking the thruway would have been faster, but that meant paying the toll, and Fell knew there had to be another way.

"No way in hell that was a lost pilot," Fell said. "That interruption last night. That was someone with some insane machinery."

"How do you know so much about radio signals?"

"I like machines," Fell said. "They make so much sense. Does your school have a computer? Mine doesn't. We're too poor." Fell went to Catskill High, across the river. "It sucks, because I really want to be learning how they work. They can do computations a million times faster than people can, and they're getting faster all the time. Can you imagine? How many problems we'll be able to solve? How quickly we'll get the right answer, once we can make a billion mistakes in an instant? All the things that seem impossible now, we'll figure out how to do eventually."

I lay there, basking in the warmth of Fell's excitement. After a while, I said: "I still think it was the Soviets. Planning an invasion."

"No Russian accent," Fell said. "And anyway I'm pretty sure the Cold War is over. Didn't that wall come down?"

I shrugged, and then said, "Thanks for the song, by the way."

Instead of answering, Fell held out one hand. I took it instantly, fearlessly, like a fraction of Fell's courage could already have rubbed off on me.

In that car I felt invincible. I could let Fell's lack of fear take me over.

But later, in Woodstock, a weird crooked little town that smelled like burning leaves and peppermint soap, Fell reached for my hand again, and I was too frightened to take it. What if someone saw? In my mind I could hear the whole town stopping with a sound like a record scratching. Everyone turning, pointing. Shouting. Pitchforks produced from nowhere. Torches. Nooses.

Space grew between us, without my wanting it to. Fell taking a tiny step away from me.

We went to Cutler's Record Shop. We found a battered old Iggy Pop cassette, which contained "The Passenger." Fell bought it. We went to Taco Juan's and then had ice cream. Rocky Road was both of our favorite.

Twilight when we left. Thin blue light filled the streets. I dreamed of grabbing Fell's hand and never letting go. I dreamed of being someone better than who I was.

As soon as the doors slammed, we switched on the radio.

"Responding to this morning's tragic crash of Continental Express Flight 2574, transport officials are stating that it's impossible to rule out an act of terrorism at this—"

"No *shit*," Fell said, switching it off.

"What?"

"The voice. They said *I could warn about the plane crash.*"

I laughed. "What, you think the voice in the night is part of a terrorist cell?"

"No," Fell said. "I think they're from the future."

Just like Fell to make the impossible sound easy, obvious. I laughed some more. And then I stopped laughing.

"Could be a coincidence," I said.

Fell pushed the tape in, pressed play. After our third trip through "The Passenger," rewinding the tape yet again, they looked over and saw the tears streaming down my face.

"It's such a sad song," I said. "So lonesome."

"Sort of," Fell said. "But it's also about finding someone who shares your loneliness. Who negates it. Cancels it out. Listen: *Get into the car. We'll be the passenger.* Two people, one thing. Plural singular."

"Plural singular," I said.

I'm sorry, I started to say, a hundred times, and told myself I would, soon, in just a second, until Fell looked over and said: "Hey. Can I come over? I don't feel like mixing it up with my mother tonight."

And that was the first time I ever saw fear on Fell's face.

My parents were almost certainly baffled by my new friend, but their inability to identify whether Fell was a boy or a girl meant they couldn't decide for sure if they were a sexual menace, so they couldn't object to Fell coming upstairs with me.

Three songs into the Graveyard Shift, Fell asked, "Can I spend the night?"

I laughed.

"I'm serious."

"Your mom wouldn't mind?"

"Probably she'd barely notice," Fell said. "And even if she did, it'd be like number nine on the list of things she'd want to scream at me about the next time she saw me."

"Fine by me," I said, and went downstairs to ask Mom and Dad.

Big smile. Confident posture. Think this through. "Cool if Fell spends the night here?" And then, without thinking about it, because if I'd spent a single nanosecond on it I would have known better, stopped myself, I added: "She already called her mom, and she said it was okay."

They smiled, relieved. They'd both been sitting there stewing, wondering whether what was happening upstairs needed to be policed. Whether a sex-crazed-menace male was upstairs seducing their daughter. But no. I'd said *she.* This was just some harmless, tomboyish girl.

"Yes of course," Mom said, but I couldn't hear her, just went by the smile, the nod, and I thanked her and turned to go, nausea making the room spin and the blood pound in my ears.

I felt sick. Somehow naming Fell like that was worse than a lie. Worse than an insult. It was a negation of who Fell was.

Cowardice. Betrayal. What was it, in me, that made me so afraid? That had stopped me from taking Fell's hand? That made me frightened of other people seeing what they were, what we were? Something so small that could somehow make me so miserable.

I was afraid that Fell might have heard, but Ms. Jackson was playing when I got back to my room, and Fell was on the floor beside the speaker, so that our hero's raspy voice drowned out every shred of weakness and horror that the world held in store for us.

We lay on the bare wooden floor like that for the next two hours. The window was open. Freezing wind made every song sweeter. Wood smoke seeped into our clothes. Our hands held tight.

Six minutes before midnight, approaching the end of the Graveyard Shift, it came again. The sizzle; the static; the chugging machine noise that slowly took the shape of a human voice. We caught it mid-sentence, like the intervening twenty-four hours hadn't happened, like it blinked and was now carrying on the same conversation.

"—out there. I don't know if this is the right...place. Time. If you're out there. If it's too late. If it's too early."

"Definitely definitely from the future," Fell whispered.

"You're so stupid," I said, giggling, so drunk on Fell that what they said no longer seemed so absurd.

"Or what you need to hear. What I should say. What I shouldn't."

The voice flanged on the final sentence, dropping several octaves, sounding demonic, mechanical. Slowing down. The *t* sound on the last word went on and on. The static in the background slowed down too, so that I could hear that it wasn't static at all, but rather many separate sounds resolving into sonic chaos. An endless line of melodic sequences playing simultaneously.

The voice flanged back, and said one word before subsiding into the ether again:

"—worthwhile—"

Control of the radio waves was relinquished. The final chords of "Blue Moon" resurfaced.

"There's our star man again," Ms. Jackson said with a chuckle. Evidently she'd had time to rethink her Air Force pilot theory. "Still lost, still lonely. I wonder—who do you think he's looking for? Call me with your wildest outer space invader theories."

"Want to call?" Fell whispered.

"No," I said, too fast, too frightened. "My parents are right across the hall. We'd wake them."

Fell shrugged. The gesture was such strange perfection. Their whole being was expressed in it. The confidence and the charm and the fearlessness and the power to roll with absolutely anything that came along.

I grabbed Fell's hand. Prayed that some of what they were would seep into me.

Fell touched my mousy hair. Sang softly: *"Is there life on Mars?"*

"We'll find out," I said. "Right? Machines will solve all our problems?"

At school, two days later, during lunch, I marched myself to the library and enrolled in computer classes.

"Shit," Fell said, pointing out the window, driving us home through snowy blue twilight.

Massive green Air Force trucks lined a long stretch of Route 9. Flatbeds where giant satellite dishes stood. Racks of cylindrical transformers. Men pacing back and forth with machines in their hands. None of it had been there the day before.

"What the hell?" I said.

"They're hunting for the voice in the night too," Fell said.

"Because it's part of a terrorist cell and knew about a plane crash before it happened."

"Or because it's using bafflingly complex technology that could only have come from the future," Fell said.

Then they switched on the radio, shrieked at what they found there. Sangscreamed: *"Maybe I'm just like my mother, she's never satisfied."*

"Why do we scream at each other?" I said, and then we launched into the chorus with one wobbly crooked magnificent voice.

My first view of Fell's house was also my first view of Fell's mother. She sat on the front porch wearing several scarves, smoking.

"Fuck," Fell said. "Fuck me, times ten thousand. I thought for sure she'd still be at work."

"We can go," I said. I'd been excited to see the house, for that insight into who Fell was and what had helped make them, but now panic was pulling hard at my hair. Fell's fear of the woman was contagious.

"No," Fell said. "If I act like she can't hurt me, sooner or later she really won't be able to."

She laughed when she saw me. "Of course it's a girl."

"Mrs. Tanzillo, I'm Laurie," I said, holding out my hand. "I'm pleased to meet you."

My good manners threw her off. She shook my hand with a raised eyebrow, like she was waiting to see what kind of trick I was trying to pull. I smelled alcohol. Old, baked-in alcohol, the kind that seeps from the pores of aging drunks. Which I guess she was.

"Don't you two turn my home into a den of obscenity," she called after us, as we headed in.

Fell let the door slam, and then exhaled: "God, she is such an asshole."

The house was sadder than I'd been expecting. Smaller; smellier; heaped with strange piles. Newspapers, flattened plastic bags, ancient water-stained unopened envelopes. A litter box, badly in need of emptying, and then probably burning. My parents were poor, but not poor like this.

"You're shaking," I said, and pulled Fell into a hug.

They stiffened. Wriggled free. "Not here."

"Of course," I said. "Sorry."

The TV was on. Squabbling among the former Soviet states. A bad divorce, except with sixteen partners instead of two, and with thermonuclear warheads instead of children. I watched it, because looking around the room—or looking at Fell looking at me—made me nauseous. A talking head grinned, said: *"It's naïve to think our children will get to grow up without the threat of nuclear war. There's no putting this genie back in the bottle."*

Fell talked fast, the shaking audible in every word. "This was a terrible idea. I felt good about us, like, it wouldn't matter what this place looked like or what you thought of it, because you know I'm not this, it's just the place where I am until I can be somewhere else, but now, I'm not so sure, I think I should probably take you home."

So Fell wasn't fearless. Wasn't superhuman.

So it was in Fell too. Whatever was in me. Something so small, that could chain down someone so magnificent.

Of course I should have put up more of a fight. Said how it didn't matter. But I hated seeing Fell like this. If Fell was afraid, what hope was there for me? Fell, who welcomed every awful thing the world had to show us. Fell was my only hope, but not this Fell. So I shrugged and said, "whatever you want," feeling awful about it already, and we turned around and went right back outside, and Mrs. Tanzillo thought that was the funniest thing she'd ever seen, and we didn't talk the whole ride home.

"That *is* what it sounds like when doves cry," Ms. Jackson said, as the spiraling keyboard riff faded out, as the drum machine loop wound down.

I'd called the song in. I wondered if Fell was listening, if they knew what it meant. How hard it had been for me to dial that number. How bare the floor beside me was. How cold. How much my chest hurt.

"This extended block of uninterrupted songs is brought to you by Friendly Honda," she said. "They're not on Route Nine. Let's stick with Prince, shall we? Dig a little deeper. A B-side. 'Erotic City.'" Her laugh here was raw and throaty, barely a laugh at all, closer to a grumble of remembered pleasure. Some erotic city she'd taken someone to, ages ago.

The song started. A keyboard and a bass doing dirty, dirty things together. Strutting, strolling. Becoming one thing, one lewd gorgeous sound that made me shiver.

I imagined Fell listening. Our minds entwined inside the song. An intimacy unencumbered by flawed bodies, troubled minds, or the fear of what could go wrong when we put them together. Small voices inside our heads that made us miserable.

What a magnificent thing we would be. If Fell ever spoke to me again. If we could make whatever our weird thing was work.

Just when things were getting good, as Prince was shifting to the chorus, the static sizzle:

"There are a million ways I could have done this. But anything else, something more straightforward, well, I thought it might just blow your minds. Cause panic. Do the opposite thing, from what I wanted to accomplish."

Prince and the star man struggled for dominance, dirty talk giving way to flanged static only to steal back center stage. I only heard one more intelligible phrase before the intruder cut out altogether, even though I stayed up until three in the morning to see if they'd return:

"—know it's all worthwhile—"

"I want to find her," Fell said, the next day, when I walked out the front door and there they were, sitting on my front steps.

I hid my shock, my happiness. My shame. My guilt. "Find who?"

"The voice in the night. The one Ms. Jackson keeps calling the star man."

I sat down. "You think it's a she?"

Fell shrugged. I had been imagining the voice belonged to a male, but now that I thought about it I heard how sexless it was, how mechanical. Could be anything, in the ear of the beholder.

Cold wind swung tree branches against the side of my house, sounding like someone awful knocking at the door. I could not unhunch my shoulders. The magnitude of my awfulness was such that I didn't know where to start. What to apologize for first.

"How would we even begin to do something like that?" I asked instead.

Fell picked up something I hadn't seen before. The size of three record album sleeves laid out in a row. Four horizontal lines of thin metal, with a single vertical line down the middle.

"A directional antenna," they said. "It picks up radio signals, but it's sensitive to the direction of the origin signal. Point it directly at the source and you get a strong signal; point it away and you'll get a faint one. Plug it into this receiver"— Fell held up a hefty army-green box—"and we can take measurements in multiple directions until we find the right one."

They talked like everything was fine, but their face was so tight that I knew nothing was.

"Where did you get that?" I asked, making my voice laugh. "And how do you know how to use it?"

"I told you, machines are kind of my thing."

"So, wait, we just turn it around until we find the signal, and then go in that direction?"

"Not necessarily," Fell said. "It tells direction, but not distance. So the signal could be three miles away, or three thousand, depending on how strong it is. With just one measurement, we could be driving into the wilderness for days." Fell produced a map from the inner workings of the complex blazer they wore. "So the best way to do it is to take a measurement from one place, draw a line on the map that corresponds precisely to the signal, and then go to another location and take another measurement, and draw another precise line on the map—"

"And the point where they meet is the probable location!" I said, excited.

"It's called triangulation," Fell said.

"Amazing. But for real. How do you know all this?"

"My uncle, he learned this from my grandfather, who did it in the war. Transmitter hunting is kind of a nerd game, for amateur radio operators. They call it foxtailing."

"Your uncle as in your mother's brother?"

Fell nodded. And there it was, the subject I'd been trying to avoid.

"He was the closest thing to a dad that I had," Fell said. "We used to have so much fun together. Didn't give a shit about sports or any of that standard dude shit. He was into weird shit like directional antennas and science fiction. Then he met this girl, and moved to Omaha with her. Fucking *Omaha*. I'm sorry about the other day, at my mom's. I acted like an idiot."

"*You* acted like an idiot? Don't be dumb, Fell—that was all me. I'm the one who should be apologizing. I didn't know how to react when I saw how upset you were. I should have stayed. I wanted to stay."

Fell grabbed my hand. I had so much more to say, and I imagine so did Fell, but we did not need a word of it.

Mom might be watching out the window, I thought, but did not let go of Fell's hand.

"What if the source of the signal is moving?"

Fell nodded. "I thought about that. I don't have a good solution. We just have to hope that's not the case, or we'll be triangulating bullshit."

"It's not the end of the world, if we end up standing in some empty field together."

We drove to the top of Mount Merino, to take our first measurement. And then we waited. Kept the car running, blasting the Graveyard Shift from shitty speakers. Across the street was a guardrail, and then a sheer drop to the river beneath us. The train tracks alongside it. We lay on the hood and looked at stars.

"You won't run out of gas like this?"

"The average car can idle for ninety-two hours—that's just under four days—on a full tank of gas, which is what we have," Fell said. "The battery will die long before we run out of gas."

I marveled at the intricacies of Fell's mechanical knowledge, but I had some knowledge of my own to share. I told Fell about my computer classes, and how, yeah, computers were incredible, they could do anything. Fell was as impressed as I'd hoped they'd be, but they kept asking me questions about the hardware that I couldn't answer. All I knew was software. Fell looked at programming the way I looked at machines: probably fascinating, but way over my head.

Fell told me about transistors, and how processing power was increasing exponentially; had been for decades. How eventually computers would be able to store as much information and process as many simultaneous operations as swiftly as a human brain. Then Fell showed me how to work the antenna, read the receiver, detect signal strength. We practiced on other radio stations, penciled lines on the map.

Then three hours passed. We were way past my curfew, and the star man hadn't shown.

"Fuck it," Fell said, at the end of Ms. Jackson's program. "Star person stood us up. We should go for a long drive. Charge the battery backup."

"Okay," I said, just assuming Fell was right and that was how those worked.

"Your parents won't mind?"

"Nah," I said, although they absolutely would, if they caught me sneaking back in, and there was a very good chance that they would because I am extremely clumsy, but that was the future and I didn't care about that, I only cared about the here and the now with Fell in Fell's car on this freezing night on this weird planet in this mediocre galaxy.

The radio show after Graveyard Shift was significantly less awesome, but we had to stick with it. Who knew whether star person would stumble onto any other stations. I had my portable radio and my headphones, so that I could periodically coast back and forth across the radio dial in search of our elusive visitor, but somehow I knew that this would be fruitless. For whatever reason, the signal was pegged to this specific station.

The new DJ talked too much between songs, and he had the voice of a gym teacher. The opening notes of "Where Is My Mind" came on and we both started screaming, but this asshole kept rambling on about a concert in Albany coming up next weekend, and he only stopped when the singer started singing.

"Goddamn him," Fell said, and then—static—then—

"—that's why I'm doing this, I guess. To tell you the future can be more magnificent, and more terrifying, than what you have in your head right now. And the one you embrace will be the one you end up with."

As soon as the voice began, Fell raised the antenna, held it out like a pistol. Turned slowly. We watched the receiver respond to the signal's varying strength, and hastily drew a bold thick line on the map when we found it. Cheered. Watched our breath billow.

"Told you he or she was a time traveler!" Fell said.

"That's *not* what that means."

"What does it mean, then?"

"We're picking up lines of dialogue from a movie, maybe. Or love letters from a lunatic. We should keep driving, wait for another one."

"It's late," Fell said. "My mom's not doing so well, lately."

The temperature dropped twenty degrees. The final notes of "Where Is My Mind" faded away.

"You can talk to me about it," I said, gulping down air as the ground opened up beneath me. "Whatever you're going through, I have your back. You know I love you, right?"

"I love you too, Laurie," but I could hear the unspoken rest of the sentence—like our minds had linked up already—like Fell knew, in a way I never would, how little love mattered.

"We'll go hunting tomorrow night," I said.

Fell nodded.

At school the next day, alone with the computer, I saw why Fell loved machines so much. Not because they were simple, but because the rules were clear. And when something went wrong, there was a way to fix it.

And the next night, hands clasped on the hood of Fell's car again, listening to Ms. Jackson with the directional antenna balanced across our thighs, I thought—if only *we* were machines. The sturdiness of hardware; the clarity of software. Not these awful meat puppets, in this awful world. Heads full of awful voices holding us back.

"I feel so good, when it's just us," Fell said, tapping into my thoughts with that eerie precision. "Our minds linked up inside the music. I want to stay there, forever."

"Maybe someday," I said, nonsensically, and Fell had the kindness not to point out that it was nonsense. We were what we were. Damaged minds alone in dying bodies.

Ms. Jackson exhaled smoke. "This one goes out to our friend the star man. Hope you get where you're going, buddy."

I groaned at the opening chords. "Starman," by David Bowie. "This song always makes me cry," I whispered, the lump already emerging in my throat.

Fell said, "I knew you were a Bowie girl."

We listened. The chorus hurt.

Fell heard me sniffle. "Hear the way his voice rises, between 'star' and 'man'?" they asked. "That's the same octave jump as in the chorus of 'Somewhere Over the Rainbow.' You hear it? Star-*man*; Some-*where*?"

Fell was right. I'd listened to the song a million times before, and never noticed. And now for as long as I lived I'd never hear it without noticing. And now I was crying. Because the song was so beautiful; because Fell was so incredible; because the world was too awful for love like ours to last.

The final chorus wound down:

Let the children lose it

Let the children use it

Let all the children boogie

And the guitar cranked up, and the background singers crooned, and we were doomed, Fell and me, I felt it as heavy as the skin on my bones, how impossible we were, how soon we'd be shattered, and then—there the voice was again:

"The future is written, you might say. What will be will be. What's the point of this? But so many futures are written. An infinite number, in fact. A billion trillion ways your story could end. I want to make sure you end up with the right future."

Fill raised the antenna. Turned slowly, searching for the signal. Found it. We drew a line on the map. We circled the spot where our two lines met.

Both of us were crying, but Fell's tears were happy ones.

Fell didn't call me the next day, the way they say they would. Nor did they come by the house. And there was no answering machine at the Tanzillo household, and no one picked up, no matter how many times I called.

I told myself this was something sacred, something practically supernatural, to go to the spot on the map where our lines crossed, where the star person's signal came from. So of course Fell was scared.

I told myself that's all it was.

I told myself that, the whole long bike ride to Fell's front door, where I knocked three times. The pounding echoed. How had I found the courage to come at all? What was I becoming?

"Quit calling my house," said Fell's mom when she opened the door. I'd only seen her sitting down before. She was taller than I'd imagined. Her long loose gray hair would have been glamorous on anyone else. "Christ, I feel like I spend half my time watching the phone ring, waiting for you to give the hell up."

"You could pick it up, actually talk to me."

She shrugged. The gesture was the same as Fell's, heavier on the left shoulder than the right, but this version oozed with cynicism and inertia instead of energy and exuberance. The news was on in the background, turned up too loud, more talking heads talking nuclear annihilation. On the way in, I'd passed more military trucks. Trailers getting set up along the Hudson River. Satellite dishes blooming like steel flowers.

"Where's Fell?"

"Not here."

"Do you know where?"

"Sometimes they go to sleep at their grandpa's place." Except Mrs. Tanzillo used the wrong gender pronouns, and clearly took great pleasure in doing so. "Old trailer, been abandoned since the man died ten years ago. Full of raccoon shit, and wasps in summer. I'll tell Fell you dropped by though." Her sweet smile made it clear she'd do no such thing, and then she shut the door in my face.

I got on my bike.

This pain, it was Fell's. It wasn't mine, and I couldn't do anything to diminish it. I could ride away and never feel it again.

I said that, but I didn't believe it. I remembered what the star person had said. About how we could have a future that was magnificent or one that was terrifying, depending on which one we embraced.

I got off the bike.

Fell couldn't see it, what a sad little creature their mother was. How absurd it was, that someone as magnificent as Fell could be made miserable by someone so weak.

Someone so small.

I knocked again.

She said nothing when she opened the door. Just smiled, like, *come on, little girl, hit me with your best shot*. And I had nothing. No practiced witty wise one-liners. Fell would have, for anyone but her.

"You're only hurting yourself, you know."

Her eyebrows rose. Her smile deepened.

"You might have the power to hurt Fell now, but that power won't last long. As soon as Fell realizes what a useless angry pitiful person you are, you'll lose that power." I wanted my words to be better. But I was done letting wishing I was better stop me from being what I was. "And Fell will leave you here, drowning in cat shit and bills, while they go conquer the world."

She said something. I didn't hear what it was.

That night I heard the star man again. Somehow I knew it was just me this time. Like our minds were already beginning to overlap, and I could see Fell lying in silence in that dirty trailer, shivering under a blanket, no radio, listening to pine trees shush overhead, while I heard the star man whisper:

"*...Two soldiers trapped behind enemy lines...*"

I stayed late after school, in the computer lab. In the library. Reading the science and the science fiction Fell had rhapsodized about. All the impossible things that could save us from ourselves. Solar power; a post-petroleum future; superfoods. Cold fusion. Brain uploading. Digital immortality. Transcending the limits of the human.

Each time I shut a book, it was the pain of waking up from blissful dream to wretched reality.

But then, blissful dream: Fell was on my front steps when I got home. Alone in the deep black-blue of late twilight. Snow fell in half-hearted flurries.

"Sorry," they said when I ran straight at them. My hug took all the air out of them.

"Never disappear again," I whispered.

Fell nodded. A crumpled map in one raised fist. "Are we gonna do this?"

"We are."

A cassette blasted when Fell started up the car. David Bowie. We drove, heading for where our lines crossed. The gulf between us was still so wide. Maybe I believed, now—that we could work, that what we added up to could survive in this world—but Fell did not. Fell still believed what Mrs. Tanzillo believed: that Fell was hell-bound, disgusting, deserving of nothing good. The miles inched past my window, closing in on the X on the map, and I had no words, no weapons to breach the wall between us.

And then: Fell did.

"Whatever you said to my mom? It really pissed her the fuck off."

"I am so sorry," I said. "It was selfish. I didn't think it through. What it might mean for you."

"No," Fell said, and turned onto Route 9. "I never saw her like that before. I went home and she didn't say a word to me. Like, at all. Except to say you stopped by. That never, ever happens. I don't know how, but what you said messed her up really bad."

"She—"

"No fucking way," Fell said, turning off the main road. "This can't be it."

We'd reached the spot on the map. We were stopped outside the Salvation Army. Where we'd met, a mere two weeks before.

"Nobody's broadcasting from here," they said.

We rolled down our windows. Snow fell harder now. Science fiction scenarios blurred in my brain. Time travel. Brain uploading.

"They'd need so much equipment," Fell said. "If we heard it on the other side of the river? They'd need a massive antenna, but there's nothing. And—"

Fell trailed off.

I looked up at the sky. Snow tap-tap-tapped at my forehead. I remembered what the star man said, the night before, to me and me alone. *Two soldiers trapped behind enemy lines.*

It was talking to me and Fell.

"The equipment's not here," I said. "Or, it's *here*, but it's not *now*."

Fell got out of the car. I turned up the radio and got out after them.

"I get it," I said, laughing, crying, comprehending. One wobbly crooked magnificent voice. "You were right, Fell. It's coming from the future."

We stood. Snow slowly outlined us.

"It's us," I said. Fell had finally infected me. The audacious, the impossible, was not only easy—it was our only way forward. "That machine voice? That's... you and me. Our two voices together, somehow. A consciousness made up of both of our minds."

Fell turned their head, hard, like they weren't listening, or were listening and not understanding, or understanding and not believing.

"Plural singular," I said. "We are the passenger."

"Plural singular," Fell said, snow falling into their perfect face, while David Bowie told us *let all the children boogie.*

They still didn't see, but that was okay. There would be time to tell Fell all of it. To say that there was so much to be afraid of—nuclear winter, ecological devastation, the death spasms of patriarchy. That the next fifty years would see unspeakable suffering. But we could survive it. Overcome it. Surmount the limits of our flesh and our mortality and our separateness. Combine into some new kind of thing, some wobbly magnificent machine who could crack the very fabric of time and space. We could send a signal back, into the past, a lonely sad staticky voice in the night, to tell the beautiful damaged kids we had been that the future would be as good as they had the courage to be.

....

Sam J. Miller's books have been called "must-reads" and "bests of the year" by *NPR*, *Entertainment Weekly*, *USA Today*, and *O: The Oprah Magazine*, among others. They've also been banned in Florida and stolen by AI. His short fiction has been published in places like *The Kenyon Review*, *Vogue Italia*, *Tor.com*, *Asimov's*, and more. He's received the Nebula, Locus, and Shirley Jackson Awards. He's also the last in a long line of butchers. Sam lives in New York City, and at samjmiller.com

MR. DEATH

Alix E. Harrow

I've ferried two hundred and twenty-one souls across the river of death, and I can already tell my two-hundred-and-twenty-second is going to be a real shitkicker. I know by the lightness of the manila folder in my hand, the preemptive pity in the courier's face as she gives it to me. I read the typewritten card paper-clipped to the front with my stomach tensed, braced for the sucker punch.

> *Name:* Lawrence Harper
> *Address:* 186 Grist Mill Road, Lisle NY, 13797
> *Time:* Sunday, July 14th 2020, 2:08AM, EST
> *Cause:* Cardiac arrest resulting from undiagnosed long QT syndrome
> *Age:* 30 months

Jesus Christ on His sacred red bicycle. He's two.

Two is, by break room consensus, the worst age for reaping. Their souls are still baby-soft and cottony, wholly innocent, but full of the subtleties and quirks that define their selfhood. They're balanced right at the teetering edge of themselves, so full of potential it makes your eyes water just to be near them.

Also, two-year-olds are contrarian bastards and it takes several hours and a family-size pack of M&Ms to coax them across the river.

These days, with the child mortality rate comfortably below 7 per 1,000 births, we don't process too many of the under-fives—some of the older reapers like to bitch about how we've got it soft, reminiscing about the good old days before seatbelt laws and vaccinations and the EPA–but six-point-six out of a thousand is still six-point-six too many. Every reaper hits one eventually.

This was my first, in my three years of reaping. I was starting to think somebody upstairs was looking out for me, shielding me in case one of the under-fives turned out to be a little boy with corn silk hair and dark eyes. In case I cracked like an egg and had to retire early.

Every new reaper is shielded, at least a little. The first dozen or so deaths we're assigned are generally people with one spiritual foot firmly in the grave: your stage-IV seventy-year-olds, your left behind spouses, your great-grandmothers who just overheard the term *assisted living* floating up the stairs.

There's something satisfying about those reapings. A routine heroism, like covering a shift for your hungover friend or shooing a trapped bird out the window. Those are the times it's easiest to believe my supervisor's speeches about the pristine order of the universe and the cyclical shape of time and the necessity of death.

(Some reapers dance around the word *death*, preferring verbs like *passing* or *ascending*. My supervisor—Raz, Reaper Recruitment Coordinator and Archangel of Secrets—believes euphemisms are a form of cowardice, and Raz doesn't recruit cowards).

But eventually you run out of easy deaths.

Eventually the courier slinks into the locker room and hands you a manila folder without quite meeting your eyes and you know you're in for it: newlyweds in car crashes; leukemia that was supposed to be in remission; restraining orders that didn't work. Or sometimes it seems fine—88 *years old, ischemic stroke, 4:12PM*—but when you arrive you find a soul so wasted and dim, so shriveled by bitterness and regret that you want to stop the clock and say: *Look, you've got a week. Try a new ice cream flavor. Listen to the Hamilton soundtrack. Call your son. Live, you damn fool.*

Except you don't because you can't, and because of the pristine order of the universe and the cyclical shape of time, et cetera. Instead you sit beside him and watch the plaque crumble from his carotid and drift sluggishly up to his cerebral artery. The fizz of electricity in his brain goes dark and the sour muck of his soul rises from his body, glaring. It's a long ride across the river that night.

So I don't come apart when I see little Lawrence Harper's name on that neatly-typed card, the curve of that 3 staring up at me like half a heart. I lay the folder in my scuffed briefcase—I was never a briefcase-carrier before, but fashion in the hereafter runs twenty to fifty years behind—and head out for 186 Grist Mill Road.

I already know how it will go: I will wait beside him in the night (does he have a bed shaped like a plastic race car like Ian did? Does he kick the blankets off his legs every night?) until 2:08AM, when the bird-wing flutter of his heart will go still. I will tuck his ghostly hand in mine as I lead him through the dark to the riverbank, and when we reach the other side I'll watch his soul disperse into the depthless firmament of the universe. It will be achingly sad but also kind of beautiful, and afterward I'll sit in the break room and drink burned coffee and cry. Leon might come by and give me the Circle of Life speech from *The Lion King* and we'll both laugh and he'll thump me on the shoulder and say *it's just the way it goes.*

And then tomorrow I'll open my next manila folder and do it again.

Not because I'm a heartless bastard; they don't recruit heartless bastards to comfort the dead and ferry their souls across the last river. They look for people whose hearts are vast and scarred, like old battlefields overgrown with poppies and saplings. People who know how to weep and keep working, who have lost everything except their compassion.

(The official recruitment policy is race and gender-neutral, but forty-something white males like me are a rarity. We are statistically less likely to experience shattering loss, and culturally permitted to become complete assholes when we do. We turn into addicts and drunks, bitter old men who shed a single, manly, redemptive tear at the end of the movie, while everybody else has to gather up the jagged edges of themselves and keep going).

Raz told me she also looks for people with kind eyes and a high tolerance for bureaucracy, who have never cheated at anything in their entire lives (poker, *Settlers of Catan*, marriage). "You can cheat a lot of shit," she says, "But not death."

Lawrence Harper doesn't have a race car bed, thank God. Instead he has a twin mattress on the floor of his parents' single-wide. He also has: a Spiderman blanket that smells like a thrift store, dusty and flowery; a plastic Buzz Lightyear clutched in one sweaty fist; reddish hair, skim milk skin; a heart that will fail in approximately eleven hours and twelve minutes; and a soul that shines like a comet streaking across the last midnight of summer.

Even for a two-year-old, it's a stunner of a soul, vibrant and hungry, bonfire bright. It's the kind of soul that might lead revolutions or write symphonies in an adult, but in a kid it mostly translates to trouble. I bet his parents spend a lot of time smiling fixedly at strangers as they haul him out of restaurants or pry him out of trees. I bet his grandma refers to him as "a handful" and refuses to babysit except in emergencies.

I bet they'll miss him like hell once he's gone.

That's what makes this job tough, of course. It's not the dead rejoining the limitless love of the universe; it's the ones they leave behind, who have to keep on trudging through the world beneath the burden of their terrible, limited love.

I settle cross-legged on the carpet, trying not to nudge the piled laundry or set off some battery-powered toy. Reapers have what the training manuals call "limited corporeal capacity," which means we can move stuff but not much, like when you're in a dream and your limbs are filled with wet sand and everything is impossibly, illogically heavy.

I figure most ghost stories are the result of clumsy reapers, although there are late night break room rumors of reapers who went rogue. Who abandoned the Department and haunted the living world until they faded into tattered wraiths. I don't know if I believe those stories, because A) what kind of asshole wants to spend eternity creeping around a Victorian mansion or an old psych ward, scaring teenagers, and B) Raz or one of the other archangels would atomize them so instantly and thoroughly there wouldn't be enough drifting motes of soulstuff left to tell a story about. Raz is the kind of sweet, middle-aged Black woman with whom you do not fuck.

I've never been tempted to do anything more than bum a cigarette or flick a light switch, myself. (Except the one time, right after my own funeral. I slunk back into my shitty, tobacco-stained apartment and took the only thing in it that I cared a damn about. But it wasn't a big deal and nobody saw.)

Lawrence stirs beneath his Spiderman blanket and sits up, his hair smeared sideways, his eyes blue, unfocused. His dad must hear the rustling on the baby monitor because he turns up two seconds later, a lanky, tired man in sweatpants. He drapes Lawrence casually over one shoulder and pads back down the hall, and for a moment I'm too choked with envy and pity to follow them. Envy because he's holding his son in his arms, sleep-soft and sweaty; pity because this is the last time.

By the time I make it out to the kitchen Lawrence is snapped into a plastic booster seat crunching off-brand Cheerios. He looks up as I enter and I figure it's nothing, just a coincidence, but then his eyes focus on me. Lawrence waves.

I've been seen before, but not often. For most people I'm a prickle at their hairline, a smudged not-quite-reflection in the mirror behind them, a strange and unwelcome awareness of their heartbeats in their ears. Reapers are the reason fewer people board doomed flights and good dogs sometimes bark at nothing.

But the way Lawrence is looking at me—head tilted, eyes flicking from briefcase to old-timey suit to beard stubble—I know he sees every single undead inch of me.

I wave back, awkwardly. He smiles. I press one finger to my lips. He copies me, then whispers "*SHHH*" so loudly that his dad laughs and shushes him back, and then they're drawn into a competitive shushing game that lasts through snack time and outside into the sweet fresh-clover smell of the July afternoon.

Their yard is several inches past overgrown and littered with sun-faded scraps of plastic. I don't feel the heat so much these days but I can tell from the wavy lines coming off the trailer that it's hotter than the hell that doesn't exist. Lawrence's dad settles into a busted lawn chair in the shade while his son wanders. I trail after him.

Lawrence picks up a stick and slashes invisible enemies, narrating a story that sounds like a combination of *Toy Story* and *Star Wars*. He tosses a tennis ball at the trailer for a while, apparently intrigued by the showers of rust that pour out from under the siding, then throws it, for no reason at all, to me.

And I catch it, like a dumbass. It strains against the insubstantial edges of my existence. Lawrence holds his arms out, waiting.

I can't quote the Book of Death line and verse the way Raz can, but I'm pretty sure there's a policy somewhere against playing catch in broad daylight with a doomed two-and-a-half-year-old, surrounded by the green hum of summer.

But like—fuck it. I toss the ball back. Lawrence misses it, because two-and-a-half-year-olds have the coordination of drunk bear cubs, but it doesn't matter. I am immediately promoted from boring stranger to Imaginary Friend and conscripted into a series of opaque games involving tennis balls and shrieking and running in circles around the trailer until even my death-cold skin is flushed and sweaty and my chest is aching, as if my heart is either mending or breaking.

By the time the game ends the sun is slanting pink and sideways and the world has softened like butter on the counter. Lawrence collapses backward onto the densest patch of clover and lies still for the first time since he woke up. I can see white streaks of cloud in his eyes and, if I squint, the red muscle of his heart contracting and releasing in that secret, imperfect rhythm. His soul blazes back at the sky, wide-open, a private infinity of possibility.

I wonder if Ian's reaper watched him like this, with something aching and tender lodged like a splinter behind their breastbone. I wonder if Ian's soul shone this brightly (I know it did). I wonder how it will feel to watch a soul like this disperse into the endless everything, scattered into a billion lonely atoms.

Raz was my reaper. She showed me my folder afterward and the card paper-clipped to it: *Sam Grayson, 44 years old, 11:19AM EST, respiratory failure resulting from small cell lung cancer.* The cancer came courtesy of a pack of Lucky Strikes a day for fifteen years or so; my personal fuck you to mortality after Ian.

I couldn't see her, but I could sort of sense her: a soft, amber gaze hovering at the edges of the hospital room, watching the labored rise and fall of my chest.

It's department policy to spend at least four hours prior to death with the soon-to-be-deceased. It's supposed to "forge emotional bonds between souls and reapers" and "encourage compassionate care"—the department has been working tirelessly and fruitlessly to combat the whole sweeping robes, menacing scythe stereotype—but Raz believes in a full twelve, even during busy weeks (flu epidemics, civil wars, the holidays).

So she sat at my bedside through the night and half a day until my clogged lungs bubbled into silence and my pulse stuttered and I drowned in carbon dioxide and cancer. I died thinking *fucking finally.*

I could see her, then: a brown-skinned woman somewhere between thirty and seventy wearing a white cable-knit sweater and comfortable Levi's.

She smiled—a professional smile, smoothed by centuries of use, but still somehow genuine—and launched into what I now recognize as a version of the same "welcome to the afterlife, kid" speech I've given two hundred and twenty-one times. It begins with some variation of "it's all right," which is an absolute lie and both of you know it, but which manages to imply that there's some sort of plan, a system in place, and usually buys you a few minutes to explain the rest.

It worked on me. I drifted, perfectly placid, as Raz explained that I was dead, and that we would shortly be stepping together into a vast and endless darkness, broken only by an even darker river, which she would guide me across. Then there was a lot of other stuff about how my soul would unravel and rejoin the spangled cosmos, and how the universe itself was love, which is all true but is still unforgivably hokey.

And then she paused and I had the feeling—even as machines beeped in ineffective alarm and my soul hovered above my body like steam above pasta water, milky and vaporous—that we were going off script.

She tilted her head, the gentle amber of her eyes sharpening. "Or," she began, and let me tell you the human brain is capable of a lot of wordless scenario-spinning in the infinite space following the word *or*. *Or* this isn't the end. *Or* this is a bad reaction to my meds and I'll wake up hungover but alive. *Or* I get a pair of feathered wings and I'll go soaring through the pearly gates and Ian will be waiting for me on a puff of cumulus, laughing his wild laugh, and these fifteen years of heartache will be wiped clean, set right, the moment my palm brushes the soft corn silk of his hair.

But she didn't say any of that. She handed me a cream-colored business card with my name embossed cleanly on the front—*Sam Grayson, Junior Reaper, Department of Death*—and offered me a job.

Just before dark, Lawrence's mom shows up in a puttering Corolla. She wears a red apron with Tractor Supply embroidered across the top and smells like rubber and chicken feed and the gray film of receipt paper, but Lawrence doesn't care: he practically teleports into her arms, face mashed against the stringy bone of her shoulder.

The Harpers clatter together into the trailer and start the dinnertime circus of bib and highchair, mac n' cheese and canned peas he won't eat, adult conversation slipped expertly between threats and pleas (*"if you spit your milk out one more time I'm taking it away—did you pay the gas bill?—two bites, baby, eat two bites of peas"*). His dad pulls on a polyester uniform and pours himself a thermos of burnt coffee. Before he leaves he kisses the back of his wife's neck and she tilts her head back, eyes closed.

I can see how tired they are, worn thin with work and worry. I can see how there's never quite enough money, how they rinse out Ziploc bags and resent the loss of milk-splattered macaroni. But I can see, too, that it's worth it. That they'll keep working and worrying and the impossible alchemy of love will turn never enough into plenty.

Except that, at 2:08 AM the following morning, their son's heart will stop and I will ferry his soul across the river and their lives will be permanently, irreparably fucked.

I want to leave. I want to step sideways out of the world and reappear back in the break room, smoke a stolen cigarette with Leon and forget all about the Harpers.

Except Lawrence would still die. Except there would be no friendly stranger waiting to take his hand and show him the way. He would wander alone into the darkness on the wrong side of the river and wisp away into nothing instead of everything.

So I stay. Raz doesn't recruit cowards or bastards, after all.

Lawrence's mom does bath and bedtime on her own while Lawrence chatters about Maui's magical fish hook and his big kid underwear and his new friend who's very tall and sad. She makes the right noises—*really? that's great sweetie!*—but she's not really listening, and I have a sudden, wild urge to shake her until her teeth rattle.

This is it! I want to say. *This is the conversation you will replay again and again for the rest of your life! You will wish you took his soft cheeks in your hands and looked into his eyes and said: I love you, Ian, and wherever you go a part of me will always follow, across that dark river and into black beyond, through every eternity.*

But I keep my fists balled in my pockets as she zips him into pajamas and plugs in his nightlight. Her last kiss is a routine brush of her lips across his forehead. "Night, love."

"Night, Mama."

The door clicks. He thrashes for a few minutes before falling abruptly and profoundly to sleep.

I watch the treacherous thump of his heart, counting out beats. I've watched enough heart failures and cardiac arrests to hear the fatal hitch in its rhythm, the tiny irregularity that will fail him when he needs it most. He's a brave kid—the kind who laughs at barking dogs and watches the garbage truck with an expression of aspirational awe—or he wouldn't have made it two and a half years without startling his heart into seizing.

But tonight something's going to scare him or thrill him. A nightmare, maybe, formless and childish, that will send his heart into an ungainly gallop. Then it will stumble. Then it will stop. His parents won't even know until they open his door in the morning, wondering why he's sleeping so late.

I see the nightmare arrive, drawing a line between the pale red of his brows. The line looks fresh somehow, like tracks in new snow, as if he'd never really frowned before. I watch his heart beat faster, *tut-tut-tut*. The delicate chambers pulse raggedly now, losing the rhythm they've practiced for thirty months. Thirty-nine months, I guess.

His heart seizes. The frown line deepens. His mouth opens as his pale skin goes from red to white to pearl-blue, and I see the first wisps of his soul rise like steam from his body.

I don't think. I don't debate or decide. I just—*do.*

I reach between his ribs and wrap my hand around his heart. It feels impossibly small against my hand, a hard apple plucked too early from the tree. I squeeze it as hard as I can with my fingers that don't exist and my fist that isn't there.

His heart shudders back to life like an engine on a cold morning. It flutters against my hand as the blue leaches out of his lips and his soul spools back into his body.

I sit beside him until dawn, watching the miraculous thud of his heart and thinking: *he's alive, he's alive* and also *oh, fuck.*

It's the failure to submit my Certification of Soul's Passage that gets me, of course. You can't forge them or fake them or forget them; when a soul disintegrates into the void it automatically generates a sheaf of papers in triplicate, signed with the last fading imprint of a soul as it leaves the world, and Lawrence Harper's soul is still very much in the world, tethered to his illegal heartbeat.

Raz finds me sitting on the pier, splashing my feet in the river of death. I'm half-expecting her to skip the small talk and go straight to the smiting but instead she sits beside me on the dry decking, the soft white of her sweater brushing against my shoulder.

She's quiet for a while. And then: "You know it doesn't work like this, Sam."

"Yeah," I say, because I do know, and what else am I going to say? That there was a beautiful boy and I didn't want him to die like my beautiful boy died? That I didn't want to ferry his soul to the far side of the river and watch it merge, however beautifully, with the infinite love of the universe? And P.S. *fuck* infinite love, give me the desperate, finite love of the living?

I don't say any of that, because I don't (quite) have a death wish.

Raz says, softly, "Would you like me to reassign him?"

Even burrowed deep in my doomed funk, I feel a flick of surprise. Deaths aren't reassigned, traded, escaped, called-out-sick-on, avoided, or skipped; your deaths are your deaths, no matter how grisly, and if you can't handle them you have a brief but blunt conversation with your supervisor after which no one ever sees you again. None of us know where you go, but it's unlikely that it's anywhere pleasant.

I look directly at Raz for the first time and find her face glowing with that terrible, bottomless compassion. She draws a Lucky Strike from her breast pocket and passes it over. She touches her fingertip to the end and it glows hot orange. "Do you still have the picture?"

I don't move. I don't breathe.

Raz knows. She knows that I flagrantly ignored the chapter in the Book of Death on Releasing Your Worldly Connections and Severing Familial Ties. She knows what I stole from my shitty apartment. She probably even knows that it's resting right now in my breast pocket, directly above my heart.

I swallow once, inhale smoke. "He was—he was a good kid."

"I know, Sam." Her voice is still so gentle. "And so is Lawrence, and it's bull-shit that they have to die, but that's how it is. It's the ugly half-bargain of living, and it's our job to make it a little less ugly when we can." She pauses and adds practically, "And we can't save every cute kid. We can't cheat death."

But I think: *I did.* How long did I buy Lawrence? How much would I pay for another day, another hour with Ian?

I don't say anything. Her voice turns considerably less gentle. "That car was going eighty-five miles an hour when it hit the ice. There was nothing Leon could have done to stop it, no matter how many rules he broke."

Leon. I never knew who reaped Ian's soul and hadn't asked. Leon is a good dude—soft-spoken and big-hearted—but for a split second I want to drag him into the river with me and hold us both under until our second and final death closes above our heads.

"I'm going to ask you again: do you want me to reassign him?"

It's a kindness. A favor, and Raz doesn't really do favors. I am obscurely warmed and almost tempted to accept—but I don't want Lawrence reassigned. His death belongs to me. However many beats his heart had left, they are mine to witness.

"No. I've got it. Thanks."

Raz leans across me, plucks the still-lit cigarette from my fingertips and flicks it into the river. Her breath against my ear is sulfurous, too hot. "Then don't fuck it up this time."

She hands me a freshly printed card with Lawrence's name on it—July 28th, 5:22AM, cardiac arrest again—and vanishes.

I run my fingertip around the crisp edge of the card and realize I was wrong. It wasn't a kindness or a favor: it was a test.

It's July 28th and I'm in the back bedroom of the Harpers' damn trailer again, watching Lawrence's heart pump like a tiny red bellows in his chest.

Except this time I've had two weeks to anticipate it. Two weeks to sit in the break room refilling my coffee from the pot that never empties, feeling the time-softened folds of the Polaroid in my breast pocket, thinking about the order of the universe and the Circle of Motherfucking Life and things you can't cheat.

This time I know exactly what I'm going to do.

At 4:00 in the morning, one hour and twenty-two minutes before he's sched-uled to die, I take Lawrence's hand. I stroke his forehead with barely-real knuckles and he half-wakes. He smiles a muzzy, sleepy smile and sinks back into sleep.

I keep holding his hand. I make sure that nightmare never comes.

At 5:23AM Lawrence's heart is still beating, red and wet and alive, and I'm smiling so hard I can feel my face splitting along the seams. I want to sing. I want to weep. I want to recite the poem I memorized in seventh grade because it was the shortest one on the list: *how do you like your blue-eyed boy/Mr. Death?*

I know I didn't cheat him, not really. Mr. Death always wins in the end. But maybe sometimes—if you're stubborn and sad and tired as fuck of the way things go—you can win a hand or two.

I stay with Lawrence til dawn, wondering idly if I should cut and run while I still can. It seems more important to stay, to watch the stubborn *thu-thumping* of Lawrence's heart, the miraculous pooling of drool on his pillow. I should have spent more time watching Ian.

I feel it when she arrives: an abrupt rise in temperature, a whiff of brimstone. I look out the narrow window to see Raz standing in the yard like the end times, like vengeance in a cable-knit sweater. I look back at Lawrence one last time and am pleased to find I don't regret a single damn thing.

I slip through particle board and fiberglass and corrugated tin of the trailer wall and stroll to Raz with my hands in my pockets. I smile at her. It's not really the time for genial smiles—I'm about to be atomized or incinerated or disappeared, whatever the hell they do with reapers who fuck up—but I can't seem to stop.

Raz smiles back. "You idiot." Her eyes are still kind. Behind her I see the faint, fiery outline of wings.

I shrug.

Raz steps forward and reaches two fingers into my breast pocket. She withdraws the Polaroid, flesh-warm, and studies it for a long second. "I knew the second you went back for this that you wouldn't last," she sighs. "A reaper has to forsake his worldly attachments, relinquish his earthly loves."

"Yeah, but..." My eyes fall on the picture, upside-down: my son at four, caught at the apex of a swing that will never fall, his corn silk hair haloed by a summer dusk that will never end. Ephemeral. Everlasting.

I shrug again. "But *fuck* that, you know?"

Raz laughs. She tilts her head. "Tell me, Sam: What would you do if I left you here?"

"Left me?"

"Burned your records. Pretended you'd never worked for the Department of Death."

"I would stay." The answer comes easy and honest. "I'd watch over Lawrence, keep his heart beating another day, another hour, for as long as I can."

"Even if it meant you could never cross the river. Even if you would fade into nothing instead of rejoining the great everything."

Would I trade my eternity for one little boy and his tired parents? The infinite love of the universe for the fleeting, finite love of the living?

"Yes." It occurs to me what absolute horseshit it is that I spent the last thirteen years of my life on earth wanting to leave it and yet now, in death, I've found something worth staying for.

Raz nods, unsurprised. "That's what I thought." There's a wistful something in her eyes as she smiles at me. "You were a good reaper, Sam. Tough enough to do the work, soft enough to do it right—two hundred and twenty-one times. I'm sorry to lose you."

She sounds genuinely sorry for whatever it is she's about to do to me. I wonder idly if it will hurt.

"Could—could you assign Leon to this case, after I'm gone? He's a good guy. I want Lawrence to be with someone who—"

Raz is distracted, rooting in her jean pocket for something. "No."

"Why?"

"Because Lawrence Harper is no longer under the jurisdiction of the Department of Death." She hands me the thing from her pocket and adds, "And neither are you."

There's a silent rushing of wings, a flick of heat, and Raz is gone. I blink around the yard, empty except for the dew-pearled lawn chair, the scattered plastic toys, the precious trash of the living.

Then I look down at the cream-colored card in my hand: *Sam Grayson, Junior Guardian, Department of Life.*

* * *

Alix E. Harrow is the *New York Times*–bestselling and Hugo Award–winning author of *The Ten Thousand Doors of January*, *The Once and Future Witches*, *Starling House*, and various short fiction. A former adjunct and Kentuckian, Harrow now lives in Virginia with her husband and their two semi-feral kids.

PROOF BY INDUCTION

José Pablo Iriarte

Paulie rushes out the elevator doors the moment they part, only to skid to a halt at the sight of his father's wife. She shakes her head, but he doesn't need the confirmation. If Tricia is out here and not in the hospital room with his father, it can only mean he has passed. He numbly accepts a hug from her.

When she releases him, a woman in a tweed jacket clears her throat. "Mr. Gifford, we are all very sorry for your loss."

"Thank you," he replies automatically, focusing on her crucifix. He swallows. "This is probably a dumb question, but what happens now?"

The chaplain draws herself up. "Now we all go back to the room where your father passed, unless of course you prefer not to." She begins walking as she talks. "You can enter into his Coda and say any goodbyes you'd like to say, or ask him any questions you have about his end."

Paulie follows her, wondering dimly if there will be fallout from the meeting he had to cancel with Professor Tappert. Paulie's father was a professor emeritus at his same university, so certainly they should be sympathetic. He doesn't kid himself about how this meeting was going to go, however. Tappert is on his P&T committee, and with his scant publication record and mediocre yearly reviews, his tenure prospects were already dim. They're even dimmer now.

Inside the hospital room, Paulie stares. He isn't sure what he expected, but he almost believes his father could open his eyes at any moment—except for the endotracheal tube stuck in his mouth. He's never been this close to a dead body before. Is he supposed to touch it or not? Paulie puts a hand on his shoulder; it feels like his father.

He grips the bed rail.

The chaplain gestures toward Tricia. "Mrs. Gifford elected not to enter his Coda. If you would like to, you can see him there."

Paulie eyes the console and cables behind the bed. "Is it really him?"

"Yes and no. The human mind remains aware of stimulus for up to five minutes after what we consider to be the moment of death. The Coda does for his consciousness what the rest of his telemetry does for his vital signs—takes a snapshot that we can look at later. The Coda allows you to interact with a simulacrum of your father, with his memories and personality at the end of his life." She gesticulates awkwardly, as though the topic is distasteful. "He can tell you if he had a life insurance policy, where the will is, things like that. The Coda cannot change in the way that a person can, however; it cannot learn or grow." Her eyes meet Paulie's. "Your father's soul is not in there. Your father has moved on."

It was early morning when Paulie put the headset on, but predawn when he blinked into the virtual environment. He had only left the hospital to go home and get some sleep about five hours before the end. Now he could almost believe he had turned back around and found his father waiting here, as though the 5 AM phone call from Tricia were just a dream.

Gone was the endotracheal tube. The room was eerily silent, with none of the sounds he'd associated with the hospital from his visits over the past week.

He met his father's eyes. "Hey."

His father smiled ruefully. "Hey."

"Are you—"

"Dead?" His father gestured toward the inactive monitors. "Apparently so."

"Does it hurt?" *Are you afraid*, he wanted to ask, but he knew better than to talk to his father about emotions.

"Nothing hurts," he said, picking at a scab on his leg. "I guess they have a way of turning that off."

"Did the doctors mess up? Should I ask for an autopsy?"

His father shook his head. "Nah. I'm seventy-one, diabetic, and with a bad heart. You're not going to win any lawsuits here."

It occurred to Paulie that Codas could be programmed to give whatever answer benefitted the hospital.

Paulie stared out the window, over the parking lot, to the eerily empty expressway. "I really believed we were close on that Perelman proof."

"Maybe nobody's meant to find it."

Easy for him to say. He'd already been beyond questions of tenure and publication; now all of that was even more meaningless for him. For Paulie, though, Perelman would have been the home run his tenure dossier needed.

He turned back toward the bed. "Okay. Well." He put a hand on the chair he'd sat in last night while his father complained about his breathing. He should say something. Something like *I love you*, he supposed. But his father had never gone in for the mushy stuff in life, so why start now?

"Goodbye, then," he finished instead.

"Bye, Paulie," said his father. "Thank you for visiting."

Thank you for visiting. The same as he'd taken to saying every time Paulie came to him since his health began to decline last year. Paulie waited, hoping this time his father would say something more, until the moment dragged on awkwardly, and then he pulled the interface off his head.

"What happens to his Coda when we leave?" he asks, leaning against a counter.

The chaplain sighs. "The equipment will be cleaned and reused, except for the actual leads that connected to his scalp, which are disposed of."

"I don't mean the equipment."

"No," she agrees. After a moment she continues. "The simulacrum itself will be digitally compressed and sent to a data storage facility."

"Will he be... awake?"

"He's not actually conscious now, so no, he will not be conscious in storage."

"Okay, well I suppose that's..."

"Mr. Gifford?"

Paulie lets his vision rest on the blinds, absent-mindedly counting. Three straight blinds. Two twisted. Five straight. The rest in a mass, discrete, but not countable from here. Three two and five. Prime numbers. Two that add to the third.

"Can he think creatively? In the, uh, simulation, I mean. Can he do math? Can he have insights?"

"Again, that's not your father in there. That's a slice—"

"Yes, I know, a snapshot of who he was in his last moments. Last night when I was here he was arguing with the nurse about whether or not he should have to wear that oxygen mask. He was capable of thinking critically right up until the end."

The chaplain winces. "I hate to remind you, but he was mistaken."

Paulie nods. "He was no doctor, but he *was* a mathematician. Can his Coda still think mathematically?"

"I suppose, Mr. Gifford. I'm no scientist."

Paulie pushes off from the counter. "I'd like to take him with me. That should be possible, right?"

She bites her lip. "This hospital is affiliated with the Presbyterian Church. While we are not opposed to the Coda on a theological basis, obviously, our ethics committee has concerns when it comes to the appearance of attributing personhood to what should be a temporary means of gathering information and comfort."

Paulie crosses his arms. "If it's not a person, then it's data. I'm next of kin, so the data should be my property."

"Technically his wife is next of kin." She holds up a hand at Paulie's intake of breath. "It is possible to take ownership of the simulacrum, with proper paper-work, if his wife agrees. You would be billed for the computer and interface, and insurance will not cover the expense. But Mr. Gifford, I don't recommend it. The healthiest thing you can do is move on. Let go."

He meets her gaze. "Thanks for the advice, but my mind's made up."

Gina wraps him in a hug when she comes home from work. "I'm so sorry," she murmurs. "I assume you told Maddie."

"Yes."

"How did she take the news?"

He thinks back to his daughter's return from school. How much harder she took the loss than he, even though he's the one who lost a father. "Not well. She's up in her room."

Gina eyes the computer console on the coffee table. "What's that?"

"The hospital let me take his Coda."

"You mean—is he in there?"

"Kind of. Not really."

She shudders. "Wow. Okay. If this helps your grieving process, then I'm all for it."

"It's not about grieving."

"What, then?"

"The Perelman Hypothesis."

She frowns. "I thought you'd given up on that when your father retired."

"He only retired from lecturing. From office hours and meetings and committees and grantsmanship. You never retire from thinking. We were working on it together. It was going to be his last big result."

"Paulie, people have been trying to prove that conjecture for ninety years. Whoever finally does will be some grad student in their twenties, using techniques that don't exist yet."

"We were close, Gina. I know it."

She meets his eye, and holds the glance a long time before replying. "And you think you're going to accomplish this by spending time inside a computer with your father."

He winces at the inaccuracies, but he doesn't correct her. "I think so," he says instead.

"Okay, Paulie," she says, though she shakes her head. "But do me a favor. Keep it in the den, okay? I don't want Maddie anywhere near it. I don't want her confused about whether Grandpa's really gone or not. Just let her grieve."

The hospital room was dark once again in the simulacrum.

"Hey. Thank you for visiting."

He nodded at his father. "Do you remember me, uh, visiting you here before?"

His father seemed puzzled. "You mean last night? Yes."

"No, I mean here in... in this thing. In your Coda."

"The last thing I remember is not being able to breathe, and my chest hurting like a motherfucker, and then I was sitting up with all the cables and hoses off, and you walked in."

"Do you understand that you're dead?"

His father nodded. "Either that or I'm suddenly cured."

"What's the square root of i?"

Paulie's father stared. "What?"

"The square root of i. In any form you like."

"Paulie, why?"

"I'm trying to see if it's really—" Paulie turned away, his fists clenched. "They say this simulacrum knows everything you knew at the last moment. This is something you could have done in your head."

"Okay, Paulie. One over root two plus i over root two. And its negation. Or would you prefer the answer in polar form?"

Paulie breathed a sigh of relief. "Okay, so I've been working on Perelman. Help me find something to write with." He started digging in drawers, but all of them were empty.

"Are you serious?"

He looked at his father. "Don't you want this?"

"Want?"

"We could still have that breakthrough. One last result to rock the mathematical world. Make everybody learn your name."

His father smiled faintly. "Your name, too."

Paulie put a hand on the bed. "Your legacy. My career. There's something for both of us here. Do you have anything better to do?"

"I guess I really don't."

He returned to searching the room, but every compartment was empty. Nothing existed in this simulation except what could be seen on the surface. Finally he hit upon the dry-erase board the shift nurses wrote their names on. He pulled a cap off a marker and tested it, half expecting it not to work as in the real world. To his relief, it left a clear line on the board.

"That's not a lot of space," said his father.

"No," he agreed. "I can't bring anything in with me or take anything out, though. Whatever we come up with has to be in small enough chunks for me to remember and replicate in the—replicate outside. So it's just as well."

"Okay, show me what you have."

Paulie started filling the little board with equations. "We know how to generate particular examples—"

"Trivial solutions," his father interrupted. "Perelman referenced a dozen himself, in his publication. We can't enumerate an exhaustive set, though."

Paulie nodded. "Right. Now, before you went into the hospital the first time, we had taken the approach of looking for a relationship between the cardinality of the Ricci set and the number of solutions it generates. We started by considering finite sets."

His father rubbed his forehead. "I vaguely remember, but this was right before things went downhill."

"That's fine—I've been working on that without you, so we don't have to repeat it, we only need to figure out the next steps. I've been approaching it as a series, trying to tie the value not merely to cardinality, but to its h-value. This feels right to me."

His father perked up at that. "Not an equation," he said. "A series."

"Right. Call it H and see what it converges to as n approaches infinity."

Gradually the board filled with arrows and sigmas and integrals.

"I wish we had a bigger board," Paulie said.

"Write on the wall. What are they gonna do, yell at us?"

Paulie stared. "Goddamn that's brilliant."

After another hour or so they hit a dead end.

"If we had a generalized solution for hyperbolic equations," Paulie's father began.

"We don't, though."

"No, but look up Brumbaugh Manifolds. Doug Brumbaugh was working on this the last time I saw him. He may have made some progress."

"Okay, that's something to try. I won't be able to hold much more in my head anyway."

"I bet if you talk to the company that makes this, they can find a way for you to email yourself from inside or something."

"No way," Paulie said. "I don't want anyone to know what we're working on here. I don't want someone to go find every mathematician who's died in the last five years and hook all their Codas up in some kind of screwed up massively parallel computer and beat us to the punch."

His father's eyes widened. "Shit."

"Yeah. Only a matter of time before somebody else thinks of it, though."

"So you might as well be first?"

Paulie chewed his lip. "Do you not want to do this? Do you think this is wrong?"

He grinned ruefully. "What do I know from wrong?"

Paulie dropped into the bedside chair. "What's it like?"

"What?"

"Being dead but being conscious. Does it make you upset?"

His father shrugged. "It is what it is."

"You had plans," Paulie said. "You were going to remodel the house."

"Guess now I'm not."

Paulie gripped the bed's footboard. "Don't you feel anything at all?" He couldn't remember if his father had ever had a feeling in his damned life.

"Would it change anything?"

Paulie flips through images on a tablet in the mortuary office. "Somebody told me you had an option to put a Coda interface in the niche with his ashes, but I don't see that here."

Next to him, Tricia winces, but she schools it quickly.

"We don't include Coda ports in the regular lineup," the funeral director says, "but yes, it is a choice we offer. This is not a service that has caught on yet. Many people find the idea disturbing, as though we are preventing our loved ones from moving on. Or preventing *ourselves* from moving on. If you elect to equip the niche with an interface, you will have to choose the special columbarium we have set aside for that. It's, ah, not near the other niches."

Paulie glances at Tricia, but apart from insisting on a fancier urn for her husband, she's let him make all the decisions.

"Do it," he says.

At the cemetery Paulie kisses the urn, and Tricia does the same. Then he watches as an employee places it into the columbarium and closes the marble cover.

A minister selected by her side of the family drones on. As far as Paulie remembers, his father wasn't religious, but this isn't for *his* benefit, after all.

On the way to the car he grabs Maddie and pulls her into a tight hug. "You know I love you, right?"

She sobs and nods against him.

"You know I'm proud of you, right?"

"Paulie," Gina says, "you're upsetting her."

"I just want to make sure she knows."

"Hey."

His eyes adjusted quickly to the dark. "Hey."

His father gestured at the silent equipment by the bed. "Guess this is the end. I had an insurance policy. There isn't much, but it should pay for a cremation. Tricia should be able to find the paperwork. You're the beneficiary."

"Yeah, we took care of all that."

"Oh. How long have I been gone?"

He stepped over to the dry-erase board. "About three weeks."

"Then... what are you still doing here?"

"We've been working on the Perelman Hypothesis.

"Are you serious?"

Paulie uncapped a marker. "Don't make me go through it all again. It's fifty degrees out, we only have so much time, and I need to walk you through what we came up with last time. Trust me, you're on board."

His father blinked. "Okay then. Go ahead."

The clock on the wall ticked off seconds, while the hour and minute hand relentlessly pointed to eight minutes after five the entire time it took Paulie to run through the connection to hyperbolic equations.

"I reached out to Professor Brumbaugh like you said, but he pointed me to the Jagadish-Rajput conjecture."

"I haven't heard of that. Are they working on Perelman also?"

"No, they're working on node forms, but their conjecture is that hyperbolic equations correspond to node forms. They've tested several hundred terms using a supercomputer and they've all checked out."

His father shook his head. "How's that help us?"

"Node forms converge. Supposing we can prove their conjecture, we can use that to prove Perelman."

"This isn't math. This is grasping at straws. A supercomputer says it works—*so what*? That's not theory. Where's the proof?"

Paulie capped the marker, even though he suspected it could not dry out. "Don't you see? If the correspondence holds, then—"

"Are you trying to give me a heart attack in the afterlife? Do Jagadish and Rajput have the basis for a theorem, or just a coincidence they can't explain? Even Euler had conjectures disproven after three hundred years!"

"Well fine then—" Paulie lowered his voice. "Fine. Help me find a counterexample, then. Or better yet, help me prove Jagadish-Rajput true, because *that* proof will make us both famous."

His father crossed his arms. "Fine. This conjecture is bound to have consequences for other node forms. Maybe a proof by contradiction is our angle."

Paulie and his father toyed with a variety of extrapolations, looking for a counterexample. At least the false starts could be erased—and Paulie wouldn't need to remember any of them when he got out of the Coda. All he'd need to remember would be a working approach, if they found one.

"The department voted on my tenure application this week," he said during a break. "They voted to advance it to the dean." Paulie suspected strongly the vote was not unanimous, which boded poorly for the next level of the process, but he kept that part to himself.

"Huh."

Huh? That was it?

"You could congratulate me. You could wish me luck."

"Okay. Good luck."

"Thanks," Paulie muttered. He added a few more lines to the board. "Maddie has a dance recital next week. She misses you a lot."

"Wish her luck too, then."

"It just...it reminds me of my piano recitals."

His father leaned on his bed railing. "Is that what this is really about, Paulie? Are you here to tell me I was a shitty father? I know. I already acknowledged that, after the divorce."

Paulie dropped into the chair by the bed. "No," he said at last. "Sorry. I keep thinking of what other people use the Coda technology for, and I keep waiting to hear you talk about something besides math or life insurance. I keep hoping you'll have something profound to say."

"I'm not the mushy type."

"You could fake it."

"You're the smartest person I ever met. You would see through any faking."

Paulie blinked. A compliment.

"I wouldn't have blamed you if you didn't want anything to do with me," his father went on, "after not being there for you as a kid. But then you made me a part of your life and we got along okay. You treated me like a colleague, so I tried to treat you the same. Now you're mad at me for not acting more like a father? I didn't think you wanted that from me."

Paulie waited to see if he would say anything else. That was about as close to "mushy" as he'd come since the night twenty years ago when he'd apologized for abandoning him.

After a quiet eternity, he got up from the chair. "Okay, well, I think I have enough to work on for now. I'll come back when I have some progress."

"Bye, Paulie. Thank you for visiting."

"Jesus, Paulie, I don't mind driving home, but if you puke in the car, you're cleaning it up."

Paulie clinks his empty wine glass against Gina's still-full one. "The free wine is the only thing that makes these parties worth attending."

She rolls her eyes. "*Our* holiday party's at the Olive Garden. You should appreciate what you've got."

He smiles. "I think that's what I just said."

"Just pace yourself, okay?"

"It's a deal."

She gestures toward the food table. "I'm gonna get some crudités. You should get some food in you too."

"I will."

As she walks away, his phone buzzes. Paulie takes another glass of wine from a server and heads to one of the standing tables.

His pulse quickens as he reads Jagadish's name in the Sender field. He skims the text, but the message is too long and too dense to try to absorb on a tiny screen. The sooner he can leave this stupid party and go home, the better.

"Dr. Gifford!"

He tears his eyes from the screen to meet the gaze of his colleague, Professor Hewett.

Her expression softens. "How've you been holding up, Paul, since, well, since your father?"

"I'm doing alright, María."

She nods and is silent for a moment, as though considering. Finally she plunges on. "How's your research going? Anything promising? I know a bunch of us have been hoping to see something new from you."

"Did I hear you say Paul's working on something new?"

Shit. Dr. Tappert. The senior professor changes course to join them as though pulled in by lasso.

Paulie chugs the rest of his wine, as much for a moment to think as for an excuse to look away from Tappert's idiot face.

"Yeah," he says at last. "I'm looking into Jagadish-Rajput."

"Oh!" says Hewett. "I met a Peruvian mathematician at a conference who was working on that. His name is Segami—you should reach out to him."

Paulie nods. "Thanks. I'll look—"

"Wait a minute," says Tappert. "I remember reading something about—please tell me you're not still tilting at the Perelman Conjecture."

Paulie's throat tightens. "It's a perfectly valid area of research," he spits out. He steps away from the table and flags down a server for another glass, hoping to lose Tappert in the process.

No such luck. "Dr. Gifford," the older professor says, resting a hand on his arm, "Perelman's a valid area of inquiry for a young man, maybe. Or for an old man, playing at being a professor emeritus. Not for a mathematician seeking tenure."

Hearing Tappert's disavowal of his scholarly value is all the confirmation Paulie needs. No way had he signed off on Paulie's tenure application.

"I disagree, Dan," says Hewett. "I have a lot of respect for people going after tough things. After all, that's kind of what math is about." Turning to Paulie, she adds, "Going after Jagadish-Rajput is perfect too, because if you don't make it all the way to Perelman, at least that's an approach that can get you some intermediary results. You just can't go silent for this long a time."

Tappert shakes his head. "It's a fool's errand. Paul, I hated to watch your father waste his later years on this, but not nearly as much as I hate to watch you throw away your career. At least your father had tenure."

Paulie slams his glass down on the table. "I really don't need you to—"

A gasp goes up around him, and Hewett points at his hand. "Dr. Gifford!"

Paulie looks down to realize that he has smashed the wine glass, and lacerated his hand. The moment he sees the blood, the pain sets in.

Some police procedural natters away on the big screen in the living room, but neither of them pays much attention. Gina makes incremental progress on her cross stitch, while Paulie rubs the label off a bottle of beer and lets his mind wander.

The officers on the screen, with their private dramas and backstories, make him think of his father—alive again in the hours Paulie spends in his Coda, and nonexistent when Paulie looks away. Or maybe the experience is more like a very lucid dream. Paulie hopes not, given how many seemingly profound middle-of-the-night insights have turned out, upon waking, to be nonsense.

Then again, he's basing all his hopes on the assumption that deduction works the same in-Coda as outside of it.

No, this is beer-fueled nonsense. The whole point of deduction is it works for any set of starting assumptions. It doesn't matter whether space is Euclidean or not—what matters is what axioms you proceed from and whether your logic is rigorous. A theorem that's true in the Coda is true outside of the Coda. And if it turns out this life is a simulation, as Paulie has seen posited online, Perelman is just as true in the reality outside this one. Even if it's simulations all the way up.

Induction. Paulie is certain that if the deductive process is solid for a reality n, then it is equally true for a reality n plus one. If he can prove Perelman in-Coda, he'll have his n equals one. He'll have everything.

On the coffee table, his phone buzzes with an incoming notification.

"Don't," Gina says.

Paulie checks his screen. "It's my work account."

"I know. I always told you it was a mistake putting that app on your phone."

"This'll only take... shit."

"What's wrong?"

"The dean's office updated my dossier." He swallows. "The School of Arts and Science denied my tenure application."

The television goes to commercials, the volume seeming to double. He can't think.

Gina strokes his forearm. "What are you going to do?"

He sighs. "I can ask my chair to appeal, take it to the provost, but as things stand right now, I don't see a reason why he would."

"What then?"

"I've still got a year on my existing contract. After that..." He shrugs. "With my evaluations and fizzling research, I'm probably not looking at a tenure-track position. I could teach community college or high school, or somehow find a job in industry, but...hell, I wouldn't even know where to begin. Being an academic is all I know."

She mutes the television. "Oh God, Paulie, please don't tell me you can't find something around here." Gina manages a nonprofit educational foundation. Paulie can't even guess at what starting over would look like for her. "I want to support you, Paulie, but you have to understand that's asking a lot."

"We've still got time before we have to worry about that." He takes a breath. "I still have one chance."

"What do you mean?"

"If I can prove this thing. Technically I'm past the deadline to add publications to my dossier, but Perelman is such a big deal, I'm pretty sure they'd find a way to let me."

She runs a hand through her hair. "Is this...is this about the math or is this about something else?"

"What else would it be?"

She takes a breath to answer, then stops and faces away. Paulie considers repeating his question, but then she looks back at him. "Is this about living up to your father? Or about proving yourself to him?"

He swallows. "It's about the math, Gina. It's always been about the math. We're close, I know it."

She nods slowly. "Okay. Prove your theorem then."

He stepped into the darkened hospital room. "Hey."

"Hey."

Paulie ran a hand along the back of the chair by the bed. "You got a nice, uh, write-up in the AMS *Proceedings*. A lot of mathematicians said some pretty amazing things about you."

"I'm not going to see it; makes no difference to me."

"No, I guess it wouldn't. You never were the mushy type."

His father chuckled. "You can say that again."

Paulie erased the shift nurse board. "I know you don't remember, but we've been trying to prove the Jagadish-Rajput conjecture."

"The what?"

Paulie began filling the board. "I'll catch you up on the broad strokes."

They were approaching a point of diminishing returns. Every visit was going to have to begin with Paulie summarizing all their past conversations, as well as the work he'd done between visits. There would come a point where recap would take all the time he could reasonably spend in the Coda. Then he would really be on his own.

"We should consider a proof by contradiction, then."

Paulie shook his head. "I tried. It hasn't gotten me anywhere. I reached out to a mathematician named Segami who's been working on a proof by induction, though. It's trivial for n equals one."

"Of course it is. Can you prove it for n equals n plus one though... Show me what you have so far."

Paulie cleared the board again, and filled it with differential topology, Vila Groups, and half the Greek alphabet.

"What about Suárez Theory?"

"How's that apply?"

"It's about group automorphisms. We might be able to apply it to these Vila Groups of yours."

"Walk me through it."

Paulie took notes while his father dictated, stopping to ask for clarifications or to offer his own suggestions. The little board got cleared four times—each time a chance to mistranscribe something or miss an assumption. But finally Paulie capped his marker and stared at their work.

"I think—" He swallowed and tried again. "I think we just nailed down Segami."

"Looks like."

Paulie wandered toward the window, with its predawn view of the empty expressway. Softly, hardly daring to say it, he added, "and that gives us Jagadish-Rajput, which takes us to—" Somewhere he had raised his voice to the point where he was practically shouting. He turned back to his father. "To Perelman," he concluded, in a more conversational tone.

"That's good," his father said.

"*Good?* Holy shit, we've slayed the dragon, and all you can say is 'That's good'?"

His father shrugged. "Paulie, I'm dead. The moment you leave, I'll forget we even had this conversation. I can't get all emotional about this."

Paulie sagged into the visitor chair. "What was your excuse before you died?" he muttered.

"What?"

"Nothing. Fine." Paulie met his eyes. "Anyway."

"Yeah?"

"I was just... I mean, I should go. Try to write this up before I forget it all."

"Makes sense."

"Maddie misses you," he blurted out. "And Gina. Gina sends her love."

His father nodded.

"Maddie had her dance recital. She did great. She was graceful and confident. She didn't get that from me. I was so proud."

"That's good."

Paulie stood. "Yeah. I should go...I was wondering if there was anything you wanted to say."

"Uh, bye, I guess? Thank you for visiting, Paulie."

Maddie squeezes cement on a plastic wing, making the clear liquid bead up.

"Not so much!" Paulie blurts out. He reaches for a sponge. "Here, let me fix it!"

"Dad! You said you weren't going to take over! This is *my* model!"

Paulie puts his hands up in surrender. "Fine, do it your way!"

Maddie frowns, chews on her lower lip, and attaches the wing.

He experiences an odd sort of reverse déjà vu, back to his first chemistry set, working through the experiments in the instruction manual—or rather, watching while his father worked through the experiments. Paulie winces and rests his hand carefully on his knee. Then he does the one thing his father never would have done. "You're right," he says. "I'm sorry. Keep going."

Maddie snaps the next piece of plastic off and trims a bit of flash from it with an X-ACTO knife. "Mom showed me a vid about your, um, the math problem you solved. Are you famous now?"

He smiles. "Famous among a very small group of people."

"That's still something. I bet you feel super proud."

Paulie doesn't answer. He's not sure what he feels. After spending decades imagining the aftermath of proving Perelman, it's possible he burned out his ability to feel anything at all about it. The reality can't match all he imagined.

"Maybe I could be a mathematician," she says. "I'm good at math. Grandpa said so too."

"You definitely are," he says. Funny how his father could say to Maddie the things he couldn't say to him. Maybe it was easier when it wasn't his direct offspring he was talking to.

He squeezes her shoulder, the n plus one to his n. Just like he was the n plus one to his father's n.

Paulie frowns. What conjecture would he be hoping to prove? That mathematical talent runs in his family? That's trivial. He thinks instead about the things he wishes he could prove. Did his father feel anything for him like what he feels for Maddie?

Deduction is useless here.

Maddie holds two pieces together and blows on them to dry the cement. "Is it true the university gave you back your tenure?" She says the word awkwardly, like she's testing out the concept. "Does that mean you can't be fired?"

"It's, ah, a little more complicated than that. Close enough, though."

She swallows. "So we don't have to move?" She focuses on the model with faux intensity.

Paulie shakes his head. "We never decided that we were definitely moving."

"But now we're definitely not?"

Paulie picks up a brush and taps the back end lightly on the table. "We're...still talking about it." Still avoiding the subject, if he's being honest.

Maddie nods and attaches another piece.

He accidentally fumbles the brush. "How about you? What do *you* want?"

"I want to stay," she says. "All my friends are here."

Everything's so simple from her perspective. Paulie doesn't know what *he* wants. Since his proof—since their proof—passed through peer review, the math world has been buzzing with the laying to rest of a decades-open question. He's gotten informal offers from schools across the country, including a couple of top-twenty departments. And, sure, his own university. Does he really want to stay someplace that hadn't wanted him?

On the other hand, Gina has her career, and Maddie has her whole life.

He squeezes her shoulder. "I'm not sure what's gonna happen, but I'll make you a promise. We won't decide without talking to you, okay?"

"Okay."

"I love you."

"Love you too, Dad."

He entered the hospital room and marveled at how unchanged it still was after all these months.

"Hey," his father said.

"Hey."

He shivered, the hospital's cool seventy degrees feeling like an ice bath compared to the warm day outside.

"You're not going to remember this, but we proved Perelman. Here in your Coda."

His father's eyes widened. "Really! Now that's something!"

Paulie nodded. "Got it published. Both our names are on it. It's all anybody can talk about—not just the proof, but, uh..."

"Proof by simulacrum? I bet that'll shake things up."

"So that's *two* things you'll be remembered for. I'm not actually sure which will have the bigger impact."

"That's something."

"Yeah."

The two men fell silent.

"You don't...I mean, you can't remember any of the things we talked about, can you?"

"I'm sorry, Paulie, the last thing I remember is not being able to breathe."

Paulie shook his head. "No...yeah, that...that makes sense."

"Did you find the insurance policy?"

"Yeah. It took care of everything. Thanks for having that."

"Good."

Paulie fidgeted with the rod for the blinds.

"Is there something else?" his father asked.

"No, I guess...it's exciting, huh?"

"I suppose. I mean, I don't get to see all that."

"I just thought you might be…"

His father inclined his head. "Might be what?"

Paulie walked around the bed. "No matter how many times I come back in here, you're never going to say the things I want you to say, are you?"

"What do you want me to say?"

"Never mind. Look, it's blazing outside. I have to get back in the car, or I'm gonna get sunstroke."

His father nodded.

"Goodbye. Dad." The word tasted funny on his lips; he didn't think he'd said it once since his father came back into his life two decades ago.

"Bye, Paulie. Thank you for visiting."

Paulie runs the air conditioner in his car for several minutes, letting it cool down inside. While he waits for the temperature to get comfortable, he checks his phone. The congratulatory emails tapered off weeks ago. In their place is a grocery list from Gina, and a drawing of a horse, against a backdrop of hearts and stars, from Maddie.

Finally he puts the car in gear and rumbles off, watching the columbarium disappear in the mirror.

José Pablo Iriarte is a Cuban-American writer, high school math teacher, and parent of two. Their fiction has been finalist for the Nebula, Hugo, Locus and Sturgeon Awards, longlisted for the Otherwise Award, and reprinted in various Year's Best compilations. Their debut novel, *Benny Ramírez and the Nearly Departed*, was published in 2024 by Knopf Books for Young Readers, an imprint of Random House. Their follow up, *AJ Torres and the Treasure of Captain Grayshark* is forthcoming in June 2025. Learn more (but frankly not much more) at www.labyrinthrat.com, or follow José on Facebook, Instagram, or Bluesky.

LAUGHTER AMONG THE TREES

Suzan Palumbo

The highway to the campground cuts through the granite Laurentian Plateau like a desiccated wound. It's been twenty-five years since I've retraced this road and, though the comfort stops along the route have been expanded and streamlined, the forest and rock remain the same; Ancient, silent and unflinching.

I was fourteen when we retreated South West on this stretch to the suburbs of Toronto—me in the back of my parents' station wagon, the emptiness of Sab's seat corroding our ability to speak. I couldn't look through the rear window as we sped away. I didn't want to acknowledge we were abandoning the search—leaving Sab behind.

Now, as I pull into a rest stop a hundred kilometres before the park, the nauseating mix of hamburger and exhaust churning my stomach, I know going back for my sister is all I have left.

We'd landed in Toronto in the late seventies with a swell of West Indian immigrants. The sepia washed prints from the time show me as a preschooler in my first snow suit or drowning in a too large hockey jersey. Typical pictures of newcomers sporting the trappings of being Canadian.

We lived with my paternal Aunt Indra and her husband in their crowded Midtown duplex while saving to buy our own place.

"We get nothing for free," was Mom's mantra. Whether she was convincing herself we had a right to be here or that leaving home for this cold, strange place was worth the sacrifice, I couldn't tell. Either way, it was the truth. She and Dad worked two jobs each, cleaning and trades respectively. They expected me to carry their work ethic to school with me when I turned four.

"You talk stupid," a boy named Michael said my first day.

"No, I don't," I snapped, offended by what my mother would have called Michael's rude mouth. A week later our teacher, Miss. Matthews called me to work with her in the hall.

"Ana, some words say "th" not "t", like "three" and "tree"." She demonstrated by placing her tongue between her teeth and blowing. "Can you hear the difference?" Her smile made me ache. Miss. Mathews was brown haired and pretty like the people on TV and I couldn't talk right.

"Yes," I lied.

We breathed lies, contorting our tongues; bending our bodies to suit the cold; feigning that we fit this place. We weren't taken in by ourselves. No one was. We flailed perpetually, unanchored.

Then, my parents had Sabrina.

Sab came home from the hospital with a crown of black ringlets and the legitimacy of a Canadian birth certificate. Even as a mewling newborn it was as if the city had been fashioned for her, unlike my parents and I who'd been transplanted too late. She crawled early and seized everything with a tiny iron fist. Old women stopped to coo at her long lashes on our summer walks. Mothers at the community centre invited her over for playdates with their Gerber baby children. I tagged along, playing with the younger kids and their toys, always deferent to adorable Sab.

"Are there jumbies in this forest?" Sab had asked on the drive up to the park. I bit the inside of my bottom lip. Relatives had seasoned us in whispers of obeah women and devil spirits who lured you to your death. I'd had the same thought but when you're fourteen, you didn't admit such childish fears to your parents. With Sab, their baby, they were indulgent.

"Nah," Dad said chuckling. "Here don't have bad spirit like that. We have to lock up we food otherwise racoons and ting go come and eat we stuff. The rest, ghost and devil, dem ting is back home foolishness."

A weighted quiet shifted into the car—one where the bumps of the station wagon's wheels on the asphalt resonated in unison with my heartbeat.

"They're real," Mom said, cutting Dad off before he could continue laughing. She hadn't wanted us to go camping; kept saying it was dangerous and dirty up until the moment we left. Her jaw flexed in the front seat. I couldn't see from where I was sitting if she was angry or in one of her moods. She had them often. She'd gaze into the distance, as if she were transfixed on someone. There was never anyone there. All we could do was wait, speaking in hushed voices until she rejoined us.

My shoulders tensed in the car.

"What you mean, Elsie?" Dad glanced at her. She stared at the highway, mouth clamped. I shivered as if an icy set of hands had grabbed my forearms. Goose pimples prickled up my arms; I rubbed them, trying to keep warm.

"Look." Sab pointed out her window. Holsteins grazing in a field slipped past us. The pressure in the car eased.

"I did cut grass for de cow and dem back home." Dad chuckled cautiously. Ma's jaw relaxed a fraction. I laughed over hard at Dad's jokes for the rest of the drive, trying to dislodge the lingering cold that had branched into my collar bone and leaked into my ribs.

Mom didn't speak until we reached the park.

The site Dad had booked wasn't tranquil or a pristine wilderness like the brochures claimed. Hair metal wafted on the breeze, along with the thick scent of bacon and charred beef patties. Kids crashed through the woods playing a violent iteration of tag or screaming Marco Polo. Still, the air was fresher than in the city and the trees were a lush green. Mom had over packed, as usual. While I helped her unload the car, Sab chased chipmunks. At ten she was still too small to help according to everyone except me.

I sat on a lawn chair when we were finished with a copy of *The Count of Monte Cristo* I'd borrowed from the library. Some kids had joined Sab's chipmunk hunt. I watched them whispering at the base of a tree. They leaned towards each other already familiar, conspiratorial. Sab could do that—make people love her instantly. They all nodded then, approached Mom as a pack.

"Can we go to the playground up the road?" Sab gestured to the ragtag group behind her.

Mom looked down, ignoring their dirt smeared faces. The creases in her forehead deepened. I smirked, bracing for Sab's incoming tantrum. We weren't allowed roam the streets at home with school friends much less a group of complete strangers in the woods. "We don't know their family," Dad said whenever I'd asked to go to someone's house.

"Okay," Mom said. She looked up and stared at me. I bit the raw spot inside my lip. Blood diffused across my tongue.

"Yes!" Sab jumped.

"But, Anarika has to come with you." I rolled my eyes. Mom sucked air in between her teeth.

"Don't cut your eye at me, gyal," she said. "Get some exercise." She turned to Sab. "Not too long and mind your sister, you hear?" Sab raced down the road with her new crew without a glance back.

"Fine," I said under my breath, bringing my book and stomping after them.

Set in rectangular clearing across from the flush toilets and hot water showers was a steep metal slide, a see saw and a set of swings. Sab and a smaller boy ran towards the swings. I settled on the park bench nearby and ignored their screeching. No one had acknowledged me on the short walk up. I didn't have the allure of a cool older sibling. I wasn't pretty or athletic. Then again, I wasn't interested in playing with these dirty kids either. *The Count of Monte Cristo* was better company. I sunk into my book, glancing up only after Edmund Dantes had discovered the treasure filled cave that would finance his revenge.

The park was silent.

"Sab?" Her name echoed, mocking me. The playground was empty. I left my book and searched the clearing. She wasn't behind the rusted slide. I circled the washrooms, flinging each door open.

"Sab!" I called, my voice fraying like tattered cloth.

Every stall was vacant.

The stench of pee made my eyes water. No, that isn't true. I was crying. My throat contracted around a sob. Could she have gone back without me? Did she remember I'd come along? Mom and Dad would kill me for letting their baby out of my sight. I slid my back down the washroom building's wall and pulled my knees up to my chest, taking up as little space as possible. What if I walked into the forest and kept going until there was no light? Until I reached a place where no one could see the disappointment I was?

A twig bounced off my head and landed next to my foot. I picked it up between my thumb and index finger and looked up. Sab and her friends were perched in a massive tree. The smaller boy huddled next to her, giggling.

"Not funny," I yelled. I stood, pitched the twig back at them and marched to the bench, drenched in the embarrassment that they'd witnessed me crying.

"Bye, Greg. Bye Ashley, Chris," Sab called. Seconds later, she was at my heels.

"It was a joke," she said, panting. "It was Greg's idea." She flopped on the bench. I searched either side of her.

"Move," I said, pushing her aside. "Where's my book?"

"Ow! What book?" She massaged her wrist. "Maybe an animal took it."

"You're the animal, Sab." I started walking back to camp. She was beside me, like a shadow, again.

"You better not say anything. I'll tell Mom you were reading your stupid book and never even watched me." I stopped, rage throbbing against the chill inside me, trembling with the effort of holding myself back from grabbing her throat and choking her until she shut up for good. She'd perfected the art of threatening to tell on me over the past year to get what she wanted. Her eyes sparkled; the trace of a smile rippled the surface of her lips.

I exhaled and left her standing there.

Back at camp, I shut my mouth. Mom would say it served me right for bringing the book and then been mad that we had to pay a fine.

That night, Dad singed chicken dogs on the fire. I crammed them in my mouth, scalding my tongue and ignoring dumb Sab. Smoke ribboned around me, drawing me closer to the crackling heat.

"Move back, Ana," Dad said. "I don't want you to catch fire."

I wanted the flames to swallow me. I wanted to burn up.

"Ana." Sab nudged me in my sleeping bag that night. "I have to pee."

"So go pee."

"Come with me."

I turned my back to her and covered my head.

"I'll pee my pants and tell Mom you didn't help me."

"Urgh." I shimmied out of my bag and unzipped the door. She was right mom would be vexed if I didn't help her. She crawled outside and moved to the left a few steps away. The night was as dark as molasses and awash in a tide of chirping insects. I couldn't make out the station wagon or our parents tent next to ours. Even the stars were dim. I grabbed the flashlight behind me and flicked it on.

"Don't shine the light on me," Sab whispered.

"Who wants to see you pee? Come on, there's mosquitoes." But it wasn't the bugs that made want to slip back inside. The darkness was heavy, as if the press of an unseen gaze draped my skin. We weren't alone. As I waited for her trickling to stop, footsteps approached. Breathing, steady but shallow carried on the breeze. It curled round the flare of my left ear and froze my spine.

"What's that? Sab asked.

I peered towards the steps but it was if an opaque cloth been drawn around our tent.

"Hurry up," I whispered. My heart smashed against my ribs. I bit fresh blood from my lip. I swung the light.

"Greg?" Sab asked. The smaller boy from the park stood there, shielding his eyes from the glare. My stomach dropped.

"What are you doing here?" I hissed.

"Ashley and Chris saw a moose by the river, wanna come see, Sab?" He spoke with a musical lilt similar to my parents but flatter, like he was mimicking them. None of the kids at the park had been West Indian, had they? In the light, Greg was sallow and thin. He wore a pair of canvass shorts and a short-sleeved button up shirt with a crest on the pocket. It looked like a school uniform. Shadow shrouded his eyes, even with the light pointed at them. When I recall his face now, the image of a yellowed skull atop an emaciated body materializes and a shudder shakes my core.

"How'd they find a moose?" I puffed myself up leaning on my age as a mark of authority.

"Let's go see." Sab was next to him.

"It's behind the trees on our side. You can come, too." He kept his boney head trained on Sab. There couldn't be any moose. Maybe some stranger was using him to lure Sab away.

"No." I planted my feet. "Sab can't go either."

"We'll be back in five minutes." He wasn't asking. This emboldened Sab.

"Yeah. Five minutes. Give us the light." She grabbed and yanked at the flashlight with the exact iron strength she'd had as a baby. I pulled back. "Come on, Ana. You're jealous he wanted to show me and not you."

I let go. Sab stumbled backwards with the flashlight in her hands. She stood up beside Greg and dusted herself off.

"Five," Greg said. He turned without waiting for an answer. I grabbed Sab's elbow before she could follow him.

"Don't go." My whisper was hoarse, pleading. She faced me, the light pointed down.

"Stop. I'll tell Dad you wrote about wanting to kiss Mia from gym in your diary."

The sick glee in her voice skewered me. My grip went slack. I watched her fade into the darkness with Greg.

I should have dragged her back or screamed and woken the entire campground. Instead, I stood outside the tent, shivering, every muscle in my body coiled with rage and shame like a spring. I crawled inside when my legs were numb.

"Why you let her go?" I imagined Mom yelling. "You supposed to protect her." I slipped back into my sleeping bag and lay awake deep into the night, waiting for Greg's footsteps; listening for Sab's voice whispering, "Let me in."

"ANA!" Mom was shaking me, bruising her fingers into my shoulders. "Where's Sab?"

"I don't know," I mumbled. She let go of me. I heard the zip door, then her yelling, "I can't find she anywhere."

I sat up and hugged my knees, my eyes still glued with sleep. The cold had trickled down my ribs and formed a hard mass in the pit of my stomach.

Dad poked his head in the tent. "Anarika, get dressed. We can't find yuh sister."

I waited with Mom while Dad drove to the registration office to get help. She paced, wringing her hands. "No. No. Not again," she mumbled to herself. When Dad returned with a Park Ranger, she went silent.

"Was Sabrina playing with anyone yesterday that she might have gone off with?" the Ranger asked.

"Yeah," I said. "A kid named Greg?" Mom flinched like the name had whipped her.

"Greg." the Ranger repeated. "Good."

The four of us went to the other campsites to ask if Sab was there.

With each "No," Mom grew more unstable, until she couldn't walk without stumbling. At one point she covered her ears as if trying to shut a voice out. Ashley and Chris' mom sat her down and offered her some water.

"Don't worry," their mother said. "We're going to find Sabrina. Kids wander off like this all the time." She was lying. I knew because a few minutes later she gave Ashley and Chris a sharp look and said, "You two stay here. No running off."

Dad and the ranger returned an hour later without Sab. No one had come camping with a boy named Greg.

The police created check points and organized a search party to comb the woods. By noon, Aunty Indra had driven up with a recent picture of Sab. Mom clung to her when they hugged, like she was about to collapse.

The picture was of Sab in a white frilly dress from her tenth birthday party. Her smile was angelic, dimpled, nothing like the bossy brat from the night before.

Officer Saunders introduced himself to us. He was tall and built like a stone wall.

"I'm your contact," he said, "If you have any questions, call me." He took us to a nearby motel. We weren't permitted to bring our gear with us. Our tent, car, all of it was part of the scene—even the bags with our clothes were evidence. Amid the flurry of interviews and police, Mom kept leaning on me. She'd never been so soft with me, not since we left back home. I was supposed to be responsible and strong. In the car she put one arm around me and rocked.

Officer Saunders interviewed us, trying to get information about what had happened to Sab. They had no leads except for what I reported about Greg. I sat between Mom and Dad when he spoke with me at the little table in our motel room.

"Did you see this boy, Greg?" "What did he looked like?" "Why would Sabrina go off with him?" "What did she say about him?" "Did you hear anything last night? "Did you wake up at all? Not even to go to the bathroom?"

I answered, "No" or shook my head to all of his questions, not trusting myself to speak. Mom and Dad leaned towards me. I kept waiting for Sab to interrupt or Dad to crack a joke. But they were breathless, hanging on my every gesture and syllable. I savoured the lurid sweetness of it. You shouldn't like this I thought and then heaved. Mom crushed me into her chest. I sobbed. I didn't deserve her sympathy. I should have been dead in the mud like Sab probably was.

"We're doing our best to find your daughter," Officer Saunders voice had softened. He shook Dad's hand. Mom got up and went to sit on the bed.

As the door closed behind Officer Saunders, I heard him say, "These animals don't watch their kids."

We were updated each morning and afternoon for the next three days. On the fourth day, a detective wanted to talk to Mom and Dad privately. I went with Officer Saunders to an identical motel room. He placed a plastic bag in front of me at the table. Inside was my copy of *The Count of Monte Cristo*, muddied and torn.

"Is this yours?" He asked, concern masking his disgust for us.

"Yes." I said, relieved I wouldn't have to say it was missing.

"Did you lose it?"

"I left it on the bench at play ground on the first day. When I went back to get it with Sab, it was gone. Where was it?"

"We founded it by the river." His faded denim colored eyes fastened on me like fish hooks. My stomach cramped. I forced myself to keep still.

"Can I have it back?" I said, stifling the wobble in my voice. "It's from the library."

"Sure." His lips rose in a toothless smile. "You know, I have kid sister. Was Sab annoying like mine?" He watched me shake my head. He didn't believe me but didn't press more. He took me back to my parents when the detective was done.

"I'm not leaving." Mom was trembling. I sat next to her on the couch. She put her arm around me to steady herself.

"What about Ana?" Dad's laughter had withered. He pointed at me with his open palm. "She can't stay here de whole time, we can't send she back to stay with my sister alone."

Mom shrunk next to me. She stared at her feet.

"Okay," she said quietly. "For Ana." Heat rose in my cheeks. I buried my face in her shoulder.

A week later, we packed our belongings that had been released and drove back to the city. Officer Saunders remained our contact. He called every week to update us on the search. As the summer wore on, his calls became less frequent. They dwindled into the winter becoming a drip that eventually dried up.

Sab's case was stone cold.

My parents went back to work a month after we returned.

"Bills don't stop even when yuh child lost," Dad mumbled the morning of his first day back.

I spent the oven hot days reading or watching TV. On Thursdays, I stayed at Aunt Indra's for company at Aunt Indra's insistence. But where I was invisible before, now, the family tiptoed around me like thin teacup. I'd walk in to a room and my cousins would clam up. "Aunties" I'd never met would sip tea in the kitchen, clucking about how sorry they were for my mama. Their pity, so viscous I gagged on it.

Mom would call me when she was home from work and I'd walk over. When Dad returned, we'd eat in tomb silence before he left to drink himself unconscious in the garage. Mom had all the time in the world for me now. In between her bouts of unresponsiveness her words were blunt and sweet. She made my favourite curries. She hugged me every night even though my longing to be tucked in had faded years ago.

Sab remained between us. Her absence slicked over my skin, like a membrane. I glimpsed her, as she was, bounding up the stairs; breathed her scent as I walked by her locked room; heard her whisper, "shut up, loser" before I drifted to sleep. I never saw Greg again. He'd gotten what he'd wanted.

One night, while looking at myself in the mirror, Sab's voice clawed up my throat reflexively. "You're ugly. Everyone hates you."

"You're a bitch, Sab." I snapped back.

A smile cracked my lips. From then on, whenever I was alone, I spoke for Sab.

There were no school hikes for me. No weeklong grade ten wilderness trip or renting a cabin at Wasaga beach with my friends when I turned seventeen. Mom kept me home from everything "wild". I was free, as long as I was caged within the steel and concrete confines of the city.

When she walked in on me and Marit, a university "friend" I'd brought home, kissing on my bed, she closed the door without a word. We went downstairs braced for a fight. Mom was sitting at the kitchen table, waiting.

"All yuh want some cake?" she asked, as if this were a cherished routine.

"Yes, thank you," Marit said. She slid into the chair across from my mother and quirked her lips into a smile. I raised my eyebrows as Mom stiffened and passed Marit a plate of coconut cake. I remember stilted small talk and Marit asking my mother about her job while being utterly charming. Mom looked back and forth between us. When Marit had licked her fork clean, we walked her to the door.

"Come back anytime." Mom was distant but sincere.

"Thank you, Mrs. Dindiyal. I will." Marit winked at me before she turned and left. I closed the door and leaned my back against it.

"So?" I asked breaking the prickly silence. "Do you like her?"

"Ana." She grimaced, like she'd tasted rancid milk. "She looks like an older Sab."

"Fuck that." I left her at the bottom of the stairs. I locked myself in my bathroom and steadied myself against the vanity. A voice bubbled up my throat. It was grittier than my earlier versions of Sab's voice.

"She looks exactly like me," I whispered. I wretched bile into the sink until the acid scorched my throat.

I moved out after graduation and survived by feeding off my memories of Sab like a maggot. I blended her voice with mine, usurped her unquestioning confidence to land a job at a prestigious law firm; transposed her charm into adulthood and used it to fuck the women I wanted. I locked pathetic Ana inside me, trotting her out for family and the occasional drinks with Marit. I flooded the space left by Sab while it ate Dad's liver and stole Mom's connection to the present.

I constructed the life I dreamed Sab would have had and lived it. Sab owned a waterfront condo and sipped champagne with top tier clients. Sab was profiled in the Saturday paper as the quintessential immigrant success story. Sab comforted relatives and said, "Thank you for coming," at Dad's funeral. Sab organized mom's move into a nursing home when she could no longer live alone.

Sab, Sab, Sab. I glutted myself on the potential of her unfinished life. Yet, the frost that had blossomed in me so long ago had fractalized, coating my intestines and invading my lungs. Sometimes, I'd take a knife to the inside of my upper arm and slide the blade beneath my skin to check If I was completely numb. The face reflected in the blade was always my own.

Soon, I only allowed Anna to crawl out of the morgue inside me to visit Mom at the retirement home.

The lights in mom's apartment were dim. She let me in, kissed me on the cheek and sat on her couch, staring at the empty park across the street.

"How are you?" I tried to catch her eye. The bouts of disassociation had lengthened. "Did you take your meds, today?" I put my hand on her lap hoping to get her attention. She didn't move.

"Do you see him?" she asked, never taking her eyes from the park.

"Mom?"

"The boy in de uniform." The tremor in her voice matched the chill that surged within me. My heart battered my ribcage like it did that night in the dark. "I was eleven." She stood and went to rifle through her dresser drawer. My stomach turned in the interval. *Don't tell me, don't tell me*, I thought. *Let it burn with you in the crematorium when you die.* My palms slicked with sweat.

She came back with an envelope. Inside were black and white photos of her as a child standing next to a boy three or four years younger than her. She flipped one of the tarnished pictures over. The words: Cousins Elsie and Greg, 1962 were written in block letters on the back.

I snatched the photo from her, my hands shaking. Greg was well fed and sturdy, nothing like the skeletal boy we'd encountered in the woods.

"How?"

"We went to play by dee river." She talked as I studied the other pictures. "It had heavy rain but I didn't want to go straight home from school and tie up the goats." She paused, allowing space for me to speak. I was frozen, my jaw locked around the truth about Sab and that night too awful to speak. "Greg's face was all bruised up like he get beat with a stick when they pulled him out de water." She swallowed. "Papa made me see him. 'Look,' he said. 'Look what your carelessness did." Her eyes shifted, tracking movement from the swings to the slide. She quivered, her eyes never leaving the park.

I put my arm around her. Exhaustion had eroded her strength. She was brittle, a shred of the mother I'd known. She'd snap if I squeezed too hard.

"I couldn't let you go to de woods after what happened to Sab. I heard him laughing, that day, after that Ranger man came."

I swallowed.

"Mama pushed me to leave. Said, 'dis go haunt you here.' You can't outrun the past, Ana, even if it's dead and drowned in another country." She fell silent. We sat in the dark, mom barely moving. I left after she'd readied for bed.

Ma passed away soon after. I cremated the photos with her. Not long after, I pushed a full cart down the aisles of the local camping outfitter. I bought the gear I needed, then texted Marit.

I stood on Marit's porch. We hadn't seen each other in nine months.

"Hey, Ana." She flashed her knee weakening smile, taking me in. "I'll help unload the car."

"No," I held my palm up. "I have to do this alone." She put her hands in the air and then crossed them over her stomach when I didn't laugh.

I crashed around with poles and spikes for the next hour in her backyard while she watched from the window. I was drenched in sweat but the tent went up. At six, she dragged me inside and plied me with pizza and beer. Her curly hair was up and her face still dimpled when she smiled. This is what Sab would have looked like, beautiful; nothing like the fraud I had become. I strained against the repulsive attraction to Marit welling inside me.

At eight, I left her in the kitchen and went out to the tent. I lay on my back listening to the crickets in her yard. A moment later Marit unzipped the door.

"Sleep over?" Mischief shone in her eyes.

"No." I looked up at the ceiling.

"Ana, we both have a lot of practice sleeping alone. You've got this portion down." I relented and she settled in next to me.

"Where are you going?" she asked.

"Can't say."

"Then why?"

"To find someone," I answered. She pursed her lips. I grabbed her hand and laced my fingers in hers—it was the only explanation I could offer her.

"You're always cold." She let go of my hand and reached over to stroke my left arm. The warm weight of her on top of me cracked the shell of ice inside me. I cupped her face and kissed her cinnamon mouth so hard it took both of our breaths away. She pulled away first. Sorrow flooded her face, making the tiny muscles in her chin twitch. I bit my lip. She knew what I wanted.

"I hate you." The words were molten. I pulled her down and we melted into each other.

On my way out of the city, a few weeks after, I mailed her my will.

The girl in the camp office is blue eyed and rose cheeked. Her sun kissed blonde hair pulled into a messy pony tail. She's the perfect poster girl for the health benefits of the Canadian outdoors.

"Keep the blue on your dash. The white you can clip to the post at your campsite," she explains as she hands me my permits. Her smile is river rock smooth. She gives me a few park programming schedules with my receipt for firewood. It's prohibited to bring your own wood in case you blight the forest with a foreign disease.

"Thanks, I'll check these out." Another lie to add to the ledger of falsehoods I've told. The exchange reminds me of Miss. Matthews. I'm fifteen years older than she was back then and the memory of her still makes me quake.

I put the firewood in the truck and rumble down the gravel roads to my lot. It's a different site, radio free and silent, on the complete opposite side of the park. But it's right.

I fall asleep exhausted after pitching the tent and wake up starving. I hike the next day. The quiet of the woods is distinct from the deathly silence of a house. It's full and I submerge myself in it.

The second night is cooler. The darkness is so damp, it sluices against my skin. I sit by the fire wrapped in a blanket late into the night, reading a copy of *The Count of Monte Cristo* I've brought with me.

"Anarika." The crisp whisper in my ear makes the hair on my neck stand. My eyes adjust. Smoldering embers are all that's left of the fire. "Come on loser," the words, breathed on my lips this time taste of ash. "Come down to the river."

Sab's standing across from me, an emaciated girl shrouded in grey smoke. Her eye sockets are stuffed with writhing worms; a rictus grin is plastered across her face. I recoil. No I don't want to go with her. I want to go back to the city. But this is a debt I must pay. I toss *The Count of Monte Cristo* into the fire. The flames rekindle, and consume it. I grab my flashlight.

Sab holds a gaunt hand up.

"No light," she hisses. I slip the flashlight in my pocket and follow her into the trees.

She walks ahead of me, smoke trailing from her skeletal frame. I struggle to keep up, tripping over rocks and twigs. The forest closes in. The air is humid, hard to breathe. Branches entangle me, ripping at my skin. They claw at my face, penetrating my mouth. I'm a bloodied mess when we reach a low cliff above a moonlit river. Sab's below me on the rocky bank.

"Come on stupid," she says in my ear. She shoves my back. I stumble down the mossy rocks and land on my hands and knees. She doesn't wait, doesn't care about my lacerated shins. She leads on, the rocky cliff face to our left and the sparkling river to our right. I stagger after her. How long have we walked? Where is she taking me? I have no breath to ask. She stops at a crevasse in the cliff and slips inside. I linger at the mouth, not wanting to trespass this space, carved by glacial ice eons ago.

"Hurry up. I'll tell the police you killed me." Her voice ricochets in the cavern and pierces my chest. I step inside. It's cold. The chatter of my teeth fills my skull. I put my right hand on the wall to brace myself. It's tacky and wet. The darkness is as black as that molasses night long ago. The space narrows as I follow Sab's voice deeper into the cave, away from the river.

"Stop," she says when I can touch either side of the fissure with my arms outstretched. "Light."

I reach for it and flick it on.

In the circular glow is a skeleton along with the smashed remains of the yellow flash light Sab took with her when she left with Greg. I kneel next to her, unable to look away. I caress her femur, her tibia, her detached jaw. They're frigid; colder than I've ever been. I rub her ribs trying to warm them. She'd been here all this time, her flesh and blood rotting away while I masqueraded who I'd imagined she'd become; when all she'd been was a dead girl in a hole.

"There's room for you, Ana," she says. "I'll tell mom if you leave."

I kiss her cheek before I lie next to her and switch the flash light off. The cave is silent. I close my eyes and relive the lingering touch of grass on my calves from the morning before. A dense cold creeps up my body, pressing the air out of my lungs. It slithers up my neck and freezes my chin. I put my hand on Sab's chest as an icy grip clutches my throat and squeezes.

· ·

Suzan Palumbo is a Trinidadian-Canadian dark speculative fiction writer and editor. Her work has been nominated for the Nebula, World Fantasy, Locus and Aurora Awards. She also cofounded the Ignyte Awards with L.D. Lewis. She is the author of *Countess*, a queer Caribbean space opera novella, and *Skin Thief: Stories*, a collection of dark fantasy and gothic short stories. When she isn't writing, she can be found exploring her local misty forests in Ontario, Canada. A complete list of her work can be found at suzanpalumbo.carrd.co

NOVELETTES

02 ARENA

Oghenechovwe Donald Ekpeki

"Where there is no inner freedom, there is no life."
—Radhanath Swami

My sweat ran in rivulets, caught between my skin and the Lycra body-suit. It slid down my spine and chest, as I regarded my enemy with detached exhaustion. Though my vision was hazy, my focus was sharp. My intention: to do murder, even a murder sanctioned and abetted by the same system that was slowly killing us all.

The man in front of me paced, fatigue showing plainly in his bearing. My body was depleted of the energy needed to carry it, and my breathing came in short, gulping gasps as I inhaled the bittersweet air. Bitter because it reeked of my own possible—no, likely—death, and sweet because of its purpose: winning a life for another, one far more deserving of it than I was. I breathed in that sweetness as if it was a promise, a sustenance of a selfish love, which, to me, was everything.

I knew my opponent was not my enemy, although he might be the instrument of my death, or I the instrument of his. The one I truly needed to defeat, our collective enemy, was unflagging: the society that broke us and engineered our existence as an inexorable journey toward death. Quick or slow, the system forced us into a profound lifelessness just so we could breathe one more day, then yet another.

I was at the arena for the second time, of my own accord, but in a trap by the society to which I had been born.

My opponent shuffled forward, all the humour bleached out of the desperate grin he wore plastered on his frozen features. A snarl spread across my own face, and I rushed at him to take life if I could, that I may cherish and gift it to another.

A small part of me whimpered and briefly wondered at the monster I had become.

A few months earlier...

The chattering in the hall faded as the speaker mounted the podium. Four thousand of us fell silent as he removed his O2 mask and began our induction into the Academy of Laws. The Head of the Department (HoD) of Property Law proceeded to tell us why we were here.

I shook my head ruefully. In the Nigeria of 2030, people still insisted on telling others their purpose, as though we did not know or could not decide for ourselves. Cursed was the one with their own will and individuality, and woe unto them if they aspired to more than the O2 credits needed to keep them breathing.

What was our daily reality? You had to pay to breathe. Since the global warming crisis had affected phytoplankton and hampered the production of breathable air, our lives were our own to maintain at the requisite cost.

Plodding along, the HoD explained to us that we were amongst the chosen few privileged to earn the Bachelor of Laws (LL.B) degree. Having studied for five years to obtain an LL.B degree, and having passed a very difficult entrance exam to be admitted to the Academy of Laws, one wondered where the "privilege" came from. Here we had to survive a rigorous, nearly militaristic regimen of study and indoctrination and only then would we be allowed to take the almighty Bar exam.

I couldn't help thinking that if I had wanted to show off superhuman stamina, I would have joined the army. Then I reminded myself that I wasn't here by choice. It was the Bar that would usher me into my position in the corrupt system where I could earn the kind of O2 allowances that would quash my CO2s. It would be a herculean journey, not helped by these pompous men making it seem like a grand privilege.

The HoD's talk prompted several students, naïve in my opinion, to ask about our rights. He informed them, almost scathingly, that they had no rights.

I inwardly shrugged. I would sort it out the way I sorted everything. Succeeding was all that was required. It didn't matter how.

The HoD introduced a second lecturer, a professor of the Commercial Law Department. Without removing his mask—which he didn't need here, where O2 generators regulated the air—he outlined the curriculum. A program that should ordinarily take three years was crammed into eight intensive months, giving room for periodic admission of new students. The more students admitted, the greater the fortune of O2 units the school made. He concluded with a reiteration of our privilege as law students. I shook my head and, slipping on my O2 mask, left the hall.

Outside, I saw that Ovoke had taken a break from the rhetoric too. She smirked when she saw me and came over to give me a hug. She felt the way she looked: delicate, as if she would crumble if I squeezed her too tightly. What was it about her fragile look that all the boys found irresistible? I held her at arm's length to inspect her as if trying to find her appeal.

She smiled at the confused look on my face, raising an eyebrow.

I never missed an opportunity to tease her, and I couldn't resist it now. "I would say I missed you, but I don't want to lie."

She laughed. "And yet you hold me like you care."

I struggled with a response, and she filled in for me. "Is it because I'm dying?"

"Of course," I agreed, hoping my off-handedness would hide the double bluff. "Why else would I care?"

She smiled again, and I soaked in her presence as we leaned against the parapet in companionable silence.

"Do you want to feel it?" she asked blandly after a moment.

"Feel what?"

"My tumour. The death inside me. I can feel it, you know."

I looked away, over the railing. When we had first met during registration for the program, she'd told me she suffered from ovarian cancer. She'd told no one else, not one of her close friends from our university days when I had been just a course mate she hardly noticed. She hadn't told her new friends here, either. Just me, who didn't fawn over her like everyone else. Me, who teased her like a brother, and never let her take anything too seriously.

The way I was around her was also her preference. Not like everyone else, who were always in puppy-mode around her, even when she wasn't ill. They didn't see what I saw: a strong, intelligent, frighteningly competent woman with teeth and claws and a mind all her own. When I saw her fight, I called her fearsome, horrifying, a raging animal in a world too delicate to cage her. When others saw her fight, they called her "brave."

It was easy then to see why she told just me.

"I told only you," she had said, "for the same reason I left home for this rigorous, unhealthy program. I don't want to be treated like I'm a sick, broken thing. I want to live before I die." And then she'd added, "If not caring is your normal, then that's what I want."

But I had always cared, even when it felt hopeless to do so, even when I didn't want to.

I realized I'd not answered her about touching her tumour. I didn't want to respond. Teasing her about death made it seem less real, but really talking about it was too hard. I had to keep pretending that I didn't care.

"Hey, mumu," I teased her, rather than humour her macabre mood on this, a day to acknowledge the new challenges ahead of us at the Academy of Laws. "We had better go in before the patrollers come looking for us."

She chuckled. "Okay, big head."

We slipped off our oxygen-filtering masks as we returned to the hall. We only needed them in the harsh, oppressive, and barely breathable air of the outside.

The lecturer, while deep in a section on campus rules, had found his good humour. I preferred him without it.

"You are not allowed to eat when classes are on. Not even to chew gum. Unless you are pregnant and carrying a kid, then you can chew like a goat. Hahahaha."

He continued on, outlining all the lack of privileges we had at our privileged school, with the interspersing of jokes, often classist. I grimaced, but some students chuckled. You knew the ones who would succeed early by ass-kissing.

Next up was Dr. Umez of property law. A man in his early forties, he rasped on about his religious, conservative principles and rules that I am sure weren't sanctioned by the institution, as strict as it already was. His last edict was that phones wouldn't be allowed when his lectures were on, and any found would be confiscated, permanently.

"Well, that's not extreme," I quipped sarcastically. "He's trying to go into phone retailing?"

Ovoke leaned closer and whispered conspiratorially, "He trades them back for favours."

I looked at her blankly, not getting her point, so she continued, "He's famous with the ladies."

My eyebrows climbed in realization, then furrowed in confusion again. "But why? For a phone?"

"He promises an easier time for them here, and better chances of passing."

I scoffed. "I have actually looked into bribing people to pass and to game the system. 'Phone Seizer' here can't guarantee anyone will pass. The scripts are marked by external examiners and people in HQ, Abuja. That's where it all happens."

"Well, the average student doesn't know that. Between deceiving the gullible and promising to make their lives hell, Umez has quite a tutoring program."

"How do you even know all this?" I asked.

"I'm a woman. It's our business, our survival, to know about people like this."

I was quiet for a bit. Ovoke touched my angry face.

"If he ever bothers you," I told her softly, "I'll kill him."

"Awww," she said. "You're every girl's dream: a psycho best friend who would kill for her. However, start with my cancer."

"I'm afraid that's beyond the reach of my goons," I said apologetically.

"Are you useful for anything?" she asked with a playful push. We both laughed under our breath.

Mrs. Oduwole was at the podium now. The Head of Hostels began by stating that the generators would be on until midnight for reading and for the making of breathable air. After midnight, we would revert to our O2 cylinders, which we must keep by our bedsides throughout the night.

The tuition was expensive but was only meant to cover the central hall's oxygen generation when lectures were on. O2 masks filtered the bad air temporarily, for the brief periods when moving between places. O2 cylinders were for longer periods when there were no O2 generators.

We weren't allowed to be in the hostels during the day when lectures were on, for any reason. She didn't care if you were a girl on your flow, no matter how heavy. And this was apparently the only example she felt obligated to give.

Another lecturer talked about modest and decent dressing, and one unfortunate girl was singled out as an example of what not to do.

The female lecturer, gesturing at the girl's long and painted nails, said, "Such is not allowed here. They are an unnecessary distraction to both ladies and gentlemen. The ladies might feel pressured to compete and focus on their looks, and the men might want to...well, we all know what men want from women."

There was a low chuckle from the students, and not for the first time I wondered at the unhealthy focus of this school to use sexist mores to try to keep everyone in their place.

"Well, we know some women also want the same from women," she continued, and the chuckle rang louder. She leaned forward now and whispered, even though she knew the microphone would carry the whisper. "So, with your nails, how do you wash your..."

The laughter rang long and unrestrained now. The girl being queried wilted in shame, and the woman moved on, having achieved her objective.

"Well, that's professional," I whispered sarcastically to Ovoke.

But she wasn't fazed by any of this. Of course, she had more immediate worries on her mind.

I had to wonder why our society still looks down on women so much. Was gasping your lungs out in between toiling to purchase filters and breathable air in an atmosphere ruined by global warming not enough? Or was the audacity of being here, daring to compete with men in the most lucrative and influential profession in the Republic, simply too bold?

At the end of the induction, students remained seated while the lecturers left. There were electronic fingerprint scanners embedded at our desks and, in order to be counted as having attended, we would have to use the scanners to sign in and out. If there wasn't eighty-five percent attendance over the entire program, you couldn't take the Bar exams. That also ensured that students were holding each other accountable.

Once the teachers were gone, the students rushed out through their exits.

Exit A was left for the Bar 1 students, the elite gang in their expensive-as-hell O2 regulator masks. They had all schooled in China and America for their LL.B. Foreign schools were attended by only the extremely wealthy and took less time—three years instead of the five in domestic schools. These elite students were generally regarded as "better" and were treated accordingly. They didn't mingle with the students from Nigerian universities. It didn't help that the Chinese government, in partnership with the CAT—Chinese American Tobacco—had donated a stash of high-quality masks for them and took care of O2 regulation in most of our institutions, in exchange for certain economic and political concessions.

The British American Tobacco (BAT) was consumed by the CAT after the Chinese had bought all the interests, infrastructure, and institutions that had been left over in Nigeria after the Weather Crises. They effectively split the country down the middle to share with American investors in an uneasy alliance. Both former tobacco companies quickly caught on and began to produce air-filtration systems, air regulators, masks, and other paraphernalia needed by all for survival.

Before the Crises, they had sold death in the form of cigarettes when life was in abundance to those who didn't care about life. But after the thinning of the air and the severe climate changes that had made the earth near uninhabitable, the industrial conglomerate had switched. Now the merchants of death sold life and oxygen because death was in abundance, and life was the commodity in demand. You had to pay to breathe. O2 credit was life. And your deficits, your debits, were in CO2. They sold to the highest bidders: the government who purchased and subsidized it for their workers, and for the rich. So there was short supply for the rest.

I made a move to follow as the peacocks trooped through their exit, but Ovoke's hand tugged my arm.

"Not that way, trouble-lover."

I smiled, and we went out through one of the other doors, heading for the hostels. I looked at Ovoke. She had taken the induction far less seriously than me, rolling her eyes through all the nonsense. She was well attuned to my moods and temperament.

"Want to take a walk?" she asked.

"Yes," I replied. "I need a break since there are no more induction classes today."

She clasped my hand as we strolled out.

A security guard was patrolling outside, and I passed him an O220 card, to forestall his inquiries. He pocketed it smartly and moved on. I bribed the security men at the gate too, and we left campus to walk illegally into the sunset of a quiet afternoon, away from the toxic Law Academy.

Weeks in, we had adjusted to the toxic institution; to the assignments and group work that ran on into late nights and had to be presented in class the next day; to the frantic, extra reading after classes to avoid being embarrassed in the randomly administered, rapid-fire quizzes; to the shaming and disgrace that followed failure to get an answer right; to hoarding our oxygen cylinders in the hostels for when the power generators switched off in the night.

We had a plethora of assignments and projects that kept us buried to our eyebrows, even on weekends. But assignments were rarely my concern on weekdays, much less weekends. And on this weekend, Ovoke was gone.

She had taken a trip home to Ikeja, where her family lived, for chemo sessions scheduled into the middle of next week.

I missed her. Taking care of her at school—buying her food, drawing her water, and keeping her company with jokes and sallies, both of which made her happy—was the one thing that kept me anchored and from snapping at the horrid attitude of everyone here.

Without her here, there was no life to be experienced. I felt acutely every pull of the thin and corrupted air. The mechanically purified and generated atmosphere wasn't much better. We hadn't had good air in a decade.

It's no surprise that Ovoke was my breath of fresh air, my reason for being able to withstand this place—for not exploding at all the verbal abuse and stupidity from lecturers, students, and other staff. I needed to stay here to stay with her.

And it was this realization that sent me on my own little detour. I needed to visit the mainland. Not that the air there was any better there. It was much worse, in fact. The people there were poor. The island that held the school campus was the part of Lagos kept for the elite, with regulated air, as seen to by Governor MC Oluwole.

You see, only the rich deserved to breathe.

Still, the mainland was home. Usually, I would take my Temperature Regulating Suit. I needed the TRS when going to the mainland so as not to suffer heat stress from the ever-rising temperatures, another effect of the warming crises of a decade ago.

But I had given Ovoke my suit, so I stood sweating, waiting for transport until one of the government-regulated Bus Rapid Transit (BRT) vehicles arrived. It would take me to the outskirts of the mainland and was fitted with its own temperature-regulation systems. Inside, I leaned back and let the cold-yet-polluted air fan my anxieties away.

I was fine until I got into the Danfo bus, the first of many on this transfer line that would convey me the last distance to my home. They were usually faulty and broke down a lot, exposing the occupants to serious dangers of heat stress.

I paid the Danfo driver O217. His bus, at least, had a marginally working air-filtration system, so we could have breathable air. I baked in the heat, but I could tell that the other passengers were not as affected. They were hardy, sturdy folks who looked like they were used to this. People who lived on the mainland but worked on the island made the trip to the high-rise and office complexes they toiled in daily, so they were used to the extremes. The island housed most of the companies and corporations that thrived in this troubled world, along with CAT, the company that owned the breath in our lungs.

I stopped at Oyingbo and took a bus going toward the University of Lagos, my alma mater. I wasn't going to my old school, though. I stopped at the university gate and took another bus to Bariga, the student community that housed most of the 100,000-student population, teachers, and other mostly junior staff that ran the institution. You only got accommodation inside the school if you were senior staff.

The hostels were for foreign students who paid top O2 credits. I was heading downtown, to the most dangerous parts of Bariga, the parts I knew were occupied by the Eiye and Buccaneer cultists.

I paid the keke driver O24. My mask was already on. I took the Ikoro, the side streets that led to the house of the friends and fellow cultists I came to see, members of the vanilla Buccaneer cult I had belonged to during my years as a University of Lagos student.

It was not as dangerous as it sounded. The Buccaneer was a cult made up of better-off kids who wanted to be dissidents. We paid the Eiye guys to handle the few infractions we got into. The Eiye was a more impoverished fraternity with their members nicknamed "bird," or "winch," for the rough and dirty crowd it attracted. They were always eager to do any jobs for the right pay, which was any pay.

I passed a few people carrying old, crude oxygen cylinders. People on the mainland here, aside those in high-profile jobs, could rarely afford filtration masks sold by CAT, so they made do with old oxygen cylinders they had to re-fill. The agencies that should have handled filtration and regulation systems here were moribund from having their initially insufficient funding further looted by officials who went on to buy high-rise apartments on the Island.

The passing folks glared at me, taking in my fine and obviously expensive air-filtration mask. To them I was a "butty," a rich kid who had lost his way—and I knew some would try to rob me, then severely wound me if I tried to resist. I looked back to see them already preparing to come at me. I flashed one of them the Buccaneer hand sign. He hesitated. I flashed the Eiye hand sign too, thus iden-tifying myself as "brother to pikin of last two years, egede number one." The guy at the head of the company nodded in respect and waved me on as "master."

My destination was the house of one of my old Buccaneer friends yet to grad-uate. It was crowded with a number of students and indigenes of the Bariga com-munity who hung out with them. Loud music blared from speakers somewhere in the two-bedroom apartment. It was old and decrepit, like most of the houses here.

The generator, running outside for electricity, powered an old air regulator which coughed out good air, marginally improving what we had. Ironically, it was ruining the good air outside, to provide for us inside. Talk about robbing Peter to pay Paul. Not to even mention the noise.

But, anything to breathe better. I could smell igbo, which had become dirt-cheap when everyone moved on to drugs and synthetic substances for highs to compensate for an otherwise shitty life. Well, almost everyone. It didn't make sense to me to smoke and damage your lungs and the most precious commodity you had: air that was in such short supply. But then, no one ever accused cultists of wisdom.

I went to my friend's room, where the smell of weed was coming from. Jaiyesimi and some friends were smoking and playing cards while another group was gambling with dice. Some had passed out on a rickety-rackety bed in the corner.

Jaiyesimi nodded at me. He had to finish his game before we could speak.

I greeted the occupants of the room in confralangua, to show I belonged. I had taken off my air-filtration mask when I got into the house, seeing as they had a regulator. But the smell of weed soon overpowered me and it was either choke or put on my mask, neither of which was a good option here; both would make me look weak. So, I signaled to my friend that I would be outside when he was done. I choked down a small cough as I stepped out. I could see them chuckle and one of them say slyly, Ju man.

Outside, I slipped my mask back on and inhaled deeply. Air was life. For this, I was content to be a "Ju man," a slur for people who didn't belong to cults in the university. Or for those who, like me, belonged merely as honorary members for protection, social and other nonviolent reasons, paying dues and not engaging in any of the requisite violent activities that gained one respect and prestige as a cultist. I had joined to be left alone. There was no middle ground in a community like this: you were either the oppressed or the oppressor.

I opted to join the latter, even as an honorary member.

Jaiyesimi soon joined me. Chuckling at something someone inside had said, he took a pull of his blunt. Looking at my disapproving glance, he put it out and deposited it in a pocket.

We both stood in silence for a while, then he asked, "How the academy be na?"

"It's fine. By that I mean everyone there isn't."

"As it should be," he chuckled. "You know, we hear gist from folks there. It sounds like the university all over again."

"Basically," I agreed. "Just more studying, more nonsense. Less time though."

"Mmm," he nodded knowingly. "More of the bad things, less of the good."

"Yea," I agreed. "The academics are really the worst. But I will sort myself out. You know I know how."

He nodded.

We were quiet again, and then he said, "I heard about this guy in your academy, Dr. Umez. Has he been bothering you?"

"How do you mean?"

"You know how I mean," he said, leaning closer. "I heard he pressures folks for sex. Has he ..."

"Wait," I stopped him, confused. "Why would you think this would be a problem for me? He pressures g— Oh! You think I'm gay, and Dr. Umez is into boys?"

Silence.

"Dr. Umez does boys?" I asked. "But he's so married, with kids, and religious, and being queer is a ..."

"… Crime with a fourteen-year jail term here and a death sentence in the North?" He rolled his eyes. "That's for the little people. Not an academy lecturer."

"But he's married, to a woman!"

"That never stopped anybody either. He's either bi or he does girls as a feint. In any case, he does both, so I've heard."

I thought back to what I had learnt about the lecturer. "Isn't he religious and a deacon at church?"

"Definitely a smokescreen."

"First of all, it's a wonder how you know so much about what's going on in the academy from here. Yes, I know gist filters down. But you know so much about the sexual lives of people there. Me, him. I am curious."

"Well, I like to check up on mine and know what's going on in the community."

"Since when was the academy part of the community?" I asked. At his raised eyebrow, I paused. "Wait, are you gay?"

I think he knew I didn't care about a person's sexual orientation. Straight or gay, bi or otherwise, as long as the relationship was healthy, who was I to judge?

He sidled closer. "Well, I could show you," he said softly, winking. "Show, not tell. Right?"

I laughed, knowing he was being playful, but also wondering if he was partly serious. It was so hard to tell in a society that didn't talk about such things openly, for fear of condemnation. "Don't ask, don't tell," I rejoinder. "This is flattering, but I prefer a partner who is cerebral."

"Are you mad?" He laughed too. "Last I checked, your grades weren't all that, so how will you be wanting a cerebral partner? And didn't you graduate with a third class?"

"I said cerebral, not academic. Also, you managed to not graduate at all."

"True," he conceded.

"Also, I'm not …"

"Right," he said.

We were both quiet after this, till I punctured the silence.

"So, Dr. Umez harasses and rapes both boys and girls huh."

"Yup," he said without looking at me.

"Dude sounds like he needs killing."

Jaiyesimi now looked at me. "Can you kill someone?

"I'm not sure. We're going to find out, I guess."

He looked at me askance. Silent.

I hesitated. "You get my text na, didn't you? O2 Arena."

His eyebrows raised in genuine surprise. "You were serious?"

"Yes na," I confirmed, irritated by the notion I would joke about something like that.

"Wetin you need money for so bad?" But he barely paused to breathe before answering his own question. "Ah … Law Academy."

It wasn't hard for him to figure out. I was a decent student when I tried. But I rarely did. School was a necessary evil for me. Something I did but had no choice.

I preferred art and writing, which I couldn't get parental approval to pursue. The only thing they endorsed or cared to entertain was a career that allowed one to get a job in the government administration as a civil servant and be entitled to O2 credits and an allocation of oxygen.

What use was a life where all you did was merely exist? So, I cheated when I could, and bribed my way through when I couldn't cheat or wing it. My dad had died in my third year at the university, and his monetary support had dried up.

Now I required five times the amount of money I had needed in the past to pay my way through the university. And I would need it all at once. So O2 Arena it was.

Jaiyesimi met my eyes sternly, and I realized he also, on some level, only thought of me as a Ju Man—faking it until I make it. Never completely all in. "You sure?"

I nodded.

"Well, na, your life, sha." He shrugged. "Make I call Papilo to carry us go."

We made our way to the underground square, led by one of the Eiye boys and my friend Jaiyesimi, to the place they called O2 Arena. It was a fighting pit, a solid Plexiglass cage, its transparent walls harder than steel. Two combatants in skin-tight black bodysuits were inside, cameras focused from every angle.

This was what had replaced selling your kidneys and internet fraud: the only get-rich-quick scheme, regulated secretly by government and top CAT officials, illegally and discreetly. The cage fights were streamed and sponsored by equally rich and highly placed folks who had an appetite for this kind of entertainment.

Thugs and all sorts of desperate people who were ready to risk it all for a huge payoff came here. Cult members came to settle squabbles. Instead of wasting a death, they came here to fight it out and at least know that one of them stood the chance to make what equalled near three decades of standard wages. Fifty thousand O2 credits, a lifetime supply of air. You fought and died to keep breathing. And this was how I planned to make money enough to sort my exams.

Jaiyesimi looked at me strangely, trying to figure out my sudden need to make such a huge gamble with my life. I ignored him.

They announced the fighters who got into the arena, glass doors sealed behind them. Pure, breathable air was provided inside so combatants could breathe well, could draw lungsful of the air they fought, and maybe died, for. The irony was not lost on the online spectators.

The fighters in the arena squared and faced off. The mic man and moderator atop the cage commentated, move-by-move, on the entire match, which turned out to be dirty, long, and ugly. I watched as the two men pummelled each other till they were almost too exhausted to stand. I didn't know them, or why they had come here to murder or be murdered, but I understood them. They were both me. I was both of them. Cultist, thug, desperate son, brother, or father—this was as fair a fight for oxygen as any of us would ever have.

One of them slipped, perhaps on the sweat on the floor. The other set to stomping the fallen, on and on. When his target stopped moving, he took him into a chokehold. The other struggled, but not for long. When he finally lay still, the victor stood up, screaming to the rafters.

Then he fell to his knees in exhaustion.

Canned cheering and applause answered him; there were no spectators live here—just the technical staff working the equipment, and thugs and cultists screening fighters or helping victors to process their payment.

The Eiye boy with Jaiyesimi looked at us both. "You don see am abi?"

I nodded. They brought trusted, wannabe participants here for a viewing, to see the action before they committed to their fate.

Jaiyesimi looked at me with disbelief. "Why you wan do this kind thing? For school? You fit read na. You fit pass on your own. And if you fail, e no matter."

I shook my head. He didn't understand. I couldn't risk it. It was not that I could not do it on my own, but if I failed, my mom and family at home, who needed the status of having a graduate from the academy of letters, would miss the income I could contribute to keeping them breathing. Not to mention the stigma of my failing. I would rather die.

The thug who brought us to the arena rapped Jaiyesimi on the shoulder. "He no get the mind." Meaning that I didn't have the guts to do this.

They were right, as I realized on the bus the next day. It's all well and good to think you can do it until you actually have to.

I had only been in school for barely a week when she called me. A week after my first trip back from the mainland. I had left after she left, because in her absence, there was not enough presences to keep me occupied. The campus was filled with students, but it was empty of companionship in her absence.

I had been lazing through the school activities with disinterest when she called me one evening, her voice such a tiny scratchy whisper, I had to strain to hear her. "Ode, I'm back."

"Oh, really?" I said, feigning disinterest. "Why is your voice so tiny? I could come see you in your room. Or should I wait for you to come downstairs?" I was eager not to seem too eager. She chuckled, no doubt aware of my ruse.

"I'm not in school yet," she said. "I'm outside. Chemo was rough and those hostels are not the best place to recover. That's why my voice was tiny, by the way."

I swallowed a lecture about how she should have stayed at home instead to rest, something she sensed. Instead I said, "Well, you were no Beyonce to begin with, so it's not like your voice is a great loss."

She chuckled and answered my unspoken question.

"My parents agreed I could lodge in one of the affordable hotels around, for a day or two to get over chemo before moving back to the hostel. So, will you come and see me there?"

My phone chimed immediately after and I received the address in my WhatsApp. Golden Tulip Hotels. I knew the place. No wonder it was affordable. It was a not too terrible place but in the more rundown part of the Island.

"Okay, girl. I'll see you in a bit. Though I have important things to do, so it won't be for a while."

"Of course, busy man," she said mockingly.

"Bye." I hung up a little annoyed that I was worried and she would know I was. I would have to deliberately delay now. Wait for a whole while before going to see her and be fashionably late, make it seem like I wasn't even going to show up.

It was 8pm when I knocked on the door of her room. She opened the door, looked me up and down then let me hug her. I held on a bit, then she pushed me away. I sat on the bed and she sat at the table, and in her scratchy voice, told me how her trip went. After a while of listening and punctuating with sarcastic quips that had her chuckling all through, she got up and pulled something from a drawer.

"What's that?"

"Neulasta."

"What's that? Are you doing drugs in addition to your cancer?" I asked, almost impressed.

She sighed.

"It's a follow-up for my chemo, to wake me up."

"Wake you up?"

She sighed and beckoned to me. I pulled closer saying, "Oooh, the sex talk."

She shook her head. "Do you know how chemo works?"

"I know what goes in where and how to use a condom."

She punched me. "Be serious." I affected seriousness and she continued. "What chemo is supposed to do is kill you."

I raised an eyebrow.

"Along with your cancer cells," she added. "It kills you and the cancer, almost. It stops before you are dead. But the cancer is weak, then you take this after." She held up what she had called Neulasta. "It's for my vitality. Wakes me back up, brings me back from the edge. Rinse and repeat, almost kill me and the cancer, I slip out of its grasp with this, leaving it to die a little more each time. Rinse and repeat, till it's eventually dead. A little game of cat and mouse."

She stopped talking. There was a lingering silence in the room. I didn't say anything but the unspoken question hung between us. What if you lose in this little game of cat and mouse?

I asked, "Does it kill your brain cells then? Cuz that would explain..."

She punched me and we both laugh.

"I'm supposed to take this by 9.30pm," she continued. "And I must take it before two hours elapse."

I nodded solemnly. "What happens if you don't take it within that time?"

"It's supposed to keep me alive, so..." she shrugged. "Your guess is as good as mine."

I swallowed.

"Come here scared cat," she said, pulling more stuff from her drawer. "I had a cannula in my hand from chemo, which I would have simply taken it with. All you would have needed to do was inject into my cannula. But it fell off you see..."

"Of course it did," I muttered.

"So I'll need you to..."

I looked at what she was holding closely now. It was a syringe.

"I'll need you to fix this new one for me."

I felt blank and empty.

"I can't break my skin myself. I'm scared of the needles."

I looked at her face now, my disbelief plainly etched in it. She smiled a little, what she must have imagined was an encouraging smile.

"You know I'm not a doctor, or even a nurse," I said. "But I'm supposed to let me get this straight, pierce your skin, fix a cannula, which I've never done before and correctly administer this drug which if I don't, you might die?"

She didn't nod; she just made the encouraging face. I groan and she proceeded to convince me that it wouldn't be that difficult.

It was difficult as hell. Her veins had collapsed from many needles and her general condition. She had what she called 'vein trauma' which made it more difficult. And I just couldn't believe how difficult it was slipping a needle into a human vein, especially for someone with no professional training. Her skin was soft under my touch and she tried to hide the tremble, then the tears as I missed the vein over and over and over again. Then before I knew it, I flung the needle away.

"This is supposed to be a normal visit. You just called me to come hang as a friend. Why didn't you warn me? Why didn't you tell me? How am I supposed to do this, which I haven't done before and it means so much, maybe even your life? How can you do this to me?"

I realized I was yelling.

She was quiet. I already knew the answers to my questions. She wanted to leave home, not stay home and get proper care and miss out on life and all that. I swallowed the rest of what I was going to say, about this being irresponsible and unsafe. She handed me another needle nonchalantly. Yeah, I realize she must be used to these kinds of outbursts. I was one of those worrying people that didn't understand the situation.

So I took a fresh syringe and tried again, and again and again. This time, I didn't snap; I just tried. But if she took my yelling stoically, she didn't take this. She was crying. And then I was crying too. She hugged me and rubbed the back of my head, saying she was sorry. I snapped out of it. She shouldn't be the strong one, comforting me. I was not the one at risk of dying.

I pulled back and looked at her.

It was an hour before the time limit for when she should take the drug. And she was starting to show signs of damage. Her eyes were dripping an odd, slimy liquid, and she was drooling too. She looked a little distant, not quite herself. Then the realisation came to me and I said aloud, "I can't do this. I'm going to get help."

She nodded weakly, as it absent minded and not present. I looked at the time. One hour more, going by the time she said she was supposed to take it.

I was conflicted as I left. Should she lock the door? What if she was in no condition to open it when I got back? Should she leave it open? What if someone came in to do something to her while I was away? Should I lock it and take the key? What if she needed help while I was gone and couldn't get out?

I slipped on my O2 mask and left. One hour to go. I stumbled through the streets, asking directions to a chemist, any chemist. It was dark, past 10pm, and I got suspicious looks as I strolled along. I stumbled from closed chemist to another closed chemist, frantic, semi-insane with the urgency of the help I needed. Then someone told me about a lady—not a chemist but a nurse. She sold drugs at home.

I rushed to the direction I was given and found the nurse. She was in her backyard smoking weed. She said she'd had a long day and just wanted to chill. She offered me a blunt. I looked at her incredulously and almost started to cry. But there was no time for that. I walked to her and said with as emphatically as I could.

"PLEASE HELP ME."

She followed me to the hotel. On the way, I explained in more details. We only needed her to administer the injection. She was high and sang all the way. But her hand was rock steady.

She asked no questions; apparently, she was used to strange, odd hour jobs. I was glad of that. I was in a random hotel with a very sick, near comatose girl and a strange, high nurse injecting something I don't know into her at my behest. I briefly wondered what would happen if she were to die. What kind of narrative would come out of this, and what kind of explanation would I give?

Then I violently shoved the thought from my mind. Ovoke ISN'T DYING.

The nurse finished her job. I gave her a bunch of O2 credits with me. All the cards I could lay my hands on. She thanked me, lingered to look back at me and

Ovoke. She opened her mouth as if to say something, then decided against it and left.

I watched Ovoke 30 minutes after. The colour came back to her. Her eyes had stopped dripping and she was not drooling anymore. I crawled into the bed and fell into a dead, dreamless sleep.

When I awoke in the morning, someone was holding me gently, cradling my head to their chest. I extricated myself and she woke. I got up, frowning at her. She smiled. I pointed at the bed.

"We're not like that. Also, did you get my consent before cuddling me?"

"Morning, grumpy."

I shook my head.

"Oh, and your breathing is really bad," she said sympathetically. "You slept so badly, I was worried all night."

"Worry about yourself, punk." I said in mock annoyance.

She smiled and got up, pulling a toothbrush from her bag. "You should call a cab now while we get ready for class. You know they usually take forever to get here."

"Why are we going to class again? After last night?" I asked. And answered it myself. "Live before you die, right!"

She beamed at me. Grumbling, I pulled out my phone to call a cab.

It happened a week after her second trio back home for chemo sessions. I had been restive. Expecting her call, thinking it was about the time she should return. I knew something was wrong. I could sense it. And I was right, I realized in dread when the call came. My breath was loud in my ears. The filter did what it was meant to, and the air that reached me was clean, but it couldn't stop my laboured breathing. My heart was thumping so hard.

My friend, Ovoke, was dying.

Ovoke's brother, Efeturi, had been the one to call; she was asking to see me.

I greeted him at the University of Lagos Teaching Hospital (LUTH) then rushed to where she lay on a stretcher outside the building. She'd always been so full of life but now she looked smaller, diminished.

How she had shrunk in such a short while, I couldn't understand. I held her bony hand in mine, rubbing it on my cheek, desperate to feel something of her as I'd known her before. Her fingers were warm, and I felt a faint throbbing as she breathed laboriously from a cylinder by the side of the bed. Over the edges of the mask, her panicked eyelids fluttered, and I couldn't tell if she knew I was there.

Her dad sat fanning her, and, while I held her and told her it would be all right, I met his stricken eyes.

She was outside, he said, because a year of cancer treatment, of chemo, had exhausted their money. They couldn't afford a ward. A bed would come at the daily cost of O2200. Getting her into the ICU and hooked up on proper machines would be even more.

So here we were. The chemotherapy treatment had been meant to kill her cancer but it was killing her instead. Now those precious, delicate lungs had stopped coping.

"So what now?" I asked.

He couldn't meet my eyes. "If we could raise the money for the ICU and a proper bed, she would be allowed time to heal her lungs. Then the cancer treatment could proceed. If not ..."

I stepped out to talk to Efeturi, leaving her parents and other brother with her.

When we came back, Ovoke was near hysterical from breathlessness and desperately thirsty. With the breathing mask briefly removed, we dribbled water into her mouth, letting her lay back. Everyone could see that it was taking all her energy just to suck what little air was given her by the mask, which we replaced after every paltry drink.

Too tired to talk, she communicated only with her eyes, and I gave her my best reassuring smile as I squeezed that fragile, tiny, bony hand.

"You'll be all right. Your dad says that you're considering surgery now."

She nodded.

I sighed, trying not to let my surprise and heartache at that news show in my eyes.

Back in school, before her chemo, we'd had a discussion about her treatment method. Chemo had burnt her out and she had lost her voice, her hair, her weight, energy, and vitality. And now she had also lost her air, the most precious commodity she, and any of us, had.

But back then, there had been an alternative: surgery. I had suggested she have the ovaries removed, removing the cancer with them. But she had refused because that would also mean losing her chance at future children.

"And what kind of life would that be?" she had asked. She was convinced that she'd be left a broken woman—a woman who wasn't a woman.

I had tried to tell her that her ability to give birth was not what made her a woman or gave her value. But even as I said it, I knew how false it would ring in her ears, as it might in mine, if I had been subjected to the other side of our patriarchal society.

She thought she would be nothing in a patriarchal society that valued men for their ability to provide and women for reproduction. I had never told her that even in such a society, she was everything to me. How could I, when she needed me to tease her, to treat her the same as I always had? When she demanded nothing could change, and I had to pretend I still cared for nothing.

"A freak," she'd insisted, "wanted by no one."

And so she had given up her air for future, unborn children. She'd risked it all. And only now could she see that her ovaries were not her, not worth her life. She was ready to let them go, if it wasn't too late.

Her laboured breathing kept me fully focused on our painful reality. I held her hands as air flowed raggedly through her damaged lungs, while she cried in between gasps, calling for her mom, and then pushing the distraught woman away when she came.

Ovoke's dad, gone for a good while during the afternoon, eventually came back. He had gotten the funds, probably by selling something, if they still had anything to sell. Whatever it had been, I could tell from his hushed conversation with his wife, and the stricken and defeated look on her face, that it wasn't good.

But it must have been enough. They would move Ovoke to the ICU. Her lungs would get the chance to stabilize while we looked for the funds to remove the offending cancer.

The surgery was a fortune, one beyond any resource the family could tap. Without it, she would die. At that moment I knew what I had to do.

I told her she would be all right. I held her hand, stroking it again lightly over my cheek. I told her I had to go get something and would be back. She gestured weakly that I should come closer. I leaned over her until I could feel each laboured, precious breath against my skin.

"I love you," she whispered in my ear.

I screwed my eyes tightly closed until the flood of tears no longer threatened. Then I smiled as bravely as I could and kissed her on the forehead. I left without telling her I loved her. There would be time later when the fire was back in her eyes and light gleamed from her smile. I would tell her I loved her then because she would know then that my love was not pity, or hopelessness, or humour.

I would tell her. But now, I had to focus on what I had to do.

Life for Life. #SaveVoke

The hashtag had spread throughout the interwebs, leading up to the fight, prompting an increased online viewership for the arena, their corrupt owners resharing the tweet, watching their bank account balance rise with glee.

Jaiyesimi was incredulous, disbelieving; his Eiye friend, our guide in this terrible place, was surprised but impressed.

And my opponent looked eager. His eyes glittered; all he saw in my place was a bag of O2 units. What I saw was life. A chance at life for the friend I loved, and I was willing to pay the ultimate price: to kill or to die.

My love and desire didn't automatically hand me the fight. I had done a little karate, up to green belt, so I took the stance and threw a flurry of punches. He took the blows, grabbing my hands and then delivering a headbutt that broke my nose and drew first blood, sending me sprawling to the floor.

There was no skill to it, no sparring strategy or technique, only experience and power.

He let me get up, perhaps disappointed by how little excitement such a victory would bring our audience. A mistake, as our next encounter had me rubbing the blood in his eyes and knocking him almost senseless.

Now we had both done damage.

I tried to take advantage of his confusion at his newfound blindness, but then it was me in a chokehold that would have ended things then and there, if I hadn't discovered a last-minute taste for human flesh. I sank my teeth into his arm, and he let me go with a brutal scream. A reverb-heavy roar from the remote spectators filled the air around us, and the announcer's words bounced off the Plexiglass walls, feverish with renewed excitement.

This would not be an orderly fight; it was a meaningless grapple for survival, for air—and drowning men didn't struggle prettily.

But I wasn't a fighter like these street thugs were, like he was. They had the crucial advantage of killing before and were ready to kill again. I had paid for protection. I had always taken the easy way out. Cheated, lied, stole. I'd never cared about anything except survival. And here I was, willing to die for something.

Someone.

I had no experience with the instinct to kill, and yet clearly this man had lived that way his entire life.

He pummelled me thoroughly, always darting back after each blow, wary of the bite of my teeth and determined to finish me without getting into close-quarters combat.

It was my reason for being here that kept me from giving up, from dying. I saw then his confusion at not having an easy kill, confusion that turned this thug's eyes into desperate rage. He caught me again in a clumsy chokehold. He was tired, but he was also eager to finish the job, to earn his fortune, to earn air—my air, my life, and Ovoke's right to life as well.

Outside the cage, I could see the Eiye cultist nod at me. I was brave, but I was done. My friend Jaiyesimi turned away. He wasn't ready to see me go.

Covered as I was in blood and sweat and tears, it was easy to slip out of my opponent's grasp. Clearly, he expected me to run then, to retreat in a futile attempt escape with my life. Instead, I went for him. His stunned response at my small rebellion was only a small advantage. With me a spent and beaten animal, there was little I could do once I had him in my grasp.

But even a wounded wolf is a dangerous thing. I still had my teeth, and his neck was bare inches away, so I went for his throat, biting through his skin into salty, coppery flesh.

He choked and slammed his fists into me repeatedly, but I held on tight, for life, for air. His blood filled my mouth and though I wanted to retch, I tightened my jaw with grim determination and felt skin and tendon cords between my teeth and lifeblood pump against my tongue.

With one final thump, he lifted me off the ground. Ovoke, I thought. I tried …

He slammed me back down.

The lights went out.

I woke days later, surprised to be alive.

Jaiyesimi had stayed by my side and recounted to me what had happened. My opponent had bled to death after he knocked me out...and I had won. The fortune in O2 units was already sitting in my account.

I was in some kind of recovery unit for the victors, but there was no time to celebrate my survival. I stumbled out of the bed, found my clothes, and rushed back to the student hospital.

I was met with numb looks and reddened eyes. Ovoke's brother's faces were filled with restrained pain. Her mother sat weeping, and her dad's defeat was evident in his hunched posture. He straightened when he saw me, letting go of his wife's hand and coming to hold me, to gently break the news.

In my absence, Ovoke had passed. Her oxygen-starved organs had finally given in. The substandard breathing apparatus that was all her family could afford couldn't sustain her through the three cardiac arrests she'd suffered in the night.

She was gone, her delicate, wild spirit, flown, borne away by the wayward winds we dealt so recklessly with. Winds which had paid us in disgruntled O2 coin, exacted in fulfilment of poetic justice, its pound of flesh.

I had fought and killed so she could breathe. Had taken a life so savagely, so pointlessly—all for her. I had the fortune in O2 units and now had access to the purest of air. But there were no longer lungs for me to put it in.

I crumbled to the floor and wept.

I walked into one of the admin offices at the Academy of Laws. The man I handed my form to was old, greying, and a bit stooped—old enough to have retired. Probably one of those who falsified their age so they could work longer.

Why anyone wanted more time in this place, I couldn't fathom. His shrewd eyes regarded my narrowed ones. His kindly smile answered the question I hadn't voiced: survival. That was why he stayed. Of course, he worked to keep breathing, for air, for a continued meagre flow of O2 units for him and for his loved ones.

Survival was overrated. I knew that now. You would live long enough to see your loved ones die.

"Son." His voice stopped me as I went to leave. "Why fill this? Why defer?" He asked, waving the paper at me.

Of course, I thought. The nosy old man wants to make sure I am utilizing my life well, not wasting my "potential."

I could try to explain the futility of it all, the fact that they were trapped here living a life that wasn't worth the O2 units it took to buy the oxygen to sustain it, but he wouldn't understand. It would shock him, my directness and honesty, my lack of respect, and brazenness.

"This isn't the place for me anymore," I told him.

His brows furrowed. "Why?"

It wouldn't be worth the O2 units it would take to explain. I had a fortune in oxygen, true, but still, every breath was precious. Instead, I raised my hand toward him, my voice raspy, Darth Vader-like, as if I had smoked a lifetime's worth of cigarettes.

"This world needs a wake-up call that might only be found in an arena of our own making."

I stepped out. The commotion was just starting.

I could hear the siren of the Reddington ambulance driving in as I stepped outside the school and into the world. After Dr. Umez didn't show up for his lecture, and they found his door locked, his calls not being answered, they would have broken in to find him slumped and unmoving, his oxygen air-filtration system in the office mysteriously disabled.

I drew in a loud, raspy breath through my own portable air system. Air that I had earned—air that was now a means to an end.

Most of us had been hiding behind these masks, telling ourselves it was because they let us breathe. It was time for the world to see the true face of things. I placed the call to Efeturi, my second in command, and, in the same raspy quality, breathed out my orders to my men.

"This world, our O2 arena, is now open."

. . . .

Oghenechovwe Donald Ekpeki is a writer, editor and publisher in Nigeria. His works have won and been a finalist in the Hugo, Nebula, Locus, World Fantasy, British Fantasy, British Science Fiction, Otherwise, Nommo, Sturgeon, NAACP Image awards, and others. His works have appeared in *Asimov's*, *F&SF*, *Uncanny*, *Strange Horizons*, *Apex Magazine*, etc. and he's been a guest of honour at Cancon, Stranimondi, the ICFA 44, and others. You can find him on Bluesky and Instagram at @penprince.

(EMET)

Lauren Ring

i. detection

When protesters take out the power at her Silicon Valley office, Chaya is at home, watching a golem pull dandelions.

The morning air is clear and cold. Chaya can hear her computer pinging alerts at her from inside her farmhouse. As soon as the dandelion patch is gone, she wraps her knee-high figurine in satin, pressing the cloth against its soft clay midsection. She lays her golem gently down by the riverside. A single tap on her phone activates the preprogrammed subroutine that wipes the alef from its forehead, leaving only the letters mem and tav—every instance in its code of *emet*, truth, becomes *met*, death.

She slips the bundle into the water, watching the satin flutter away in the current as the golem returns to the wet sediment. All that is left of Chaya's creation are smears of ochre on her fingers and lines of code on her hard drive.

Chaya wipes her hands on her jeans and heads back to her daily bug tickets, ready to find out the day's fresh disaster. Working from home has its perks, but maintaining her plot of land would be impossible without the help of her golems.

After a few false starts, Chaya has the bestowal of life down to a science. Each morning at dawn, she molds assistants from clay, connects them to her wireless network just like any smart watch or Bluetooth dongle, and passes them the day's variables: a list of chores, with each step painstakingly defined. The golem in charge of the dandelions finished early, but there are others of various sizes lumbering about the yard, carrying eggs from Chaya's chicken coop and clearing loose stones from her long, winding driveway.

Chaya stumbles over a heap of dandelion roots on her front porch and swears. She has forgotten to specify that it must dispose of the roots on her compost heap, not just wherever they happen to land once plucked. Another tweak for her chore list. There is less and less time for quality assurance these days, and Chaya tries to pour as much of that time as possible into her code for Millbank Biometrics.

"Sorry I'm late." She slides her headset on before she even sits down, logging in to the morning standup.

"No worries. Headquarters lost power just now, so I'll be taking over until management can find a hotspot." The sprint leader smiles as he speaks. Chaya will never understand how her coworkers can be so cheery, not with the bug tickets stacking up and the release date approaching. Millbank has contracts with social media platforms, telehealth doctors, and even law enforcement agencies, so management has been very clear that there's no postponing this release. Still, Chaya doesn't want to seem unmotivated. She smiles, too, and taps her mic back on.

"That's the third time this month. Is everything all right over there?"

"It's just the privacy protests again. Legal still thinks we're only collateral, since the office complex also houses a few major surveillance vendors. There's nothing to worry about—especially for you, Chaya."

The privacy protests rose up to oppose the expansion of surveillance and shrank after the laws passed, but are ramping up again now that the implementation date approaches. Even Chaya has to admit the new guidelines are uncomfortably broad. Thanks to lobbying from the deep-pocketed tech companies on Millbank's confidential client list, neither consent nor search motive will be necessary for facial recognition, anywhere in California. The protesters may not know the names behind the change, but that doesn't stop them from cutting power lines anyway.

It's more of a nuisance than anything, at this point. Chaya is tucked safely away in the countryside, and she doesn't blame the protesters for trying to protect themselves. Millbank's software is relentless. She wouldn't want to find herself on the wrong side of it.

"We're heading into crunch time," the sprint lead adds. "If we just keep our heads down and push a little harder, we can get a stable build ready by the Phase Two launch date."

There are a few cheers. Phase Two has been a long time coming. It's an upgrade to Millbank's facial recognition, a comprehensive system that can detect and identify faces even at significant distance. Phase One, which is over a decade old now, is glitchy and unrefined enough that a particularly shadowy rock could probably trick its neural net. Millbank has advertised Phase Two as "unstoppable."

Their new system is scheduled to launch on the same day as the new surveillance legislation is implemented. If the power keeps going out, Chaya will have to work overtime to make that happen.

At least she'll have her golems to help her. She wonders if her mother envisioned this use case back when she taught Chaya the word of creation, but decides that this is an unproductive line of thought. There's no time for tears today.

"Let's go around and check in with everyone. Chaya, would you mind going first? Camera on, please."

"Sure, one moment." Chaya spots a golem on the video preview screen, climbing up to patch her roof, and tilts her monitor to hide its sunbaked arm. "I'm on bug reports today, and if I have time after that, I have some margins to fix."

Someone else speaks up next, their face lit green with microphone activity, and Chaya switches off her camera again.

"There's a protest here in Los Angeles now," her coworker says. "I'll try to keep reviewing everyone's code, but there's a chance they might take out our power, too. I'll keep you posted."

When the meeting ends, Chaya switches back to her task list and settles in. She works on the front end, coding the screens that clients will see as they install Phase Two. No proprietary algorithms or dramatic decisions for her. Just realign this and double-space that. She may not get much recognition, but if anything ever goes wrong at Millbank, it won't be her fault.

Between meetings, Chaya keeps her head down as instructed. She is distantly aware of something happening in another branch of the company, something hushed and urgent and protest-related, but she is never pinged to discuss it. This is not the first time such a thing has happened, and Chaya has learned to know her place. Head down. Push harder. There are bugs to fix, even if the truth of what she is doing gnaws at her like water eroding clay. She's safe out here in the countryside. If she wants to stay safe, she has to do as she is told.

Chaya was four, old enough to mold Play-Doh but not too old to try eating it, when her mother taught her how to craft a golem. She pulled and prodded the neon dough into shape while her mother guided her hands. Slowly, the lump took the form of a squat figure, with stubby legs barely large enough to support its weight.

"This is a golem," her mother said. "Golems come to life and protect those in need, just like in the olden days I tell you stories about. Do you remember the stories?"

"It looks like Lolo," Chaya said, giggling. Lolo, a pink dancing elephant, was Chaya's favorite virtual character. She formed an elephant trunk on the golem's face and smiled.

"Be serious, Chaya," her mother scolded, pressing the trunk back into formless pink dough. "You must respect this gift. We are the only ones who can raise golems."

With a slim wooden stick, her mother carved the word *emet* into the golem's forehead. When she finished the last letter, the little pink creature shivered to life. Chaya stared at the dark cracks that suggested its features.

"Give it something to do. It will listen to you." Chaya's mother set aside her carving tool and began crafting another golem out of hunks of bright green dough.

"Dance," Chaya ventured, thinking of Lolo.

The figurine burst into jerky motion, twisting and shaking. Chaya clapped, thrilled, but the golem kept dancing and dancing until pieces of itself splattered across the kitchen table. The scraps of Play-Doh jittered around until Chaya's mother took her thumb to a piece of crumbling forehead and wiped off the alef.

"Why did it fall apart?" Chaya, distraught, tried to meld the pieces back together, but it was too late.

"You never told it when to stop. A golem will do exactly what you tell it to do. Nothing more, nothing less." Her mother brought the green golem to the center of the table and retrieved her carving tool. "Don't worry. You can always try again."

ii. alignment

It's night by the time Chaya signs off, and her back aches from sitting hunched over all day. Lines of code scroll past her inner eye every time she blinks. She frees herself from her desk and walks outside, pushing through the chill and the tickling caress of the tall grasses. The night is as thick and as comforting as river mud.

Fresh clay from a riverbank is the best for building golems. It has the ideal consistency, damp enough to sculpt but thick enough to hold its form and not crumble to pieces when it dries. Chaya has tried all sorts of materials and mostly anything will do, but hers is a life of iteration and efficiency. Less input, more output.

Chaya finds her golems huddled at the very edge of the water, waiting for deactivation as instructed. She deactivates them all at once, watching as they slump back into inanimate masses, then begins to dispose of them. There isn't enough satin left to wrap them all in. Her mother always used satin and it feels disrespectful to use anything else, but it's too late to drive into town. She wraps the last golem in a blanket of thick reeds and slips it into the dark waters.

The next morning, Chaya sculpts two golems. At lunch, three. They aren't supposed to be used for frivolous things, she knows that, but the motion of the work and the texture of the clay soothe her anxiety even when she runs out of chores for them to do. Hebrew glyphs are becoming as familiar a sight in her farmhouse as the scripting brackets on her dual monitors.

Near the end of the day, an unexpected meeting invitation arrives in her inbox. It's not that she hasn't been flooded with last-minute schedule changes already, but this email was sent by the legal department and the meeting begins in ten minutes.

A chill like the river runs down Chaya's spine, even though she can't think of anything she might have done wrong.

Attached to the invitation is a document filled with unfamiliar faces. They are numbered from one to thirty-six, and the email also contains their associated faceprints. Chaya can identify a few of them from the news as protest organizers, but most of them she can't place at all. Unable to focus on her half-written code,

Chaya stares at the faces until the meeting begins, burning every last detail into her mind's eye.

When she logs in to the meeting room, she is greeted by several rows of faces that she does recognize. Chaya wasn't the only one to receive the invitation: There are other front-end engineers, back-end engineers, and even customer-service agents on the call. She is relieved to see more coworkers trickle in until what feels like the entire company is present.

"Thank you all for joining me on such short notice," the rumpled-looking legal representative says. Faint chanting is audible in the background, seeping through the protective walls of the Silicon Valley office. "Law enforcement has asked us to check every face that our servers process for a match to the attached faceprints. Hopefully we can refine this in the future—engineers, I'll be speaking to your managers—but for now we'll need to manually review any flagged match with a confidence of at least ninety percent."

Confusion spreads across the faces on Chaya's monitor. If her camera was on, she is sure that she would see the same expression reflected in her own frown. Tracking protesters isn't exactly what she signed up for when she applied to Millbank. Sure, it's what their software was ultimately going to be used for, but *she* wasn't supposed to have to do it.

"Are there any questions?"

Chaya expects someone to ask what crimes these people committed, or what is going to happen to them when the information is turned over to the police, even though she already knows the dark answer to that. She expects questions about ethics and precedent and nondisclosure. At the very least, she expects someone to ask how they are supposed to check every partial match from every instance of every client's software without neglecting all their other work.

No one asks any questions, though, not even her manager, so Chaya stays in line and keeps quiet. She sets the thirty-six faces to display on one of her monitors and returns to her code. What else can she do? She's only one person, after all.

Chaya was thirteen, but only just, when she cried hard enough to frighten her bat mitzvah guests. Tree shadows flickered against the walls of the courtyard, picked out in wheeling, staccato bursts of red and blue. Through the glass windows of the banquet hall, she could see one of her friends crying in the back of a police car. He was in the grade below her at school, one of the only Black boys in their suburban district, and always traded snacks with her at lunch. Seeing him behind a barred cruiser window didn't feel real.

"Dad?" Chaya turned to her father. "Can't we help?"

"An officer told me their system identified him from a photo booth picture that someone here shared. I didn't argue. It's best not to get involved." Her father knelt by her chair and laid a hand on her knee. The pink tulle of her dress was stained with teardrops.

"But can't we tell them they're wrong? He's not even a teenager yet. There must have been some sort of mistake." Chaya wanted to go to her friend, but surely her father knew the right thing to do. He was an adult, after all.

"Technology doesn't make mistakes, Chaya. Their system saw what it saw. I'm sure they'll let him go once he answers their questions. Why don't you go ask the DJ to play some happier music in the meantime?"

"Mom?" Chaya looked over, desperate for a different answer. Her mother didn't respond. She hadn't been herself lately. She walked heavy and slow, dragging her feet, and her mood turned sour in a heartbeat. Chaya had hoped her mother would call for justice and action like the heroes in her stories of their ancestors in Prague. She could even build a golem, which she hadn't done in weeks, but she only stared at the ground. It was as if she had retreated into a shell of her own making.

"I'm just trying to keep you safe," her father said. "You'll understand someday."

Eventually, the police released her friend. He darted for his phone and made a tearful call. Chaya stood up, ready to comfort him, but her father caught her eye and motioned for her to return to her chair. Obedient, trusting, Chaya sat.

"I'm okay, Mom," she overheard her friend say in a shaky voice. "Some engineer called them and said it was a false positive, a glitch or something. They're gone now."

Just before dessert was served, a minivan pulled up where the police car once parked. Its headlights were dull and yellow. Chaya's friend walked outside without saying goodbye to her. His parents held him tight, their family safe and whole out by the car, and the lights from the DJ's booth shone on their tired faces. Then they left.

"You did the right thing," Chaya's father told her as they drove home that night. Her mother slept soundly in the passenger seat. Chaya kicked off her shoes and picked at the tearstains above her knee. "I'm sorry your friend had to deal with that, but sometimes there's just nothing we can do."

After that night at the bat mitzvah, Chaya and her friend drifted apart. He didn't bother telling her why. He didn't need to. Eventually, Chaya pushed aside her regret and let herself believe her father's words.

iii. extraction

With only two weeks left until the release of both Millbank's system update and California's new legislation, Chaya wants nothing more than to stay at her keyboard. Unfortunately, her refrigerator is empty, and her tiny plot of farmland is nowhere near subsistence, even with the help of her golems. Some things can't be fully automated. Chaya signs off at dusk and heads into town, shopping list in hand.

The road is long and dark, but quiet, and mostly empty. Every once in a while, sleek cars with low profiles streak past Chaya's pickup truck. When she leaves the countryside, clusters of buildings begin to appear, and the long shadows cast by orange-hued streetlights rove across her face with every turn.

Under cover of night, workers are beginning to hang new cameras. Their digital eyes will open soon to watch over the state, just like their active counterparts in the most crowded urban centers. Chaya's code will guide the agencies that guide their lenses. For now, they sleep.

"Welcome in," a tired clerk says as Chaya enters her favorite grocery store. It may be far, but it has a kosher section, and that alone is worth the trip.

They don't have any satin. Chaya takes a few extra produce bags and murmurs a preemptive apology to her golems, then loads up her cart with fresh fruit and vegetables before moving on.

A crash in the hot-food aisle draws her attention. She hurries over to find a customer struggling with a basket brimming over with food and jars of canned goods, some of which have tumbled to the linoleum below. The customer has a Star of David necklace, smooth brown skin, and a kind, round face that seems somehow familiar. They look more frightened than Chaya would expect from a simple grocery store spill.

"Don't worry," she says, kneeling to gather the dented cans. "None of them broke open."

"Thanks," the customer says, but they don't relax. Chaya hands over the cans. Their basket is full of staples, all rice and kosher noodles and canned beans, mixed in with a strange combination of face paint and permanent markers. "I appreciate you coming over to help. Fuckin' techies down the aisle didn't even pause, but then, you know how they are."

"I'm an engineer," Chaya points out, bristling.

"Oh. Sorry." The customer shrugs. "Most of the folks I meet around here are just out for themselves. It's nice to see that isn't true of everyone."

Maybe it's because she's feeling defensive, or maybe it's just time passing, but either way, something clicks in Chaya's mind. The customer's face falls into place in her memories like a vector map aligning. They are one of the thirty-six on Millbank's watchlist.

"I do my best," Chaya manages to reply. She glances around for security cameras. What if someone sees them together? No one at Millbank will believe that this customer is a total stranger to her. She feels exposed, vulnerable.

"Hey, do you live around here? There's going to be a surveillance protest in Silicon Valley in a couple weeks. It would be nice to have some tech allies show up. If you're interested, I can send you the details."

Chaya thinks of Play-Doh and protection, girls and golems. She thinks of sirens outside a bat mitzvah.

"I'm just passing through," she says, and flees.

On the drive home, Chaya can't take her mind off that stranger and their basketful of groceries. She didn't see their face through the system, so she has no obligation to report them. They didn't appear to know that they're being hunted, but Chaya signed a nondisclosure agreement, so she does have an obligation not to tell them. Doing nothing seems like the best path, but her hands are trembling on the steering wheel.

The stranger's face haunts Chaya all through the week and into the weekend. She wishes she could ask her mother for advice, but she can't, and that only makes everything worse. All she can do is toss and turn in bed, staring at the evergreen shadows on her wall. One day she prints out the full Millbank watchlist; the next day she shoves it in her compost heap. In the evening she prints a dozen more copies that she folds and unfolds like a ritual. Everything seemed so much simpler when she was young.

By the time the week of the Phase Two release arrives, Chaya is too overwhelmed to worry about the watchlist or the protests anymore. Messages are flying everywhere, priorities are changing, and the video calls are never-ending. When she finally sits down for a late lunch, her brain is so stuck in code-mode that it's easier to set up a golem than to microwave some leftovers. There are fresh chicken eggs on the counter. She writes a quick script instructing the golem to scramble them, then activates it.

Instead of cracking an egg, though, the golem sits on the floor, alive but still. It looks almost contemplative. Chaya frowns and checks her code. Her mind isn't in the right place today. She probably forgot to specify what to do with the eggshells or left out the location of the carton.

The code reads: (emet)

Nothing could go wrong there. The activation word was tried and true, more tested than any part of Millbank's software. Chaya scrolls down to the chore list, expecting to see her messy egg-scrambling subroutine pasted in from the other window.

The code reads again: (emet)

Her heart skips a beat. She whirls around, but the golem has already left.

Chaya finds it right where she expected it to be, doing exactly what she told it to do. The golem is down by the riverside, digging its nubby hands into the damp mud of the shore. Beside it, a lump of clay is slowly taking shape. *Emet*, the golem was instructed. Truth, yes, but also the word of creation. By absent-mindedly passing the activation word as a task for her golem to complete, Chaya has created a physical quine: a self-replicating program, writ large.

She sits back on her heels and watches the riverside rise. Golems of all shapes and sizes emerge from the shore, all with the same intricate forehead inscription. They each sit a moment, contemplative. They each build one more golem. Then they slump back into a waiting posture.

Chaya's mother once told her the story of the original golem of Prague. That golem was created to protect the Jews of the city, but when the threat was vanquished and the golem was set to chores, it broke free of its master and rampaged through the city. Chaya's panicked thoughts jump to scenes of destruction, her desk in pieces, her flock of hens scattered.

There are ten golems on the shore, with an eleventh half-built. They are peaceful and still, for now, but they've dug huge gouges in the riverside. Chaya grabs her phone and tries running her deactivation program.

The chain reaction stops. *Emet* turns to *met*. A dozen golems sit lifeless on the riverbank, looking for all the world like an army of terracotta soldiers.

She doesn't want them. Power, truth, creation—all of it just complicates her simple life. The golems should be used for something greater, by someone greater, not commanded to scramble eggs by a tired engineer who has missed Yom Kippur two years in a row. She feels the indent-eyes of her creations fixed on her, judging. Finding her wanting.

"Don't look at me like that," Chaya shouts. She knows what happens to whistleblowers, and it's not a cushy job offer with the option to keep working from home. Nothing to gain, everything to lose. So why can't she get the protests and protesters out of her head? Why does she feel unmoored in her own life, which was once so comfortable?

Chaya crushes the replicated golems beneath her fists, destroying the words on their foreheads entirely. She can make her own lunch.

When she returns to the river that night to clean up the golem shards, Chaya wraps their clay pieces in watchlist printouts and lets the truth sink to the bottom of the river.

Chaya was eighteen, the number of life, when her mother fell ill. Her family had only just switched insurance carriers when a delayed physical turned up the cause of her mother's constant fatigue. Tumors. Cancerous, metastasized, and the scariest adjective of all: preexisting.

"It's policy," their agent explained, avoiding eye contact with Chaya and her father as he passed them the denial of coverage letter. He turned back to his computer, flicking through documentation. "I'm sorry. I can't help you."

They took her to the hospital anyway, sinking college savings and retirement funds alike into Chaya's mother's medical care. It was nowhere near enough. They ran through even the most desperate lines of credit available long before a surgery slot opened up, and by then she was no longer a good candidate anyway. Against the wishes of both father and daughter, Chaya's mother was moved home for hospice.

Her room, once quiet, became a hub of activity. Golems toddled in and out, carrying stacks of clean dishes and scraps of damp cloth. The room smelled of bedsores and candles. While Chaya's father retreated, unable to watch his wife succumb to disease, Chaya stayed by her side as much as possible.

"Dad says he's not going to call the hospital anymore," Chaya complained late one gray afternoon. Her mother was sitting up to sip her tea, a rare sight and a welcome one, but her hands quivered around the mug. Dark circles stained the skin under her eyes, and her wrists were so thin the bones showed. When she spoke, her voice was little more than a whisper.

"That's probably for the best, at this stage."

"It's not fair," Chaya said, incensed. She balled her hands into fists at her sides to keep herself from crying again. "We should send out the golems. They're supposed to protect us, right? That way we can make the hospital treat you."

Her mother set the mug of tea aside and pressed her thumb to Chaya's forehead, tracing a pattern on her skin. Chaya didn't need a mirror to know what she was spelling. The three Hebrew letters of *emet* were as familiar as a kiss.

"There," said her mother. "Now you have to do what I say."

"Mom, I'm not a golem," Chaya protested, but she sat still and waited for instructions all the same.

"Don't go after the hospital staff. This is something too big to fight with a few clay dolls, and I'm afraid it's too late anyway. Just be brave, and don't lose sight of the truth." Chaya's mother stroked her forehead so gently that it took Chaya a moment to realize what she was doing. Her thumb brushed over the place where the alef would have been. *Met*.

When her mother died, Chaya buried her by a river under a veil of satin. The funeral was attended only by Chaya, her father, and a few sturdy golems, commanded to carry bags and offer tissues. Their clay was damp and salt-stained from Chaya's tears as she sculpted.

They lowered the casket in with tender precision, then each added a shovelful of dirt. Even the river was quiet, as if in respect. When Chaya's father sobbed and clutched his chest, Chaya knew just what to say to absolve him of his guilt.

"Sometimes there's just nothing you can do."

iv. comparison

On the day before the Phase Two release, Chaya's breakfast tastes like ash. She chokes it down anyway, staring hard at her monitors, keeping herself busy. Busy is good. If Chaya stays busy, then she can't think about the watchlist flags or that night at the grocery store.

Next on her task list is a series of last-minute requests from Millbank's existing clients. Some of them look strange. Most of them look unnecessary. It's a little too late to be changing things, so Chaya pings her manager, asking if they can reprioritize the requests. Won't the clients be satisfied enough with a revamped system? Shouldn't they focus on actual errors?

Not my call, her manager replies. *Sales says these are our biggest accounts, and they already promised the changes.*

There are no client names attached, but it's easy enough to tell who wants what. It must be a social media company that wants their match-results page to look prettier, and a police department that wants the accuracy rate estimation to be moved to a different screen. The request that really stings is from a hospital that uses Millbank for their check-in system. They want insurance documents to be the first item displayed upon identification, not medical history.

Chaya isn't naïve. She has seen the protests, heard the news, lost her mother. She knows what horrible chain reactions these changes will contribute to. But they're so small, if you don't know what you're looking at, and Chaya has already spent months improving Phase Two for these companies. Everyone has. Given the size of Millbank's team, no one will even know it was her. She's not even a cog in a machine, she's just a drop of oil that helps the cog turn.

As she types, implementing changes and submitting them for review, Chaya glances out the window to her wrecked river. A gentle breeze kicks up ripples that smooth out the gouges in the shore. Her golems did exactly as they were instructed, and still they were destroyed. No, too passive: Chaya destroyed them. She did it, all on her own. How long had it been since she had done anything without being told to do it?

The longer Chaya works, the more doubt creeps in between chair and keyboard. Her rapid-fire typing slows.

She's not so different from her programmed clay. Input to output with no evaluation in between, listening to anyone who commands. Chaya thinks of the stranger in the grocery store, with their basket full of small things. Was the face paint they bought meant to protect them from recognition? From the new system Chaya worked so hard to build? It won't be enough.

On her personal computer, Chaya opens a private window and searches up the protests for the first time. They have their own website. Alongside a summary of California's upcoming legislation change, the drastic extension of surveillance, a video from a past protest plays. Every face in the video is covered with a solid black box.

"Give what you are able, help where you can," says a distorted voice. The protester is holding a megaphone, and Chaya can see the glint of a silver chain just beneath the black box of their face. "We may not be able to defeat this bill, but still we cannot abandon the fight."

It's a line from Pirkei Avot, sort of. Chaya's stomach twists. That could be her out there, if things had gone differently, but instead she is sure the speaker is the Jewish stranger from the grocery store. The stranger from the watchlist.

Her inbox chimes at her. She has a new private message from her manager at headquarters, where the wi-fi is out for the fourth time.

Chaya, do you have enough time for some capacity testing before the release?

It's either that or finishing these client requests, Chaya points out.

This is more important, her manager writes back. *I'll pass on the details from management. Thank you for being so reliable.*

That would have been a compliment, once. It's more of a back-end question, but she's asked Chaya. She trusts her, maybe even values her input.

Chaya values her golems, and yet they are disposable.

She pulls up the most recent server statistics for Phase Two and stares hard at the numbers. Millbank has already tested for typical levels of demand, and even some surges, but now management is requesting performance beyond even the previous peak. It can't be a coincidence that they're asking now, right before the surveillance bill goes into effect. They want to scan the protests, and tomorrow is going to be the biggest day yet.

There's no time left for stalling. Chaya wants to think it's not her fault that she sits safely at home, that she has no power and no alternative to complicity, but the truth is, she isn't a golem. Even doing nothing is a choice that she makes.

The army she raised from the riverbed comes to mind, but there is no one physical enemy for them to fight, no way for clay to overpower willful ignorance. Instead, Chaya recalls her mother's tales of massive golems and Nazi forces. The golems offered protection. They took the blows while her people fled, living to rise again another day. They were not the heroes, they were shields that the heroes could wield. The last words her mother ever spoke to her ring in her ears.

Chaya has been so focused on protecting herself that she has lost sight of the truth of whether or not she is the one that needs protecting. The government isn't coming for her right now, but there are other people in danger.

With one final look at the riverside, Chaya sets her fingers back on her keyboard and re-downloads the watchlist faceprints. She reaches for her clay and begins to mold a prototype. It's human-sized, one of many to come. Chaya will work until her riverbed is scraped empty—after all, she has a lot of lost time to make up for.

She'll test Millbank's server capacity, all right. She'll do exactly what they asked, in a way they never anticipated. Tomorrow she will find out if it's too late for change. Today she prepares.

The clay takes shape under her steady hands.

Chaya was twenty-five, still so young, when she interviewed for a position at Millbank Biometrics. Her hands shook as she passed her resume over the desk. Millbank was her last chance to take the first steps toward a bright future.

"It says here that you last worked at a synagogue," the interviewer said. She wore red lipstick that looked like blood against her white skin, along with a lapel pin that said *#girlboss*. "Can you tell me more about what you did for them?"

"Web development, mostly. Their public site and internal pages are all my work." That role had been local, a compromise for her father, who still desperately wanted her to keep living at home. He wouldn't be happy about this interview, either. Chaya tried not to think about that.

No matter what her father wanted, Chaya needed to get out of the house where her mother died. Her memory was a blessing, but there was more to life than memories. Her father wouldn't let her change anything, let alone build golems, even though they were Chaya's strongest connection to her mother. He claimed it was for safety, but he was always afraid. Chaya's mother had wanted her to be brave.

"I see. Excellent." While the interviewer typed something on her laptop, Chaya smoothed the grief out of her expression. "Here at Millbank, we're all about teamwork. Tell me about a time when you set yourself aside for the good of the company."

Teamwork was a softball question, something off every prep sheet. The interviewer liked her. Chaya rattled off a prepared answer about crunch time and setting aside work-life balance. She was willing to do anything to get the job done. All she had to do was make that clear, and the job was as good as hers.

They ran through a few more easy questions before the interviewer checked her watch and closed her laptop. She smiled, and Chaya's heart soared.

"Well, everything looks good to me, but I'll have to consult my team before we make any final decisions. Oh, and smile for the camera on the way out. We'll need to scan your face and run it through our system for background checks, but I'm sure you have nothing to worry about."

Chaya looked into the dark mirror of the camera lens and grinned. No more fear, no more hardship. At Millbank Biometrics, she was going to make her mother proud.

"We'll be in touch," said the interviewer.

v. recognition

Computer programs are just like golems. No matter what, they always follow their instructions. Millbank intends to tell their system to detect and identify every instance of the thirty-six watchlist faces, so that's what the system will do. The engineers have done their job well, and Phase Two can handle the estimated protest turnout with ease.

Chaya can't change the program anymore, but with enough time and clay, she can change what it sees.

She works all night and into the morning, perfecting her code. It's not the sort of thing she can check for bugs easily, but she does her best, testing and testing until her floor is more mud than wood. One of her monitors shows scrolling code while the other displays a sandbox version of Phase Two, set to a disconnected version of the facial-recognition system.

Next to Chaya stands a golem of gray mud and beige clay, built taller and broader than herself. With rough movements, aided by a sharp stick and a dull rock, it is carving its own head. The resulting features are little more than the suggestion of a face, but that's enough for Chaya.

She has fed the faceprints from the watchlist into the golems' code. Instead of a generic suggestion of eyes and nose, her creation bears an approximation of one of the thirty-six suspects' faces. Chaya checks each carved golem's face against her test environment at every angle and lighting setup she can manage. Photographed from a distance with a hat and a mask, the golem could easily be mistaken for human. It just needs to be mistaken for the right human. When the readout displays a match, she instructs the golem to smooth its face clean of everything but the Hebrew on its forehead and start again.

By time the gray-white light of dawn breaks through her curtains, Chaya is satisfied with her creations. She masks her face with dark cloth, loads her trusty pickup truck with as many golems and buckets of pure mud as she can fit in the bed, and heads for the freeway. The streets are jammed with vehicles. Half the streetlights are already out. Chaya leaves her truck at a gas station when she arrives, as close to the wave-dampened shores of the San Francisco Bay as possible. Once the protest starts, she's going to need all the mud and clay she can get.

As Chaya waits under the soft layers of low-lying fog, she idly sculpts with her clay. Not a golem, for once. A small elephant from the depths of her memory. It reminds her of her mother, even if she doesn't quite remember why, and that gives her a quiet sort of strength.

She can't make out the words from the megaphone-wielding marchers yet, but she can see them spaced out among the front lines and hear the rhythmic way in which the other protesters echo their chanting. It sounds like a song, or a prayer. They break through the fog like so many rays of sunlight, then disappear again as they continue on down the street.

Chaya pulls her phone out of her pocket and is unsurprised to see that her notifications have maxed out. Most of the messages aren't even directed at her. It's release time for Phase Two and everyone is scrambling to launch. She doesn't bother to read further, just loads up her home-brewed golem application and initiates the last element of her plan.

The code begins: (emet, emet)

Each golem will create two more golems before moving on down the chore list to sculpt a face assigned by its birth time. The series is a geometric progression of creation, and the golem decoys will quickly grow to rival the human crowd. Once they've served their purpose, Chaya only has to initiate the deactivation subroutine, erasing every alef with a single tap and collapsing her golems back into inert clay.

Chaya watches with pride as her pre-prepared golems dig into the soft, yielding mud from the heavy buckets in her truck bed. They build quickly, then mold their own faces as the newborn golems turn to the sediment of the bay. Some sacrifice themselves in the waves to retrieve raw material, but two more golems rise in the place of each lost to the water, stronger and streaked with grass and stones from the shallowest shores.

As the first disguised golems head out into the city, looking directly into the watchful eyes of every security camera and drone lens they pass, Chaya checks her messages again. Soon the disturbance will start overwhelming the manual reviewers, then the servers themselves. As she scrolls, she heads toward the city center. The marchers are all wearing masks or thick paint, and they carry signs with all manner of witty quips and emotional pleas. The long shadows of the nearest buildings stretch down the sloped street behind them, making each protester look for a moment as tall as a skyscraper.

Lots of weird data coming from the bay, one of her coworkers reports.

Chaya was supposed to test capacity, can anyone reach her? asks another.

I think she's out sick, a third engineer replies. *This data does look off. Let's set anything coming from a mile radius of that area to disregard for now. I'll push the code.*

Chaya's heart sinks. Her golems are doing their best, and they are fooling sensors where they can, but they are still clay. They can't travel fast or far. They aren't enough.

She lugs a bucket of mud and a golem to the city center anyway, hoping that bad data in the middle of the crowd will at least make Millbank block out more of the protest. On the sidewalk of a street barricaded with sandbags and reflective tape, she hears something familiar.

"Go ahead, take whatever you need," the stranger from the grocery store says to a line of protesters. They are standing by a table stocked with food and a sign that reads *mutual aid*. The stranger is wearing a mask and a layer of face paint, but there are packages of kosher noodles on their table, and their voice is unmistakable.

Chaya approaches them, golem in tow.

"I made it," she says.

"I'm sorry, have we met?" The stranger pauses in their work and leans forward, peering at Chaya and her golem. Chaya takes a deep breath before unraveling the cloth around her head, exposing her bare face to the protest organizer. She lifts the hat of the golem as well so that they can see the word *emet* etched on its forehead. Its face matches theirs.

"You invited me. I'm here to help."

"Hold on a moment." The stranger steps away from their table and pulls Chaya to one side, shielding their face with their body. "You know it's not safe to show your face, right?"

"Trust me, I know. That's why I disguised these golems, to divert attention. Only, they can't get far enough." Chaya's shoulders slump. "I just wanted to tell you that I tried."

"Golems in disguise, huh." The stranger's eyes dart between Chaya's golem, the bucket of mud, and the other decoys filling out the crowd behind her. They don't panic at the realization that Chaya's companions are animate clay. Perhaps their mother once told them the same stories that Chaya heard from hers as a child. After a moment's thought, they place a hand to the golem's cheek, then rub the residual clay between their fingers. "I think I know how we can make this work."

It's simple enough, in the end. Each recipient of donated items gets a miniature golem and a request to pass it along or leave it by the side of the road somewhere. Even if they don't fully understand, the protesters are agreeable enough to take a clay doll with their food and face paint. They may not trust Chaya, but they trust the protest organizer, and that is enough.

As they march, bike, and drive away, Chaya updates her code, setting various time delays for the golems. Already the data is starting to shift. A human chain far greater than anything Chaya could have done alone will stretch across northern California and beyond. The miniatures they scatter will build full-size siblings, prompting sightings of the thirty-six in so many places simultaneously that the servers will crash and the search will have to be postponed. By then, the protest organizers can hide. By then, Chaya can put in her two weeks' notice. By then, the golems will have faded back to dry dust.

For now, as her coworkers start to panic and the protest surges forth, Chaya is just another face in the crowd. It's a different kind of anonymity than at Millbank, where she was known but ignored. Here in the streets, here where no one is alone, Chaya's actions are her voice. It has already taken her far too long to speak up. No matter what the future holds for her and her creations, it will be a future she has chosen, and she chooses truth.

....

Lauren Ring (she/her) is a perpetually tired Jewish lesbian who writes about possible futures, for better or for worse. She is a World Fantasy Award winner and Nebula finalist, and her short fiction can be found in venues such as *F&SF*, *Nature*, and *Lightspeed*. When she isn't writing speculative fiction, she is most likely working on a digital painting or attending to the many needs of her cat, Moomin. You can keep up with her at laurenmring.com.

THAT STORY ISN'T THE STORY

John Wiswell

Everything Anton owns goes in one black trash bag. His ratty yellow sketchpad, which he bought to draw the other familiars when he moved here, and only ever used three pages of. The few shirts and khakis that he paid for with his own money, before Mr. Bird took control of his finances. A broken pocket watch he'd found dangling from the side of the Queensboro Bridge, on the first day he really considered ending himself, and had instead rescued the watch with the intent of one day learning how to fix it.

Anton never did fix that watch. But it is leaving with him.

He heads for the stairs that will lead him out of the townhouse. It'll be the first time he's gone outside in so long it feels like he's never been outside. Time outside the gothic damask flock wallpaper and blacked out windows still doesn't seem real.

"Where are you going?"

The voice comes from the rear room, the one next to Mr. Bird's, where the twins sleep. Liquor and jasmine incense waft forth as one of the teenagers emerges. Both Pavla and Yoana look and sound so similar, with their gossamer hair and legs as thin as their arms.

This one is Pavla, recognizable because she always wears red arm warmers, because her elbows are where Mr. Bird bites her.

He bites Anton in more intimate places.

"Aren't you supposed to be getting his Manets out of storage?" As Pavla asks, she touches the inside of her arm through the arm warmer, as though to protect it from a thought. "He's going to flip his shit if you don't have them hanging when he gets back."

Anton lies, "I'm on my way."

She rubs her eyes and looks at his garbage bag. "What have you got there?"

"Nothing important."

The sleepiness drops off her tone and for a moment her voice is thin and hard, like Mr. Bird's. "What are you doing?"

A car horn blares from the street outside the townhouse. He needs to hurry up. Grigorii is outside and probably as scared as Anton is. He has to be out of here before Mr. Bird returns.

So Anton hugs his garbage bag and goes for the stairs. The thick oak front door of the townhouse is ajar, letting orange sunlight spill over the coat rack and end tables of their parlor. It leaks up the stairs, and Anton pauses on the last step above it.

Instinctively he checks the windows, with their blackout curtains nailed in place. The rest of the townhouse is dim. Mr. Bird has banished the sun from this place, cloaking it in a peaceful, suffocating dark where Anton and Pavla don't have to think.

The sun is intruding because of Anton's doing.

Pavla says, "Don't do it. You'll burn."

Anton tells himself, "It's not true."

It's not true, not that a fact helps a feeling. Anton urges himself. Mr. Bird goes outside. Walter, the senior familiar, often goes with him. They survive.

A bulky white man steps into the light, and Anton's chest seizes.

Anton says, "Mr. Bird? No, you're early."

It isn't him. It's Grigorii, tall and chunky in odd directions. He moves like he doesn't care; Grigorii has an ugly charisma. His face is splattered with risen moles, acne scars, and asymmetrical dimples. He is comfortable with his face and his faded One Piece hoodie and running shoes that he wears to every occasion.

"I'm double parked, dude. Let's hit the road."

Anton says, "I'm sorry. You should go home. It was a mistake to call you."

Pavla sneaks closer to the stairs, still shy of where the sunlight falls. She demands, "Who the hell is he?"

Grigorii eyes her. From his tone, he has no idea who he's talking to. "I'm a friend of Anton's since high school, and I'm a reason you should step away from him."

Anton says, "Seriously. You need to get out of here. Before he...before the owner gets home."

"To quote the Bible, 'No fucking way,'" Grigorii says, and lumbers inside. He makes the terrible mistake of entering this place. Mr. Bird has probably seen everything. He's probably furious.

"Seriously, man," Grigorii says, "I am not going anywhere without you. If I get a ticket, that's on you."

"He'll be home any minute."

"And if he comes for you, he comes for me. Let's go."

"You don't understand."

Grigorii stretches out one of those lumpy arms with palm extended, to touch Anton. It's an offer of touch. Such an unusual thing, for touch to be an offer in this house. Anton forgot it could be an offer.

Anton grabs his hand and they run, leaving Pavla swearing upstairs. She doesn't follow them into the light.

Their escape is a dented currant Kia Rio with a broken front bumper and a trash bag covering one broken side window. Anton goes for that door and tosses his own trash bag of belongings inside.

Grigorii asks, "You still like the Electric Six?"

They are not the first words he thought he'd hear upon escaping. The question is so alien it feels like being struck in the face by a hammer, or like an invasive bite. Briefly, Anton wonders if he's bleeding already. That will happen.

A black town car trails up the street toward them. Sleek and black, with that short club of a man Walter at the wheel. Mr. Bird's senior familiar. Anton knows who sits in the tinted windows and the shadows of the rear seats.

From inside the Kia, Grigorii pops the passenger door open. "Come on, man."

Is blood spotting in Anton's jeans? He gropes at his thighs, unsure if the moisture is sweat on his palms or if he's bleeding. The car is getting closer. Mr. Bird definitely sees him.

Anton sinks into the car. He clutches his seatbelt until they are doing forty in a twenty mile zone. He's too worried to turn around, and too afraid not to fixate on the rearview mirror.

The black car stops in the middle of the street. A rear door opens, and a dark thing peers out. There is no seeing any detail of that figure—no detail except for his mouth. It is open and sharp. Distance doesn't change how clearly Anton sees the teeth.

They drive to one of the thousand little towns that keeps the city fed. Grigorii's place is tucked behind a salt barn, near a depot where the district parks its vehicles and keeps supplies for winter storms. Grigorii's place itself looks like the mutant child of a double-wide and a single-story kit house, made from faded white aluminum with a slanted roof like the building is tipping its hat to them. The colorful light of a TV flickers through the murky windows, which look like they haven't seen a sponge in their entire lives.

Grigorii says, "Welcome to my estate. You'll have the east wing to yourself."

Anton hugs his trash bag and follows Grigorii. The house is even smaller on the inside, more a living room/kitchen combo with a few doors that must lead to cramped spaces. It's a house of unpainted white walls with the occasional brown or greasy scuff. A Hispanic kid sits on a couch cushion on the floor, playing retro videogames on the TV. There are four couch cushions and no couch to be seen.

The kid twists around on his pillow to face them. He has lopsided ears, the right almost two thirds bigger than the left, and his black hair is raked to the left. He gestures at Anton with the game controller.

"Hey, is this the new guy?"

Grigorii says, "Yup. In the flesh."

The kid rolls backward, getting his shoulders to the floor, then springs up to his feet with his arms outstretched as through awaiting applause. The controller is still in his left hand. "Hey. I'm Luis."

Suddenly Anton feels too tall. Luis is the same height as him, and Anton still wishes to be smaller. He doesn't deserve to take up as much as space as that poise and swagger.

He says, "I'm Anton. Pleased to meet you."

"So formal," Luis says. "You got any stuff? I can help bring it in."

"I packed light."

"That's cool. I didn't have anything when my uncle kicked me out, either. So you lived with some fucked up people?"

Anton remembers feeling the sun on his skin and thinking he'd die on contact. He remembers it so intensely that he might still be standing in the stairs of Mr. Bird's townhouse.

Escaping was an illusion.

This is all a lie he's telling himself.

He says, "Sort of."

"What were they like? Did they make you do fucked up shit?"

Yes, this definitely isn't happening.

Anton is somewhere in the townhouse. He's in the archives, finding the right paintings for Mr. Bird. It was stupid of him to think he could get away. He feels the slickness on his thighs—the sign that Mr. Bird is here and mad at him.

Grigorii steps in. "That's not the story we're telling today."

Grigorii is so close that his hot breath falls on Anton's shoulder, cutting through his shirt. It grounds him in the moment. The crappy little house tucked behind a salt barn is tangible, and so is the meaning of the people inside it. His friend extends an arm like he wants to touch Anton to reassure him, and he does not take the touch. It is another offer of touch. That intent is more reassuring than touch could be.

Anton tries to focus on the intent, despite dreading that shadows and teeth are nearby and that his pants are full of blood.

Grigorii says, "Anton's an old friend. His family was there for me when I needed something. My house is going to be here for him, just like it is for you. We don't have much room, so we give each other space of ideas. Right?"

Luis nods ruefully and sets the game controller aside. He says, "My bad. Sorry. You sure there isn't anything I can carry for you?"

The bleeding feels real. Anton asks, "Actually, do you have a bathroom?"

Anton means to check himself in the bathroom mirror.

There is no bathroom mirror. There are three small white shelves holding supplements and amber pill bottles like the inside of a bathroom mirror. The mirror itself has been removed, leaving empty hinges behind.

Subconsciously he listens for Grigorii and Luis's footfalls to trail away from the bathroom door, like they might hear his guilt. It's a genuine fear that sticks to his ribs. Pavla and Walter would've mocked him for it.

He sits on the toilet and spreads his thighs to check himself. There are many holes in his skin, most like the shapes of melted Tic-Tacs. The holes form the circular shapes of three bite marks—two on his right thigh, and the newer one on the left.

They are not healing. The two oldest bites are maybe eleven months old and have never sported a scab. He'd hoped they might close up after he fled. They are not closing.

At least they are bloodless tonight. That is all the relief Anton gets.

Mr. Bird's bites only bleed when Mr. Bird is near and upset with his familiar.

This means Mr. Bird isn't nearby. Not nearby yet.

Anton runs a fingertip over the holes in his skin, worrying them. He dreads that they will start bleeding at any moment. He stares so intently that he doesn't know he's panicking until someone knocks on the bathroom door.

"You okay in there, man?"

He spends hours apologizing for the noise he makes next.

He is not up to chatter. The couple times Luis asks him about superhero movies leave him in tears. The raw thought required is too much. Should he pretend to have seen a movie they consider essential? Will liking Captain America more than Batman upset one of his hosts? When he actually does care about something, is he effusive enough to hold up his part of the talk?

Grigorii drops the yellow sketch pad in Anton's lap along with a few colored pencils. "Literally had these leftover for ten years. Can you believe it? They waited for you."

Gripping them feels familiar and nostalgic. Anton had these pencils in high school. A third of them are merely nubs of pencils. Grigorii kept his nubs.

They sit on the stray sofa cushions, all arranged around the TV. The guys play Terraria, a videogame that seems to be about digging a tunnel to Hell so that you can build a house. It's in the retro style of graphics that were old before Anton was born.

Luis offers him the controller. "You want to play?"

"No thank you."

Grigorii says, "Anton's a gamer. He used to be a beast at Smash Bros."

Luis says, "This game is more chill than Smash."

It's a multiplayer game, but they don't own any other devices to play it on. Rather they take turns with their one controller. Grigorii likes to build ladders up to the clouds to face harpies for treasure underground. Luis is more into mining for metals and building traps. Digging one single block in front of a door means no monster can get in. Instead they fall in and are stuck in the shallow hole.

The door of their actual house has no pit in front of it. Anton watches through the window, looking in the creeping shadows of dusk. Any of them could be Mr. Bird.

Grigorii says, "How am I supposed to fight the Eye of Cthulhu with all the NPCs living on the top floor?"

It's another of those sentences that feels like it belongs in another plane of existence from Anton. He scrutinizes the fort they're building in the game. Luis has disco balls and fire places in every room. The place has no symmetry, and too few ways to get between the chambers. It's boxy, with patches of wood and gray stone for walls and ceiling. It's a mess of pixelated good intentions.

Anton has the nub of gray and brown pencils. He sketches a sleek revision to the fort, with a ladder up the center of all the floors, like an elevator. It can lead down into all of Luis's tunnels. Everywhere, there will be a torch. Then they'll be safe.

He nudges Grigorii with the sketch pad and gets a nod of approval. The three of them start redesigning the fort.

"And a door there," Anton gestures to the wall of the top floor. "To throw bombs down when monsters come."

Luis drops the controller to put both his hands to his scalp. "You mad genius."

The quickened pulse. The rapid flight of his eyes between pad and people and game. It's been so long since excitement wasn't coupled with fear. When they slay a giant flying eyeball with fangs, all three of them grab each other and shake wildly. It's terrifying and Anton doesn't want it to stop.

Grigorii has four jobs altogether. From 7 AM to noon he's the cook at a gastro diner called Breakfast For Breakfast. Anton thought they'd be eating gourmet pancakes every day, but Grigorii can't stand breakfast food.

"Not after making it this much. I'd rather eat my hand than a waffle."

For the rest of his week, Grigorii mows the grass around the town hall and the cemetery, and separates papers from plastics at the town dump, and almost ironically he drives a ride share.

Luis has two jobs—he works at the dump as well, and bags groceries part-time.

These are the things that just barely keep food on their table. Not that they have a table. They eat off old plastic egg crates. He starts to draw again, trying to get the holes in the egg crates right, so eventually he can draw the holes in himself.

During this whole time, no question is asked. Grigorii lets him coast without a nudge. Anton could hide in the house and draw and play Terraria for weeks.

But doing their dishes and laundry and scrubbing the windows is simply not enough. It'll be Luis who asks when Anton is going to pitch in, and when the answers are vague, the resentment will grow. The advice helplines he calls tell him not to rush himself. They do not understand what it is to bleed when you disappoint someone.

"Calm down," Grigorii says. "You're making that buzzing sound again."

"I need to work. If one of you gets hurt, we've got nothing."

"Well, lucky you. This town's getting gentrified to fuck."

"How does that help?"

"Where there are rich people, there is work they don't want to do."

Manual labor is a gift. Lugging jugs of weed killer and spreading soil is not so different than building pixelated homes in Terraria. They are both distractions. Much as he doesn't think about his own existence when he plays the game, he ceases to exist when he hauls and aches and works. It's a peaceful oblivion that pays bills.

There are so many showy second homes, and Grigorii knows some of the owners. The nearest properties are an eight mile walk, which Anton can abide. After a week, he's pulling fourteen hour days without a complaint.

The homeowner is a white lady, Mrs. Walsh. She sips limeade and tequila with a generous smile, the generosity of which is that she is smiling for him at all. He knows the dynamic. He knows to show gratitude.

"Kids today don't have a work ethic," she says, shooing Anton to the road. "You're different."

Without thinking about it, Anton knows he doesn't have a work ethic. The helplines have taught him better. He has a habituated trauma that requires him to do something or face consequences he's too afraid to think about. If anything, it's a relief that Mrs. Walsh's kids aren't like him.

He is thinking again. He needs to stop that.

He says, "Thanks, Mrs. Walsh. It's a beautiful property. I'll have the slope finished soon, and then we can start on that garden."

The eight mile walk home will be easier in a week, when Grigorii frees up and joins him. They'll drive together. That'll mean more sleep, too.

Fifty yards into those eight miles, he recognizes a town car parked along the wrong side of the road. Its black hood has a grainy polish so that it lacks any luster, in moonlight or daylight. Its windows are tinted so deeply that pedestrians couldn't see what was done to passengers inside.

His pants are wet. The cloying warmth seeps out of his bites, soaking through the fabric. It brings with it the anticipation that a blow is coming. He cringes in expectation.

The other familiars are here. They've been waiting for him. The twins, Pavla and Yoana, are on either side of the senior familiar, Walter. They wear sharp satin suits over starched linen shirts. They wear the kind of uncomfortable, thick rings that left indentations on Anton's fingers to this day.

Pavla says, "Get in the car and come back with us and I'll try to smooth it over with…"

Walter raises a hand with one finger and Pavla stops talking. Her eyes go from his finger, to the car, to her shoes. A little stream of blood trickles down her left cuff and across the heel of her hand. That means her bites are bleeding, too.

She and her sister have to leave Mr. Bird, too. Anton should argue with her and convince her that leaving is possible.

Not that she'd dare listen to him now.

Walter is a gangly man, barely out of his teens, younger than Anton, and broader. His limbs are thin enough that it's easy to miss how wide his shoulders are, and how long his reach is. His teeth have started to sharpen, although his are nothing close to Mr. Bird's.

He has been Mr. Bird's familiar the longest. Mr. Bird is frequently unhappy with him. He'd wanted Anton to take over, allegedly since Anton was more decisive. The idea of becoming Mr. Bird's right hand is what finally made Anton run. It's something he's worked hard not to think about.

Walter says, "You took something of his."

Anton shifts on the side of the road. The crumbling asphalt tilts under his footing. "I didn't. I swear."

Walter points at Anton's chest. "You. Your time is his time. You made the same deal we all did."

Anton pushes the soles of his feet against the asphalt, letting it break. "You can't make me come back."

"You are going to make yourself come back," Walter says, with the edge that Mr. Bird usually speaks in. "It's for your own good. None of us could live without him."

"I'm alive. I'm fine."

"You're shaking. You were shaking the day he and I found you, too."

Is he shaking?

He clutches his right arm. Yes, he is.

Was he shaking before Walter said he was?

He's not sure.

Walter says, "He's not doing this to hurt you. You were nothing before. We were all nothing. Are we not good enough for you? Where's your loyalty?"

That word. 'Loyalty.' It makes him think of Grigorii's ugly face, and the one time he and Anton went on a date and how bad it went, and how they were still friends the next week, and how years later Grigorii came and double parked to save him.

Walter asks, "What made you think you could survive without him?"

"That story is not the story I'm telling today."

The blood flowing on his thighs slows, as though it's clotting. It's still forming dark circles in his pants that are visible in the waning daylight.

He refuses to relent. He thinks of his new home, and the sketch pad and game night waiting for him. The linoleum floor of Grigorii's place is more welcoming than Mr. Bird's memory foam bed. If his brain is going to lock up, it is going to lock on those feelings.

Walter says, "If you don't come with us, there will be consequences. We know where you're nesting now."

The mental image of that linoleum floor now floods Anton with cold dread. What could be happening in their home right now? Is that house on fire? Is Mr. Bird waiting in the town car, or is he across town ravaging Grigorii and Luis? Is there any life left eight miles away?

No. His bites are bleeding. That means Mr. Bird must be here, not there.

A speck of red wells in the white linen of Walter's shirt. It peeks out behind beneath his suit jacket.

Anton often wondered where Mr. Bird bit Walter. Now he knows.

This means Mr. Bird is furious at them all. He must still want to replace Walter.

Pavla and Yoana move to the rear door of the car. They open it and stand, waiting for Anton to submit. To come to the place no one should call home.

Anton says, "I have work in the morning."

Pavla and Yoana watch him leave, walking to a different home.

There is no sleeping tonight. Anton lies on the floor and pretends to rest while he watches the window. There are noises in the night, deeper animal sounds than any raccoons. There's a warbling buzz, like a flock of nocturnal crows are clearing their throats.

He doesn't dare go outside. Not in all that dark. They could be anywhere out there.

First thing at sun-up he inspects the front door in case any carnage or omens have been left there. There's nothing there except garbage and the pair of beat-up lawn mowers they need to tear open and fix.

This doesn't make sense.

Anton pulls weeds the next day. His neck feels made of fraying rope from all the times he checks behind himself. As best as he can tell, the car and the familiars don't show up.

Monday morning is the same, if harder to get through because of the brain fog. Anton needs to sleep or he'll never survive this life. He cuts the shit out of his hands working, and that is a sign that he needs to focus on what really matters.

Everything will be fine.

It's not until Tuesday that they come for Luis.

Anton moves slowly. He creeps through the front door, physically feeling like whatever happened to Luis will ooze out and suffocate him. It is a tangible panic he has to fight to walk through.

Luis sits against the wall, using one of the sofa cushions as a back rest, watching Captain America: Winter Soldier for the hundredth time. He turns his attention from Steve Rogers to Anton. The motion makes the wadded bandage on the side of his neck crinkle.

Anton asks, "What happened?"

"Random accident," Luis says, muting the TV. The heroes keep fighting wordlessly. "I was working near the highway. Clearing brush and crap. I paused to catch my breath and somebody bumped into me. Car almost wiped my shit."

"Somebody hit you?"

Anton can see it happening. Scrawny Luis rubbing his eyes, and a shadow lunging out of the trees to toss him in front of traffic. Walter had warned that there were going to be consequences.

"The driver said he saw a white girl. Neither of us was exactly looking at her, you know? She ran off. Wouldn't be the first meth head running around out here." He shrugs, then winces and touches the bandage. "I'm just getting my mind off it. Want to play Terraria?"

It was a woman, then. Pavla and Yoana could have done it. Mr. Bird has his familiars do everything for him. They are his hands.

So he's showing Anton. Showing him how a familiar is supposed to behave.

Anton asks, "She pushed you into traffic?"

Luis says, "Nah, man. If somebody wanted to yeet my ass into traffic, I would've known. This was, like, I would've thought I tripped if the driver didn't tell me she was there. And I dodged the car with my super reflexes. Chill."

Too much doesn't make sense. Anton leans against the frame of the front door, mulling the attack. Why did Mr. Bird order Luis to almost die? He is the sort to burn down this house with all of them inside it. The only reason Anton isn't dead already is that Mr. Bird wants him back.

Luis scratches at the adhesive of the bandage on his neck.

Before he knows it, Anton is approaching him. The bandage is a sanitary white rectangle. There's no seeing what is underneath. Judging its size, Anton feels his own mouth, for the size of his teeth.

Anton asks, "Did you get cut in the fall?"

"Yeah, cut myself up. I don't know what I fell on. My luck."

"A scrape?"

"Nah, it got me deep." Luis mimes stabbing himself in the throat with a sword, with a comical expression. "Must've been a rock."

That expression and that mental image tell Anton that he has to go back to Mr. Bird. He has to go trade himself to protect Luis and Grigorii from what may have already happened.

Anton kneels over Luis, looking for any blood spotting through the bandage. None is visible.

He asks, "Could you show it to me?"

Luis says, "What?"

Anton is crouching over Luis now, trying not to look manic, trying not to look like someone whose heart is about to rupture out of their chest. "I need to...you know, can I make sure..."

"Grigorii already looked at it. I'm good."

"Did it feel like something bit you?"

Luis looks aside without turning his body. "I'm trying to watch a movie here. You mind?"

Anton isn't thinking. The thoughts are too heavy to lift. Action is easier, and he has to do something. It's for Luis's safety.

Luis reaches for the remote, and Anton reaches for the bandage.

"Man, quit it."

"I'll go back to him. He can't take you. I promise, I promise, I promise."

"Dude! Fuck off of me!"

One of Anton's hands nests in Luis's t-shirt, and the other goes for the bandage. He yanks at both, and Luis shoves him in the chest. Anton rocks backward, then surges forward again. All he can see is the loose bandage and the infected pink flesh of the cut underneath. He can't see the size or shape of the injury.

He needs to see it closer. He needs to be sure that he didn't get this boy cursed.

Thick arms circle Anton's belly and he is in the air, a flying feeling that reminds him of when Mr. Bird used to hit him. His throat buzzes, and he promises that he'll go back if they don't take Luis.

No one is hitting him. Grigorii is here, dragging him away from the house. Anton tries to explain, and he can't. Not through the hysterical shrieking that overtakes his mouth.

The two of them go for a drive. Anton is terrified that Grigorii is taking them to the city and will dump him at that dark townhouse. It would be right. He's a problem that needs to go back where he came from.

And he needs to go back. His pain can plug the hole his escape made. He should've taken the ride with Walter; then nobody would have attacked Luis.

They don't visit the city. They roll a few miles into the pines, to the view of a trail that is half hiking path and half knotty tree roots that serve as natural stairs. The entrance is decorated with used Solo cups and cigarette butts. Grigorii stays in the car, taking a long drink from his old water bottle that he refills from the tap every morning. Its label is long gone.

There are so many shadows under the pines. Any of them could be Mr. Bird.

Grigorii says, "You need therapy. I know you do, and I wish I could afford it for you. It's a shithole country."

"You don't owe me anything. I'll be fine."

"Man, you're clearly scared. I can see the fear when you're happy. Does my place make you feel unsafe?"

Anton whips his head back and forth. "No. No, no."

"Did I do something to make you scared?" Grigorii sets the water bottle aside. "Because I don't think Luis did anything. He's a sweet boy. I'm not entitled to know all your shit. But I need to know what's setting you off like that. That can't happen again."

"I wouldn't hurt him."

"You were hurting him. I need to know what caused that."

Anton owes him so much. Even if Grigorii doesn't believe him, he deserves to hear what he wants to hear. How can he shape it so that he'll understand?

"There's a man. I mean, he's not a man. He's sort of…"

Anton trails off immediately. There is no way to describe the shadows with a mouth that controlled his life for three years.

Grigorii asks, "If he's not a man, what is he?"

"Let's say he's a man."

"Okay. This is the guy that ran the little cult you lived in?"

"He preys on certain kinds of people. Immigrants. People without families. I think his oldest member was a drug addict."

"Well I'm glad you're out of there."

"I think I should go back."

Grigorii rests a broad palm against the backrest of Anton's seat. His fingers sink into the cushion. "Buddy. That is not happening."

"I don't know."

"When you called me, you said you were going to die if you stayed."

He had phrased it like that. It had felt too much to confess that he'd kill himself if he stayed.

Now Anton wonders if killing himself is the answer. It would give Mr. Bird no satisfaction. No returned slave. And it will give them no reason to keep harassing Luis and Grigorii.

"Anton," Grigorii says. "Speak to me, man."

The car is real. His friend is real. The conversation is real.

Anton speaks. "The three others tracked me down. They caught me on my way home a few nights ago."

"Holy shit. They came out here? You should've said. I've got a baseball bat they can meet."

"They said I had to come back or there would be consequences."

"They said you had to do what they said or they'd attack Luis?"

"Not exactly."

Grigorii worms his tall body around the driver seat so he can face Anton dead-on. There's no escaping his warm, overworked eyes.

The man says, "Look. I'm not attacking you. I put you up in my place. I got you out of that cult. I'm listening to you now. So come with me, okay?"

Anton breathes. "Okay."

"What did these people say? Exactly?"

The exact phrasing is murky. A series of panics has mashed it up like a bad remix in his head. He knows a few things about it, though.

"It was short. They didn't have to say much."

"Was it specific?"

Anton thinks. No, it wasn't.

Anton speaks. "No. It wasn't."

"Did they say they'd push somebody into traffic?"

"No."

"Did they say they'd attack one of us at work?"

"They didn't have to say that. People make vague threats all the time."

Grigorii falls into his seat. "Yeah they do. Do you remember my mom?"

Mrs. Caravaggio is an ancient story. Anton has to search into the dusty archives of his mind for a vague image of that woman with the constant smell of menthols and the beautiful black hair. The last time Anton saw her was middle school. When Anton's family had sheltered Grigorii, they didn't see her all that year, or ever again. She disappeared into the chasm that was her life.

Anton says, "Yeah, I remember her."

"She was the master of vague threats."

"She was?"

"Whatever happened, she said she planned it. One time she said if I didn't scrub the basement floor, she'd have to punish me. Two days later our power got cut because she spent all our money doing whatever else, not that I knew. She said that was my punishment for not scrubbing hard enough. It worked, too. I begged her to bring the power back."

Anton squeezes his hands together into one messy fist, and looks between his fingers, in the miniscule gaps, as though he'll find himself inside.

"The threats meant that when there wasn't food, it was my fault. When Dad didn't come for his weekend, it was my fault. It made me paranoid."

How many times has he begged Mr. Bird for forgiveness for things he didn't do? For things he didn't do wrong?

The answer is not in the miniscule gaps between his fingers.

He asks his friend, "What happened to your mom? Do you ever see her?"

"That story is not the story I'm telling today, man."

Anton breathes. "Right. I'm sorry."

"I'm telling you what I did for me. What you've got to do for you. She doesn't matter to the story of how I survived."

"I just don't see how you survived. If she controlled everything in your life, what did you do?"

Grigorii holds out his palm, with all its calluses and grime. It's another offer of touch. "You know that part. I came and lived with your family."

"They don't want me anymore."

"Yeah, but I do."

The drizzle makes working on the Flemings' new shed futile. It's an unusually chilly precipitation, and so Anton quits early. His body is beat anyway, sluggish like it has the brain fog instead of his head for once. At least he can use some of the plastic tarp as a poncho for the long walk home. If he's lucky, Grigorii will leave the cemetery early and drive along this road on the way.

Around the first bend, still in sight of the Flemings' property, Walter waits under a black crocodile skin umbrella.

The car is parked on the shoulder of the road. The rear left window is open a sliver. A gloom festers inside. Anton strains to see the mouth, to see the white of the teeth that long for his flesh. Already his jeans are damp with warmer things than the rain.

Walter's acid voice splashes him. "You're coming with us. Now."

At first Anton licks his lips and averts his eyes to the ground. The old habits of weakness.

It's a smaller 'us' than before. Walter stands alone on the road, and perhaps with Mr. Bird in the car. Anton has to wonder where the twins are. Is Luis safe? Is this a distraction to keep him away until they've attacked?

Anton says, "I have to get home."

"This isn't an offer. This is what's going to happen."

Anton tells his feet to get moving. A puddle grows underneath him.

Walter says, "You're going to help us find wherever Pavla and Yoana ran off to. Your leaving made them think they could leave, and you're going to show them you made mistakes. That none of us can live without Mr. Bird."

It's too much in too few words. The twins can't have left Mr. Bird, and they can't be utterly missing. Mr. Bird knows everything about them. He has to know where they are. He made them try to kill Luis.

Unless being forced to attack Luis was too much. Unless that is why they ran.

Anton mumbles, "I'm going home and taking a hot shower."

He imagines the warm beads hitting and streaking over his face. It will be the opposite of this rain. He thinks on it, refusing to let his mind cave to the panic or stillness. If he focuses, he can feel the warm water on his legs.

Walter says, "You're going to make them come back or there are going to be consequences."

The young man shifts as he threatens Anton, revealing how badly he's bleeding. Four ugly circles of gore leak through his undershirts, streaking down the fabric like little red ties.

Despite the coverage of the plastic tarp, Anton's trousers are soaked. It's especially wet along his inner thighs. Warmth trickles from the old bites, streaking down to tickle the backs of his knees.

So Mr. Bird is furious with them both.

"Get in the car," Walter says, "or there will be consequences."

"More consequences?" Anton asks. He can't get Grigorii's mother out of his head, that vague memory of a woman who used vagueness to seem omnipotent. He looks for her face in the partially rolled down window of the car. All that lurks there are shadows. He says, "I don't believe in your consequences. I believe in a shower."

Walter says, "If you don't come with us right now, we are taking Grigorii Caravaggio."

Anton digs his heels into the road. "What?"

"You won't know when Mr. Bird will come for him."

"You can't."

"You won't know if it's when you're together and you'll have to watch, or when you're apart and there will be no one to hear him weeping. Mr. Bird will sink his teeth into Grigorii's flesh and make him a familiar in your place."

Anton's arms drop, and the plastic lowers to his hips. The cold drizzle blots at his hair and face. This is too much.

He says, "You won't. Grigorii's not weak like us. He won't break."

Walter sneers with crooked teeth. "It won't be hard to take away the things he relies on. He'll be weaker than you in no time. And it will be your fault."

Can Anton run away?

No.

He's unsure if he can walk. He's unsure of everything because anxiety cuts through everything, feelings chewing ideas and dragging them into the mire. He so badly wants his mind to shut off, to kill those awful visions of where Mr. Bird will bite Grigorii. He wants to finish building the Flemings' shed, and build a dozen more, and play Terraria and watch a movie on constant loop so that he doesn't have to think anything.

Walter says, "You're not better than me."

Blood is streaming from the bites on Anton's thighs, coating his calves and pooling in his socks. He doesn't know if he can bleed out and die standing here.

As badly as he wants the apathy of not thinking, apathy is not an option.

Walter says, "You're not more deserving than me."

That scorn sounds pathetic. Anton hears it, and sees Walter condescending at him, and can only imagine himself and Walter spewing the same scorn at Pavla and Yoana. They're supposed to be the hands of a monster. They're supposed to do a shadow's work.

Anton says, "I never said I was better than you."

The wind shifts rainfall, and a pair of drops slant under the umbrella, spattering against Walter's chin. He says, "You people think you can walk away and live a better life, and you've got dirt under your fingernails to show for it. Right now you're standing in line, in the cold, hoping for another day of backbreaking labor. You think it makes you better than me?"

His teeth are more crooked than Anton remembers. And they're duller.

Anton asks, "Is that what Mr. Bird beats into you? Is that what he says when he leaves new teeth marks on your heart?"

Walter is bleeding so badly under his suit jacket that it looks like he's wearing a red shirt with white bleached spots. That is the cherished place where Mr. Bird wanted Anton to be standing. He could have the honor of chief among sufferers.

Anton says, "I had to leave. I didn't want to do what you do."

"Get in the car."

"I thought he'd kept it secret from you. But you know it, don't you? Did he tell you that he wanted me to take your place, or did you figure it out on your own?"

Walter throws the crocodile umbrella into the road. It rolls in a minor wind. "I've run his household since I was fourteen years old. You think you could do what I do?"

Anton pulls his cheap plastic sheeting over his head again, making a cloak that crinkles. His hair is slick enough with rainwater; he refuses to get any wetter. "I don't want to scream at people, and drive that shadow everywhere, and pretend I don't care when he does what he does. How does it feel to stalk and scare gay boys into coming back to work so they can replace you, Walter? Does it make you think anything is going to hurt you less?"

The rumble of the car's engine is joined by a buzzing. An awful panoply of chirping sounds swirl from inside the tinted windows, inhuman and ravenous. They flow from every dark part of a drizzling world.

Smothered in that noise, the two familiars bleed together. Anton refuses to look around for wherever Mr. Bird's shadow may be, or where his mouth is cursing them. He focuses on the young man in front of him.

"I'm not better than you, Walter. Me, and Pavla and Yoana, we're not one ounce better. And we all walked away. That means you're capable of leaving, too."

"What made you think you could leave?"

"That's not the story I'm telling today."

The drizzle soaks Anton's pants so thoroughly that moisture drips off his shoes. It's a mixture of water and worse, leaving reddish brown tints in the puddles behind his feet. It marks where he's been after he leaves.

Of course he apologizes. But apologies are not enough.

For most of two weeks, Anton never lets himself be alone in the house with Luis. If Luis is home, then Anton waits outside for Grigorii. He never forces the boy to be alone with him. He will not become that kind of specter.

With some favors, he gets work with Grigorii. Every second he has eyes on him is a relief. It means that if something will happen, it isn't happening now. The present tense is a sort of refuge.

Together they flush out and clean gutters. He learns how to prune different kinds of bushes, and how to cover his mistakes in ways that look artistic enough for affluent people to praise.

Near the end of the two-week period, when he's saved up enough money, he stands in the doorway of the house. He faces Luis, like he needs to be invited inside. A different invitation happens.

Anton says, "You want to hit the bar with me and Grigorii on Friday? All you can drink on me."

"I could do that."

"There will be plenty of people there. Thought it might be fun."

He doesn't say what will be fun about it. He shifts, letting more daylight into the doorway.

Luis pretends to keep watching Winter Soldier, but he's clearly following Anton out of the corner of his eye.

That's fine. Anton goes outside to sit in the sun, on the rough-hewn tree stump that scrapes his legs. He has a sketch pad and an active mind. He fills these hours by summoning old hours, drawing himself walking out of that dark townhouse, and Grigorii's clunker driving them away from New York City, and himself digging other people's gardens. There are parts of the story he wants to draw, wants to draw as badly as a kid wants to breathe when he's made a dare to stay underwater, but every time he tries to draw his thighs he gets the scars wrong. It's been so long since he's had the nerve to actually look at his bare thighs.

But he has his sketch pad, and the nubs of pencils, and time.

He also has an aluminum bat resting next to the tree stump. Just in case.

Friday is St. Patrick's Day, which is Luis's favorite holiday. He glibly explains that the Irish got potatoes from South America to every patron in the bar—and explains it more than once to some patient women. Anton and Grigorii linger nearby to make sure he doesn't get in over his head, and so hear half a dozen increasingly dramatic versions of the story of how he got the scar on his neck.

Anton tries to give Grigorii space. The man wants to chat basketball and gripe about work with other locals. What matters is that he can see Grigorii being safe, and that Grigorii sits in a well-lit part of the bar. No shadows will encroach.

With that amount of security, Anton goes and does foolish things. Foolish things like flirting.

In the shoulder-to-shoulder cramp of this St. Patrick's Day, there is Julian. Julian is a big man with glasses and a fine navy pinstripe suit, like a Puerto Rican Clark Kent. His soft voice carries in the booming crowd. He's adorable from the moment he accepts his drink by waving both hands excitedly, as though accepting a newborn into his arms.

Thanks to all his exposure to Luis, Anton is able to converse casually about Marvel movies. That takes them to art, and Anton makes himself talk about his pencil sketches. He tries to show Julian the nicer pieces, the ones that don't require him to tell a hard story.

As he thumbs from sketch to sketch, Julian leans in exquisitely close such that Anton finds himself hoping. Upon seeing Anton's sketch of his Terraria base, Julian goes all high-pitched. They argue about whether Terraria or Minecraft is better until the bar closes.

The truth is that he's still too hurt inside to be sure if anyone can be attracted to him.

That's why it helps to have friends.

Luis slaps him on the shoulder. "Getting after it, son. When are you two getting married?"

It's so bewildering and so exciting that he doesn't think about how long the shadows were in the parking lot. Not until the next morning.

Julian lives in Brooklyn. He knows eight thousand better places to eat than the diner and two fast food places near Grigorii's.

"The big guy can come too," Julian says. "I've got a coworker that is starving for a man."

Julian takes them to a burrito joint that is basically a closet, but where the food tastes like God. They go for tapas in this place with a view of the river.

Their third date is at a Turkish restaurant that is spacious and so dark that a Goth would complain. The dark doesn't bother Anton. Not at first.

They watch as a waiter wipes down what will be their table when the app on Julian's phone buzzes. The waiter has an equally chic and shaggy haircut that looks familiar from behind. Then the waiter turns around.

It's Walter.

Anton is falling into the intense dark of the restaurant. He clutches at anything, one hand snagging Grigorii's sleeve, the other catching Julian's. They get him by the elbows and raise him. He's sure his pants are full of blood.

Walter hasn't seen him yet. He is busy setting out cloth napkins and silverware.

He's different. It's like looking at an earlier draft of a person. His eyes are more sunken and carry greater distance. Simultaneously, his whole body is thinner, such that his button down shirt and vest are baggy on him. Every exposed inch of his flesh is coated in a thick, unhealthy perspiration. Like he's sweating something out of his system.

Julian asks, "Are you okay?"

Anton stands free of their support. He brushes the thighs of his pants, which are surprisingly dry. He takes a couple steps into the restaurant, until Walter glances at him—and then another two seconds, until Walter sees him seeing him.

Walter's head snaps at him in a wicked double take. He looks ashamed, and frustrated, jaw setting like words are trying to force their way out.

"I need some air," Anton says, bumping into Julian's side. "Can we go somewhere else? You said there's a good Vietnamese place?"

Grigorii smiles mirthfully, even though he moves to stand between Anton and the waiters. "I always wanted to try Vietnamese."

They roll home after 2:00 AM. Getting up for work tomorrow morning is going to suck.

Luis is passed out on the cushions with Terraria running. His character gets eaten by zombies, dies, respawns, and is eaten again, over and over. From Luis's snoring, he doesn't mind.

The one thing Anton needs before bed is a piss. Through blurry eyes he unzips and pushes his pants lower than he meant to. It's probably the inebriation that makes him look at his bare legs for so long.

He pushes an index finger at the bites on his thighs. His fingertip doesn't fit inside them anymore. It's been so long that he took their ugliness for granted and hasn't checked them. They have shrunken and closed, and turned a pale pink of old scar tissue. They don't look like they've bled in an eon.

Is this a cosmic prank?

His phone buzzes and he hits his head on the wall. A needle-stick puncture of anxiety hits him. This is Mr. Bird. This is the revenge.

His thighs still aren't bleeding.

It's Julian's number.

"I had a great time tonight," turns into, "We should see more of each other," which turns into, "I know this sounds sudden..."

Anton rubs wetness from his eyes and asks, "What's sudden?"

"It started in college. Every spring, my best friends get together in a cramped cottage in the Carolinas. A nice part of the Carolinas. The food is grotesquely expensive, but I can cover you, and besides, Latisha brought her boyfriend last year, so why can't I bring mine? Will you think about it?"

Thinking used to be dreadful. It used to be.

"It'll only be a weekend," Anton explains. "I'll come home."

Grigorii is so chunkily proportioned, with such expansive arms, that he gives unbelievable hugs. He holds Anton to his chest and says, "You go wherever you want, buddy."

It will be a road trip. Hour after hour of Gipsy Kings and Alejandra Guzman; pricey satellite radio and Julian only wants two bands. They'll make a short detour in Delaware to pick up Latisha and her guy.

Anton takes half a deep breath and asks, "Can we make a second detour?"

He shows Julian the route. Julian's eyes bug out. He says, "Further into the city? At midday? We'll literally die."

But Julian is willing to risk death for a kiss.

The detour takes them through a pristine borough that Anton has not missed.

Anton says, "Take this left."

Five blocks after that left is the townhouse.

On the upper floor, the blackout curtains sag from two windows. One has come loose entirely from its fixtures, exposing a triangle of the interior to the scourge of sunlight. Sunlight does kill some things.

The front door is shut firmly. Its blue paint is chipped and flecking away, like the lines of roads on a state map. In fact the whole townhouse's exterior paint job has faded from walnut brown to a sandy color with the same veiny cracks. The building has never looked so dry.

The shadows of the townhouse are shorter than any other. All the townhouses on this street are a uniform height.

Anton studies the shadows, sketching them in pencil in his thoughts.

It begins with a meager sound, like a heartbeat under the building. The blackout curtains crumble, and the glass panes tip inward. The front door yawns and melts from its hinges, lapping the parlor like a tongue. Julian is looking the wrong way, and so he misses the entire townhouse collapsing into a plume of unruly dust.

Julian startles in the driver's seat. "What the hell was that?"

Anton fishes out a fresh sketch pad, settles it on his thighs, and opens to a clean page. He takes a pencil and says, "Let me tell you a story."

....

John Wiswell is a disabled writer who lives where New York keeps all its trees. He is a Nebula and Locus Award winner, and has been short-listed for the Hugo, World Fantasy, and British Fantasy Awards. He is the author of two novels: *Someone You Can Build A Nest In* and *Wearing The Lion*.

JUST ENOUGH RAIN

P. H. Lee

1. The Funeral

I wasn't surprised when God showed up for Mom's funeral. They'd always been close.

He slipped in the back during my eulogy in the form of a stranger. I don't think that any of the various relatives noticed Him. For all they knew, it could have been some old flame of hers come to pay his last respects.

After the service, as the various relatives were clearing out, I thought someone should say something, so I approached Him. He was standing off to the side of the room, sipping a glass of water.

"It was good of You to come," I said, taking care to capitalize the Y.

"I wouldn't miss it," He said, and sipped His water again. "She was a great lady, your mom."

"She was." It was a bit awkward. I hadn't spoken to Him since that failed prophetic vision the summer I turned 15.

"Do you remember the first time she had cancer?" God asked.

Did I remember? "Of course."

"Do you know what she said to Me, when I sent down a dozen angels to carry off her sarcomas one by one? She said 'I need to check with my oncologist before I try any alternative medicine.'"

I didn't laugh, but I smiled. "So what did You do?"

"What else could I do? I waited for her to check with her oncologist and then I sent down a dozen angels to carry off her sarcomas one by one."

"Thanks for that," I said, and meant it. Another two decades.

"You're welcome," said God. "Least I could do, really."

We stood in the awkward silence for another few seconds.

"So," God finally broke the silence, "about that…"

"Yeah?" I asked.

"I was thinking about bringing her back to life."

My knees buckled and I nearly pitched over. God held out a hand to steady me. "You were WHAT?" The spot He'd touched my dress began to glow faintly.

"I was thinking about bringing her back to life."

"But, why?"

"Don't you want me to?"

"Of course I do, I mean, God, what I wouldn't give for another day with her, but." I stopped, noticing what I'd just said, and blushed. "Sorry."

"Oh that?" said God. He dismissed it with a wave of His hand. "It's not a big deal. You're not really taking My Name in vain if you're actually talking to Me."

"I mean aren't there other miracles You should be doing?" I couldn't believe I was saying. Mom always told me I'd gotten twice the family argumentative streak, but was I really going to argue with God about His miracles? Particularly when He wanted to bring my mom back to life?

"Should? Like what?" asked God. He seemed genuinely curious.

"I don't know: ending world hunger?"

"You already have all the food you need to end world hunger."

"Sure, but if we just give the food away, it collapses local agricultural prices." God shook His head skeptically. "Is that really true, though?"

"You don't know?"

"Economics isn't really My forté."

"Okay, how about bringing peace to all humanity?"

"Every time I get involved in politics," said God, with a touch of regret in His voice, "it goes *completely* off the rails."

"There must be something!" I said, still not quite believing that I was having this argument.

"Oh, there is, I'm sure. Probably a lot of things. But this is an easy one. I liked your mom. We were close. I miss her already."

"So do I," I agreed, trying as hard as I could not to ask about the afterlife.

"So I'll bring her back from the dead," concluded God, His eyes shining. "Easy."

"Why are you even asking me, then?"

"Oh, I wanted to make sure it was okay with you. You weren't relying on an inheritance or something like that?"

"No!"

"Just wanted to check," He said, then snapped His fingers.

From inside my mom's plain pine coffin, I heard her begin to move.

"And by the way," added God on His way out, "if you ever want to talk again, let me know. You've got my number, right?"

I did, indeed, have His number. But I wasn't paying attention to Him anymore. My mom had just sat up out of her coffin and was looking around, about as surprised as you might be if you woke up at your own funeral.

"Annie!" she shouted at me. "Go get me a dress!"

"Mom?" I couldn't quite believe it.

"These funeral clothes have absolutely no backside. You still keep that emergency dress in your trunk, don't you?"

2. Honi the Circle-Drawer

My mother used to tell us the story of Honi the Circle-Drawer. "He's our ancestor," she'd always say. "You can look it up in the Talmud."

Long ago, in the land of Judea, there was a great drought. When the month of Adar had passed and rain had still not fallen, the people came to Honi, who was beloved by God like a member of His own household, and said "We pray to God for rain, and none comes. But you, Honi, are beloved by God like a member of His own household. If you pray, surely it will rain."

Honi prayed for rain, but no rain fell.

Thereafter he went outside and drew a circle in the dust and stood inside it. "Master of the Heaven and Earth," he said, "Your people have turned their faces toward me, who You love like a member of Your household. Therefore, I swear this oath by Your holy name: I shall not leave this circle until You have mercy on your people and grant their prayers for rain."

Thereafter, rain began to lightly trickle down, just enough to fulfill the oath, but Honi was not satisfied.

"Master of Heaven and Earth," he said, "this does not grant the prayers of your people. I shall not leave this circle until You send enough rain for them to water their crops and fill their cisterns."

Thereafter, it began to rain in great torrents, soaking everything, tearing the roofs off of houses, sending great rivers through the streets. It seemed like the Great Flood had come once again. But Honi was still not satisfied.

"Master of Heaven and Earth," he said, "I did not ask for a harmful rain either, but a rain of benevolence and blessing."

Shortly thereafter, the rain lightened and began to fall in a standard and appropriate manner. Honi, finally satisfied, left his circle.

3. Phone Calls

After God brought my mom back from the dead, they were closer than ever. For a while, they talked all the time, but eventually they settled on a long phone call every Saturday afternoon, which drove cousin Miriam up the wall.

Mom wouldn't say what exactly what they talked about. "He's very busy," she'd say vaguely, "under a lot of stress."

"You could call Him sometime," she would add, when I pushed her. "He aways asks about you."

I did think about calling Him. But then I thought about that failed prophecy, the whole Conversation we'd have to have, and ugh.

For the most part, though, Mom had other things on her mind. "You know," she'd say, as if I hadn't heard it a hundred times before, "one of my great regrets was dying without getting to meet my grandchildren."

"Mom," I'd say, "you're still alive."

"Only because of a miracle, dear," she'd say, "and we mustn't count on miracles. What happened to Brett, anyway? I liked Brett. Good Jewish boy. And a doctor!"

"Brett threw plates when he got mad, Mom. And he wasn't a doctor; he was a nurse practitioner. There's a difference." And he never let me forget it.

"If he can prescribe medicine, he's a doctor in my books!"

"It wasn't going to happen."

"Well, when is it going to happen, Anat? You're thirty-eight years old, you know. Your ovaries aren't getting any younger! And after 35 fertility—"

"I know about fertility rates, Mom. I'm just busy with the new job and the new city and I haven't met the right person yet."

"Listen," said Mom. "I'm being serious."

"You think I'm not being serious?"

"Sweetie, listen. Your whole life, you've been struggling just to get your feet under you. It's not your fault, but you're here, you made it. You've got a good job, you're in a new city, you've even got a condo you love."

"You say that, but—"

"But nothing. I know it's not perfect. It's never going to be perfect. I'm telling you, all the things that you wanted to do, everything you've been putting off until you got your life together, whether that's getting married or having kids or, I don't know, writing a novel, I don't care. Whatever it is, for you, now is the time that you get to do it."

I thought about it. I thought about the kids I wanted to have with Brett before he started throwing plates. I thought about the Rimbaud notebooks in the back of my closet. I thought about that time when I was 15, the prophecy, and then I needed to stop thinking.

"Of course," Mom continued, "even if it isn't your only goal, you can still have kids. I'm not saying you have to choose. We have feminism now! You can have it all!"

"You're just saying that because you want grandkids."

"Anat. I'm 68 years old. Of course I want grandkids. Take it as a given."

"Can't you just put in a word with your pal God? He helped Sarah conceive when she was 90."

"Anat Bethesda Meagel! Don't joke about this!"

"I'm not joking, Mom. He already brought you back from the dead."

"Well, honey. You know what they say: God helps those who help themselves. So maybe you should start helping yourself. If you get what I mean."

"Mom, don't be gross."

"I'm just saying."

"Mom, I love you, but I'm hanging up now."

That weekend, she called again.

"Hi Mom, it's not a great time, I'm in the middle of cooking dinner. Can I call you back?"

"Oh, that's fine, I just wanted to let you know that I brought up your problem with God and He said He'd see what he could do."

"My problem? What problem?"

"Your problem finding the right guy, of course."

"You told *God*? Mom. Isn't He busy ruling the heavens and the earth?"

"Well, He said He'd be happy to help."

"Of course He did! Look, it's just not a good time for me to be dating right now"

"Annie, it's never a good time for you. Just tell me you'll keep an open mind, okay?"

"Mom!"

"Okay, okay. I can tell that I'm not wanted. Cook your dinner, cook your dinner. Love you."

"Tell Dad I love him," I said. And then "I love you too."

4. The Butterflies

I was fifteen when I saw God for the first time.

I mean, it wasn't the first time, not really. I'd heard Mom talk with Him on the phone. And He'd been at my bat mitzvah, of course, sort of nebulously hanging around the back in the form of a golden cloud. And, of course, in the broad sense, God is everywhere, and every person is His image.

But none of that really mattered. Because when I was fifteen, I saw God for the first time.

It was morning and I was walking up the hill to school and thinking about my crush on Andy Tanaka and then there He was, right in front of me, in the form of a pillar of fire, in the angle of a beam of light, in the fullness of the creation and endurance of the world. I staggered and fell to the ground and the entire time I couldn't take my eyes from the vision of His form.

He said: "Hello, Anat."

But when God said "Hello, Anat," I didn't just hear "Hello, Anat." Instead, here is some part of what I heard: Every name that I have ever had, every name that I would ever have, every part of my nature fundamental and superfluous, every woman who had ever had my name, all of my mothers and their mothers and the whole of my family back to the years before we even had names, before we even were people. Every implication and meaning and every echo of my name Anat, from the incense-filled temples of Canaan to the streets of occupied Paris.

I heard all this and so much more than this at once, echoing through my head. I slapped my hands over my ears, trying to shut it out, but all of the implications and interpretations and understandings just kept reverberating, louder and louder.

God didn't seem to notice. Then He said: "I'm worried about the butterflies."

When God said "I'm worried about the butterflies," I heard the fragility of a butterfly's wing, the twists of air against it as it flies, the shapes and storms that those twists became, the caterpillar that the butterfly was, the pupation that created it, each and every mark on its wings and the chance and evolution that put it there, the image of the butterfly to the human eye and its beauty and poetry and triteness, the great swarms of monarchs resting in the branches of my thought, each meaning that the words might take, each way I could have turned them into scripture and into prophecy, every misinterpretation, all the cults and all the heresies that might spring up from them—people praying to butterflies, breeding butterflies, eating butterflies as sacrament—the ancestral tree of life, the fundamental genetic connection between me, as I live (the divine image) and every butterfly (every one its own divine art) as they lived, a thousand other things, a million, the bonds between all life everywhere, all of it living and all of it dying, the bonds between the stars and the sun and the Earth that I could feel spinning underneath me, that I could feel rocketing through space, the whole of the universe, even beyond the edge of our event horizon, the entire eye of God.

I screamed.

"Anat," said God, concerned, but I couldn't hear Him. Still screaming, now crying, I tried to stand, stumbled, tried to stand again, and when finally at the least I'd scratched and scrabbled to my feet, I ran. Not to school, not back home, but just away, out, as far away as I could get. I ran until I reached the edge of town, and I kept running, into the cool damp of the old municipal forest.

It was already dark by the time my mother found me there, curled up in a tree stump and still crying myself hoarse and wet and gross.

"Anat!" she yelled, and ran towards me.

"Mom," I tried to say as she hugged me, but no sound came out.

"What happened?" she asked, and then looked into my eyes.

I tried to tell her. I really did. But I couldn't fit it into any words I knew.

"Was it God?" she asked. "Did He say something to you?"

I nodded.

She hugged me again.

"I'll talk to Him," she said, in a voice that made "talk" sound like murder. "This won't happen again."

"Mom?" I finally managed to say.

"Yes, honey?"

"Does it ever get easier?"

"It does," she said. "But it isn't ever easy."

5. The Light Rail

I was on the Blue Line, reading *The Guermantes Way*—the new translation—when I noticed him—her? them?—sitting across from me, beautiful.

It was their skin, I think, that caught my attention. Strong, muscled, but still soft as a feather. I sucked in my breath and, without thinking, bit my lower lip. There was no question of going back to *The Guermantes Way*. I just sat, and looked at them, beautiful, God they were beautiful.

Then, just as we left Elmonica/SW 170th, they stood up—tall, broad-shouldered, the slowest curve of their chin—and unfurled their wings of holy light, almost the length of the entire train car.

"Oh no," I said, but I couldn't look away.

"HARK," they said, their voice filling the entire railcar. "BE NOT AFRAID, FOR I AM A MESSENGER OF THE LORD YOUR GOD."

Some people were fumbling with their phones, but most of them just gawped, open-mouthed. I felt the cold-warm rush of embarrassment and I wanted to hide under my seat almost as much as I wanted to keep staring.

He'd sent an angel. Of course He'd sent an angel.

The angel turned to a slightly paunchy man—nice curly hair, though—in glasses, khakis and a polo shirt. "DAVID ELIAS RUTENBERG," it said.

David blanched and looked for all the world like he'd just had a dream about taking a final exam in his underwear. "Y-yes?" he finally managed.

The angel pointed to me and I tried my very best to blend into the seat cushion. "THIS WOMAN, ANAT BETHESDA MEAGELE, IS SINGLE. SHE HAS A GOOD JOB AND SHE'S EMOTIONALLY MATURE AND READY FOR A COMMITMENT. YOU SHOULD ASK FOR HER NUMBER. SO SAYETH THE LORD."

David stared at me, and swallowed hard. His face was covered in sweat.

"TAKE HER SOMEWHERE NICE, NOTHING TOO FANCY, IN THE $20-30 RANGE," continued the angel, just when I thought that this couldn't get worse. "ARGUE ABOUT WHETHER TO SPLIT THE CHECK BUT THEN PRETEND TO GO TO THE BATHROOM AND SECRETLY PAY."

David, still sweating, gave me an appraising look that made me instantly aware of every wrinkle and sag. "She's, uh" he started.

"YES," said the angel, turning their magnificent gaze upon me. "HURRY IT UP."

"She's a bit old for me, isn't she?"

The angel snapped their gaze back to him. "WELL YOU'RE NO SPRING CHICKEN YOURSELF, DAVE."

Dave looked like he'd just swallowed a toad. "I-is that also the word of G-G-God?" he managed.

"NO, DAVE, THAT'S JUST A SIMPLE OBSERVATION THAT ANYONE COULD MAKE. YOU'RE NOT EXACTLY GOING TO LAND A SUPERMODEL."

"Uh, well," said Dave, and pulled the emergency brake.

After we'd all filed out of the halted train—Dave had taken off running—I sat on the bench of the Merlo/SW 158th stop and started to cry. The angel sat down next to me, their shining wings filling the shelter awkwardly.

The angel reached out and gingerly patted the back of my head. "THERE THERE," they said.

"Am I really," I paused to sniffle back a wad of snot, "that horrible?"

"DAVE DOESN'T KNOW WHAT HE'S MISSING."

"It's just even when God Himself gets involved, I still can't get a date!"

"IT'S NOT YOU."

"I know, but, I mean—" I sniffled a little bit more. "Men are terrible."

"OH HONEY," said the angel, "YOU HAVE NO IDEA."

I looked up and remembered all over again how beautiful they were.

6. *Phone Number*

"Okay, listen," I said, when God picked up the phone. "You have to ask me before you do something like that."

"It's good of you to call to thank me," said God. "So when's your date with Dave?"

"I'm not going on a date with Dave!" I yelled, "because Dave is a humongous jerk."

"I'm sure you'll warm up to him. He's a good guy once you get to know him. Eventually this will just be your meet-cute story."

"We're not going to have 'a meet-cute story' because he said, and I quote, that I was 'a little old for him.'"

"He'll get over it."

"Then he pulled the emergency brake just to get away from me!"

"Oh My Me," said God. "That didn't go as planned."

"How did You not already know this," I asked God, "aren't You supposed to be omniscient?"

"Oh sure," said God, "but I like to leave things up to all of you sometimes. It's fun have a surprise or two."

"Please refrain from using my love life as Your entertainment."

"No promises."

"So, speaking about my love life—" I said, trailing off. My heart was racing. Was I really going to do this?

"Oh?" God sounded curious.

"Can I get the number of the angel that You sent?"

There was a silence at the other end of the line.

"Can I get the nu—"

"I heard what you said," said God. "I was just very surprised."

"I wanted to ask them on a date."

"I figured." God still sounded, not exactly angry, but not definitely not happy.

"So—?"

"So, just let Me clarify: you want Me to give you the angel's phone number so that you can ask them on a date?"

"More or less."

"That seems like a lot to ask."

"I would have said that sending an angel to fix my love life was a lot!"

"Well, your mom was really worried about you."

"You mean she was worried about grandchildren."

"Well, you know how she can get."

"Oh, yeah, absolutely."

"So, about this phone number thing—"

There was a pause. "Yes?" I asked.

"I don't think I can do that."

My heart collapsed. Damn it. And just when I'd found someone I liked.

"Why not?"

"Well, the last time we tried it, it really didn't work out."

"I'm not talking about having kids! I'm just talking about a dinner date!"

"*You're* just talking about a dinner date, but your *mom* is talking about grandkids."

"Sure, but—"

"Look, we really shouldn't risk it."

"We can use protection!"

"I don't even think that angels have phones."

"Okay, God, but You're the one who has to tell my mom why her daughter is still single at 38."

God paused for a long time. Finally, He spoke.

"I'll think about it."

7. I'm sorry

Eight days later God called me back.

"Okay I've been thinking," He said.

"Oh?"

"And I think that I owe you one."

"You what?"

"I owe you one. From that time."

My skin suddenly went cold and my stomach immediately reminded me of the precise burrito that I'd had for lunch.

"So we're talking about this now?" I asked.

"I just want you to know that I'm sorry," said God, with genuine contrition in His voice.

"No," I said. "No, I'm not ready to deal with You saying 'I'm sorry.'"

"But I am," said God. "It was too much for you, and I knew it would be too much for you, but I hoped…"

"No!" I said, almost yelling into the phone. "You're not sorry! I'm the one who's sorry! You had a message for me, a mission, and I was young and stupid and I didn't want to think about it and now it's gone, it's too late. I read about the butterfly sanctuaries, about the monarch die-offs, and I know… that I could have…" I could hear the words, I could feel God's meanings in my mind, even twenty two years seven months five days later, but I still didn't know how to say them.

God didn't reply.

"Do You know what it's like? Do You know what it's like to have had a purpose, a meaning in your life, a divinely-appointed task for you and you alone and you've already fucked it up because you were fifteen and you were scared and you didn't understand?"

"I know," said God, because of course He knew. I could feel His reticence, holding back the fullness and truth of His words.

"What am I supposed to do now? It's one thing if I was just like everyone else, wondering if life had a purpose, if I had a purpose. But I'm not. I haven't been like everyone else for a long time. Because I know that my life had a purpose, I'm absolutely certain of it, more certain than anything, and I know with the same certainty that I lost my purpose and I'm never getting it back.

"Anat," said God, and I could hear the echoes of His voice, that first time He said my name. "That's not what your purpose is."

I was stunned. God didn't say anything, either. We stayed on the phone in silence for a moment and then another moment.

"What?" I finally managed to croak out.

"I didn't make you just so you could tell people that I was worried about the butterflies. Or anything else."

"What?" I croaked again.

"I don't create things for only one reason. I certainly don't create *people* for only one reason. I created you in My image, with the capacity to dream and think and create and convince and destroy on your own. I made you, like everyone else, to find out what you'd make and what you'd become! To take a person and turn them to only one thing would be…" He stopped talking, seemingly reaching for a word, before finally saying "Well, I wouldn't do that."

"Then why?" I started to ask.

"Because your mom was telling Me about you," said God, "and I wanted to meet you. So I said hello. I was just trying to *make conversation* and I've given you some kind of permanent existential crisis. So I am sorry. That's true even if you're not ready to deal with it yet."

I didn't say anything. Then I just said "okay."

"So here's the angel's number," said God, and told me. "But don't say I didn't warn you."

8. First Date

The angel and I met at a tapas bar right off Waterfront Park. It was a summer evening; we sat outside. I was wearing that yellow sundress that probably shows a bit too much cleavage. The angel's wings lit up the entire block.

"So," I said, staring at the angel's gorgeously defined collarbone. "What do you do for fun?"

"PERFORM THE PRECISE WILL OF THE ALMIGHTY, PARTICULARLY WITH RESPECT TO HEALING AND RESCUE," said the angel.

I looked at their face, which was impassive.

"I mean, other than for work?"

"EXECUTE THE TASKS THAT GOD HAS GIVEN ME."

Okay, so this isn't going well. "So do you ever dance on the head of a pin?" I ask.

The angel looked at me. Their eyes! "GOD HAS NOT COMMANDED ME TO DO SO."

"So, any other interests?"

"GOD'S COMMANDMENTS, PARTICULARLY WITH REGARD TO HEALING."

I looked at the angel, then looked down. I was not going to be able to make a smart decision while I was looking at that jawline.

It felt like pulling off a band-aid.

"You are so, so hot," I finally said to them, "but I don't think this is going to work out."

On my way out, I stopped by the front desk and paid the bill. It was the least I could do. Anyway, I was pretty sure that angels don't carry money.

The next morning, I got a text from the angel.

REALLY ENJOYED LAST NIGHT, it read. WANT TO DO IT AGAIN SOMETIME?

I ignored it. A few hours later, I got another text.

WHAT'S UP? it said.

I left my phone behind when I went out to the gym, and when I got back I found that the angel had sent a series of escalating messages in all capital letters.

IS EVERYTHING OKAY?

WHY AREN'T YOU RESPONDING?

WHAT IS THIS EMOTION WHEN YOU WON'T TEXT ME BACK? IS THIS WHAT HUMANS CALL "ANXIETY?" IT IS VERY UNSETTLING.

I AM CONFUSED. DID I ERR?

I SEE NOW THAT I MUST HAVE ERRED. I AM NOT USED TO ERRING. GENERALLY I ONLY ACT ACCORDING TO GOD'S WILL, WHICH IS ABSOLUTE. YOU CAN UNDERSTAND THE CONFUSION.

I ENJOYED SEEING YOU. DESPITE MY ERRS, I HOPE TO DO SEE YOU AGAIN.

ANAT? ARE YOU GETTING THESE?

I'M SORRY FOR MY ERRS.

I HAVE DISCUSSED THIS MATTER WITH MICHAEL AND GABRIEL, I NOW UNDERSTAND THAT I WAS "BORING" AND NEED TO "HAVE INTERESTS" AND "ASK YOU ABOUT YOURSELF." I APOLOGIZE. I WILL DO BETTER NEXT TIME.

NOT THAT THERE NEEDS TO BE A NEXT TIME.

I UNDERSTAND NOW THAT I SHOULD NOT HAVE DISCUSSED THIS MATTER WITH MICHAEL AND GABRIEL. THAT WAS A VIOLATION OF YOUR PRIVACY AND I APOLOGIZE.

BUT I REALLY WOULD LIKE TO SEE YOU AGAIN.

ANAT?

I scrolled through the phone, and sighed. They really were trying. And Mom was always saying I'm too quick to judge. And they were really hot.

Fine, I text back. But you're paying.

9. Second Date

For our second date, we met at the Korean place in the strip mall near my condo, because their broiled fish is amazing and if things went wrong again I wouldn't have to take the train home.

By the time I showed up at 7:05 the angel was already there, wings furled this time. When I stepped in the door, they stood up out of the corner booth and waved.

"ANAT! YOU CAME! I'M OVER HERE!" They were wearing some boot-cut jeans and a white T-Shirt that read "I knelt before Man on the Eighth Day and all I got was this lousy T-shirt" and fit very tightly. Mrs. Pak, the waitress—she's the only one I've ever seen working here, and she always remembers my order—caught my eye and gave me a big smile and a thumbs up.

Without the wings, wearing a T-shirt, in the dim light, the angel almost looked like a human, but not quite. There was still something about them, something a little too perfect.

"I WAS TOLD TO 'DRESS DOWN' SO I COULD 'KEEP IT CASUAL.'"

"It's a good look on you."

"THANK YOU," replied the angel. Was that a blush? They gestured to the booth seat and I slid in.

"SO," said the angel, "WHAT'S GOOD TO EAT?"

"What isn't good to eat here?"

"IT'S JUST A BIT CONFUSING."

"First time eating Korean food?"

"YES."

"Well, why don't we start you with bibimbap?"

"IT'S ALSO MY FIRST TIME EATING."

"First time eating what?"

"ANYTHING."

Oh, I told myself. Right.

"I AM USUALLY SUSTAINED SOLELY BY THE WILL OF THE DIVINE."

"Oh?"

"BUT I AM ALSO VERY EAGER TO TRY BIBIMBAP."

"My friend Katherine says that bibimbap is the perfect food, because it has a little bit of everything. It's a pretty great first food to eat."

"BUT WE'RE JUST TALKING ABOUT ME AGAIN. TELL ME SOMETHING ABOUT YOURSELF."

Of course, I thought. Now it's awkward again.

"Look," I said after an awkward moment. "I'm sure that someone told you that you have to ask about me, and it's not exactly bad advice, but you can't just make open-ended demands like that. Ask me a real question about something you're curious about." Someone needed to drive this date and it certainly wasn't going to be the angel.

"IT'S TRUE," said the angel. "GABRIEL DID TELL ME TO ASK ABOUT YOU AND NOT TO TALK TO MUCH ABOUT MYSELF."

"It's okay to talk about yourself!" I said. "I want to know about you, too. But let's try this again. Ask me a real question, about something specific that actually you want to know."

"YOUR BOOK," said the Angel. "ON THE TRAIN. YOU WERE READING A BOOK. WHAT WAS IT?"

In Search of Lost Time! "Only the greatest novel ever written!" I started in. "Proust is writing this novel where it seems like not a lot happens, but it's about how ultimately we live in our own memories, but also that those memories are imperfect and incomplete and ultimately cannot contain the joy of actual lived moments in time. So in a way the lack of action—and the self-absorption of the main character—is fundamentally underlining the premise of the book."

"INTERESTING," said the angel. "HUMANS EXPERIENCE TIME SO DIFFERENTLY FROM ANGELS. PLEASE, TELL ME MORE."

"Are you sure I'm not boring you? I studied French Lit in college and can go on and on and on about *la Recherche*."

The angel cocked their head sidewise and looked at me. "WHAT WAS THAT?"

"What was what?"

"YOU SAID THE SAME NAME, BUT IT SOUNDED DIFFERENT."

"Oh, yes, sorry, *la Recherche* is the French name. Or, I mean, it's a part of it. The full original name is *À la recherche du temps perdu*. The English titles are 'In Search of Lost Time' or 'Remembrance of Things Past.'"

"WHY DID YOU SAY IT IN FRENCH?"

"Oh, I don't know, just habit I guess? When I'm talking about the translations I use the English names, but when I'm talking about the original I use the French."

"SO YOU'VE READ THE ORIGINAL?"

"Of course! I wrote my senior thesis about it!"

"BUT IF YOU'VE READ THE ORIGINAL, WHY WOULD YOU NEED A TRANSLATION?"

The angels eyes were wide and curious.

"It's—uh...—hard to explain."

"OH NO! IS THIS A *SENSITIVE TOPIC*? I HAVE VERY CLEAR ADVICE TO AVOID *SENSITIVE TOPICS*."

"No! I mean, it's not that sort of thing. It's just, whenever I read a new translation, if it's any good, it gives me some insight into the novel that I never had before."

"WHY? ARE THE WORDS DIFFERENT?"

"Sort of? Like I said, it's hard to explain," but the angel is so curious about it that I keep trying to tell them anyway: "There's no such thing as a perfect translation, right? Because languages aren't all the same. So every translator has to make choices about what words to use, which show the reader how *the translator themselves* read the original text, as opposed to other translators. So I read the new translations as a way of getting a deeper understanding of the text, because I get to read it through the translator's eyes, which are different than my own."

"HUH."

"Or sometimes I just get really mad about some specific verb they got wrong—I mean! Not that they got wrong! It's more that they had an interpretation that I wouldn't..." I trailed off, embarrassed.

The angel looked thoughtful for a moment, or maybe bored.

"I'm sorry, most people probably don't to spend their date on a lecture about the semiotics of translation."

"NO!" said that angel. "YOU HAVE DONE NOTHING WRONG. THIS IS FASCINATING. IS THIS WHAT IT'S LIKE TO KNOW ANOTHER LANGUAGE?"

"What do you mean?"

"WELL, I ONLY SPEAK ONE LANGUAGE. SO I'VE NEVER REALLY UNDERSTOOD WHAT IT'S LIKE TO KNOW MORE THAN ONE."

"You're an angel! How can you only speak English?"

"I DON'T SPEAK ENGLISH. OR FRENCH."

"What do you mean, you don't speak English? Then how are we talking?" " I SPEAK THE TRUE LANGUAGE OF ALL CREATION. I SPEAK THE LANGUAGE THAT WAS SPOKEN IN THE TIMES BEFORE THE GREAT TOWER, THE

LANGUAGE WHICH EVERY BEING OF GOD'S CREATION CAN UNDERSTAND WITHIN THEIR VERY SOULS."

I thought for a moment, and I realized that, even though I understood their words, the sounds that the angel was making weren't anything like English or any other language that I knew. It was amazing, and I was about to say something, to ask some question about this miracle that's happening right in front of me, but Mrs. Pak was already there to take our order, and it seemed rude to make her wait.

The angel looked askance at the sizzling bowl of bibimbap in front of them.

"I CAN EAT THIS?"

"Yeah, just... pass it over here." I pulled the paper cover off my chopsticks, stuck them into the bowl, and mixed vigorously. The angel watched me until I passed it back to them.

The angel lifts up their chopsticks and split them apart uneasily.

"Do you need help with your chopsticks?" I asked.

"I AM ENDOWED WITH THE ENTIRE GRACE OF GOD," said the angel. "I CAN USE CHOPSTICKS. I AM MERELY SAVORING THE MOMENT."

"Try it! I want to see what you think."

The angel took a deep breath, nabbed some bulgogi, bean sprouts, and rice with their chopsticks, and stuck it awkwardly into their mouth. Their eyes went wide. They tried to say something, but all that came out was "MHRGWLD OR ICSOUS."

I laughed. "Chew and swallow, then talk."

The angel's eyes sparked with realization. They chewed and swallowed, then spoke. "THIS REALLY IS DELICIOUS!"

"Isn't it?"

"IT HAS ALL OF THESE DIFFERENT TEXTURES AND FLAVORS, BUT IT'S NOT CONFUSING. THEY ALL WORK TOGETHER."

"Try some of the banchan."

"ARE THESE CUCUMBERS? THEY'RE AMAZING."

"Cucumber kimchi, yeah. And those are the fishcakes. They're even better."

"So, tell me something about yourself." We'd been talking about food for almost twenty minutes; time to change the subject.

"THERE'S NOT MUCH TO TELL, REALLY. LIKE I SAID BEFORE, MOSTLY I PERFORM THE EXACT WILL OF GOD THE ALMIGHTY, PARTICULARLY WITH RESPECT TO HEALING."

"Okay, sure, that's your job. But what about your interests? Your hobbies? Do you ever do anything just for you?"

"WELL," said the angel. They looked off to the side, embarrassed.

"Well?" I asked, leaning in.

The angel leaned over and cupped their hand around their mouth. "DON'T TELL GOD I SAID THIS," they began. I could feel their breath on my cheek. "SOMETIMES, WHEN I'M ON MY WAY TO PERFORM DIVINE HEALING, LIKE, IF I'M IN A HOSPITAL..." They trailed off, but stayed leaning towards me with their hand cupped.

"Yes?"

"SOMETIMES I HEAL OTHER PEOPLE IN THE HOSPITAL. NOT JUST THE ONES I WAS SENT TO HEAL. BUT OTHER PEOPLE WHO NEED IT."

Oh! My heart. I looked up into their eyes and smiled. They smiled back—that mouth!—and then they looked away.

10. Fourth Date

After the fourth date, we were making out on my couch. I held up a hand. "Hold on a moment."

"IS SOMETHING WRONG?" asked the angel, and stopped.

Mom always said nothing before the fifth date, and the idea of taking off my clothes in front of this embodiment of physical beauty... But Mom also told me to "help myself," and it had been quite a while since... Anyway.

"Do you want to take this to the bedroom?" I had to look away to ask, but I looked back after.

The angel stared at the carpet. "OH, WELL, I MEAN, THAT IS..."

I felt a rush of embarrassment. "It's all right if you don't want to! I don't want to pressure you."

"NO," said the angel. "IT'S NOT THAT IT'S JUST. YOU KNOW. I REALLY LIKE YOU."

The rush I was feeling was no longer embarrassment.

"LIKING SOMEONE ELSE IS STRANGE. I HAVE ALL THESE NEW FEELINGS. I'M ANXIOUS THAT YOU WON'T LIKE ME IF YOU SEE ME WITH MY CLOTHES OFF."

"Oh honey," I said, and stroked their hair. "You have nothing to worry about."

The angel's wings lit up my bedroom as bright as day. "I guess there's no option for lights out with you," I quipped, and they looked puzzled. "Just a joke," I explained.

"I COULD LEAVE MY SHIRT ON," said the angel. "I CAN HIDE MY WINGS UNDER A SHIRT."

"It's fine. You're beautiful this way."

God, they were beautiful. God.

God! How was I going to explain this to God? I looked at the angel, fussing with their pants anxiously, their soft hair falling down in ringlets. God was a problem for tomorrow.

"COULD YOU TURN AROUND?" asked the angel, "I DON'T WANT YOU TO SEE ME TAKE OFF MY CLOTHES."

I turned around, and began to get undressed myself. The angel's light, somehow, became even more intense.

"OKAY," said the angel, and I turned around.

Their human guise—clothes, but also skin and eyes and everything—lay in a pile beneath them. What remained was a great cloud of a thousand different hands, in each hand a different eye, in each eye a different name of God, all wreathed in light and holy fire.

"THIS IS ME," said the angel, with a voice that seemed to come from everywhere.

I stepped forward, took one of the hands, and kissed it. "You're beautiful," I said, and meant it.

The next morning, I woke late and the angel was already out of bed. I heard noises in the kitchen and made my way out to check.

The angel was in the kitchenette, making breakfast. They had their clothes and skin back on, but were wearing them loosely, with a few spare hands and eyes poking out. Not wanting to disturb them, I padded softly across the room and curled up on the couch to watch them.

"ANAT," said the angel when they finally noticed me. "I HAVE MADE YOU BREAKFAST." They gestured to a stack of pancakes nearly four feet high.

"I see," I said, and smiled.

"I WAS NOT SURE HOW MANY OF THESE PANCAKES A HUMAN MIGHT REQUIRE," said the angel, "SO I USED TWO BOXES. I HOPE IT IS ENOUGH?"

I slipped off the couch and over to the angel. I wrap my arms around their back and kissed their hair. "It's lovely," I said, "but I really only need three."

"OOPS," said the angel, and turned to kiss me back.

11. The Rest of the Story

It was a Thursday night, alone in my pajamas with delivery Pad See-Ew, and I'd just ignored two calls from God. So I called my mom.

"Anat!" she said. "Are you okay?"

"What kind of question is that?"

"Well, you never call unless something's wrong. I'm always the one who has to call you."

"Mom! That's not fair!"

"It's true. The truth is extremely fair."

"I'm calling now, aren't I?"

"Did you get fired? Was it because you had an affair with your boss? Are you pregnant with your boss's lovechild? Is his wife suing you for custody?"

"Mom! No! I'm fine! I promise!"

"If you're fine, then why are you calling?"

"Can't I just call to talk to my mother?"

"Anat, as much as I would love that to be true, and as much as you would love for me to believe that was true, we both know that it's just not true."

"Mom! This is why I don't call more often!"

"Okay! Okay! What is it that you wanted to talk about?"

"Do you remember that story you used to tell?"

"What story? The one about your father and the Roosevelt Elk—"

"No, no, the one about Honi. And the rain?"

"Oh, yes, that one. He's our ancestor you know. It's in the Talmud."

"Yeah, I remember. Anyway, it was a slow day at work today and I thought 'Hey, I wonder if I can look up Honi online?'"

"So you're saying you *were* fired. For slacking on the job."

"Mom! No! It's fine. Even the lawyers—just let me finish."

"Finish! Finish! I'm not stopping you."

"Anyway, I found this site, Sefaria—it turns out that the entire Talmud is online now, amazing, right?—and I found the whole Honi story. Why didn't you ever tell us the rest of it?"

"The rest of it? What do you mean?"

"There's a whole second part, about the rain continuing to fall, and flooding all of Judea. And since you're not allowed to pray for a miracle to stop happening, Honi can't fix it, until he goes up to the temple a sacrifices a bull in a gratitude offering and then the waters recede. And then, after that, they almost excommunicated him! For being disrespectful to God! Even after he saved them twice."

"Oh, is that how it goes?"

"Mom!"

"Anat, I'm an old lady. I can't remember all the stories I told you, even if they are stories about our ancestors."

"You're not old. You're sixty-eight."

"I'm a card-carrying member of the AARP. I am officially an old lady and you can't take that away from me."

"Anyway, I wanted to ask you—why didn't you tell us the rest of the story? When we were kids? Why only tell us the first half?"

"Oh, honey, I don't know, really, it's just a story—"

"But it's not a story, is it? You always said that Honi was our ancestor. And you're friends with God right now. I bet you wouldn't even have to stand in a circle to get Him to make some rain. So I don't think it is just a story. I think that it actually happened."

"Okay, fine, it probably happened. Why does it matter, anyway?"

"Because I want to know why you didn't tell us the rest!"

"Why is this a problem for you? Did your therapist say that you have an attachment disorder and it's all my fault?"

"Mom!"

"Look, honey, I truly don't remember. If I had to guess—and it's really just a guess—I probably didn't want you to be scared for me. You were always so timid, and you would listen in on God and me. I didn't want you to think that we were going to get flooded, or cursed, or excommunicated. Who even knew that Jews *could* excommunicate people?"

"Don't change the subject."

"I'm not trying to change the subject! I just don't understand why this is such a big deal for you."

"It's just. It's so hard. And I don't think I ever knew how hard it was. For you. Or for me."

"What's so hard?"

"Being friends with Him."

Mom didn't reply for so long that I thought she'd dropped the call.

"Mom? Are you there?"

"It is hard," she said. "But it's worth it."

"Is it, though?"

"Oh yes. Honey. You don't get it."

"What don't I get? He honestly seems kind of high maintenance."

"He's just lonely."

"How can He be lonely? He's God! He's literally worshipped by more than half the planet!"

"Well, sure. A lot of people worship Him. And some of them love Him. Some of them might even obey Him, although I'm skeptical. But does anyone listen to how He's feeling? Do any of them spend quality time with Him? Do any of them call Him just to catch up?"

"Still—"

"Still, nothing. Sweetie. He's lonely. He needs friends and, better or worse, we're what He's got. I'm not saying it isn't hard. It is hard. We might get flooded. We might get excommunicated. And, regardless, a lot of other people won't understand. But it's important. And He cares about us— about you. He tries His best."

"I know, I just—" and stopped. I wasn't ready to talk to God or my mother about it.

"So who is the guy?" asked Mom.

"Who is what guy?"

"The guy you met. The one you're not mentioning."

"Mom!"

"What?"

"Did God tell you something?"

"Oh, no. God didn't tell me anything. He's 'respecting your privacy,' believe it or not. But I can still tell. A mother always knows."

"I have not 'met a guy!'" Which was technically true.

"It's fine; it's fine. Tell me when you're ready."

"Good night, Mom."

"Good night, sweetie. I love you."

I sighed. "I love you too. Say hi to Dad for me."

I hung up, and looked at my phone. I pulled up my contacts. My finger hovered over God's Name. But I clicked the phone off and set it down. Not tonight, I told myself. I'd tell Him soon. But I wasn't ready.

12. *Translation*

"CAN I ASK YOU A QUESTION?"

It was a lazy Sunday in bed a couple of weeks later. I was nestled into the crook of the angel's arm, still half-asleep. I smiled. "'kay."

"WHAT'S IN THOSE BOXES IN THE BACK OF YOUR CLOSET?" One of the angel's hands came flying out.

My notebooks. I buried my face in their shoulder. "uuuuuuuuugh."

"IF IT'S TOO PERSONAL—" started the angel, but I cut them off.

"No, it's fine, it's just, you know..."

"WHAT DO I KNOW?"

I sat up. "Old dreams that I'm never put the time into."

"WHAT'S WRONG WITH THAT?"

"It's embarrassing."

"IT IS GOOD FOR HUMANS TO DREAM. IT IS EXTRAORDINARY THAT YOU CAN."

"Not if you don't follow through."

"EVEN IF YOU DO NOT, YOU WILL HAVE GROWN AND LEARNED IN THE ATTEMPT."

Ugh. "Can you can it with the positivity for a second?"

"SORRY. I DIDN'T MEAN TO—"

I reached out took the angel's hand; interlaced our fingers. "It's fine; I'm sorry. I'm just being touchy."

"THIS IS CLEARLY IMPORTANT TO YOU."

I didn't say: Is it, though? If it was really that important, wouldn't I have made time for it?

"WHAT IS IT?"

"What is what?"

"YOUR DREAM. IN THE BOXES."

I sighed. "It's poetry."

"YOU'RE A POET?"

"No! I mean, they're not my poems. They're translations."

"OH! OF *La recherche?*" The angel very carefully pronounced the French specifically.

"No, I'm not... Even I'm not ambitious enough to try to translate that whole thing. Anyway, it's not poetry. No, it's Rimbaud."

"WHAT IS RIMBAUD?"

"Rimbaud is wild! He's this brilliant French poet from the 1890s. He starts writing amazing poetry when he's only fifteen. By the time he was 20 he'd run away from home, had a torrid abusive affair with Verlaine—who was also a brilliant poet—completely changed the face of poetry in western Europe. Then he swears off of writing, tries to become a soldier, ends up representing a French coffee concern in Ethiopia, just in time tragically die young of cancer."

"THAT'S A LOT."

"I know, right? Anyway, he's been translated about a million times, but I after I moved back to the US I was looking for a way to keep my French sharp so I started to translate some of his poems. And there are really some ways that translators have gotten them—"

"WRONG?"

"No, they're not wrong, but just some of the implications in French, I don't know—"

"I SEE."

"It was a dumb idea anyway. I'm not a professor or a poet. It's not like anyone is going to be interested in my translations."

"I'M INTERESTED IN THEM."

I looked at the angel. "Why? Can't you just read the original poems in your perfect language?"

"I CAN. BUT I WANT TO READ THEM LIKE YOU DO. THROUGH YOUR EYES."

...Really?

"I WON'T IF YOU'RE NOT COMFORTA—"

"No, it's okay." I stood up and walked over towards the closet in bare feet. "I'll get you one. But they're really not very good!"

"WE'LL SEE."

"Don't say I didn't warn you," as I hand them one of the black-speckled composition books.

"I WON'T."

I came home from work that Monday and the angel had all my notebooks spread out around the living room—each one with a hand or two leafing through it—along with my *Collins Robert Unabridged Dictionary* (three hands on that one, with another circling around) and a bunch of other hands scribbling angelic glyphs on the remains on my printer paper.

Thud! I dropped my bag. "What?!"

"ANAT!" said the angel. "YOU'RE BACK!"

"What on in G—" I stopped myself.

"I'VE BEEN READING YOUR TRANSLATIONS," said the angel, gesturing to the chaos. As I looked at them, the hands looked up, made eye contact, and waved. "THEY'RE REALLY GOOD."

I held my face in my hands. "Oh no."

"I MEAN IT," protested the angel.

Not helping. I didn't look up. "I know you do," I muttered into my palms.

"LIKE THIS ONE," said the angel, holding up a notebook, "ABOUT THE BOAT. YOUR TRANSLATION ISN'T JUST REFLECTING THE ORIGINAL MEANING, BUT IT'S ALSO DISCUSSING THE DISCONNECTION OF THE POST-MILLENNIAL GENERATIONS FROM THE IDEALS AND VALUES OF THEIR PARE—"

I walked over and hugged them, mostly to get them to stop talking.

"I'M SORRY," said the angel. "I GOT CARRIED AWAY. I CAN CLEAN THIS UP."

"It's okay," I said. "This is just a lot."

"YOU'RE GOOD AT THIS, ANAT. YOU REALLY ARE."

I blushed, but didn't say anything.

13. *Good News*

Six months later, I called my mom on Friday after work. The angel was in the kitchen, working on dinner, listening in.

"Anat-honey!" she said, "is everything all right? You haven't been in a car accident have you? If you were in a car accident make sure to get—"

"Mom! I'm fine. I just wanted to share some good news."

"Good news? Are you finally ready to talk about that guy you've been hiding?"

"Yes, Mom. Fine! You were right. I met someone."

"You met someone? Oh, honey! That's fantastic."

"Mom, you don't have to fake surprise. I know you've known for months."

"Sweetie, I have been waiting for this moment for years. I am going to savor it and you're not going to stop me."

"You know what? That's fair. Savor away."

"So tell me about him."

"Well, they're very considerate."

"That's great. Is he Jewish?"

"Yes," I said.

The angel looked at me: "technically i'm not," they whispered.

"More or less, anyway," I added.

"Is he a doctor?"

"Yes, they're also a doctor."

The angel's look intensified.

"Technically not, but—" I began.

"Sure sure," said Mom, "whatever they call them these days."

"Anyway, I think I'd really love to bring them down to meet you; they've heard so much about you."

"Oh, honey, that would be lovely. How about next month? You could both come down for Pesach!"

"Great. I'll book tickets."

"Anat? Is there something you're not telling me?"

The angel, overhearing, made a gesture with their hand. "it'll be okay," they whispered uncertainly.

"All right, Mom, you're right. I have some more good news."

"More good news? Really?" She sounded skeptical.

"But you have to promise me that you'll be the one to talk to God about it."

"Sure? Honey: What is it?"

Here it comes. "Well Mom," I said, "you're going to be a grandmother a little sooner than we expected."

"Oh honey! That's great to hear. But—" She cut off.

"But?"

"I don't mean to complain."

"What is it?"

"Isn't this all a little sudden?"

What was I going to say? That I thought I'd missed my life's purpose and then it turned out I hadn't? That I spent my whole life too worried that I was going to have to run out into the desert and be a prophet to form attachments, and now I was in deep, serious, committed love with an actual angel? It was all too much, so I just made a joke. "Well, you know what you said about eggs after 35."

"I know, I know, but I just want to make sure you're making the right decision here. How well do you really know this guy, after, what, six months?"

"Eight months." Had it really only been eight months?

"Eight months is not a long time, sweetie."

"I know, Mom. But just... Please trust me. Sometimes things just fit together."

"I bet things fit together *real* well."

"Mom!"

"Sorry, honey. I'm just so happy for you."

"I'm happy for me too." It felt weird to say it, but it was true.

"But you should really be the one to tell God."

"Mom!"

"What? He hasn't heard from you in forever."

"It's just... it's not that simple, okay?"

"What is it?"

"Well, it's just. It's not exactly that I met a guy."

"What do you mean? Is this one of those new gender things?"

"No— I mean. Not exactly—" the angel was looking up from the stewed eggplant to give me a confused expression, "It's not *not* that, but it's more that—they're not really—"

"Anat. It's okay. Take a deep breath and tell me."

"They're not really a guy. They're not really a human at all. They're an angel."

"Oh, honey. That's so sweet of you to—"

"Mom. I mean it literally. They're literally an angel."

...

"Mom? Are you there?"

"Anat. No jokes."

"It's not a joke."

"Do you really think that this is a good idea?"

"I mean, I know that there were—I know. I know. But I really love them. And they really love me. And it just feels *right*."

"Okay. But, Anat, you have to tell Him."

"Mom! You promised!"

"Look. Honey. I know. I know it's hard. But He should hear it from you. And I think He might surprise you."

"You think he might surprise me? Mom, the last time this happened He literally flooded the entire world."

"That's from the Book of Enoch! It's apocryphal!"

"That doesn't mean it didn't happen!"

"Even if it did, honey. This is different."

"Is it?"

"Well, Anat. I don't know. Are you going to use this baby into a weapon?"

"What?"

"Are you?"

"Of course not!"

"Because that's what happened last time."

"Mom..."

"Are you going to start a cult with her? Are you going to sacrifice her? Are you going to treat her like she's anything less than human?"

"No! Mom!"

"Because if you're worried about what happened last time—"

"That's not what I meant."

"You're going to love this baby?"

"Yes!"

"Then it's different than last time. If 'last time' even happened."

"Still... He told me not to."

"He tells lots of people not to do lots of things. And most of us do them anyway."

"Still."

"Plus, He likes you. You're friends. And He trusts you."

"Mom, I just don't know if I can—"

"You can. You're just scared. And that's okay. You have to tell Him, though. I love you. But I'm not that one you should be talking to."

"Mom—"

"I'm hanging up now. I love you. Your father says hi."

I looked at my phone. I looked over at the angel, who was busy wrestling with the dutch oven. I reached out and opened my contacts, scrolled down until I found His Name.

I squeezed my eyes closed. I could hear the rain outside; beating gentle and arhythmic against the window. I reached out and made the call.

. . . .

P. H. Lee lives on top of an old walnut tree, past a thicket of roses, down a dead end street at the edge of town. Their work has appeared in many venues including *Clarkesworld*, *Lightspeed*, and *Uncanny Magazine*. From time to time, they microwave and eat a frozen burrito at two in the morning, for no reason other than that they want to.

COLORS OF THE IMMORTAL PALETTE

Caroline M. Yoachim

LEAD WHITE

I will always remember the view of Paris from his window. Snow, pure and untouched, softens the outline of the buildings and covers the grime of the streets. White, the color of beginnings. His canvas is primed and ready to be painted, and stark winter sunlight glows bright on his undead skin.

The studio is cramped, drafty despite the heat radiating from the stove. One corner is clean and lavishly decorated, the rest a cluttered chaos of painting supplies and personal effects. He studies me intently as I take in the room, evaluating me much as he did at the Café Guerbois when I'd first caught his eye.

I wait for him to ask how I came to be in Paris. Artists are so very predictable that way—no trouble at all accepting this pale immortal creature as one of their own, but a woman of my mixed ancestry? Utterly implausible.

"You should hear the stories they tell of you at the café," he says. "If Émile is to be believed, you arrived here as a ukiyo-e courtesan, nothing more than paper wrapped around a porcelain bowl. A painter—he will not say which of us it was, of course—bought the bowl and the print along with it."

"And the painter pulled me from the print with the sheer force of his imagination, I'm sure," I reply, laughing. "Émile is a novelist and can hardly be trusted to give an accurate account. The reality of my conception is vastly more mundane, I assure you... though it does involve a courtesan."

"A grain of truth makes for the best fiction." He waves his hand at a worn-looking dressing screen. "Nude, but leave the jewelry and the shoes. I'll paint you on the chaise. We'll have three hours in the proper light, and I will pay you four francs."

"Victorine gets five!" I protest from behind the screen as I get undressed.

"Victorine is a redhead."

I step out from behind the screen and go to the chaise, running my fingers along the elegant curves of the walnut frame. The cushions are firm and covered in soft green velvet. I arrange myself carefully. Hopefully he will like what he sees. Often what the artists demand is a relaxed-*looking* pose that is hideously uncomfortable. Like novelists, they require only a grain of truth. The rest is purely of their own creation.

"My name is Mariko, by the way, but everyone calls me Mari." As if I could pass for a French girl simply by changing my name. Though, particularly with the artists, there is a fascination with all things Japanese. Several of Hokusai's views of Mount Fuji decorate the wall behind me, the ukiyo-e prints crammed together with neoclassical portraits and a few realist landscapes of the Barbizon School.

He remains facing the window, his attention fixed on the snowy landscape.

"I'm on the chaise," I tell him, and finally he turns.

"Bring your left hip forward. No, not that far. Bend the leg a bit more, yes." He paces back and forth, frowning. "Turn your head to face the canvas."

I smile knowingly. "Like a Manet."

His frown deepens into a scowl.

"Don't like a model that talks while you work, huh?" I've posed for that type before, honestly not my favorite sort of job, there to be seen and not heard. If the artist is talented enough I can still pick up a technique or two watching them work, but—

"I don't like being compared to other artists."

I laugh. More of an ego than usual, this one. Though perhaps he's earned it. If Victorine was to be believed, he's been painting since the Renaissance. "Then you must paint me so well that I forget about the others."

"Tilt your head into the light." His voice is softer now, and he steps forward to cup my chin, shifting the angle of my head ever so slightly to refine the pose. "And look at me intently. Intensely. As though I were the one naked on the chaise."

His touch sends shivers down my spine. It feels as if he is reaching into me, beyond the surface of my skin. Intimate. I'm not above a dalliance with an artist if he pleases my eye, or if I need the money or a place to stay... but this one is different.

His eyes are as dark as the Seine at night, darker even than my own. I'm laid bare before him in more ways than my mere lack of clothing. The canvas is reflected in the window behind him, and he is painting me in deft strokes of vivid color—as other artists have done before him—but this time the image holds the promise of an understanding. His skill with the paint is breathtaking; his movements simultaneously wild and precise.

It is exhilarating to watch him work.

My back aches and one leg is going numb, but I'm disappointed when he sets down his brush.

"You did better than I would have expected."

"Oh?" I stretch and, still nude, go to take a closer look at the canvas. Even with the work unfinished, I can see that he is more talented than any of the other artists I've known, and his intensity sparks my interest, draws me almost inevitably closer. "There are other poses I could show you, if you like?"

"Hmmm...?" His gaze is fixed on the canvas, studying a streak of bright winter sunlight that cuts across the upper corner.

I'm about to give him up as hopeless when he turns to look at me. I'm lost in the darkness of his eyes, drowning in the intensity of his attention. I can barely breathe, but I repeat my invitation, "I could show you other poses."

"Yes." He sweeps me into an embrace that is strong and cold. White. He is snow and I am determined to melt it.

The sex builds slowly, deliberately, like paint layered on a canvas in broad strokes—tentative at first as we find our way to a shared vision, then faster with a furious intensity and passion.

After, when other artists might hold me and drift off to sleep, he dissipates into a white mist that swirls in restless circles around the room, chilling me down to the bones when it touches my skin. His mist seeps into me and pulses through my veins for several heartbeats. I feel energized, an exhilaration more intense than watching him work, a connection closer even than our sex.

He withdraws, and I am diminished. I hadn't known until this moment what I was lacking, but now I am filled with a keen sense of my incompleteness. I long for him, for the sensation of vastness I felt when we were one.

He does not return to the bed.

I sleep alone and wake to windows white with frost.

VIRIDIAN GREEN

The park is vibrant green with budding leaves and delicate spring grass. Birds are singing, the sun is shining, and my lover sets up his canvas on an easel in the shade.

"Must we really have those other girls?" I ask.

"You on your own isn't enough for a picnic," he answers.

"I used to be enough, all on my own." I sound like a sullen child. I'm tempted to tell him that for composition's sake he should have *more* models, some of whom should stand to balance out the towering height of the trees, or that the setting he's chosen bears too strong a resemblance to Monet's *Le Déjeuner sur l'herbe*, which was in turn inspired by Manet's notorious painting of the same title...but instead I bite my lower lip.

"I'll let you sit in front," he says. "And I'll take you to the Louvre afterwards."

I sit at the edge of the white picnic blanket, taking great care to crease my skirt at an awkward angle. I open the book that I have brought—*Orgueil et Prévention*—and I cannot help but marvel at the degree to which Mr. Darcy resembles my immortal artist. I shall have to ask sometime if he's ever made Austen's acquaintance, though if I recall correctly from his occasional ramblings on history he'd spent most of the relevant time period in Verona, trying to hide both himself and his paintings from Napoleon's army. Or was it Venice? I have such difficulty keeping it all straight, I truly do not know how he is able to recall several lifetimes worth of memories.

The three models he's hired are chattering incessantly about the latest fashions—tassels and bustles, hemlines and hats. The three of them have no opinions of their own and are simply parroting some column from *Harper's Bazaar*, as if Americans knew anything about fashion beyond having the good sense to look to Paris for guidance. They mock my choice of reading material and attribute the poor taste in literature to my being Portuguese, and I do not bother to correct them. They will shun me as an outsider regardless, and I have no desire to make friends with such insipid tarts.

"Suzette, lean in towards Claire, yes, better." He paints a few strokes and then strides over to where I am sitting to fix the hem of my dress so it drapes more gracefully. He gives me a pointed look. I return his silent rebuke with a look that is halfway between 'apologetic' and 'fuck you for inviting these other girls'. That might seem like a big range, but as a model I've learned to do a lot with my expression.

He laughs, and goes back to his canvas without taking away my book—though my reading it will render my pose too similar to a painting of Morisot's depicting her sister—and these wretched girls make it hard to focus on the text. One of them complains that there are ants in the grass, and another that being in direct sunlight will burn her glorious fair skin. I try not to grit my teeth. I'm supposed to have a serene smile, as if this was a delightful picnic with friends. Self-absorbed shallow friends that I have never met before and who will not leave off of talking so that I might read my book in peace.

Now the third has joined the first two in their complaining. He is quite clearly not painting their faces right now or he would tell them not to move their mouths, which would be dearly welcome.

"And honestly why wouldn't you try," the least irritating of the three is saying. "After all, youth is fleeting if you're mortal, but if you can get someone like him to turn you—" She waves her hand in the general direction of the canvas.

"Keep your hand on the blanket," he says, not responding to her words.

"He doesn't turn models," one of the other women says. "That one's been at it for over a year now and if he won't even turn her—"

"I'm right here, and I have a name," I say. I turn the slightest fraction in the direction of the irritating woman before I catch myself.

"Don't move your head," he tells me.

"Wouldn't it be glorious to be young forever?" asks the woman who had declared her own fair skin glorious and I wonder if she even knows any other words.

She's wrong, anyway. Contrary to what everyone assumes, I have never asked him to turn me. Not yet, not yet. I do not want to die into being forever young. If he turns me now, it will be so that I remain a beautiful object to adorn his canvas, and I have grander goals.

"Keep your expression soft," he says.

Only then do I realize that I am scowling down at my book.

"Wonderful, Suzette," he adds.

Suzette is younger than I am and has a classic Western beauty. Wonderful, Suzette. Wonderful Suzette. What will happen when I am too old to be his model?

He remains forever fascinated with youth, and rarely paints women beyond a certain age.

I do not want to be the art, I want to be the artist. There are women who manage to do both, yet I hear them so often described as models who paint—and this despite the fact that their talent far outstrips the men... who sometimes do appear in each other's paintings, but never once do you hear *them* categorized as models. No. They are painters who did each other tribute and documented each other's lives in masterful works of art.

Think of the time I would have to develop my art if he makes me immortal. So many of my hours are lost holding perfectly still to be immortalized as an object in someone else's paintings. I want it desperately, the gift of so much time. But when to do it, that is the trick. Eventually he will lose interest and cast me aside, but if I die into immortality now I will be horridly young. Not to mention the question of children, which I do not believe I want, but I am reluctant to give up the option.

Suzette laughs, but I have lost the thread of their conversation so I do not know why.

What if I have missed my moment? If his fancy turns to this woman with her *glorious* fair skin glowing like a diamond against her emerald green dress, where will that leave me?

By mid-afternoon I am hot and hungry and his attention is fixed only on his work, on capturing the grass and the grapes and the girls. I can smell the fruit practically baking in the afternoon sun, but I am determined not to move or even complain. I do not even turn the pages of my book, reading the same ballroom dance on an endless loop, angrier each time that the Bennet sisters are having a lovely time dancing while I am sitting. in. the. sun. not. moving.

"Take me to dinner when we're done?" Suzette asks him boldly out of nowhere.

I hold my breath.

"Oh, I'm done with your part now, you can go," he answers, not looking up from the canvas. "All of you can go, I have what I need from you."

Suzette flounces off, the other two models following her at a distance, giggling.

I let out a soft sigh of relief when they are gone.

"I'm doing the trees now, and then after that the bowl of fruit, so you can go with them if you like," he says.

"But what about the Louvre?" I demand.

"Another time," he says. "I have to finish this before I lose the light."

His promises are a perpetual first day of spring—like daffodils that remain forever buds.

CHROME YELLOW

I have no trouble convincing Louis to take me to the Salon. He is both a painter and a critic, and *unlike a certain other artist with whom I have parted ways*, he showers me with attention and treats me as a person rather than merely an exotic object to be painted. We are quickly separated in the jostling crowd, for as usual half of Paris has turned out to gawk at the paintings which hang from floor to ceiling.

The immortal artist—and yes, I am sufficiently petty not to name him even now, for his artistic legacy does not need more help from me than I have already given—is here at the Salon, of course, though I am pleased to note that despite him having taken part in perhaps a hundred Salons, the hanging committee has placed his work poorly. Not at the ceiling, quite, but high enough to strain the neck should anyone wish an extended viewing.

"I was quite fond of Naples yellow," he says, speaking loudly to some potential patron over the general buzz of the crowd. "The paints now are so exuberant, which has its place of course, but there's a subtlety to the older pigment, and I do sometimes miss the ritual of mixing it myself."

His words trail off as I approach. Perhaps it is only my imagination, but for a moment his edges blur, as though he is fading into mist. Even the merest suggestion of it makes me ache with longing. He was stealing away my life, but in those moments, in that process of the taking, I felt so complete. And who hasn't chosen, at one time or another, to do what feels good in the moment, even knowing that they might live longer if they were more virtuous?

"Mari," he says. Only the name, nothing more.

The painting that hangs behind him is titled *Woman, Reclining (Mari)*. Being familiar with his other works, I know that the reason my name appears in the title (shortened and in parentheses) is not because he believes my name is in any way important to the piece, but merely that he has many other works that bear the title *Woman, Reclining*.

I study the woman on the chaise, illuminated by the bright winter light streaming in through the window. The painting captures things about me that other artists have missed. There is a wry expression on my face and a bold invitation in my eyes.

He has changed the decor of the room. Gone are the eclectic mix of ukiyo-e prints and neoclassical portraits that would have been the perfect background for a woman of my parentage. Instead he's created miniature renditions of his own paintings from the past several decades. The entire composition is a collection of his work, and my form is but a piece in this collection.

"What do you think of it?" he asks.

I shrug, knowing full well that his question is a bid for my approval and my indifference will infuriate him.

"I've captured you so beautifully, and your response is to shrug?" He knows that I am baiting him, and his voice is light, but he cannot keep his face from falling.

"Yes, I should be so very honored, to appear here in the Salon," I say, unable to match his lightness. "Naked, no less."

"Ah, so that is it then," he says. "You had another painting refused. This is the third time?"

"The fourth." I'd thought to hide that unpleasant fact from him, but he was, as ever, a keen observer. "My style is not so rigidly traditional as to please the jury. And I—"

"—have a great deal of company." At some point during our conversation Louis has jostled his way through the crowd to join us. He catches my dismayed expression and hastily adds, "But your work is far better than that of the others who have been refused, of course—"

"This is Louis." I interrupt him to make the introduction before he can start ranting about the failings of other painters. "He writes for *Le Charivari* and, as you have heard, he appreciates me for my art and not only for my looks."

"Good."

With that one word it is now *his* indifference that infuriates *me*.

"My latest attempt at pleasing the jury was a harvest scene of two women working in a field, deep in conversation—"

"Which against my advice you signed only as Mari," Louis interjects. "You should sign with your surname if you want the jury to take you seriously."

"My father's name has no place on the art he so thoroughly disapproves of. Besides, it would be too similar to Camille's signature, and you've seen how everyone confuses Manet and Monet."

Louis opens his mouth to argue, then thinks better of it. Instead he starts ranting about Monet, and neither he nor my immortal artist notices when I leave. Half the reason I had asked Louis here to begin with was to make my immortal artist jealous, and he does not seem to care.

I am invisible, even as my naked form hangs upon the wall. As a model I am a footnote in the story of the artist, and as a painter I cannot win over the Salon jury. What I want most of all is to be remembered, but I cannot even manage to be seen.

VERMILLION

"Surely he will change his mind and paint you again?" I'm sitting with Victorine at the Café Guerbois, nursing my coffee as she sips absinthe. It is Thursday, and Manet is here, presiding over his Batignolles group—this is no coincidence, of course, for I am familiar with their usual schedule... and, having parted ways with Louis, I could use the work. The smoke-filled air inside the café still holds the day's heat, and by all appearances the discussion at Manet's table is similarly heated.

Victorine gives a bit of a shrug. "Perhaps. And what of your vampire friend?"

My eyes widen. "Victorine! You must not call him that. People will think he drinks blood."

"As you like," Victorine replies, "but that doesn't answer my question."

"I want to be the artist, not the art. Surely you of all people understand." I take a sip of coffee and try to hold back my jealousy that she is taking art classes at the Académie Julian.

"You and I," she says, "do not have the advantages afforded to women of means and social standing. Morisot and Cassatt need not give music lessons or pose nude to pay for paint. Surely *you* of all people understand *that*."

 I bristle at her tone but the observation is true enough. Worse, a young woman with fine features and a striking green hat has entered the café and captured the attention of the Batignolles group. Renoir in particular seems quite taken with the girl, who looks not a day over fifteen.

"What you need," Victorine continues, paying little mind to the new arrival, "is to make a connection with an art dealer. You've had no success at the Salon, but Paul Durand-Ruel has had some success selling paintings in America, where the tastes are less refined."

"What a horrid thing to say!"

Unrefined. My paintings? I should stay in hopes of getting work but I cannot bring myself to spend a moment more in her company. I storm out of the café, my mind churning with accumulated insults. Victorine's barbs, the indifference of the painters I had hoped to charm, the deplorable youth of the woman in the green hat.

The heat rising from the cobblestones makes the world shimmer, as though the air itself is melting. It reminds me of all the times my immortal artist turned to mist and everything around us melted away. I crave the cold white snow of that first winter, the thrill of his embrace.

I am on his street before I have even truly decided to see him, and I knock upon his door quickly, before I lose my courage.

He is there, and Suzette is not, thank God.

"I wanted..." I trail off into silence because I am not entirely sure what I want, and I am even less sure that he is the one who can bestow it. Recognition? Respect? A way to be seen as more than an exotic courtesan who graces the canvas of painters.

"Time," he says.

He is staring at me, dissecting me not into shapes and angles or light and shadow but deconstructing my ambitions and my dreams, seeing a pattern that I cannot because once, centuries ago, he was not entirely unlike me. A mortal artist, striving for something greater, grasping without knowing what it was he sought.

"Time?" I echo weakly.

"Where were you, before you came here?"

"At the Café Guerbois," I admit.

"Trying to secure work from Manet and his lackeys, no doubt." He scowls at the mere thought of Manet, which I find rather heartening, that even he, my immortal artist, is jealous of his rivals.

"I need money for paint," I tell him.

"Ah, and now we are back to time again," he says. "Immortality is, obviously, all about time. When you come right down to it, time is the thing that everyone most values, even you mortals who have so little of it. You simply shift it around instead of trading it directly. Three hours of work for five francs, which then can be used to buy paint.

"An art collector is hoarding time. Time spent by the artist applying paint to the canvas, yes. But there is more to it than that. Each successive painting contains something of the time that went into all the previous canvases, not to mention the time spent studying, practicing. And the art holds other time as well—the model that sits for the painting, holding a pose for hours on end. Time that she has devoted, perhaps, to keeping a certain figure, or creating an appealing hairstyle."

I scowl. "Time spent building the resentment that burns in the model's eyes as she glares at the painter."

He tilts his head, thoughtful. "Perhaps."

"The other girls say you have never turned anyone." The words slip out before I can stop them, my heart racing, knowing the conversation is in dangerous territory now, territory that I have always scrupulously avoided. "They say that you drain away your models' lives and leave them with nothing. That all you care about is light and paint."

"Light and paint. Legacy and time." He leans in so close that I can feel his breath against my ear as he speaks. "You have a good eye for light, and with time you could master the rest."

"No one tells Jean that he has not mastered the rest, or Jules. People praise them for work that is nowhere near what I do." I gesture at his wall, largely covered with the works of his fellow Frenchmen, paintings ranging from brilliant to mediocre. There is a sunspot on the back of my hand, a single dark freckle that I had never noticed before.

"Time," I whisper.

"I cannot give you everything you want," he admits. "But I can give you time."

This. This is why I have always been so careful to avoid this conversation. I have always known that he would offer. And that I would accept.

"Yes."

He dissolves into mist and seeps through my skin. It is different than it always was before. His impressions of the world are mine to take, not mere glimmers at the edge of my perception but a clear vision of his entire being, like slipping into a photograph that holds his centuries of experience, living through a lifetime in an instant. Everything I have thirsted for since our first meeting—knowingly and not—all of it is here in this moment of connection. I am complete as I can only be when he is with me, and I absorb all that I can, drinking from him as deeply as I dare, taking him into myself and pulsing with the sheer power of it.

There are but wisps of white mist remaining when I realize that I must let him go. When he withdraws he does not steal a part of me, as he always has before. Instead he leaves behind what I have taken.

He has given me the gift of time.

Energy courses through me like a vermillion flame. I am no longer a mere model from whom he draws inspiration, but an artist, immortal. Time stretches out before me and I long to take him to bed that both of us might burn hot with passion.

But he has vanished, just as he did that first night, winter white and cold. As he always does when I most crave his presence.

I wait the entire night, but he does not return.

COBALT BLUE

I paint the English Channel at Étretat, shortly after sunrise. The sun is a fiery vermillion and the water shimmers cobalt blue. It is roughly my hundredth impression of a sunrise, spread across the year on whatever days I can gather up the energy to greet the dawn with my easel at the shore.

I have painted skies both cloudy and clear, water in a variety of hues. When the tide permits I paint from the beach and include the white cliffs, and when the tide is high—as it is today—I paint the vast expanse of the channel from atop them. Sometimes the dark silhouettes of ships break the line of the horizon, and sometimes there is fog, a thin white mist that gives me shivers not entirely accounted for by the crisp morning air. Monet set off a movement with his *Impression, Sunrise*, painted not far south of here. Monet, and before that Manet, changing the world of art forever. Or so the historians like to spin the tale, imposing order onto the chaotic jumble of the past, pulling a single narrative thread from the fabric of time. Providing a focal point, like the bright orange sun that hovers above the water. And their focal point, of course, must always be a man.

"You could have painted a hundred portraits of me, and instead you paint the sunrise." Victorine has come up the trail behind me, carrying her own easel which she sets up next to mine. Her hair is like the sunrise reflected on the water, vermillion streaked with silver. She arrived here last week, at my invitation.

"Manet painted the definitive portrait of you years ago," I say, teasing.

"And Monet painted the definitive impressionist sunrise," Victorine replies, "Yet you seem to have no issue painting those. Besides, *I* painted the definitive picture of me. They showed it at the Salon. Honestly it is unfair that you should be immortal and I am not. Clearly I am the one with all the talent."

Her voice takes on an edge of bitterness as she says it, cobalt blue tinged green, like the underside of a wave in the bright light of a midday sun.

"I would turn you if I could." I hadn't known how precious the gift was that my immortal artist gave me, or how rare—he had gathered time for all the centuries of his existence, and even so had only barely enough to share his gift with me. The process had nearly destroyed him, leaving him unable to take any form but mist for over a year.

"Then paint me," she says. "Give me that at least."

I cannot paint her without stealing precious moments of her time, and I cannot bear to lose my oldest friend. She is already slipping away so fast.

"Please," she says. "Just this once."

I let her convince me because in my heart of hearts I long to paint her. I direct her to an outcropping of rock and have her look out over the water, her face glowing in the morning light. Her dress is a pale blue, the perfect contrast for the orange-streaked sky, and, of course, her hair.

The wind has freed a lock of it and when I go to pin it back in place the edges of my hands thin into mist and I can feel her energy, the wildness only barely contained beneath her skin. Where my immortal artist was cold and white, she is a fiery vermillion, and this neatly composed painting is entirely wrong.

"Let your hair loose in the wind, and take off your hat." I tell her, my fingers still brushing against her face, the tiniest sliver of my hands still within her, our energies pulsing together, her passions tempting me to drink deeper, to take more of what she unknowingly offers. So sweet and heady, this sensation of pulling her out of herself.

I force myself to withdraw and she gasps.

She stares off into the distance and for a moment I am not sure if she heard my request.

"Is that always what it's like?" she asks. "The thrill and then the loss."

"Yes."

Victorine removes her hat and takes down her hair, then tousles it—carefully but with a result that looks careless. The hat she lets dangle from her hand. Everything about it is exquisite, and I paint in frantic dabs of color to capture it before we lose the light. Victorine holds her pose flawlessly, and I know from experience how difficult it is to stand so long, especially in the sun. I highlight the graceful curve of her shoulder, the determined set of her jaw.

I have always signed my paintings Mari, but this painting of Victorine captures her with such honesty that on impulse I sign this one with a name I have not used since my mother died—Mariko. In red as a nod to tradition, but spelled out in the French alphabet for I do not trust my ability to write the kanji even for my own name. That, too, is honest—an admission that I am of neither world and of both.

"This is your best work so far," Victorine says, admiring the painting. "We can go in turns—you shall paint me and I shall paint you. It will be a series of a hundred portraits and historians will speculate about—"

"No, I cannot. Never again." I know the longing she feels. It was cruel of me to paint her. Cruel of me to invite her here, to ease the loneliness of being fixed in time as the world keeps passing on. And in truth, I hunger for her as much as she does for me, for the taste of her humanity. I can feel my fingertips thinning into mist, reaching out for her... but no. Already her life flits away far too fast, and I will not speed her to her grave for the sake of my art. I will find another way.

"I cannot stay, knowing what I will not have."

"Take the portrait, if you like." I turn away from her and look out over the English Channel, pretending that I don't care what she chooses.

She leaves without another word. She doesn't take the painting. The water stretches out before me, an endless chasm of blue.

CADMIUM YELLOW

My work is on display at the Art Institute of Chicago, thrilling for the venue but disappointing for the exhibit—Cassatt merits an exhibition composed entirely of her own work, but I am tucked away in *European and Oriental Art*. Still, they have invited me to the opening, and I have done my best to look fashionable though I cannot pull off the yellows that are quite popular this season and the angular lines of flapper dresses are better suited to women who are straight where I am rounded. Never have I paid so much for so very little fabric, though I must admit the beadwork is lovely and the freedom of movement compared to the dresses of my youth is divine.

The exhibit is laid out so that I must walk through the European artists in order to reach my own work, and I am startled to encounter a painting with which I am intimately familiar—*Woman, Reclining (Mari)*. It is, to my surprise, exactly as I remember it from the Salon. By now the varnish should have darkened and the yellows should have shifted brown, for he had favored the cheaper chrome yellow during that period.

"I had them restore it." He has appeared from nowhere. Like the painting, he is exactly as I remember from our last meeting—only his clothing has changed. "It seemed fitting, given the subject. An unchanging painting of an unchanging model."

He means it as a compliment, but I am half a human lifetime away from being the woman that graces his canvas, and no longer mortal. To imply that I am static and unchanging simply because I do not physically age... I had thought him more insightful than that.

"I'm surprised to see you here," he says.

"And I you." I'm flooded with emotions. Surprise, yes, and also a longing that I thought I'd put behind me, that old familiar yearning to connect with him, to let our energies flow together and feel the pulse of time itself. But I pity him, too, because for all his success as a painter, he is not keeping up with the world, and his popularity is fading. If he cannot come up with something new, he will be swept into the past as a historical footnote, or perhaps be forgotten entirely. "What are the odds that we would finally be in the same exhibit, after all these decades?"

He shakes his head. "What I meant was why Chicago? Why not San Francisco or Seattle? You could blend in there."

"The handful of Japanese living in Chicago are a curiosity, like kimonos displayed in a department store. People aren't as hostile to me here as they might be on the West Coast because they do not see me as a threat. I've taken up correspondence with a young artist there—Chiura Obata, who is doing some promising work—and he says resentment for the Japanese community there is building. Besides, it isn't my intention to blend in. I want to be remembered."

There are three of his paintings in the exhibit, and the other two both feature Suzette. Time has not been kind to these. The thick strokes of paint are cracking, darkened in places with grime, faded in others from light.

"Yes, but you want to be remembered for your art. Being so out of place will only distract people from your paintings—"

"And yet you are also here, some 300 years older than everyone else." I tire of looking at Suzette, indeed I tire of looking at his paintings at all. I drift deeper into the exhibit as we continue our conversation, searching for my own work. It is quieter here, away from the growing crowd of patrons who have not yet made their way this far in. "Why must I blend in when you do not? Why is your story so much easier for them to accept than mine?

"They can see themselves in me. Envision themselves as immortal. I am what they wish to become. You are the foreigner they fear. The outsider."

"And a woman besides," I mutter. "If I don't carve out space for myself, they will steal whatever inspiration they like from my culture and my art and erase me from the conversation entirely."

There is only one of my paintings on display, which I had been excited about before I'd known that they had three of his. My sole piece in the exhibition is the painting of Victorine, standing on the rocky shore, surrounded by the cobalt blue of sky and ocean, and seeing it I am filled with sadness.

"Have you seen her lately?" he asks. "Victorine, I mean."

"Not for many years, though she writes me letters occasionally."

"She must be very old now, yes?" he says. "She and Monet are the last of your mortal cohort. It is easier to bear after that, the fleeting nature of the lives around us."

His expression is sad and I wonder about *his* mortal cohort, the people he had known when he was still alive. He never speaks of them, which I thought was for lack of memory but perhaps he is trying to avoid the pain of his loss. I put a hand on his shoulder, cold against cold. When he does not speak further on the subject, I turn my attention back to the exhibit.

The curators have opted to hang my painting at the transition point, the very edge of the European artists, for though I am French—or was, at the time of the painting—they clearly do not see me as having been truly European. Worse, they have placed my painting alongside two others, not a trio of my own work but with a pair of paintings that share the same model—Victorine's self-portrait... and Manet's *Olympia*, which bears more resemblance to *Woman, Reclining (Mari)* than it does to Victorine.

"Of the three of you," my immortal artist says, "Manet has captured her the most realistically."

Of course he would think so, for he sees the world through the same male gaze that Édouard once did, antiquated and narrow, dismissive of women. To him, Victorine was a model and a prostitute, elevated only by her inclusion in Manet's painting. And I was similarly unchanging in his view, an object to be painted.

"All three paintings have elements of truth and falsehood," I argue, "for each artist comes to the canvas with our own artistic vision and personal biases. How we wish for the audience to view the subject, the context in which we are working, the details we choose to include. And what is truth, anyway? We cannot capture the entirety of a person's life on a flat piece of canvas. No matter how skilled the painter there are only hints—suggestions which the viewer of the painting will fill in with whatever it is that *they* believe..."

I cannot quite articulate what I want to say, perhaps that there is no underlying truth at all, only a myriad of perceptions, each slightly different from the rest.

"Yes," he agrees, "that is exactly what you are missing, the ability to draw upon the perspective of the viewer, to give them an experience that is both familiar and new, to evoke in them a shared experience. That is the thing you must learn—to depict the universal truths."

"Your truths are universal but mine are not." I say, and he nods as though I am agreeing with him. "I've lived in two countries that do not consider me one of their own, and the lesson I've learned is that *I* must adapt, that *I* must learn to act as other people do. I did it as a young girl in the French countryside, and again when I came here. They will not make allowances for me as they have done for you—I am not permitted your eccentricities. I must behave as they expect, always, flawlessly."

"You say the right words, but you don't believe them," he says. "You are fighting the inevitable, the world is what it is, and you are who you are. It cannot be helped."

"But the world can change. It has changed. And so have I. You're the one fighting the inevitable, not me."

"There's no audience for what you do, this blend of styles and inspirations and...perspectives," he says, convinced that he can sway me to his way of thinking if only he can find the right words, the proper argument. "It's too complicated, muddled—like mixing too many colors, overworking the paint."

"When other impressionists were influenced by Japanese art there was an audience for that. Monet, even now, is painting a grand mural of his beloved water lilies, in a garden inspired by Japan."

"Monet's paintings are relatable."

Relatable. Monet filters the world through a background that these art patrons understand. European. Male. He is relatable in ways that I will never be. My mere existence requires an explanation—how is it a woman like me came to be in France, why am I in Chicago and not San Francisco? If the story of my life focuses on the art it will be rejected as implausible, but if I pause to explain the truths of my existence the story is no longer universal.

Patrons and donors file past, many of them stopping to stare at Manet's painting, which is here on loan from the Louvre. It remains provocative even now, though there is less scorn and more admiration in the bits of conversation I catch. They barely glance at Victorine's self-portrait, or at my own painting.

None of these mortals has ever met Victorine, so the truth of the depiction matters to them very little. They only experience the art, whatever it might convey, and their attention is drawn to a naked form, a confrontational stare, a famous artist's name.

I don't need to capture the truth of my subject, I need to capture the attention of a broader audience, convey a deeper underlying truth... and I do not know how.

ULTRAMARINE

It's a cold March afternoon in 1927 when a Western Union courier hands me the small yellow envelope of a telegram. It comes from a woman I've never met, though Victorine often mentioned her in letters. It bears sad news that I have known for quite some time was coming.

I had planned to paint the sunset from the shore of Lake Michigan today, so I force myself to go out with my easel, but the colors are wrong. Rosy pastels streak the sky above the water. Some other night I might have found it beautiful, but tonight I cannot think of anything but vermillion, and I let the light fade to the deepest blue without so much as opening a tube of paint.

The world has been a week without her in it, but her death did not become a truth for me until the telegram arrived. She is the last. Even Monet has ceased his endless paintings of water lilies, having passed in December. I've not seen either of them for decades, but tonight I feel the loss as keenly as if I'd sat with them yesterday, all of us gathered at the Café Guerbois, Victorine and I engaging the men in passionate discussions on the purpose of art, the role of the model, and whether critical outrage was an attack on the honor of the painter, this last being a topic that always irritated Manet.

They were my cohort—Édouard, Émile, Claude, Paul and Camille, and of course Victorine. I met them not knowing that I would outlive them, and without having the distance that knowledge brings. My immortal artist was right—I don't get quite so close to mortals now, I no longer see myself as one of them. But I'm accustomed to navigating a world I do not feel a part of, a place where I am unlike all the others. This has always been my truth.

I sit all night beside my canvas, a lonely vigil for the last of my cohort. The sunrise is reflected on the square windows of the city skyline. It's a fitting tribute. My memories of her life are fragmented as if by steel and concrete, everything but the fiery window-glass moments are lost to the passage of time.

I cannot paint the sunrise. Vermillion is her color and she is gone.

If my immortal artist is to be believed, I will grow accustomed to this. The pain that burns sharp within my chest will fade to a dull ache, not just for Victorine but for all mortals. Their passing will be easier when their lifetimes are but the merest fraction of my own. I will never share the length of history with them that I do with my immortal artist, and by comparison the loss of such shallow relationships will seem trivial. Or so he says. He is an ass, of course, and making excuses for his own inability to connect with those around him.

But the fact that he is an ass doesn't mean that he is always wrong. Those things he'd said at the Art Institute, what if all of it is true? Maybe my perspective is muddled with too many influences, perhaps I have failed to synthesize such disparate parts into a cohesive whole. Maybe the failing is in my execution.

I have outlived my friends, my colleagues, and for what? All my paintings combined have not garnered the renown of *Olympia* or *Impression, Sunrise*. I am best known as the model from *Woman, Reclining (Mari)*, and maybe my lack of success is not—as I have always told myself—because I am a woman and an outsider, but because I am lacking in talent.

Even being immortal, which should be simple enough, is a task that I am failing for I cannot bear the thought of stealing time from mortals whose lives are already so fleeting. I take just enough here and there from models—always with their consent—to maintain a human form, but if I cannot create beauty, cannot leave my mark on the world of art, their time is wasted, and nothing is so precious as time.

I've never done a self-portrait, but I am determined to purge these wretched truths. I paint the portrait and quite literally put myself into the work, thinning my fingertips into mist and leaving a sliver of my very being in the darkest shadows of ultramarine. I create the portrait in shades of blue, abstract and dark, shadows overpowering the light. I call the painting *Futility*, and I do not sign my name because despair is never done, it is unending and can never be complete. Critics will no doubt call it a feeble imitation of Picasso, but I cannot bring myself to care.

ALIZARIN CRIMSON

I'm still fighting the ultramarine depths of despair some fifteen years later, when I meet Joshua at the Club DeLisa. We get to talking, a fragmented conversation to fill the space between sets. He's a singer and he used to play trumpet in a swing band, up until he got caught in Chicago by wartime travel restrictions. Little Brother Montgomery and The Red Saunders Band are playing tonight, along with a comedian and some dancers.

"I love the music, but what really brings me here is the energy. It reminds me of the Café Guerbois—in Paris. I used to go there with some artist friends of mine, painters who wanted to push boundaries and create something new." There's something about him or the music or the energy of the club tonight that compels me to keep talking. "The way the musicians build on each other, changing the nature of music, it fills me with nostalgia. They have a passion that I've been missing for a long time."

He gives me a strange look. "You're one of those immortals, like Pops."

"Yes." I'd heard him play once, back in the 20s before he moved to New York. I hadn't realized he was immortal, but that did make sense of all the tall tales and inconsistencies when he talked about his childhood. I can't help but wonder who turned him.

"You must really be something special then," Joshua says. "Show me your paintings?"

"Only if you'll sing for me." I'm flirting without meaning to, leaning in close as we try to talk over the noise of the club. He has the same vibrancy the performers here have, and I long to taste him, to connect at a deeper level.

We stay late, almost until dawn, drinking beer and discussing everything from the gorgeous poems in Georgia Douglas Johnson's *An Autumn Love Cycle* to Archibald Motley's vibrant paintings of nightlife—both in Paris and here in Bronzeville. Our conversation turns to the war, and he talks about the delicate dance of supporting the war efforts while simultaneously pushing for civil rights for Black folks here at home; the Pittsburgh Courier was calling it "the Double V Campaign." At some point he mentions the Japanese internment camps, and we both go quiet for a moment.

"Must be hard," he says, "having family on both sides of the war."

"Honestly I've always felt more French than anything else. But I'm defined by what other people see, not by who I am. I have so little connection to Japan—to me it is courtesans in a ukiyo-e, brightly colored kimonos in Paris shops, faint memories of warabe uta my mother sang for me a long long time ago. And yet I'm still the enemy."

"Tell me about it," he says, and both of us drink.

Joshua walks me home, and I invite him to come in. I haven't had anyone over in ages and there is clutter everywhere. I scoop up fabric scraps from the assorted seamstress jobs I've been doing on top of waitressing to make enough money to pay the outlandish rent—so high it's illegal under rent control but who am I to challenge the landlord? And he knows it, knows just how far he can push and get away with it. Boarding at the Eleanor Club had been cheaper *and* the shared bathrooms there were cleaner... but I couldn't bring men home with me. I sigh. There are always tradeoffs. "Sorry about the mess."

He laughs. "You don't have to—"

"I do." Not so much for the mess but because I need to shift my focus away from his delicious energy. He is too much temptation, but I can't bring myself to ask him to leave.

While I try to tidy up, he studies the art on my wall. The oldest piece is a woodblock print, *Night Scene in the Yoshiwara*, by Katsushika Ōi, one of the few tangible items I have that belonged to my mother. I wait for him to guess, incorrectly, that it is my work, but he turns his attention to a far more recent piece.

"Is this?" he asks, leaving the question unfinished.

"The Tanforan Assembly Center." I set down a handful of empty paint tubes. "Chiura Obata sent it with his last letter. Sumi on paper. I'm not sure how he managed to get it past the censors, maybe smuggled it out with one of the couriers that brings him art supplies. He's starting an art school. I don't know how he can make art in a place like that."

"Maybe the art is what saves him, the thing that keeps him from breaking. Besides, if you wait for the world to be perfect, you'll be waiting forever."

He's right, of course. There is always something—a war or a plague, a widespread catastrophe like the Great Depression or the more personal tragedy of a friend's passing. Being immortal, it is so easy to put off the work, to drift aimlessly because there is no urgency without the ultimate deadline of death. "The frustrating thing is that Chiura can make art when I cannot. That he's stronger than me even though I'm the immortal one. I'm angry about the camps but I'm not forced to live in one. I have only the most tenuous ties to Japan. My mother died more than a lifetime ago when I was young."

"After Ma died, back in '37, I couldn't..." Joshua waved his hands as he searched for the right words, "I just couldn't anything. I'd open my mouth to sing and nothing came. There was too much joy in a cheerful song and too much sorrow in a sad one. Ma sang the blues like nobody's business, taught me everything I know. She was 43 when she died and I was so angry with the world for taking her."

"I'm so sorry."

"Yeah. Well it's not about strength. Music is the thing that saves me, usually, the thing I escape to. But when Ma died, everything I tried to do reminded me of her, and the pain was still too raw."

"So what did you do?"

He laughs. "Enlisted in the National Guard. Powered through basic combat training. That's probably not going to work for you, Mariko. But mostly what I needed was time. I found my way back to music again, and you'll get back to the painting. That's where your heart is."

"How do you know, you haven't even seen my paintings—"

Then I notice what he's looking at.

Futility.

I never even tried to sell it, and I haven't finished a single painting in the decade and a half since I'd poured my depression onto the canvas in blue paint. It's a painting of my heart, and my heart is broken. The canvas isn't hung or even framed, it simply leans against the wall in the darkest corner of my apartment.

"This is amazing," he says. "Powerful."

As he studies the painting—intensely, intently—I can feel the barest shimmer of a connection, a faint suggestion of how it might feel to take a fragment of his life, and like a shark frenzied by a drop of blood in the water I am suddenly overwhelmed with need.

I draw him close and we kiss, deeply, bodies pressed together. I tremble with desire and with anguish, for I am determined that I will not consume him. "No, this is wrong, I have to stay away from mortals. You burn so bright, so briefly."

"Are you protecting us, or are you protecting yourself from the pain of losing something so fleeting? How can you paint if you refuse to live?"

"I can't," I admit.

"It's okay," he whispers, his breath hot as fire against my skin. "I want to know how it feels, how you feel. Live with me. Everything in this one moment."

I slide out of my dress. "We can have the one without the other. I've heard what people say about immortals, about stealing away people's lives with sex. That's not how it works."

"Never?" He unbuttons his shirt.

"Almost never."

We have sex in broad strokes of fiery vermillion shading into crimson, building to a deep connection, something beyond the raw intensity of our physical passion. I transform into mist at the moment of his climax and bask in his passion, his energy, his health, his life. When I withdraw, I try not to take anything with me, though I'm not sure I entirely succeed.

Unlike my immortal artist, I do not disappear into the night. I return to human form and sleep in Joshua's arms.

In the morning, I start a new painting. A Black man, talking to a woman who has her back to the viewer, both of them standing under a streetlight in front of the Club DeLisa. The streets are empty save the couple, and I paint the center of the canvas in a realist style reminiscent of Edward Hopper, but as I move out from the light into the shadows, surrealism creeps into the painting—the buildings in the background morph into barbed wire and the full moon hangs crimson in the sky.

I title the painting *Night Club* and sign it Mariko. It is both bleak and beautiful. Chiura would be proud. At Joshua's encouragement, I sell it to the Art Institute of Chicago, along with *Futility*.

Full of life and finally painting again, for three months I am the happiest I can remember being since I became immortal. Then Joshua is called to service with the 370th Infantry Regiment. He goes to a training camp in Arizona. In his last letter before he ships off to Italy, he proposes.

I accept.

ZINC WHITE

When Joshua returns from Italy, he brings me a gift. An enemy parachute, salvaged by a fellow soldier. He'd traded some cigarettes and a pair of wool socks from one of my care packages to get it. There are twenty panels of useable silk in the canopy once I've discarded the burnt bits. The material is thin and slippery and difficult to sew, but I manage to make myself a wedding gown. The color is a delicate cream, a beautifully warm tone—zinc white mixed with cadmium yellow and the barest hint of alizarin crimson.

It is a warm August afternoon, and raining, which they say is good luck for weddings. Ours is a quiet Sunday afternoon affair. A few of our musician and artist friends attend, and three soldiers from his company. No family because all of mine passed away before Joshua was born and none of his relatives that live near Chicago approve of our relationship. He wears his uniform and I wear my gorgeous parachute gown. Looking at us, no one would guess that I'm three times the age of my groom.

The cake is a cardboard cutout, but Joshua surprises us all by opening it up to reveal a stash of Hershey's Tropical Chocolate Bars he'd saved from his rations, enough for each of our guests to have one.

They are not at all what I expected, difficult to chew and far less sweet than what I remembered of the chocolate I'd tasted before the war. I must have made a face because Joshua laughed. "Why do you think I had so many left?" He lowered his voice to a conspiratorial whisper. "And these are the *new and improved* variety."

We can't afford a honeymoon but we both manage to get Monday off work and we spend the entire day holed up in our apartment, newlyweds basking in the joy of being together after spending so much time apart.

It isn't until I leave for work Tuesday morning that I see what has happened, sprawled across the top of the Chicago Tribune at a corner newsstand: *ATOMIC BOMB STORY!* The news is a stark and chilling white—the flash of the weapon itself, the coldness of a headline that speaks not of the people killed but of the power the American country now wields.

I let the white consume me. I transform into mist and careen through the streets of Chicago, then out over the vast ultramarine depths of Lake Michigan. Yet even here I cannot escape the war, for I find myself sharing the sky with warplanes from the naval air station, pilots training to fly in formation and land on aircraft carriers. Pilots not unlike the one who flew the plane that dropped the bomb.

What right do I have to feel this pain, I, so distantly removed? I feel guilt for being free instead of interred, for being American instead of Japanese, for failing to connect with my mother's country. Her country, never mine.

And then, Nagasaki. The city where my mother was born.

There are no words to describe the horror. I am only at peace when I transform into mist, mingling with the clouds above the city. It would be so easy to remain this way, to disperse in the atmosphere, to thin into nothingness. I am immortal, yes, but only so long as I choose to endure.

If not for Joshua, I might never have returned to human life. He is my anchor in the endless sea of time, my shelter from the nightmare storm of mushroom clouds. And I, in turn, am his calm harbor when the flashbacks hit, his comfort from the pain. We fight together against our demons from the war, stronger for being able to lean upon each other.

I paint Nagasaki in abstract, a monstrosity of crimson and white. It is passion and anger without form, in a style I have not mastered, and the result is garbage. I destroy canvas after canvas, unable to paint but determined nonetheless to try.

"Would it help to talk about it?" Joshua asks.

I'm painting over a ruined canvas, making it ready for my next attempt. I stop partway through, leaving streaks of color in between the broad stripes of white. "They're the only ones who start with a blank white page. Their story is the default, invisible, a crisp new canvas. Our stories, our history, our pain—that's color already on the page and we have to work around that, we have to explain why there's a burst of crimson seeping through where our people bled, why there's a vermillion rage underneath the calm surface of white."

"And then they'll tell you that they don't want your explanations because it complicates the story, sullies the art. They're always erasing the past—that's how they get that fresh white page they like to start with."

"Like snow covering the filthy streets of Paris," I say, remembering the time so long ago when I looked out the window of my immortal artist's studio. I wonder where he is right now, where he's hiding from the war, for that has always been his way, to withdraw when the world of mortals was too intense or dangerous. "The memories are harder to visualize now, there are so many of them and they blur together. I suppose I wasn't meant to remember more than one lifetime."

"You should write it down," Joshua says. "Tell your story."

"I thought they didn't want my explanations." I study the canvas, partially repainted.

"Since when do you care what they want?" he replies.

"Never. And always." I leave the canvas to dry, my previous failed attempt still showing in the gaps. It is better this way, somehow, with white to cover the things too horrible to bear. Pain avoided and erased. There is truth to that, in the things we hide, the things we omit, the things we do not even think to include. Words unwritten.

I title the painting *History* and sign it white on white, nearly invisible, erasing myself before anyone else can.

EMERALD GREEN

For thirty years I live an almost human life. I can't bear children, but after the war there are so many orphans, and particularly unwanted are the mixed-race children, the children most like me. We adopt Midori when she is four years old and Joshua is forty and I am one hundred and six.

They grow and change and age and I—well, I don't age but having them as a family alters me forever. I learn more about Japan, my interest spurred not by my past but by Midori's future. She looks like I did when I was young, and I want her to have the connection to her birth mother's country that I have always lacked. I try to give her a sense of belonging to both places instead of neither—and it strengthens my own connections as well. Maybe what I needed, all this time, was an excuse to explore a culture that never felt like my own. But it seems fitting, somehow. As a tree grows, so too do its roots.

It trickles into my paintings, as everything always does. Art has a way of absorbing all that I am—in its content and technique, but also more literally, for ever since that ultramarine night of losing Victorine I always leave a fragment of myself in the paint. In one color of each painting, as the emphasis, a focal point. When I paint my family, I am in the crimson, the color of love and passion.

The mortals around me begin to see the truth in my paintings. It is the most miraculous of things, for as I pour myself into the paintings they begin to sustain me, stealing brief moments from the audiences that study them, only the tiniest sliver of time from each but adding up to eternity as my popularity grows.

Three precious decades, vibrant like springtime, warm as summer, beautiful and fiery even in the autumn, when I know that Joshua's eternal winter is near.

He is laid to rest in Graceland Cemetery. Whatever my immortal artist might say, Joshua is no less for being one lover of many, our marriage no less meaningful to me for being a smaller fraction of my existence than it was of his.

On a sunny spring afternoon, I go to visit Joshua's grave. I'm sitting in the shade of a cherry tree, reading the latest John le Carré novel—Joshua had developed a fondness for spy stories in his later years and sharing a book seems more fitting than leaving behind a bouquet of wilting flowers—when my immortal artist finds me.

"I tire of the endless cycles," he says without preamble, "the constant turmoil of the world."

We've exchanged the odd letter here and there over the years, but I haven't heard his voice since we'd shared an exhibit at the Art Institute, for he travels widely and hides from mortal society for years at a time. He can't stand such newfangled technology as the telephone or the ever-present cars, never mind flying from one place to another in planes. No, he travels by shifting into mist, he communicates only by post, and hearing him again for the first time in so long I am struck by how thin he sounds, almost hollow. Like an echo of the immortal artist I once knew.

"Hello, old friend." He hates when I call him old, and I love to tease him. As usual, he doesn't take the bait.

"There's an impatience in the mortals now, as they rush through their fleeting little lives, and all I desire is a peaceful time to paint. To retire to a garden, perhaps, as Monet did in his final years."

"Then find a garden, or make one." I remember something Joshua once told me. "If you wait for the perfect moment, you will wait forever. Even we immortals paint in stolen bits of time, for the demands of the world expand to fill whatever time there is, no matter how vast. We must fight for it. For art. For time. Even when our lives are endless."

"I am weary of the fight."

I realize that I can't remember the last time he's exhibited a new painting, and his more recent letters have not mentioned models or even lovers, only his travels. "You've stopped painting."

"You've finally won them over to your way of seeing things, your muddled mix of influences, that complex stream of new ideas and techniques." He stares at a mausoleum in the distance, and I wonder if the pillars remind him of ancient Greek ruins.

"I'm persistent," I tell him.

"Stubborn."

"Yes. And I've learned to care less what others think." I run my fingers over Joshua's headstone, letters and numbers cut deep into the granite, shadowed in ultramarine.

"Is that the man you married?"

"Joshua," I say. "He died a few years ago. I miss him dearly. But I'm glad he's here and not in one of those crowded city cemeteries like the ones in Paris with graves practically stacked one atop the next. He loved plants. Trees. Gardening was one of his many attempts to escape from the horrors of war. We had a beautiful garden out behind the house. It looks a mess now because I've never been able to create plants from anything but paint."

"He was also a painter?"

I shake my head. "No. A musician, a composer, a civil rights activist, and, for a time, a soldier. He was the one who suggested I take control of my narrative, preserve my memories in writing. I haven't quite the knack for prose that Émile did, of course, but I want to have a record of my past."

"You've kept your connection to the mortals," he says, his voice wistful. "Yours was the last generation that really moved me. The last to draw me in."

He speaks of my entire generation, but I'm better at seeing the negative spaces now, hearing the words that aren't said. No one since me has moved him, there is no one but me in his heart after all these years... and I have well and truly moved on.

I can't help but think how far we've diverged. He is tradition, isolation, stagnation—all things I see within myself but which I fight so hard against. It leads me to think about duality, the way we often divide ideas so neatly into opposing pairs. Artist and subject. West and East. Life and death.

When I return to my studio, I paint a canvas on both sides: one a lively picnic in Burnham Park and the other a funeral at Graceland Cemetery. The grass of both is a vibrant green, and instead of placing opposing elements on opposite sides of the canvas I jumble everything together. There are hints of death at the park, and life in the cemetery. Even the style of the painting is a chaotic mix of impressionism and realism, ukiyo-e and abstract expressionism.

I call it *Two Worlds*, and it is what some consider my greatest masterpiece.

TITANIUM WHITE

The latest fashion in Paris is voluminous and flowing, with hidden pockets and hooded capes. A decade ago it was sleek minimalist cuts in patterns reminiscent of Rothko. It's fascinating to watch the way trends disappear and return, the throwbacks and the updates, the new combinations and perspectives.

The city itself follows a similar cycle, though far more slowly since a building is less easily changed than a frock. The arrondissement of my mortal youth is recognizable again, recreated as a historical preserve. They've managed to keep something of its underlying character, though the streets are far too clean, and the towering mid-millennium arcologies block the morning sun and make the light all wrong.

The Café Guerbois is a museum—a static recreation of the buzzing artistic scene it once was—but there's a dive bar around the corner called le Salon des Refusés where artists gather in their various groups and have heated discussions on the nature of art.

I sometimes go on Thursdays.

The new generation isn't weighed down by centuries of history, the experience of how far we've come. Their basis of reference is the time of *their* childhood, not of mine. They are at once refreshing and infuriating, and they inspire me to push forward—in my paintings and in my life. My once-immortal artist would have liked this bar, for the nostalgia of it if not for the modern conversations. It is strange to think of a world that doesn't have him in it.

The Musée de l'Orangerie houses the last remaining trace of his existence— *Woman, Reclining (Mari)*. The museum has continued to restore it for centuries, using the best technology and the most skilled conservators.

On the surface, the painting is much as I remember it, faint though the memory is. But he is gone from it, the paint that he himself applied replaced bit by bit like a colorful Ship of Theseus until little of the original remains. His other paintings are lost, and have probably long since crumbled into dust. Poor Suzette. She'd thought herself immortal at least in paint, but that tribute is fleeting. History has forgotten her, even as a footnote. It's hard to imagine that once upon a time I'd been jealous of the attention he'd paid her, so many lifetimes ago. And jealous of him for being an artist when I was a model. Now his painting is preserved, not because it was painted by him, but because it is the earliest known depiction of me.

Time eats all things in the end. Entropy brings everything back to white—a chaotic jumble of all the colors mixed together, if you paint with light. Now even my once-immortal artist has succumbed to the unending white. An artist must struggle to find meaning, to put order to chaos—and he no longer wished to fight.

He is a mist too thin to ever recohere; the strongest notion of him that remains is the splinter of his being that lives on in me. His model and his student, shining so brightly that I can never again be placed in his shadow.

In honor of his passing I paint *Entropy* in a palette of colors I mix myself, using formulas from both ancient times and modern, carefully applying the colors so the painting will change as it ages—chrome yellow that darkens to brown, red lake pigments that quickly fade, an ordivant green that will darken through emerald and into a deep blue over the course of several hundred years. I put myself into the titanium white, mist into paint, adding nuance to the crisp bright hue.

It is a self-portrait, though my physical likeness is not in it. It is historical painting, though it does not depict any recognizable moment in time. Even the signature will shift, as mine has over the centuries—briefly it will read *Mari* before the rest of my name emerges. *Mariko* means truth, so this appeals to me conceptually: over time, the truth will be revealed. Then eventually the letters will fade until only the M remains. The details of history, given enough time, are mostly forgotten.

I have the Musée de l'Orangerie display the painting in carefully specified values of light, with strict orders never to move it, repair it, or alter anything about the painting or the room. Its true glory cannot be appreciated within a single human lifetime, but mortals flock to see it nonetheless.

And even now the doubt remains, the lingering fear that I will be forgotten. Perhaps the time has finally come to share my story. I've been writing it in dribs and drabs ever since Joshua suggested it, the words accumulating like dabs of color on a canvas. There are moments I choose to describe and moments that I omit, deliberately or otherwise. When you outlive everyone you've ever known, there's no one to remind you of the things you've forgotten, and no one to contradict your version of events. I find myself always returning to white. Beginning, again and again.

WHITE

This is not the end. I'll leave my mark on the blank page of history, and I'll paint the world in colors so bold and bright they cannot be ignored.

There is beauty in my truth, and I have so much to share.

....

Caroline M. Yoachim is a three-time Hugo and six-time Nebula Award finalist. Her short stories have been translated into several languages and reprinted in multiple best-of anthologies, including four times in *Best American Science Fiction and Fantasy*. Yoachim's short story collection, *Seven Wonders of a Once and Future World & Other Stories*, and the print chapbook of her novelette, *The Archronology of Love*, are available from Fairwood Press. For more, check out her website at carolineyoachim.com.

NOVELLA

AND WHAT CAN WE OFFER YOU TONIGHT

Premee Mohamed

1

The dead girl woke and asked for her perfume and we gave it to her and she slept again.

And when she did so I felt glad I had not let anyone rifle through her things as often happened before the funeral. Someone might have been wearing her scent at the ceremony but no one was.

So now she lies on my bed with her bluewhite hand curled around the glowing vial. The one thing she wanted.

Nero sniffs, leans a shoulder gingerly against the doorway, avoiding his newly-implanted wings. "They do that with dinoflagellates, you know. It's nothing special."

"Don't be jealous," I tell him. Of course he cannot help it, he is very young, and anyway we are all of us a little rattled right now, I would say that none of us are really acting like ourselves, not *really*.

Someone needs to tell, someone whispers just outside the cracked door of my room, and someone whispers back *Shhh! What is wrong with you?* and someone else adds *What the* fuck *is wrong with you?*

For now I think the secret is safe. But the owners of our House will find out at some point. Not from me and not from my fellow courtesans, and need has nothing to do with what we do anyway. Does it. Ever. Has it. Ever.

Nero gets up to stand watch in the hallway and that leaves me in here with the dead girl who is not dead.

2

This morning we crept out to the abandoned church, a dignified flotilla, ten and twenty and thirty and at the last perhaps forty boats bobbing in the dark with our red lanterns, and for a moment it was pretty and calm, Nero smiling for the first time in days, balancing lightly in the prow and holding up his light like a statue, and *Sit down, sit down, fool,* the hisses from the back, the others disliking the rocking on the flat oily water, and then the church loomed ahead, a grand jagged ruin bleeding rust into the slowlapping sea.

We made mooring on silken ribbons and entrusted the boats to the god of the beautiful dead. The steps have been vanishing year by year but we still splashed up the last few and passed through the great doors and down the aisle, the coffin already waiting on the altar. And inside some of us walked and some of us paddled, not thrashing or kicking overmuch, so that the sound of the sea could enter also.

Our church has been our church for generations. No one knows how it all began: this dark procession, the laying out of the body. It occurred to me that these things—to prepare the dead, to gather in the act of mourning—are among the hardest to shift in a people. That they move slowly and stubbornly, and that people cling to the practices they know for centuries, millennia, through famine, war, assimilation, invasion, colonization, plague, decline, despair.

What cataclysm drove us to this broken place? Was it whole then? I feel certain it wasn't. Our rituals are too set in stone.

Cemeteries in the city have been mostly built over, the standard practice and the standard process: leveling, compaction, low areas filled with waste, high areas brought low. The few left are guarded like prisons, and only for the use of the very rich.

No one says anything about that, no one ordinary, everyone just puts their dead into a canal. Lots of those around. Free, too. Once, I know, there was an idea of eternal life, or life after death, but everyone has abandoned that idea except them, the rich I mean, who are like another species.

We have not even given our god a name. Maybe in another thousand years.

On the thick particleboard of the coffin we placed flowers, and on the damp and crawling walls we hung the necessary artifacts, each giving as tradition specified: something about the deceased, but also something of ourselves. A single earring, rendering its mate back at the house useless; one glove; a painting or a scrap of sheetmusic; a lock of hair; a prized lipstick. To represent her finest skills, those of which she was most proud, some illustrated the walls in grease-pencil, or tacked up the packaging of toys or whips, hoarded specially for memorials and set aside for these days.

And the priest did not bid us be quiet, because we are told to be quiet often enough. And he also gave us no name for that reason, because it is only in mourning that we use the names we like instead of the names we were given when we were purchased. Each part of the ritual has a purpose and each successful step has a consequence for the dead. So for duty's sake we played the game as it was necessary to be played and the priest blessed the final piece and placed it on the flat glossy lid of the coffin.

It was nearly sunrise, the funerals always happen at sunrise, that too is our tradition. Someone once said: *Yes, now, when we are set free, like fairies in a story, from our bondage, and fly the wide woods...* but that itself is a fairy story. We are still bound. This place is the only one we can visit, and the owners of the House look away from our transgression like they look away from death, and the sky is blueblack as a bruise and the water is the same and between them, very often, is a single knife-thin slice of gold sun more beautiful than any metal and any gem at House of Bicchieri and more beautiful than any of us and more beautiful than any of our clients.

And one of the new girls was crying and disoriented, she had been sick on the boat; and luckily her dress was still clean, because we must present ourselves in the church as clean and proud. But she said, *This isn't how funerals go, this isn't how they go,* and someone questioned her, and was stunned to discover that she had attended one as a little girl; and I too was stunned. Till I began at the House I had never heard of a funeral. I repeat: you paid your respects to the family and you gave a few credits if you had them, and then the body was weighted and sunk in the closest canal.

Instead this girl crying, saying this was not what she remembered. Her family must have been wealthy. I wondered how she had come to the House. Not something we ever ask, that's the rule; that information is only offered freely, and only to friends. For you don't climb to us. You fall only, you don't climb. She had fallen, or been thrown. Now she would never rise again. A long sad time, never.

Someone comforted her, and we clambered upon the rounded backs of the pews to begin the last of the rites. Someone passed around a bag of sweets. Someone passed around a flask of liquor. Wrists rose pale in the darkness and were blessed with a dab of scent. We were defiant, we were dressed for no client, scented for no client, we had lit up our implants and fed our hair for no client. Only to honour the dead girl, who we all loved.

And the priest said, *Blessed are the bodies,* and we said, *Whose bodies.* And he said, *Yours. Yours.* And the girl who had been crying looked up all surprised and dried her face and recomposed herself.

Good girl. You fell far, I wanted to tell her, but you have fallen into our arms, and we will carry you as best we can. Hence this secret ceremony, hence the priest we pay from our own earnings, hence the boats, the finery, the coffin itself. The House will not let us have this and the city will not let us have this but have this we must for those very reasons.

In the distance small red lights, looping regular patterns like the flight of a moth, a govvy cull in the Lows. Popular neighbourhood for it. They can get their quota in a day or two, and laze around the rest of the month. A curse upon their name, a pox upon them, we could not be touched by a cull, the House made us safe, but all of us had left someone behind. May they sicken and die. May they go unremembered.

And the priest said, *This, your friend Winfield,* and at hearing her name she stirred and sat up and pushed open the coffin and flowers spilled off her like water, roses, jasmine, lilies, honeysuckle, and the ugly rip they had made to fake an 'autopsy' tore open its lazy stitches and filled with blossoms.

No one screamed but we are trained to control our screams and in looking back actually I was very proud at our silence, which was stunned but absolute.

And she tried to get out of the coffin but could not. The priest fainted. We climbed from the pews and propped him up out of the water and took her home.

3

Give her to me, I said then, and because I have been in the House for so long, because I am nearly thirty years old, they obeyed me. Or obeyed my seniority at any rate. Before the ceremony I hissed and whisked people away from her room; now I probably will not need to. Even those who did not attend and do not know what to fear will have the vague knowledge that if the road to mortality runs two ways now, that if she is not alive, and she is not dead, her room is certainly filled with numinous spirits.

I asked for her without a plan in mind but we'd better do *something*. Demand is high to get in the House of Bicchieri, maybe the highest in all of the city, and the owners will not let the room languish without an occupant for long; it's not making a profit while it's empty of a warm and willing body.

I leave Winfield on top of the silkstitched duvet, hoping she is comfortable (hoping she will die again and solve this) and speak softly to such as I think I can trust, and they agree to pack up her things, conceal them piecemeal in their rooms, and safeguard them till we know what we are dealing with here.

No one says: But what *are* we dealing with? The answer is too terrible.

A girl who was dead, and then was not. A girl who was dead in a fridge for a week, and was torn open, and finally, grudgingly surrendered to us for our rites. The owners threw us the 'autopsy' as a sop, because we complained, and because, they said, it would stop the whining... like scraps to a pack of dogs.

Fake, I thought then, and now I know for sure. They never did an autopsy. They didn't hire a medical examiner. Just ripped her open themselves, maybe with a steakknife from the kitchen. Forged the death certificate and sent it to the city. We could not protest, not without evidence. But the evidence is on my bed.

Awake again, Winfield touches the incision gingerly, its edges the colour of her low-cut gown. Her flesh shimmers like an opal and for a moment I think we should not have buried her in it, although I suppose we could not have known she would end up resembling it, like a chameleon, like a cuttlefish, that same bluish-silver fabric. There is no blood, not a drop. She says, "Jewel, is that you? You're all aglow."

"It's me, and I'm not. There's something wrong with your eyes, my lovely. Among other things."

"I died," she says. "He killed me."

"Who?"

"I don't remember."

Well.

Well. Well. We all thought as much, but I am struck with a sick full-body thud all the same. The way you hate to hear that you are right about an abomination. I take her hand, and eventually Nero comes back in and she takes his hand too, though he squirms, and she tells us that she was dead, but is no longer dead, and none of it makes sense, none, and we are asked to accept it and we do, because she is calm.

She tells us that she flew through a strange version of our city-state which floated on a maze of salt sand, not water; that something spoke to her and gave her life back, though not instructions. That she was in a place of instruction, not of apotheosis, not of prophecy; a sanctuary not because it was safe but because it was sacred. And she awoke in the sea-rotted cathedral and she knew it from other funerals and she looked for us and we were there.

"We'd never leave you," I tell her.

Nero says, "I'd rob you, but I'd never leave you."

Her first real smile. Winsome Winfield, who commanded the highest prices in the entire House, who got to keep that crucial five percent bonus from every client because of it, who was actually allowed to receive tips, spreading them among us with unthinking largesse, her wrist always buzzing with a new name on her waitlist, lunging and scuffling for cancellations like the suitors of Penelope... Winfield who had been here only two years and was not considered 'used up,' though the owners never said that about us, and they never called us whores or escorts or hookers or sluts, always courtesans, because we were in a house, a capital-H House.

In a House you are safe, even pampered. You have healthcare. Three squares a day. Clean air. Your own room. Security cameras. You might have a career of twenty or thirty years if you are lucky and fit and diligent and obedient.

Or this might happen. Something like this. As had happened a few times before.

"*Did* you rob me?" she says, and Nero looks at her solemnly, *How could you think that of me*, and he says, "Only your earrings."

"Give them back, darling."

"But you—" he begins, and I nearly kick him before he stops on his own, cheeks reddening under the golden-brown skin, the dyed-fire brows. His ears positively glow. *But you won't need them now*, he wants to say, *because you are dead*.

I want to say, *What will you do now?* Which isn't much better and I am so bad at this, I am so bad at saying the needed things, the obvious things. She cannot work here, and you have to work to live; no one else can look after you, because no one else has anything any more. There's no such thing as a mutual-aid society like in the old days when welfare stopped, there's no aid now, no one has anything to give. Just mutuality without the actual exchange of money or goods. The city is like the canals which keep it alive: filled with garbage and killers, a terrible silent deadly striving beneath the surface, regularly dredged, its leavings crushed and processed for value, then discarded.

Had we not all seen, growing up, cull after cull after cull, had we not taken in with infant ears that if you didn't have the chip saying you were a worker, if your employer did not verify it, you were fair game, you had less value than a rat (for there are bounties on the rats now, both North and South halves of the city decreed it last year, ten credits for a tail), you only have value here, somewhere *like* here I mean, and I can say none of this.

No one says: My God, what are we going to *do* with you.

She cannot stay here, it is an impossibility. The waiting list to get into the House of Bicchieri is miles deep, no, an ocean abyss, you could wedge a mountain into it and watch it simply sink down into the darkness forever. In hours—because they know how long our ceremonies take—her room will be rearranged, sanitized, depersonalized, and reassigned. Tomorrow, or perhaps the day after tomorrow at the latest. She has nowhere to hide.

For us to reveal to the owners that she is not dead might simply mean they kill her again: for not being dead enough, staying dead enough, for what she knows and has seen, for what they did.

So she exists in this space where she cannot exist and cannot be allowed to exist. Not by any of us.

In a few hours, the clocks will strike and our appointments will begin and there is just nowhere to put her and for a second I feel a wild rush of despair that stings my eyes like a splash of canal water illuminated for a second by a sign: bright, chemical burn, replaced with darkness, why couldn't she just be dead, why, we mourned her, we performed the necessary acts, our secret rites that belong only to us, we risk our lives to properly look after the dead, and now she is back, and she has ruined everything, why couldn't she just decently die, we *cried* for her.

And I can feel Nero's thoughts drumming on the back of my neck, Nero who loved her, who loves everybody (he cannot help it, he was bought so young), who is a little mad with despair right now too. Finally, he says, "Maybe the roof?" and I think for a minute, maybe, it's not unused but it's not frequently used, being less prettified and landscaped and manicured than the rest of the place, of course there are some clients who like that, but she will not be found, I think, by management at any rate. It could be a temporary refuge.

I put her perfume into a pocket of her dress and lace it up again where she has opened it seeking her bloodless lie of a wound. "Up we get," I say, "uppy-up," and Nero and I drag her down miles of silent hallway to the great gilt elevator. A shadow, at the end of the hallway? Someone fleeing? No, just an optical illusion, caused by the double mirrors I think. We are all paranoid even though we are all on the same side.

She lolls against us as the elevator clanks and jerks upwards, the noise an affectation, like so much else here (the stupid gazebos, the pergolas, the marble fauns that I hate, the benches poised coyly behind the loathsome topiaries, the picturesque fields of poppies and lavender against the ruthlessly sprayed, clipped, combed, compacted, dyed, and soundproofed turf).

The decorative brass grid of the cage leaves marks of fern and seashell on her bare, bluish arms. I imagine the three of us from behind like a court portrait rendered in oils: the three heads leaning together, the gold and the silver and the black. In life we are paid to imitate art.

On the roof we are struck with the wind, warm and humid, and the smell of the city: rotten, curiously chemical though, like a mouldy battery rather than mouldy food. The sky is indigo and the buildings below us are the same and the canals and the sea some miles away are the same and it is like being caught and tumbled in a great monotonous wave there in the wind with no walls around us and the hard golden light of the sunrise that was supposed to arrive as the priest finished the speech is here now, flung sideways and approaching with startling speed, amidst the small fiery lights of factories, boats, homes, and the glow-backed fish that live far below and sometimes rise just before dawn to lip the surface of the viscous water.

Winfield holds us in the noise and the openness of the wind and Nero and I put our arms around her waist, she feels light, emptied out, how could they, and I begin to say, *What will you do?* and she says, "I am going to kill him."

And the wind rips her words away and carries them around us and I picture them like small furious birds of prey, their talons piercing something furry and struggling.

Nero has the good sense to keep silent for once. I too say nothing. We watch the sun come up and then embrace her and return to work, taking the stairs down, tapping our wristbands against the clock, we are paid by the hour as well as per client, this is a good House, not like the others, we will always be safe, always looked after, and I think: When we go back up there she will be dead again. Not: When we go back up there she will be gone.

4

But after our shift ends, of course, she is gone.

"Oh, bleeding Christ." My hands leap to my mouth. I picture only the wind picking her up, light as she is, using her expensive opal-coloured gown as a sail, we always bury the dead in their best, their very best, carrying her away in her best.

Then I shake my head, and practicality descends. She's young and she's pretty and she's dead but she's not a fool; she will have hidden someplace, and because the security system is largely infrared based to keep out vermin of various species and credit ratings, she can likely come and go at leisure. She is scheming, planning, to enact her revenge; she's good at this, savvy, she sees technology as toys.

Hiding. Spying. Trying to fill in that gap in her memory... the owners will have records, it is part of the understanding they make with our clients: phone numbers, addresses, maybe more. Or will Winfield find her enemy some other way? Is she beloved of a god now, will the god help a favourite out, like in the stories? Possessed by sharp-eyed Apollo, and sending out silver arrows. Possessed by owl-eyed Athene, and swinging your sword with such force and speed as would kill Ares himself. Or someone possessed by him. Why do I keep thinking about possession? The gods don't need our bodies.

"Do you know who it was?" Nero says, as we huddle out of the wind and pass a stik back and forth (unflavoured, unscented, the only kind we are allowed).

"No," I tell him. "But I can guess."

"Me too."

There is a slate, a menu of options... not many. Which tells you something too. The clients are sometimes permitted, for an extra fee, to take us off the property, for meals or 'cultural events' only, such as humiliating an ex-wife, and so I have seen the full range of restaurants the North city has to offer (we cannot cross the river), and I know the more expensive the establishment, the smaller their menu, and the most expensive ones have none at all, you eat what they give you. Someone else picks. You don't pick.

So we know this is a small menu. It was a man, a wealthy man, even more so (I think) than our usual clients, whose net worth generally veers into the stratosphere anyway; we are not one of those Houses where any ordinary family (our own, say) could save up for a few months to gift someone a trip to visit the expensive whores. It would not be possible.

Even more rich, even more elite than usual. Hm. But perhaps something else too... the way it was hushed up so quickly, the way we heard through the whisper walls not even the faintest hint of reparations, settlement, to the House that we've previously seen for the accidental death of a worker while with a client.

Something else, something... I don't know. Politically connected, perhaps, or neo-nobility from somewhere else, or the heir of one of those big conglomerates, you know the ones. Big. Like they bought planets and suchlike, like *moons* belong to them, or their family. Someone the owners do not just pander to, like everyone else, but also fear.

Of the clients I have seen coming in and out of the House, perhaps just five or six fit the description... I shake my head. "We're not going to help her."

"No, of course not."

"We're not murderers."

"No, no." He hunches over and his golden curls flop into his eyes, sweet Nero whose real name he's never revealed, purchased as Ganymede two years ago but of course there are a thousand Ganymedes in the city, what a cliché, rechristened as soon as he'd stepped in the door (the back door; front is for clients only), *You don't want him*, the owners had sniffed, *mistaken for one of* those, and that's what it means to work here: we are precious, rarefied, you don't want to be confused for something *not* that. The disdain dripping from their words, so your shoes slip on it.

Because if you are confused for *one of those*, if you fuck up: back out you go. Back out there to the city, sink or swim. And if you don't swim, immediately and strongly and far, far faster than all the others thrown out with you, you're cull fodder. We still say: bird in a gilded cage. But better a cage than an oven.

I slide my arm around him, avoiding the warm healing tissue of his new implants, and I put every bit of authority into my voice that I can. "No. She's on her own. We're not like that." Because if you say it, it becomes true.

"Of course we're not." He empties the stik, sets it on the thick black gravel, presses down with his thumb till it crumbles. The wind will pick up the scraps. Safety first.

I stand, pull him up, look down automatically. Down there, the filth, the lights. Something nagging at me. "When we first got her. Someone outside the door said *We should tell.* Or something like that. *We need to tell.* You were closer to the door, did you hear that?"

He nods uncertainly. His eyes are golden rings, matching the glow of his hair. You could almost read by those eyes, they become so hot and bright when he is agitated.

"Who said it?"

"I don't know," he says. "You know how it's hard to tell. With whispers. But... do you think..."

"No. It's nothing to worry about. We're not like *that* either."

"All of us?"

"I don't know. I hope so."

5

Back inside we eat and nap, work out, endure the weekly medical (brisk as always, unremarkable as always, the phlebutton the only good part, watching the little sphere fill with red), lounge in the library, cuddle in front of the viewscreens, cocoon in our rooms.

Two hours till my next client and I think I will read and nap again, we are always a little tired, it comes from the weird shift system and your body simply never gets used to the constant changes, but I open my door and the scent comes at me, she doesn't like citrus, says it smells too much like disinfectant, other fruits, herbs, fig, blackberry, sage I think, pine resin, like the trees along the Singing Walk.

Winfield says evenly, "Did you know that they had cameras in here?"

I shut the door and press my thumb to the lock. "They're fakes. To make the clients behave. You know that."

"They're not. As it turns out. So now you know too."

I turn instinctively, though of course that's the worst thing to do if she's right, and stare at mine: the round lens shiny and clean and fake, comprising the mouth of the jar held by the simpering gilt cherub in his nest of flowers above the door.

For more than a decade I have been told it was fake. I pass a hand suspiciously in front of the lens. "Win."

"I deactivated it," she says. "Then erased the recordings. They'll have to buy new ones for a couple of rooms. You, Iris, Samira, Flyboy…"

"You know he hates that. How?"

She tosses her hair impatiently and I wait, cringing, for a clump to fall to the floor, she is dead after all, but nothing happens; and she looks radiant, not alive, something else, brimming with light. The light of vengeance, I think with a little twist of envy. The light of fury. In my aubergine-wallpapered room with its inkily figured ferns, the bloodred duvet, the sepia headboard and floors, she is the brightest thing.

She says, "I broke into the study. Serpentine's study."

Miss Serpentine, I almost say, then laugh. Of course she doesn't have to use honorifics of any kind for the owners now. "But what good…"

"They had all the recordings, exterior and interior. And it shows viewcount. So I knew I was the first one who had accessed it. Actually I don't think they watch them, mostly, on off-hours," she adds, her voice filled with bile. "Just with clients. Later."

"Lawsuit city," I murmur.

She snickers. "A whole city of lawsuits. Skyscrapers, arcologies of lawsuits. Floating colonies of lawsuits. Anyway, I'm sure they don't let a single image get off the grounds."

"But they had him."

"…They had him. With me."

My knees give and I collapse onto the bed next to her and instinctively, as we all often do here, we take each other's hands. Hers is cold and dry, but strong, and a strange irregular pulse beats in her wrist. But she is dead; no one could have been emptied out like her and not be dead.

I squeeze her hand. She squeezes back. What can I say to her? She has seen her death, she saw herself killed, that is what she meant by *With me*. What beats inside her? No, stop it. She saw herself killed. She will never forget that, not for a single moment of her renewed life. She sought out and watched her murder and she really means to do this, whatever this is.

"He held me down, he held his hand over my face," she says. "Over my mouth and nose, till it was done. It was not an accident."

"He wouldn't have told them it was," I tell her when she has told me the name, and I am obscurely proud that he was on both my longlist and my shortlist. My ears are ringing. "Someone like Pederssen, he'd have *bragged* about it. He wouldn't be afraid of anything the owners could do to him. They would have been afraid of him."

"No."

"Of him not coming back. Of losing his business."

"Oh," she says flatly. "Maybe. Maybe."

"People like him," I say, "don't have scandals. They have amusing little diversions." Then I remember I am speaking of her murder, and fall silent. I have said hateful things today. "I'm sorry."

"Don't be. You're right."

There's a very simple food web here, I think. Predators, prey. Prey fights for its life, as she must have fought. And out there somewhere, mother, father, family, friends, not even aware that she was here or dead. In any other world we would call him a monster and do what you do to monsters, which is kill him; but because he is who he is, we protect and revere him, we fawn at his feet, we forgive him his rampaging and ravaging, we go so far as to maybe kill those who would kill him. Imagine Beowulf showing up only to discover the Danes protecting Grendel, guarding him while he eats their people.

Her voice is steely, distant. "All the same, proud as he is, he won't come back here for ages. But his life is an insult on this Earth. I won't wait. I'll hunt him down like a rat. Go into the city and make him bleed."

"Win, no. Let it go."

"Let it *go*?"

"All right, we've been dancing around this. But I'm going to say it." As I speak she pulls her hand from mine and places it in her lap, staring at the wall. Our heads are twinned in the great mercury mirror, expressions identical. "You came back. We don't know how. And I'm tempted to say we don't know why either, but what if *why* is to give you a second chance at life? To do something else, something... meaningful."

She snorts. I flush when I realize it, humiliated that line insinuated itself into my speech: something the owners, Serpentine and Jasper (they like mineral names, and are always changing them) say. Especially in the early days of each new purchase, when people are disoriented and empty, ready to be filled with their apparently inspirational talks, like pouring poison into a cup.

They say that we *are* doing meaningful work: that we are generating profit, not everybody can do that you know, that we are employable, not everybody is that you know. That we are providing company and comfort, listening ears, welcoming orifices, that we are using both body and mind to help others in this awful wreck of a city, that we are a small shining light of civilization as well as civility, that we are a torch held aloft the darkness and separate from it because of our intent to do good in the world...

I thought I had ignored those speeches. I certainly scoffed at them when they were given. Now I see they were grit and have become, inside me, a pearl. Misshapen, I suspect. Not nice and round. "You're a miracle. A medical miracle. Probably among other types... how many are there? But look, darling, you can't waste this chance. No one else has ever gotten it. You're absolutely unique in the history of the world and you're just going to... to get yourself killed again. Or worse."

"Worse?"

"Well, I don't know. Use your imagination. Like the movies." I watch us in the mirror, meeting her eyes. "Captured. Studied. Vivisected!"

"But nothing hurts now," she says dreamily, and stands, and trails a hand over my head. "How dare you tell me not to, Jewel. *Darling.* How dare you. Maybe this is precisely the reason I was brought back. Maybe a god asked me to come back and be the hand of justice. Maybe a god said: *Not everybody deserves to be alive. But you do. And he doesn't.* Hmm?"

I stare up at her, the clinging dabs of perfume glowing behind her ear. How we had loved her when she came, I thought. Instantly, unstintingly, and because of this: because she said the things we thought in our worst nights, the things we whispered through gritted teeth into the pillows, she was like a cold clean air blowing through the dust and fug and musk of the House. She was the only person who seemed unafraid.

"Pederssen can try to unmake me," she says. "But he cannot unperson me. I will always be who I am. And you will always be who you are. A coward, huddling in this House with her safe little job, afraid of the city. Afraid of what I might bring to you from it. Contaminating this place. That's what you're worried about. Isn't it?"

"I'm worried *for* you. You've already risked enough, breaking into the study, doing what you did. You'll be caught."

"Liar. Look at you. You're worried about four square inches of skin. You're worried about the light on your wristband. I'm not afraid of the city."

"You should be. What neighbourhood were you from again? West Jovia? We used to call that Redlake. You know how bad it was. It's worse now. You've known it long enough to know what it can do."

"Survived it long enough. And will again." She smiles, as if I am forgiven. Now her teeth look like her dress and her skin: polished, iridescent. "I'll go. It seems there is no help to be found here."

"Winfield. Don't."

"I'll come tell you when I'm done," she says. "We can have a party."

"*Don't.* Think of the rest of us. If you..."

"I'll see you later, Jewel."

When she leaves, I get the sense (fleeting, inevitable) that a safe-box has just been emptied of its contents; I feel robbed.

6

For days I read the news with a certain horror, the horror of anticipation, as if earthquakes or hurricanes had been predicted, and I suppose it is almost the same thing, it is the same feeling because it is the same thing: What will she bring upon us if she does what she says she will do? It would be like an earthquake.

Well, she'd better not, that's all I'm saying. She wouldn't do that to us, her friends, put us out on the street. (Briefly. *Briefly* out on the street. Then we will be off the street, and in a canal.)

But there's nothing, there's never anything, and I find I have to scour all the sections, we still get a newspaper, we are not allowed personal devices you can search, so even absent from us she is an inconvenience: his murder not on the front page? Perhaps an oversight. In the Business section, because of his family's business? No, not there. Books, perhaps? Why? Well, he wrote books, didn't he. He wrote those self-help books. Finance? What's the difference between Business and Finance? And so on.

"You're very up on current events these days," someone chirps behind me a week later at breakfast.

I turn: not someone I know—not new, I don't think, I've seen her a few times, but she works in the other wing where I don't often go, as you have to cross through the atrium where a girl hung herself eight years ago. She is young, sly-looking, pretty; her hair writhes slowly around her shoulders, its reticulated pattern like fall leaves. "Do you need the paper, darling?"

"I'd love the entertainment section if you're done with it."

I fish it out, hand it over. If my instincts have kept me alive this long, I think, I should obey them: and there is something a little off about her brittle brightness, something that is not the play-acting we often do. "Long way to walk for the comics, isn't it?"

"Oh, no no. Miss Serpentine and Mister Jasper reassigned me to the East wing. There was an empty room. So lovely to have a window."

"I quite agree."

Win's room. You, I think. You whispered in the hallway after the funeral. You, just a few feet from my door. Who corrected you? Who defended you? Are there *factions* now, in this place where our unity is the only thing we have ever counted on to stay alive? "And you can buy good little plants at Klaas for your window-sills," I add, referring to the House store in our wing, the only place we can spend our money. "They can order in plants from the city if you want something special... someone did show you where it was, didn't they?"

"No! I'd love a tour."

I refold the paper, meet her eyes for a moment: bright violet. A mod colour that was popular when I was a teenager. Comes with its own set of assumptions. "Well," I begin, and stop as I catch—not quite, my intuition catches, not my eyes, even my nose, the harsh smell of blood and nanofluids—the merest blink of the medical capsule traveling at its top speed through the transparent glass tube that runs along the ceiling of the Great Room, where clients rarely look.

The others glance up at the subsonic whine of eaten air, then snarl and flinch, protecting their breakfast or books, as I rush from the room, past the stranger, hiking up my skirts with both hands, till I am pressed against the tingling force-field of the infirmary steriglass, ill with a different dread.

7

"No," Nero says, "it doesn't hurt, it's fine," and Miss Serpentine and Mister Jasper smile and coo over him, their investment, soon he'll be tuned-up and waxed to a high shine again, never you fear my dumpling, my honeycake, and I wait till they sweep from the room, favouring me with their most brilliant smiles, as matchy-matchy as surgery and injections and delicate layers of painterly cosmetics can make them, as brilliant as diamonds, and I lean over the railing of his bed. There is an awful stink of blood still, and disinfectant, harsh artificial lemon.

Nero weeps and hides his face with one hand and reaches for me with the other, groping the air till I take it and press it to my face. I will not ask him what happened; it is clear enough. The new wings on his back—the best, the most expensive, the most natural that can be made, the envy of any real bird in the sky—were ground zero of this attack.

One is bandaged and apparently intact, but the other is clearly broken, carefully splinted into a frame of small articulated metal and plastic pieces, like spiders protectively cradling the long white arc. His face too is battered, one eye puffed shut.

The wings are new, yes, but they are stunningly tough; they are crafted, feather by feather, out of the stuff once used in bulletproof vests. Someone did this on purpose. Someone held him down and did this. Someone put him facedown on the floor at some point and wrenched the wing open as he tried to protect it and then someone twisted till it bent and then broke.

No accident. Not even a pretense of an accident.

"My teeth are all right." He chuckles through his tears, gathering up the loose strands of his composure. "I think that's the important thing."

"Yes, you still have your million-dollar looks. You vain beast."

"I know."

"You peacock. But oh, your..." His dark, rosy face is ashen from pain. I want to weep too, it must hurt so badly, and they never give you enough drugs here, as if the threat of lying unmedicated after a beating would prevent the next one. We should be used to the world in which the victim is punished instead of the instigator but something inside us still cries out that it is wrong, not just logically wrong, causatively or chronologically wrong, but wrong in some other way as well. Something deeper. More cellular.

I kiss the palm of his hand, unharmed but bearing a teardrop-shaped splatter of blood. "Who was it?"

"What does it matter?"

"It might have been..." I hesitate. "Well, I don't want to say revenge. But a... a warning. Maybe. More than a slap on the wrist. Because you and I are the ones who... all right, listen, just now while I was eating breakfast—"

The window darkens, and we both draw away instinctively, startled more than actually frightened, and he yelps as the splint on his broken wing adjusts itself with an affronted little hydraulic whine.

Winfield slithers into the room with boneless ease, a joyful swing from the top frame belying her bared teeth, a filthy avenging angel in this spotless place, her bare feet squelching onto the tile floor. Her hair is lank, the opalescent lilac strands matted together like lace. She looks delighted with herself. "Tell me who did this."

"Thank *God* for this catheter," Nero says when he catches his breath.

"Who?" She leans over the hospital bed, grasping the railing. She no longer smells of perfume and the flowers of the grave, but the city: smoke, trash, fish, the clinging gloop of canals. "I'll have a word."

"Don't," I say. "We're all in deep enough, Nero. Someone is passing things to the owners, someone in the House, spying on us... you don't know what'll happen. Retaliation."

"You haven't done anything wrong," Win says, not looking at me. "Ignore her. Tell me."

He stares up at her for a long moment, half-defiant, a contrarian, now that he has been asked he certainly will not tell, he might have told us before, then seems to come to some kind of conclusion, you can almost hear him think, *Retaliation, you say?* and light flares green and gold behind his eyes. "Draavik."

Even in my anger I find myself unsurprised; he's slapped a few of us around. There is a lazy cruelty to him that no one doubted would become intentional, deliberate, to one of us, or perhaps to one of his wives back home, or his kids or his dog or his employees or maybe all of them. Whoever was within reach when he decided to stop toying about with his impulses and take off their muzzles.

Winfield straightens, meets my gaze. "I won't kill him," she says. "Princess. Look at you. Look at your face. No, I'll just teach him a lesson."

"First murder, now this? You've got to knock it off, Win. This won't get you any closer to Pederssen."

"I haven't done a murder," she says. "And this is just a friendly chat. Help him see the error of his ways."

I hesitate, chewing on my lip, and glance back over my shoulder to see if anyone is watching us through the steriglass. Little spy with her cheap purple eyes. Now I know of her existence, and now she must know I know. Good old predictable Jewel, reading the paper every morning, sitting in the same place, getting the same breakfast. Outwit her by zigging where she wants me to zag. Can I? I move in a straight line every day.

Win smiles, taking visible pleasure in my worry. "Help me. Come with me. See for yourself."

"See..."

"What it's like." She leans on the bed, her face nearly meeting mine. Bones are visible now beneath the shimmering fabric of her gown. "What I do now."

"What?"

"I send messages. I'm a poet, really." She glances up at the ceiling for a moment, pretending to compose something. "Come with me and send a sonnet to the rat you think is running around the House. Tell them: I'm not afraid of you. Tell them: I know what you're doing. Tell them: And there will be consequences for this. For Draavik. And for you."

Oh. Now that. *Would* be something. But.

I waver, still clinging to Nero's hand. His face is a sunrise: filled with impossible, malicious delight. At the thought of someone not just sticking up for him, I think, because we all do that when we can, but someone getting back at the bully. Bursting, if even for a second, that bubble of money and power and arrogance and invulnerability that surrounds them... and I feel it, I feel what he feels, as if it is being conducted through our skin, breathed in with the harsh stink of lemon. I feel it and I want it. I want to see it, at least. I want to see a moment's justice.

Draavik won't have gotten far, I think, that small practical voice inside me that I hate, that makes the others call me *Auntie* and *Grandma*. He would have spent how long in Serpentine and Jasper's office? Drinking gin with them and watching their hands flutter in apology, oh *no* had he perhaps damaged his fists on their thoughtless courtesan's face? Did that awful boy's blood stain your lovely suit? How can we make it better, Mr. Draavik?

God I hate him. I hate him.

Not justice, no. She won't mete out justice. But as close as we can get, because no one else is handing it out these days either, the so-called authorities are not for people like us except in the sense that we may sometimes be on the receiving end.

Nero smiles, seeing our faces, he is so good at that, the one who spent years reading people in a split second so he could stay alive. "Oh Win," he says sweetly, "I do abhor the use of violence."

"Well we won't tell you about it then," she says, pleased. "See if you can sleep. Work on your horrible novel. We'll be back before you know it."

"Bring some good drugs!"

Winfield smirks, and leaves the way she came in, swift and almost boneless, the flick of a snake.

When we are alone his face slams shut like a door. "God this is fucking nuts," he says. "Jewel, you're not really going out into the city with a zombie vigilante."

I look down at her dirty bare footprints on the floor, and smudge them carefully with my shoe. The cleaners will crawl around here soon enough and get the rest. "Don't say it like that."

"But you're *not* though. Not really."

"We'll be fine. And you, you heard nothing, you saw nothing. You were off your little curly-headed gourd on painkillers, and I was upset and went back to my room."

"Yes, yes you were. Needing a good cry at the death of beauty. Heartbroken at what happened to my face."

"Passive voice," I tell him as I leave. "Remember we said to watch for that. You hack."

"I'm going to write you into my book so I can kill you," he calls down the hallway.

"Yeah yeah."

8

I want to change before I join Winfield outside somewhere (but where? she didn't say, expecting me to know) but at the same time, I am seized for just a second with her madness or Nero's contrarianism, *why*, goddammit, why, if she is swanning about the place in her expensive finery, can I not do the same? Well, lots of reasons, good ones, not least that I don't have anything but expensive finery in my wardrobe, but I don't care. In my crimson gown flecked with golden ferns I go, and I tell myself that even though the colour of the silk is as loud as a shout, my passage will be entirely unheard.

Where did the spy go? I wish I knew her name. At any rate I don't spot her as I slink swiftly through the House, trying to look both distraught and busy, though of course that doesn't mean she's not around, and slip into the Long Promenade and through the door that leads down and then over and then out into the hangar, a strange great dim high-ceilinged cavern which seems to be moving restlessly all over its surface like the skin of an animal shivering in its sleep, an illusion created by dozens of gray-suited mechanics and laborers and dozens more gray-enamelled cleaners labouring along on their little treads keeping the dust off the gleaming craft, polishing even the struts of the roof.

No one looks up as I pass. We aren't forbidden from the hangar, no one can fly anything here anyway, and we've all visited now and again with a client; a stray courtesan here or there doesn't attract attention. Its main appeal is that it has a small exterior door leading to one of the lawns which the mowers use and which therefore is left unlocked on the inside, and I take this, casually, and shut it behind me with a discreet click.

The world is too big. I have been inside too long. This is not like the roof, bounded by its neat white stucco, making us safe up to chest-height, this is like... a sky, a mile of grass on either side, the trees too tall, a hopping thing that startles me for a second: a crow furricking in the turf. God what have I done, I turn and the door is locked of course, I turn back and Winfield steps out from behind one of the trembling cedars, smiling, twigs in her hair like a dryad. "I knew you'd come this way. Did anyone see you?"

"I don't think so."

"Tell me about this spy."

I talk as we go, my voice wavery, and I hate this tremolo, it shames me. Why can I not be as brave and careless as her? (Because I am alive, because I am still alive.)

The sky is slaty and still and dull, punctured by occasional agonizing stabs of light. As we head towards the wall separating us from the city I glance back at the House: a stacked white monstrosity, artfully stained to appear mottled with age rather than pollution; the saccharine prettiness of its lawns; the white-gravel path to the elaborate, insectile front doors; the bare-breasted and bare-bottomed statues littering the place; the self-conscious placement of each tree and flower. My home.

Some people, I think, some people pay so much money not even to take my clothes off and come against my thigh, but just to be here, physically here, just to breathe a moment's clean air, smell the chlorophyll.

And for a second I ache for it, to just turn and go back, I feel love, what feels like genuine love, for the white walls, the golden lights, knowing my little room is up there, a sanctuary with a lock on the door to keep out the monsters, and it overpowers my anger and it overpowers my glee and I smell something sour and terrible: fear coming out of my pores, the broken-down molecules of it, the acrid metabolites of it, so that a dog could nose me a mile away.

I say nothing, do nothing, follow Winfield's quick-moving back, the silvery silk stained and spattered like a map. I'm here now, and I must push down the fear for a little while at least to help her, if that is what I'm doing. See, I think in a vague way at the rest of the people in the House as it retreats behind us, see, I am not so old, I am not so hardened in my ways.

In fact I feel ten years old for a second. No, nine. The last year of adventures, because you become eligible for the cull at double-digits (your band goes dark that morning, you can be targeted, it's all legal, all above-board).

Nine, when you could still climb the rooftops, play pretend, form your little gangs and mobs, speak your secret language, leap and know that even a long fall could be survived, the way a spider can fall from a height. No going back from that birthday. And no going back from this. There's a gap in my schedule right now, it's true, and as such I won't be missed, but if I am late for the client that arrives at noon, that will be observed and reported. And there will be consequences.

Deal with that when it happens, I tell myself firmly. Be the sensible one later. For now, be someone else. You're always two things at once anyway. All of us are.

We find a gate in the wall, hidden behind a thick wall of ivy that shades, as designed, from black at the top through violet, red, pink, orange near where it brushes the grass. With insulting ease Win reaches through the pink and punches in a passcode and we are through, and I don't need to ask whether she has busted or zapped the exterior cameras, she moves with such confidence, as if she does this a dozen times a day.

The gate shut behind us, we trot down a long set of concrete steps slick with moss and lichen, I had forgotten how high the House was set above the city, and then we are at street level, and back in what used to be our home.

It has been long enough—let me think. Eight months? Ten? that I stop in my tracks and gape. Winfield pauses patiently while I do this, so that we do not get separated. Safety in numbers. Survival, really. I wonder if she felt like this too that first morning, sneaking out and back here.

The city, the city. I forgot all this so quickly, my mind let it evaporate... no. It was not a passive thing. I pushed it down on purpose, but kept it all. As real and solid and vivid as this, something you could touch and smell, all of these details—the signs, the snarled ivy and thorned weeds, the rat shit, broken-down buildings, trashcan fires, tilting streetlights, the city doesn't look after any of these people, the city doesn't *want* to look after them or even itself because it does not see itself as a home, not a workplace either, just where people happen to be, temporarily, making money for people who live elsewhere. Because there is nowhere else to live now but a city. Because there is nothing but cities. But in the House, you are supposed to forget about the city.

"It hasn't changed," Win says.

"No. Just us. It's all relative."

"All relative," she agrees.

We are surrounded by narrow streets and water of various depths, and I spot one of the great strange armoured indigo-coloured fish always waiting to suck down a little boat, the kids sitting on the ledges and bollards keeping one eye on it as they dangle their fishing lines in the thick water, a mudlark just down the block from us oddly familiar, was she here when I lived here? shuffling, eagle-eyed, with her long clawed tool probing into the overflow gutters alongside the canals, something about her gait I feel sure I know, and the last time, the last dozen times, I have left the walls, it has been on the arm of a client, and I saw this place, my old home, for just a split second between the wall and the copter, the wall and the hover, the wall and the car, the wall and (on at least one memorable occasion) the carriage.

"Don't freak out," Win says.

"I'm not."

"Uh huh."

My heart pounds. Can you die of this, can you die of memory? I take Winfield's hand as she pulls us out of the shadow of the wall, get it over with, people nodding to us interestedly, *It's not often*, you can hear them think, *that the little decorative songbirds hop free from their cage there... look how fast they're walking, they must have been sent out for something very important.*

"Up," she says ten or twelve blocks later, and we climb a ladder bolted to a crumbling brick building dotted in a thousand colours with the eager lichen that eats dirty air, and I feel like I am climbing into my childhood, climbing back digit by digit, job by job, and she laughs at my laughter as we surmount the roof and wind carefully between the beds of soil and plants protected by barbed wire. I remember these rooftop gardens and am secretly pleased that they have not changed; it is like seeing an old friend whose face lights up with recognition just as yours does.

The old woman in the little cinderblock watchtower at the far corner watches us cross but makes no move for her shotgun, swathed inside her tightly-wrapped tea-brown blanket, fringed tassels draped over the visible trigger. Winfield must have been here before, or maybe this is her headquarters now, and I suppose a dead-now-alive girl is no weirder than anything else you have seen if you are old enough here, and we're not a threat to the plants or to the shacks around them where people sleep.

We move to the very edge of the roof and Win removes a brick and takes out a pair of binoculars.

"I bought these in the market," she says, as it runs through its flickering, glitchy initialization. "One of a kind. Here we go." She presses a button on the side, and laughs as she peers through them. "Oh, it's too easy. It's too easy from up high. What's the saying? Is it shooting apples in a barrel?"

"Is it shooting *ducks* in a barrel?"

"I don't think so. Why would you put ducks in a barrel? Apples, at least, you can... here."

She hands me the heavy, sticky device and shows me how to focus the view. At first there is only chaos, a storm of different-coloured pixels. And then it fades to gray, and a small, dark-red clot of pixels marches confidently away from us, down the cross-street. "How did you—"

"Reprogrammed the infrared sensor to switch between heat mode and credit rating," she laughs. "It's unbearable. I had to recalibrate it a few times. Lot of hustlers out there with fake numbers."

I swing the binoculars down. In the slow stream of traffic you can see it, the artifice of Draavik's car, dinged-up with stick-on rust, dents, scratches, entire areas of paint programmed to be 'missing,' and, though I cannot hear it over the din, I bet there's a beautifully-composed and artificially-responsive engine noise. Trying to blend in. Oh no we can't let the *poors* see us can we. No, we just go in, and beat up boys, and leave, squeezing our way through this disgusting *rabble* till we reach the big clear roads where the poors cannot afford the tolls, and then home, to our ethereal mansion on the hill, propped above the layer of smog and fug like a stylite's pole in the desert, above all that, do you see, we're *above* all that...

"Oh, I hate him so much," I sigh. "I hate all of them."

"I know."

"God. So *satisfying* to say what I fucking mean sometimes."

"You should try being dead. You can say anything you want any time you want. And you don't get written up."

"Mm. Pros and cons, though, darling."

"Swings and roundabouts."

The car is moving slowly for now, but I swing up the binoculars again and widen the field of view. "The road opens up in about two... hm. Three miles."

"No, there's construction there."

"There isn't anything. Look."

She doesn't, and frowns. "Come on. Bring those."

We climb down a different ladder on the other side of the roof, scraping my palms in the rush, and jump down five or six feet into a shallow drift of muddy sand. I remember these too: meticulously scraped up by the streetcleaners and set aside for the local brickies and builders, trying to shore up the more obviously collapsing buildings where possible. Nothing goes to waste in the city.

A group of kids scatters as we approach, not afraid of us exactly but startled, I think, by unexpected novelty: two strange women, one in questionable shape, in long gowns of silver and red.

"Hey!" Win calls, the twang of her neighbourhood accent returning. "Who wants to earn a coupla stiks?"

Two boys and a girl return in curious little hops, like sparrows, the others showing nothing more than the soles of their runners. Win taps the inside of her wrist. "Two now. Three when you get back."

The taller boy shakes his head. The other, his grey t-shirt smeared with fish guts, opens his mouth and closes it again. The girl, smaller than the other two, shrugs, and taps the inside of her wrist the way you do, the return gesture, just above her wristband. The flesh where the wiring is embedded looks puffy and white, as if her hands have been soaking in the canal. How it goes. She says, "What you need, ep?"

Win gives her the stiks: a local brand, I notice with a faint, faraway pang of yearning, and flavoured. Ginger! No, we're not allowed. Let me minimize my sins, it's bad enough I'm out here in the first place.

The little girl pockets them and looks up expectantly. Win digs in her pockets for something else, a small dark disc scribbled with circuitry, and says, "Ep-ep, I need you to go put something on a car."

"A car?"

"One car. With a monster in it."

9

For the dead travel fast, she says, but we have taken too long on our mission of justice, heading to Draavik's, doing what she declared needed to be done, returning. It is twelve-fifteen, I am late, I am filthy, I am wild and roaring with exhilaration, I am much changed in ways I have not even realized, I do not wish to think of them, my hair is disarrayed from the getaway flight in our stolen hover (a fizzing heap of rubble now being disassembled by an industrious hive of pickers and their kids, the rest in a canal over in Upper Yarlen), it will take an hour to make me presentable, two to make me worth my fee, and of course I have been noticed, and Serpentine and Jasper do not even bother calling me into their office to reprimand me; they simply have one of the maids bring me a letter on a brass tray engraved with skulls and flowers.

Yesterday, I think, such an envelope would have killed me. Before even opening it I would have sobbed, pleaded innocence, found excuses, sickened myself with guilt and worry, and started planning an elaborate compensation to the client I had failed... today, I tear it open and suffer the slow revolution of my stomach, once, twice, because you do not abandon the habits of obedience and self-umbrage so easily, the owners of the House of Bicchieri are *disappointed*, they are *hurt*, they are trying to understand that perhaps I did not feel well after my friend was taken for medical care (there's that passive voice again), but the client comes first, always, the client always comes first (yes, and usually only, thank you), so they have no choice but to take a fine from the account that pays my wages, room, and board, because it's not about you, do you see, and it's not about him, it is about our *reputation*, which we need in order to keep operating, but since it is only your first major offense, we are being lenient, because we *do* care about you, we care about *all* our employees.

Bastards.

The actual number is on the back of the letter, and for a moment through my shocked and ringing ears I feel a neutral curiosity about this. I have been here for eleven years and never heard the precise amounts, we do not usually talk money, it is seen as crass, something only poor people do, won't Winfield laugh when I tell her what they have docked me...

But the number winds me like a punch and I have to look at it again when my vision returns, see where the decimal point falls.

For several minutes there is no sound anywhere but the noise of my heart, gulping and palpitating as it falls into my guts. Stop it, I say faintly. Be reasonable. Stop overreacting.

What have you done, I say, as if I have left my body, as if I am addressing this slumped sallow dirty thing clutching the pristine paper from several feet away. What have you done, you fucking fool. All this for a... for a violent lark, a prank almost.

Oh my God. Oh my God. Oh my God.

Stop it! It's just a number. It's just... it doesn't mean anything. It's just money.

No it isn't. It isn't just money. It's the food I eat the bed I sleep on the roof over my head my medication my showers my

Stop! Panicking won't do you any good.

I'll go to them, I'll tell them the truth, I'll—

Stop it.

Oh God oh God. And for a second I even think, and there's a little high giggle that certainly did not come out of my mouth, that I should kill myself, that maybe I'll come back too, like Winfield, maybe her god will speak to me... there's nothing more dangerous (the city teaches us) than someone who's got nothing left to lose.

But someone who's got nothing left to lose who is given a generous, open-ended offer to earn it all back with hard work is not dangerous at all. Is desperate, groveling, speechlessly obedient. Splayed heart and soul for inspection and approval (and money, always money).

You can take extra shifts, the letter says. Flexibility is very important to us (ha!). Immediately I start doing the calculations. I could cut out lunch and dinner, just eat breakfast (the meal that puts me the least in the hole anyway), so that's two hours back, not quite two hours... an hour and forty minutes. No more naps.

How long can you survive on two or three hours of sleep a night? Amalthea does it. Elizabeth does it. Or they say they do, I don't know. I could train myself to do it.

More than a decade and I haven't learned anything here, have I. No I haven't.

And it's all been taken away. But I could get it back.

If I just behave. If I forget everything I did today, everything that's happened, put my head down, get back in the traces, back to work. Forswear and disavow it.

Is this worth it? Worth the stunned glee in Nero's eyes when I tell him what we did, show him the video, or worth his stunned silence when I tell him what it cost me?

No, of course not, says the prim little Jewel inside my head: the pocket expert in her white lab coat, who often says sensible, data-backed things and is very good at math. Of course it's not worth it. You fucking idiot. You impulsive fucking idiot. As if you were in love and had lost all your damn sense. Aren't you ashamed of yourself?

Yes, I tell her. I am. Very. It turns out. Yes. Ashamed beyond belief.

Was it worth it? What does worth mean? says the little Winfield inside my head, a fairly new resident.

You're one to talk, I tell her. You still decked in your silk and your gold.

I take a couple of deep, heaving breaths, and gather my things, and go to see who can lend me a few credits so I can buy a hot shower. I stink of blood and canals and no one will want me. There's still much to lose, there's so much to lose. You have to choose what constitutes an acceptable loss. I can do that. I'm the fucking adult around here.

10

Weeks pass while I keep my head down. Win, meanwhile, does the opposite of whatever I am doing. The city is in uproar and she is photographed wearing a full-face mask of black that I recognize, at once, as a piece of engineered cashmere sliced from Draavik's suitjacket as we left his mansion.

She had laughed doing it, the real trophy was the video I had taken on her phone, the one we surreptitiously showed Nero in his hospital bed, but she had wanted something she could touch. Disgusting, I thought then. Worse now, I think. That bloodsoaked scrap of cloth pressed to her face the way Pederssen's hands had been, how could she stand it?

But her posture tells the true story: more than erect, actually arrogant, no more charm school 'top of the head to the heavens!' but pelvis out, a snarl behind the oval of soft black wool. Beautiful Narcissus saw his own reflection in the pool and drowned, unable to resist his loveliness. You're so beautiful, he said, and took a breath to say something else, but what he breathed in was his death.

That would never happen to Winfield. She conceals the beauty of her face. In that small and apparently utterly still mythological pool she would see only this darkness, two eyes burning behind it like coals.

The act of covering her face said something else, too; it said *See who I am*. Because we all knew it was her, and that meant the owners did too. It could not be anyone else but her. Even if she was dead.

"Those two won't do anything," Nero says when I show him the paper, folded to the photograph and stained somewhat with jam. "How can they? It's impossible. No one will believe them. They'll be put away."

"Where?"

"I don't know. Wherever they put people like them."

"The canals would be too good for them."

"Yes. Poor fish. Think of the fish, eating them. But I suppose they're used to garbage on the menu." He perspires with pain as the broken bone heals, as the nerves find new places in the crushed synthetic material to grow into; he looks unsteady, nauseated. I or a few of the others visit him daily, cajoling him to eat. I cannot really spare the time, I am working flat-out, exhausted, but somebody's got to do it. He won't eat if we don't watch.

I am angry at the thought that somewhere, Draavik's broken arms and legs must be nearly knitted back together, as good as new, maybe better than new, while he is being lavished with drugs; they have machines that do all that, robots. To the rest of the city the medicine of the rich looks like magic. I hate it. I hate him. I hated the sounds the bones made as they broke, I stumbled over the bodies of his guards and retched into one of his potted plants when Win did it. I hated his screams because they meant he lived.

Pederssen lives too and I hate him too. I am filled with so much hate sometimes that I wonder that whatever rich bastard grunts and pants above me cannot smell it coming through my skin. But maybe that's how you get rich or at least how you stay rich: you ignore that smell, which is given off by everyone around you. If you're rich you can always buy something nicer to smell.

"Her name is Georgia," Nero murmurs, and forks up a piece of ham. "Your nemesis."

"She's not my nemesis. She is, at best, a minor pain in my ass."

"Well, she's a terrible spy," he says. "She's got a big mouth. Can't shut up. Iris is looking after most of Win's jewelry now? And she says your little stool pigeon spends all her time searching Win's room for it. And asking about her. 'Oh, who was here before me? She had wonderful taste. She must have been lovely!' Bullshit. Win had the taste of a brain-damaged magpie."

I roll my eyes. The spy, unsubtle as she is, must be getting frantic now without anything new to bring to the owners. I've been a perfect straight arrow, a dead-end with a blank wall. No secret doors here, I would tell her if I confronted her.

But I am all done with confrontation and conflict. I am all done with vengeance and payback. Everything is paid back, the accounts of morality are squared away now, and I need to put my life back together after what I did. "Win won't come back here," I say. "No matter what. It's over."

"I know. She's smarter than that."

"I'll come back tonight," I say, and kiss his forehead, leaving an expensive rainbowy print. "You have to eat."

"I eat."

"Pretend you're a monster fish," I say. "Or pretend that you're an ordinary fish. Eating monsters."

"Don't patronize me, whore."

"Go on and starve then." I flounce out to his hooting laughter. These micro-performances keep us going, they always have, we all of us love the tiny one-act plays enacted over the last spoonful of jam at breakfast, a new pair of shoes, the glossy surficial frivolity of our ordinary lives. This place, the House of Bicchieri, was a restaurant once, centuries ago. Then, and I think this is important, it was a theatre.

Winfield is not play-acting though; she is doing something else, something deeper, older. A tragedy, in five acts. And she knows it, too. Out there in her shredded gown and her stolen mask.

I think of our mad rush back to the House in Draavik's stolen hover, skimming the canals, shrieking as the gelatinous water splattered up at us in slow-moving lumps, dislodging startled fish, nine-legged frogs, floating garbage, semi-sapient mats of algae. The little wooden boats dodging and rocking in our rippled wake, their curses and cheers following us because it seemed that we were persecuted and that is who and what you cheer for in the city. Freedom. The freedom to be covered with filth, and to move fast.

I think: Hamlet? Othello? Macbeth? Who are you, my strange new friend? What died, and was replaced by the words of a god?

I think: No. It doesn't matter any more.

11

One client with a two-hour appointment cancels and I find myself temporarily adrift, paid my percentage of the cancellation fee, so not technically not making money, but boneless and limp at the audacity of free time, of having money but not doing the work, not even the work of sitting in one of the stupid gazebos listening to some ass in a suit talk about his stock portfolio and smelling the lavender (and if you don't think it's work listening to a man talk, come take one of my shifts sometime).

I head out to the pool, clamber into an alligator floaty, stare up through the discreet gleam of the dome above us. Insects don't like it but birds don't seem to mind, and today there are several sparrows and one radiant starling, its natural iridescence multiplied and refracted through the coating on the plastic as if it has been dipped in oil. Where is your flock? Whoever saw a starling by itself? This is an omen, I tell myself. I'll have to ask Nero what it means.

But it is an omen, because a few minutes later Serpentine and one of her assistants, which she goes through at a rate of about four per year, enter the dome.

Serpentine claps her hands, so heavy with rings that it sounds like a drum riff. All around me damp and sleepy heads rise from lawn or water, indolent, fuzzy with pool chemicals, so that I think of bees coming out of the flowers on the lawn. "Everyone? Everyone! Special announcement!"

Here it comes. It what? I don't know. She's looking right at me, though she's not facing me: I study the sleek sunken paperwhite face, the richly leonine mass of her hair over the long embroidered caftan.

Right at me. You can tell even through the sunglasses, her gaze like two hot points of light on my skin, and I will myself to transmute into something heavy— lead, mercury, particarb, stone—and sink to the bottom of the pool. Inhale. Narcissus dead drowned turned into a flower, oops.

But I float and smile, in my white swimsuit printed with oranges and lemons. Here it comes.

"We're holding a fête!" she says, smiling broadly. What beautiful teeth she has.

It takes me a second to parse what she said, as I stared. Well, all right. A party? All right. We like parties. I do wish I had money for a new gown, new shoes, new gloves maybe (gloves are very in this season). I'm nowhere near paying back my fine though, and only just (maybe in the last day or so) at the point where I don't need to borrow money from people to eat. All this, for one strike. My first strike in eleven years. You see how they do it.

"What's the occasion, Miss Serpentine?" Georgia calls. "Have we been very good?" Several of us pucker our lips sweetly at each other: *Asskisser*. Iris chuckles and submerges to hide her laughter. The water surges around me as she swims in circles, which is another way of laughing, like a shark.

"It's Miss Aventurine now," Serpentine-now-Aventurine snaps. I sigh, and wonder if Jasper has changed his name too. She says, "It's a new occasion. Something that I think we'll make a bit of a tradition. Traditions are important, you know. Only humans have those. Not animals. So it's meaningful, developing a new one. We're calling it a Celebration of Life. And guess where it'll be held?"

Passive voice again. But even before she speaks, I know. And something hits me square in the gut, something with weight and mass that I did not think was real in the sense that it possessed those things, or real in the sense that it really existed: blasphemy. The profaning of something sacred. No, there is nothing sacred to us... *yes, there is*. There is the one thing. Of which we never speak, because it is ours, belongs to us, and someone has told her the secret, the location, maybe even (Christ!) our rituals and our... but that's why she said it. A tradition.

The spy? No, even she would not have. Would she? It is unfathomable. I feel again that thing I tried to push down: this hunger for revenge that has no single name in our language. The way it lights up every nerve ending like being struck by lightning, so that all I can think of is telling everyone else to look away, and striding over to Georgia, and holding her head underwater till she is dead.

Stop it.

Stay calm.

It is too much to hope that Aventurine will burst into flames upon stepping across the threshold, or that the long-abandoned structure will fall in on her (and Jasper too, don't forget him, they move as one, they hunt as one). Such things are for old stories. But if you were the devil, and you set foot on sacred ground... and of *course* it's not sacred, her entire body says, her smug tone as she talks. Of course it's not sacred. Nothing that belongs to *you* has any whiff of the divine. You cannot create such a thing and so it is ours to take and sully.

I have been to twenty funerals there, nineteen deaths. My friends, my enemies, my competitors, my students. People who had wept with me and eaten with me and bled with me and tried to build our little shelter against the great cold unfeeling night of money that presses down on us in this House. We have nothing to love but each other.

You cannot feel love, says the speech under Aventurine's speech. You? Not you. Not any more than an animal can.

For a second I am wild with anger and I wonder how I ever thought of self-destruction when it is so clear that it is the world that needs to be thrown off something high, and that is when I know: they are throwing a party there not just to break us and hurt us and insult us without recrimination, because that is what bullies like to do, but to lure Winfield there and trap her. The House is a cage, after all. They know about cages.

Winfield will know. That it is a trap, I mean. But sometimes what you want in the trap is worth the crunch of the iron jaws around your leg... I lie very still and dabble one hand in the water, my mind racing. Sometimes you want the bait more than you want to live.

Of course they will invite Pederssen and of course he will come. Even if he knows Win wants her revenge, he will still come. To gloat and to be invincible and untouchable: to be the new god of our church. You're allowed to hate gods, after all. Because they are allowed to smite you.

They will catch her no matter how wily she is and they will kill her again or put her away or simply take her apart, for science or for sadism, and life will go back to normal.

"Jewel!"

I shade my eyes with my hand. Aventurine is standing near the edge of the pool where I have drifted in my silent, pondering panic. My face must scream murder. I rearrange it into something obedient and pleasant. "Yes, Miss Aventurine?"

"I'm putting you in charge of the entertainments. Do let me know if you need any guidance."

"Of course. Thank you for the honour." I've done that before, there should be nothing strange in the request, nothing sinister. There are only five or six companies to call around. They send their demo troupes (singers, acrobats, contortionists, anatomists) and you pick a few acts.

But she keeps staring at me, her smile unceasing. Don't, I think. You'll ruin that expensive thread-job that smoothed out your nasolabial folds last year.

That's a lot of money. It's hard to erase the marks of human emotion. That's our money, you know. Earned on our backs. Stop staring, you gargoyle. Stop it. You know I was a friend of Win's, you think I'm in cahoots with her somehow. The escaped courtesan who crisscrosses the city on rooftops and canals, who walks underwater unafraid of drowning, who steals and lies, who rescues people, ends fights, stabs rapists, who the people love, who you hate. The shameful secret you share with her and him binding you all together. One big happy.

You know it's her. You know it's me. But you don't know what she can do now. Do you?

It doesn't matter, her smile says. Whatever she is, she will be a prisoner. And thanks to her you will be punished in whatever ways don't affect our profits. Making you clap for a dancing dog act in your sacred place would be a start. Or maybe making you beg...

"Do a good job," she says, "and maybe we can have a little chat about your... performance improvement plan. Hmm?"

Play along, she means. Dance for us and we'll throw you a coin. Aiming for your face. "That would be lovely, Miss Aventurine."

We remain silent as she leaves, the assistant tossing one last, desperate look back at us. The sun through the dome makes their shadows multifarious: like they are centipedes walking upright.

Now they will be watching me, I think, and Nero too, and a few of the others. To see how we will give Winfield this news.

But they will watch in vain. She'll find out, but we will not need to give her this information. It will escape from the House like radon and something inside Win will be set off and beep. I know it.

Somewhere across the city, she has looked up and said: *He will be there and I will kill him.*

12

"Not just him," Nero says when I come to his room the day before the party. His wing has been deemed healed, and it certainly opens and closes, and looks nice, but he winces horribly as he flexes it. "Them too. S... Aventurine and whatever the hell he's calling himself this week. Agate or whatever."

"Them? No, I don't think so."

"Yes. When have you ever known her to take half-measures? Look at what she does to people in this city who fuck people up. Look at what she did to Draavik. An eye for an eye. And then some."

"Well, yes," I say uneasily. "But that wasn't because she got carried away, darling. I was there. It was because she knew you had saved for the wings for so long. Because you had gone without."

"Nearly a year," he muses. His room is dim, fragrant, spotless; only the faux-baroque ornamentation of the moulding, and a dozen bottles of creams and unguents on his vanity, catch the light. His wallpaper is like mine, purple verging on black, with twisting, tumbling designs worked in some kind of flocked stuff. He doesn't have a window, even the tiny token one that some of us have, just an enormous blistered mirror that takes up an entire wall, its gilt frame carved with leering faces.

We sit together on his chaise, fists between our knees, hunched over as if we are in great pain. He says, "This is something else, isn't it? It's one thing to just rough people up. Hell, I've got a whole list of clients who like that kind of treatment. She could make a mint if she came back. *Get your licks from a dead gyal!* But murdering him. I don't know. I thought she'd have given up by now. When she realized he's too hard to get to."

I nod hopelessly. That is what the fête has done to me, I think: taken the last of my hope. For what? For everything. I thought I had a future once. But she will take it away if she comes. "What are we going to do?"

"What?"

"About all this. About her. Tomorrow."

He doesn't move, but I feel his dense familiar body withdraw from me anyway, retracting like the poked eye of a snail from a salty fingertip. The body produces these salts; there's nothing you can do about it even if you do not mean offense. That's the impression I get, in those few hurt seconds: that his very soul is pained, and must flee me. "If you're going to say something you'll be ashamed of later," he says evenly, "then don't say it."

"I won't then."

"Good."

He thinks I'm a coward, a traitor. He thinks I will sabotage Win's mission somehow, that I will collude with the owners to bring her down and stuff her in a cage, that I will shove Georgia aside to grovel at their feet hoping for redemption.

Do you think so little of me, I want to say, then check whether I would be ashamed of it and so fail his test: Yes. I am ashamed.

Like you're so much better than me, I want to blurt, like *you're* the one setting some kind of moral standard. You set her loose on Draavik. You did that.

Can't say that either.

So, by his metric, there's nothing left to say. I get up and go back to my own room.

13

Here is where we are expected (not even requested: *required*) to show off our wit and talent and potential. Here is where we must say to clients: We're not like those other houses. Small-h. Brothels really. With their tacky little escorts. What *you* want is a courtesan. What *you* want is to get what you pay for. Our entire demeanour must say this at all times.

I am in a couple of different kinds of pain and I conceal everything under my most dazzling and calculated act: a veteran of the house, experienced in things you've never heard of (no, I assure you, you have not), capable of astonishing feats in a one-hour session, unbelievable perversities in two. Educated, erudite, able to converse on numerous topics, offer advice, stock picks, a listening ear, as well as the warmth and softness of my plump, welcoming golden body. Eleven years, yes.

But I am in pain and the pain is an insult cutting into me like a scalpel, red-hot, even white-hot, but refusing to sear my nerve-endings shut. The bastards have drained the church and reinforced the iffy ceiling with carbon-fiber struts, cheap-looking and ugly against the ancient dignified wood, the name of the man-ufacturer clearly visible in ultra-reflective white against the gray hexagons, as if we've plastered the place with ads. They have unbolted the pews from the floor and shoved them to the periphery of the room, a jumbled mess. The altar where we place the coffin is a buffet table. All our votives and candles are gone, decades of painstaking placement and shuffling and arrangement. The small narratives we made on the walls are painted over in flat black.

The place has been profaned and every time I look around and see what they have done I feel the double-punch of *How dare they* followed by *How dare I be offended*. It's not a real church. It's not a real religion. It used to be some-thing once and then we took it over because they said we could have nothing else, nothing. I am angry and then I am angry that I am angry. And all of this I have to shove under the cool surface of my smile, and hold its head there till it stops struggling.

Nero has acquired a fan club, people cooing over and even petting him: his curls, his wings, the thick silk of his suit which is cut so closely I am not even sure he can sit down in it; he stood in the bow of the yacht on the way here.

He looks, to a trained eye, half out of his mind with insult. Like me, I think. But also like me, he knows better than to drop the act. Our sanctuary has been vi-olated, the soul driven from it, but we go on. Dancing with clients, complimenting their outfits, asking after the health of their portfolios. Feeding them little tid-bits from the buffet table, sweetly declining sips from their drinks (no one wants to hear all our alcolarms go off at the same time; the roof will collapse from the noise, reinforced or no).

Win hasn't come and it is nearly midnight, when our coaches will turn back into pumpkins, and probably the bulk of the guests will begin to trickle in. The party has been going on for hours already. Since sunset, and the slow dissipation, by agonizing increments, of the day's heat and humidity. My makeup feels like it's going to slide off my face in a single unit and plop onto the floor. Like the cream tart Samira dropped earlier, causing (forcing, really) us all to make the same joke at the same time.

I hold down a hysterical giggle and accept a waltz from a client too tall for me to even see his face in the dim light. He stinks of some metallic cologne, as if under his tux he is a robot sweating molten aluminum, and his hands are small and wet. The music, from floating speakerlights, comes down ghostly and slow, like snow rather than sound. Particle, wave. Great gusts of incense like the hot scented breath of a dragon occasionally blow in from the loaded braziers outside, meant to cut the stink of the lapping water.

We're slumming it, the guests say, and giggle in scandalized delight. Oh, *isn't it risqué*. Some of them, Agate is saying, through peals of laughter, sneak down here and throw parties after funerals. Oh, like when we have wakes, someone else says. Can you *believe* it? Aventurine says. Isn't it perfectly adorable? Monkey see, monkey do. Gales of laughter. Imagine creeping down here. Leaving the House and. When there are three enormous, lovely rec rooms to. And they can. Or they could. But instead.

Nothing is holy to you, I think, and that is all right: make it be all right within yourself. Nothing is holy to me either.

Not after going to them, and telling them everything I knew about Winfield and where she hid and hunted and swindled and traded. Not after I prostrated myself trying to bargain for her strange small reinstituted life. (Hers, I said. So it would sound less craven than mine. So I would not have to say out loud *What must I do to regain your favour and keep my job*.)

Please, I said, in the darkness of their study, surrounded by their trinkets, the fan blowing their hideous scent at me. She's made mistakes. Please go easy on her.

Jewel, we are honourable people, Aventurine said proudly, and in the circle of her voice I had heard myself included: We all, *and* you, are honourable people. We'll keep our word. And you are so worried about your friend. Well of course you are. We were nearly out of our minds with grief too. You remember that.

Well, no, I thought. I still think: No. I don't think so.

I told them she would come by water. I told them she stole hovers and boats. But I did not tell them about this church and our secret post-death necessities. That was someone else. We are all ragged with rage and insult at the blasphemy, we all feel that our insides have been torn out and picked through, to have these rich fucks dancing in our holy place, mocking our broken-down sanctuary.

I didn't have much to trade anyway, I imagine myself telling Nero defiantly, hotly, my face aflame with rectitude. I'm trying to save her. It's barely more than the papers have been saying anyway. I did nothing wrong.

There's no god that can hear us but I still think again and again as I twirl in circles, God I wish tonight were over. God please let it be over. Please in my next blink let me wake up in my room, in my own bed, on fresh sheets. No atheists in ratholes. Isn't that the saying?

Agate and Aventurine sometimes favour me with their smiles and I swing wildly between genuinely relieved pleasure, and a disgusted flinch, as if I have been threatened by a growling dog. Showing your teeth means different things at different times, I tell myself. Calm down. Nothing lasts forever. This party won't last forever. This hateful charade.

You people can't love, they said when I spoke to them in their study. Not *real* love. So it is not that you loved this place or your silly games. It's something else.

Was something else. And you'll feel whatever that is again. For something else. Later.

All right. If that's true. If. Then get through tonight.

I am handed off, smoothly stolen into someone else's arms, a gallant thief: Nero, tired and haggard under an artful coating of glitter. "God, my feet fucking hurt," he says. "Is this over yet? Have they made their point?"

"Mine too. And these are my best shoes. Iris even put foam in the back. Fuck these rich fucks."

"Ugh. Not without an appointment."

We dance through the other couples, barely moving. My back hurts too, and my neck. And my face, from smiling. I lean on his silken lapel and close my eyes for a moment, the closest thing I've felt to rest for about twenty hours. Annoyed, the collagen armature of my bra implant senses the change in position and hoiks everything up into their preprogrammed position, a twang of pain in my back where it attaches. Stay perky! Stay up! Fuck *off*. I hope no one heard the hydraulics.

With every minute that goes by we are safer and Winfield is safer. Go be a hero somewhere else, I hear Nero think. Go beat rich people up somewhere else, I think.

I don't know if I'd call it heroism. Maybe it is. I don't want to think about it. What does it mean to kill a murderer? Why does she get to be the one who does it? Maybe because she is the only one who can? Maybe being a murder victim gives her the right? This must be the first time it's ever happened. But I don't know how to make any of it sit right in my head. We were more accepting of her resurrection than her lust for vengeance, and what kind of people does that make us?

He's killed others, I'm sure he has. I have only glimpsed Pederssen a few times in person, sometimes in the paper, but if you had asked me, beforehand, whether he would be the one who caused one of our dawn funerals, I would have said yes. No hesitation.

There are no courts, there are no lawyers. Those are things we read about in books, so I know they were real at some point, but not any more. There is law but it does not apply to everyone, and that itself is enshrined in law. The law says: Only you and you. Not you. People could not fight it when it happened not merely because fighting it was outlawed but because they were too hungry and too ill and there was simply no recourse; because if you had to choose between a fight you could not win, and trying to feed yourself and your family, you made the choice. An easy one. I had done it, growing up. Most of us have.

Another yachtful of people must have arrived; I feel the room increase in density, the cross-currents change. New scents, another stifling cloud of incense billowing in as if it had an invitation too. The way a crowd is a crowd even when it is entirely silent and you're not looking at it, so that you cannot be surprised by it when you turn a corner and see it. My childhood: spent trying not to be surprised by things, and failing.

"Oh, Christ," Nero whispers into my ear. I don't need him to tell me what he's seen; the skin between my shoulderblades itches as if something is about to be driven into it. The feel of a healing implant. Something small but sinister, something that could go very wrong, kill you. I resist a powerful urge to reach up and scratch, worried for the fingertips of my borrowed lace gloves.

My stomach feels cold and heavy, sinking with a certain liquid grace, like cold water coming down from melting ice. Whatever happens next will not surprise me, I think, and then it does happen and I am not surprised.

"Oh, Mr. Pederssen! How was your trip here?" Agate cries.

"Did you enjoy the quartet? They came very highly recommended," Aventurine adds.

They think boot polish gives you magical powers and the more you lick the closer you come to god. It's not money they want. Already they are rich, by any stretch of the imagination. They want other things from him, things you cannot measure, and they want them desperately. If it were the other kind of fête they'd be fellating him right now, here in the church. Or, more realistically, getting one of us to do it. Gratis.

Nero says, "There's the bait. Look at him."

"No, I don't want to look. Just tell me."

"Well, don't then. Smug enough to make you puke onto my nice new suit. Because they helped him cover it up, they're on the same team, they're *buddies*. They're not ashamed. Why should they be? It's not like we're real people."

"Nero."

"It's not like he killed a *person*, you know, Jewel. He just busted a business asset."

"*Nero*."

"Like breaking a chair at a bar. Oh, God," he whispers in a new tone, fresh horror, "brace yourself, darling."

But I don't need to, I am already comprehensively braced, my back is ready for this, my tits are ready for this, their internal cantilever creaks and groans under the strain of how straight I am standing and how ready for the blow to come.

The owners appear as two gleaming skulls in the gloom, a brief glitter of teeth, and then I am moved bodily out of Nero's arms and placed in position to dance with Pederssen. The acrobats swoop and soar behind him, sparkling like dragonflies, like the big blue and gold ones that pick up dropped food on the canals before it can sink. I note this mechanically, wondering if I am about to drop dead, my heart is beating so fast.

Pederssen is much bigger than I remember him being and this seems relevant not merely in the sense that I feel intensely and personally and viscerally threatened, as if I have placed my hand into the jaws of a street dog, but in the sense that it forces a movie to play in my mind that I have not seen and am therefore forced to imagine: the way he held Win down with one hand and covered her face with the other until she was dead, the way it would have cost him no effort, the way merely the size of his hands and the weight of his body would have done it, the way he would have ignored her kicking and pleading and scratching and writhing until it all stopped.

His face is monstrously pleased, the expression so twisted under his blonde-and-silver hair that it looks as if it's been transplanted from another species. Some kind of bird or lizard. Blandly lipless, the effect of a smile given by the malevolent shape of the jaw. Don't talk to me, I think. I'm not responsible for what happens next if you do.

He says, "I've heard so much about you, Jewel."

"Oh, how flattering," I say automatically. Absolutely automatic: like jerking the hand back from a flame.

"I'll have to remember to book an appointment later on to find out if it's all true."

"Oh, it is true. All of it."

"You know, your owners speak very highly of you," he growls, leaning close. His breath is loaded with whiskey. Heavy enough on the smoke to be the exhalation of a dragon. He doesn't seem drunk, look drunk. My hand creaks in his. "Of your... experience. Compared to some of the other bitches. Do you find that's helpful? Hm? Experience versus youth?"

"Well, I think many people have natural talents at a young age," I say, and try to correct the high, panicked note in my voice, Winfield, he's talking about Win, they would have told him that she and I were friends, or something, what did they tell him, he knows, what does he know, does he know what he's here for? Does he know that? "But of course, training is helpful for all skills."

"They can't train you to want it. Can they. You just do on your own. That's why you do this. I know. They told me." His hand on my back moves down, squeezes a handful of flesh through my dress. I keep dancing, my face inches from his leer. "Hmm? Dripping for it. Aren't you. Not like her."

"Oh, Mr. Pederssen. You do know how to work up a girl."

His grip on my hand tightens, with both hands he is leaving bruises, his jeweled rings snagging both skin and fabric. He will draw blood soon from somewhere. A space clears around us, and I wonder about it till I realize that the others are subtly and gently and I hope unnoticeably steering their partners away from us, from the circle of contamination. The stink of murder. Nero, his curls visible above the crowd, looks at me despairingly before he is whisked away.

Under Pederssen's tuxedo jacket several weapons gleam in the low light, the glitter of metal or nanoceramic or LEDs, I am not sure, tucked into the flat silk pockets where other people might carry pills or creds. He doesn't need any of that. People of his level, people in the stratosphere of money, they carry their wealth with them in a way they never have to touch. How many bodyguards did he bring? To a party of indolent courtesans and other tuxed fucks? Two, maybe. Three. As a matter of habit, not because he fears the revenge of a dead girl. Why would he? Why would anyone? No, he is enjoying being bait that will never be touched.

My God, maybe she is not even real, maybe her resurrection is something we made up. Maybe she died and was properly interred and I have been hallucinating from grief this whole time... but if so then maybe I can say something to him. Not something cutting, hurtful. He cannot be hurt by people like me. But something. In the gloom his eyes hold a stunning amount of light: blue but an engineered blue, like a satin dress, like a sapphire. The last thing Win would have seen.

I open my mouth and we crash through the ceiling.

Not in the abstract. Not metaphorically. It's so fast that my brain races to capture and register what is happening: things in the body move at the speed of chemicals, not light.

Panic. Weightlessness. Pain. Noise. Impact. *Impact*: then the sudden absence of all these and a thin high scream, mine, and gravity reasserts itself. I crash hard, something jabbing into my leg with a pop as the skin parts, and then I am rolling uncontrollably sky-sea-roof-sky-sea-roof and falling before I can process what I glanced at for just a second and what it might mean and then I have hit the thick icy water like a slab of concrete.

Breath knocked loose and escaping in thick bubbles, I kick instinctively but is it up? Where is up? Where has up gone?

I don't have much air left. Seconds. Water opaque as paint. A void.

A second later I figure out which way is *down*, in the utter darkness: because my gown is soaked and it is pulling me at speed like something has grabbed my ankle and is swimming as hard as it can for the ocean floor.

I can't hold my breath any more.

I will not come back. Not like Winfield. Up there on the roof of the church, gar-rotting Pederssen with the line she had tethered to the ancient steeple, his fingers already whitening, her shock realizing that I had reflexively clung to him when she snatched him, that we had flown up there together for no reason other than that I am always afraid to be alone, always, three angels ascending to heaven, ha ha, and now I am sinking, dying, I open my mouth and inhale and the kicking stops like a switch has been flicked and it *burns*, how can water *burn*, I deserve this, I deserve this.

> *if a god lives here help me please help me*
> *if there is one maybe she will understand that*
> *i have always thought that the punishment for any offense should be death*
> *because i grew up seeing people die all around me in front of me i grew up thinking*
> *a mistake meant death and because it was everywhere it must be all right*
> *the grownups wouldn't let it happen if it wasn't all right to happen*
> *if there is a god help me at least tell me which way is up if there is*
> *a god do you know my friend do you know what you did to her do you*
> *it hurts it burns*

14

Light returns and I realize I am no longer in motion, perhaps have not been for some time. There is a stillness to everything, not just the negation of momentum but new inertia. My dress is soaked, ears full of a high steady tone. Light above me: not the moon but strings of coloured bulbs. Hovering? No. Tacked to the crumbling wood of some huge dark edifice.

Yes. A party. I have not gone far then, we are still at the church, I might still be alive.

I heave a dozen rattling breaths and spit and cough, and the thick rank water oozes from my mouth and nose. "Still going?" someone says near me, Nero squatting on the boardwalk next to me, flanked by two others, only half-paying attention, glancing back at the doors of the church, where people are congregating slowly, curiously, holding up gadgets or adjusting their glasses to film something within, as if they were watching a house on fire.

I croak out the obvious question.

"Not me," he says. "I didn't see who. Just look for whoever's wettest, I guess. But we'd better stay out h—Jewel, stop. Stop. Don't go in there!"

I shove him aside, clockworking back inside the church on stiff, numb legs, leaving a trail of blood behind me where the torn-up roof tore me up in turn, my chest on fire, lungs on fire, throat on fire. Am I dead? I don't know. But I'm moving. Someone catches at my trailing wrist, the strap of my gown, seeking to slow me. I slap them away without looking. From festive light into darkness, the music stopped, no one inside, the few in the doorway with me staring, solemn, unmoving.

Did I hear screaming or did I only imagine it? Regardless, it has stopped. Cables dangle from the ceiling like viscera, some containing the bound and struggling forms of the bodyguards, *She will come by sea*, I said, and she must have known I would say that, I am transparent, useless. If she asks later I will say: No, I lied to the owners with care and precision. I knew you better than that. I knew you wouldn't bother fighting his people, but would simply take him out of the place. Nobody else would have known that. Only me. I fooled them good, didn't I?

Coward, traitor.

Pederssen is motionless on a thick quilt of blood. Did she cut his throat? I can't tell in the gloom. There is a lot of blood, but he is a very big man. And it's still spreading.

No one weeps; no one speaks. Winfield, glowing as if she has doused herself in her perfume, stoops and flips open his jacket, finding things, discarding them. Each rattle sounds like a gunshot as the weapon hits the wooden floor. We few gawking witnesses flinch, wince, as if we have been shot. It is too loud for this solemnity.

Murdered him in our sacred place, how fucking dare you too. How dare you. Why did you not do it in his house. Why here, in the trap.

But she has circumvented the trap somehow; no bodyguards lunge for her, no rentacops get out their tasers and deafeners. And what are you going to do against the dead anyway. It is as if we have all agreed to this: all agreed to disarm ourselves and allow this to happen. Not justice but revenge.

One murder in here appears to be enough. She glances at Aventurine, Agate, holding something small and dark in her bloodied hands. "Outside," she says. "Now."

Pederssen croaks and gurgles and we draw back, startled, is he resurrecting too, will he try to kill her in retaliation for killing him in retaliation for killing her, who will win the prize in this tontine—he reaches into his hip pocket and we scatter in silence, flocking like starlings away from the door, the shot is dull rather than sharp, a *phut*, another, *phut phut phut* until it's gone ten times and she is hit more than once, the other projectiles, whatever they are, thudding into wet wood, pinging off carbon fiber, but she doesn't look back, continues to shepherd the owners outside, down the aisle of the church towards me, a reverse wedding, not the joining of two lives but the ending of them. I can see all of her ribs as she approaches.

My heart is stuttering, all rhythm lost. It's too much. I cough, tasting salt, motor oil, iodine, other things. If what you have done is unforgivable you may as well just keep doing unforgivable things, her posture says, hips swinging, pelvis front. If no one's going to forgive you *anyway*. You may as *well*.

This is something the old Winfield would have said, I think with a sudden twitch of pain, the pain of memory. Maybe she did say it and that's why I'm thinking it. She did something unforgivable with a client. Maybe gross, or humiliating. But then you *may as well* do it again.

"I'm sorry." She halts a few paces from where I pant and cough and drip and hold out one hand as if it'll make a difference. "I didn't know you were there. That he still had you."

"Forgiven. But Win..."

But what? Agate and Aventurine are not merely accomplices in many murders. They're practically murderers themselves. If you cover it up the murderers keep going and going and going... how many lives have they thrown away as having less worth than the lives that took them? Telling people, *It's all right if it happens at the House of Bicchieri. We'll make it all right.* How many of my friends would still be alive?

I am shivering, I probably am in shock, I don't know who pulled me out, I didn't hear the voice of a god, I wish I had seen her face, I wish she could have appeared and told me it was going to be all right. "Please don't."

"Don't what?"

"Don't... kill them too."

She stares at me, honestly baffled. A moment passes. There's not much to think about, I suppose. Not more than about a moment's worth. "Get out of the way, Jewel."

"If you do this, you're no better than them."

"Thought you might say that." She brushes past me, shoving them through the door and onto the rickety boardwalk where my wet outline still shines in the party lights like a heap of wet laundry was deposited there. "What a boring saying. When has that ever convinced anyone? In a movie, maybe. I don't *care* if I'm better than them. It's not a contest."

"Winfield!"

Nero finally manages to grab me as I follow them, the three figures receding to where the last yacht bobs prettily in the unclean water. She glances back at me only when they are cornered between the end of the boardwalk and her, holding the gun or whatever it is she took from Pederssen's jacket. It looks a bit like a gun, a tiny one.

A quick, neat death. Much nicer than hers. She is so kind, the gun seems to say. Isn't she kind?

My heart will not slow, my whole body stings as if it's full of salt, and now at last my leg has started to hurt, though I know it has been bleeding for a while. People gather around me, enemies and friends. In the dark, clouded night, everyone seems to hold their breath. Maybe they think it is part of a show, our guests. Maybe they think this is modern art. One of the entertainments I arranged.

Nero is holding my wrist, his hand icy and slick. "Stop her!" he whispers.

"You stop her!"

She's still watching us and I don't know what to say. She'll laugh at whatever it is. Whatever moral high ground I try to find. And she'll say: You only said that to try to save your fucking job. That's what you want.

And I'll have to deny that it's the case, which it isn't, mostly, but it would not be fair to say it's entirely, it's just another thing I'll have to panic about after tonight but it is by no means first in the queue. The white boat gleams like a pearl, all its lights off except the ones marking out its body to others, bright red and green.

Wait. Maybe. Wait.

She's raising the gun. They face the water, unmoving. They haven't pleaded for their lives and I think that's probably good. It wouldn't stop her. But if I. Wait. Yes and the glow of their wristband displays. For they have them too. We all do. It proves that we're people worth keeping alive. That's how it works.

"Win!"

She doesn't turn. "What?"

Too many people are looking at me. It's a show, I want to scream. It's just another kind of show. I think I was *dead* a minute ago, all right? Fuck off. Go home. All of you. All of you.

"Don't kill them. Just... take them. Across the straits. To St. Maddwell. Take the boat, and take them across. Take their bands and dump them there."

"Why should I..." But the gun falls to her side, her finger loose on the trigger. Now Aventurine does protest, an incoherent wail. She's always been a little quicker on the uptake than her husband.

Strip their rings and necklaces and earrings away, their cards, their identity, their connections, whatever prestige or power they have accumulated by throwing us to the wolves for fourteen hours a day. Their House that lets them kill us and hush it up and starve unless we fuck our way into handouts. Strip that away. Let *them* starve. Start over from the bottom. And see how it goes.

To live well, they say, is the best revenge. But if it's suffering she wants in her revenge, why not let them suffer in the way that only life can manage?

Win chuckles, turning it over in her head, admiring the logic. She can make it, I think, so that they will never be able to access what they've got here. Lock them out. And why not?

She says, "*Well.* I've always wanted a yacht."

15

I don't know if it's a victory. There's nothing in the papers (and I am eternally curious as to who hushed it up; there is nothing scandalous about attending a party held by a House, nor is there about a public murder, but I suppose I must concede that there is about getting murdered, specifically, by someone you've murdered).

No one owns up to pulling me from the water. Weeks later, when I finally pluck up the nerve to ask, Nero says only that he saw me already on the boardwalk in the commotion as about half the party fled at Win's entrance, diverting smoothly around me like water around a stone. "Maybe it was a god," I tell him. "Winfield's god."

"Maybe. Are you a saint now?"

"You wouldn't respect me if I was a saint," I tell him. "And anyway, get thee behind me." He's got his eye on a new implant, horns. The ones that light up. Modelled on something exotic and long-extinct whose name I forget—ridged, delicate, spiraling horns in the catalogue. "You'll be Satan."

"I will not."

"Yes you will. An actual Satan. Like in a medieval manuscript."

"Well then we can charge extra."

"People will not pay extra to sleep with Satan."

"Will so." He drums his fingers on the windowsill, humming. I hate that we have become the new Aventurine and Agate, but it was true, infuriatingly, pathetically, inevitably true that we did still need jobs, and the code for everyone's wristbands had to be kept valid.

I dug into the reserves as soon as Win unlocked them, and tried to fix what I could (the two were sitting on a dragon's hoard of credits, the fuckers, as we'd always suspected despite their weepy speeches about operating on the slimmest, the most monofilament-whisper of margins every quarter).

We cancelled every appointment, in essence firing our clients; we're surviving on savings now. It was terrifying but necessary, and the fear we felt assured us we were doing the right thing. And a few of them contacted us quietly afterwards, promising nothing more than financial advice. "We could live on dividends," Nero said, and I said, "Some life."

Many of our friends left too, and I gave them as much cash as I could, even the loathsome Georgia, and wept when their wristbands blinked out of our system. Iris told me it didn't mean anything certain: only that they were out of range, perhaps returned to family or friends, or had picked up another job, not that they were dead. "You're too soft for this job," she said, but would not take it when I offered it to her. "It has to be you." At least I've got a secretary, I told her, as Nero sneered at me over the intercom.

We're actually making some money, even after everything, by opening up the South and the East Walks as botanical gardens, charging a nominal entrance fee for the clean air, the stupid gazebos, the faux marble statues of fauns and nymphs, the fountains, the flowers. I suppose we'll see how it looks in the spring. But even now, with everything fading and sere, people flock to it, rub their faces on the turf, photograph the drying ferns.

Win hasn't sent word.

Maybe she did kill them. No one here is a saint. And no one wants to be here. Not even those few of us who took pride in being good at what necessity had forced us to do. But it's the world we live in. It's the only way to survive: protect what we have, hold one another close and hold one another up.

Nero turns back from the window. "Are you busy later?"

"I'm a pimp, sweethead, I'm always busy."

"You can't call yourself a pimp. You're a girl."

"Well, a madame, then. And I just run the place, I don't... look, get to the point, Satan."

"I was thinking."

"I bet."

He flaps his hand impatiently at me. "About the church."

Even now the mention of it brings a rush of blood to my face that does not resemble grief but something else. Humiliation, embarrassment. Like someone reading my diary out over a megaphone. The sensible one, the one who never rocks the boat, suddenly exposed and vulnerable. Nero nods, seeing whatever it is that confirms what he wants to do: the flush, the tears. "We should take care of it," he says.

"Do you think so? Why us?"

"I don't know. Who else?"

16

I make him wait until nearly dawn, and we sail out there unremarked, unescorted, half-expecting at any moment to see Winfield drop from the broken rafters like a silver-gowned ghost. "Like the Phantom of the Opera," Nero says when I tell him. "But no. I don't think so. She'll be happy in St. Maddwell. It's a whole different setup over there."

"Is it?"

"Different enough, I think." He narrows his eyes. "Someone's waving. Do you know them?"

"Where?" I follow the line of his arm to a distant little flat-bottomed boat, sitting high on the sluggish, oily water. Again a pale flash of palm, a glimpse of a face in their lantern. The mudlark I saw in the city, the silhouette I keep telling myself I remember. I open my mouth to deny it, but if you see someone twice, if you nod at someone, isn't that enough of a connection these days? "Yes, a bit." I wave back at her.

Wet as the church is, steeped from foundation to windows with seawater, it still burns: hotly at the top, subdued and smoky at the bottom, twisting with curious colours from the centuries of salt, lichen, moss, chemicals, pollution, everything we deposited in it, everything the world deposited on it.

We tether the boat upwind and watch, the lanterns warm and pink on our cold hands, it is not faith that is burning, it is something else, and I don't feel sad as it begins to collapse and vanish, it feels natural and good, like an animal sliding into the sea from the beach, ready to swim away into the medium it has always preferred.

What will we do for funerals now? Where will we make our secret ceremony, we outcasts from everyone else's traditions? I suppose I can ask about it when we get back, if there is somewhere we might begin to pray to a newer god, one who brings girls back from the dead to grant their greatest wish.

We hold our hands over the tiny candles and make smalltalk about the unseasonable weather as the flames begin to die down. It is supposed to snow next week. I believe it. It smells like snow.

. . . .

Premee Mohamed is a Nebula, World Fantasy, and Aurora award-winning Indo-Caribbean scientist and speculative fiction author based in Edmonton, Alberta. She has also been a finalist for the Hugo, Ignyte, Locus, British Fantasy, and Crawford awards. She is an Assistant Editor at the short fiction audio venue *Escape Pod* and in 2024, she was the writer-in-residence at the Edmonton Public Library. She is the author of the Beneath the Rising series of novels, as well as several novellas. Her short fiction has appeared in many venues and she can be found on her website at www.premeemohamed.com.

NOVELLA & NOVEL FINALISTS

THE 2021 NEBULA AWARD FOR BEST NOVELLA

And What Can We Offer You Tonight

Premee Mohamed

Fireheart Tiger

Aliette de Bodard

Fire burns bright and has a long memory...

Quiet, thoughtful princess Thanh was sent away as a hostage to the powerful far-away country of Ephteria as a child. Now she's returned to her mother's imperial court, haunted not only by memories of her first romance, but by worrying magical echoes of a fire that devastated Ephteria's royal palace.

Thanh's new role as a diplomat places her once again in the path of her first love, the powerful and magnetic Eldris of Ephteria, who knows exactly what she wants: romance from Thanh and much more from Thanh's home. Eldris won't take no for an answer, on either front. But the fire that burned down one palace is tempting Thanh with the possibility of making her own dangerous decisions.

Can Thanh find the freedom to shape her country's fate—and her own?

A Psalm for the Wild-Built

Becky Chambers

Centuries before, robots of Panga gained self-awareness, laid down their tools, wandered, en masse into the wilderness, never to be seen again. They faded into myth and urban legend.

Now the life of the tea monk who tells this story is upended by the arrival of a robot, there to honor the old promise of checking in. The robot cannot go back until the question of "what do people need?" is answered. But the answer to that question depends on who you ask, and how. They will need to ask it a lot. Chambers' series asks: in a world where people have what they want, does having more matter?

Sun-Daughters, Sea-Daughters

Aimee Ogden

One woman will travel to the stars and beyond to save her beloved in this lyrical space opera that reimagines *The Little Mermaid*.

Gene-edited human clans have scattered throughout the galaxy, adapting themselves to environments as severe as the desert and the sea. Atuale, the daughter of a Sea-Clan lord, sparked a war by choosing her land-dwelling love and rejecting her place among her people. Now her husband and his clan are dying of a virulent plague, and Atuale's sole hope for finding a cure is to travel off-planet. The one person she can turn to for help is the black-market mercenary known as the World Witch—and Atuale's former lover. Time, politics, bureaucracy, and her own conflicted desires stand between Atuale and the hope for her adopted clan.

Flowers for the Sea

Zin E. Rocklyn

We are a people who do not forget.

Survivors from a flooded kingdom struggle alone on an ark. Resources are scant, and ravenous beasts circle. Their fangs are sharp.

Among the refugees is Iraxi: ostracized, despised, and a commoner who refused a prince, she's pregnant with a child that might be more than human. Her fate may be darker and more powerful than she can imagine.

The Necessity of Stars

E. Catherine Tobler

Plagued by the creeping loss of her memory, diplomat Bréone Hemmerli continues to negotiate peace in an increasingly climate-devastated world, ensconced in the UN-owned estate Irislands alongside her longtime friend and companion Delphine.

The appearance of the alien Tura in the shadows of Bréone's garden raises new questions about the world's decline. Perhaps, together, Tura and Bréone will find a way forward... if only Bréone can remember it.

The Giants of the Violet Sea

Eugenia Triantafyllou

On the toxic planet Lethe, humans from the Mediterranean once settled after leaving Earth.

After many years away from home, Themis returns to the seaside village she fled from, to attend her brother's funeral and solve the mystery of his death. Torn between her mother's legacy as a tattooist for the dead and her own need for independence, she finds herself entangled in a conspiracy involving venomous dolphins, two conflicting cultures, and aliens with their own hidden agendas. Will Themis find her place in the small society of Tafros or will she be swallowed by her own memories and whatever killed her brother?

THE 2021 NEBULA AWARD FOR BEST NOVEL

A Master of Djinn

P. Djèlí Clark

Cairo, 1912: Though Fatma el-Sha'arawi is the youngest woman working for the Ministry of Alchemy, Enchantments and Supernatural Entities, she's certainly not a rookie, especially after preventing the destruction of the universe last summer.

So when someone murders a secret brotherhood dedicated to one of the most famous men in history, al-Jahiz, Agent Fatma is called onto the case. Al-Jahiz transformed the world 50 years ago when he opened up the veil between the magical and mundane realms, before vanishing into the unknown. This murderer claims to be al-Jahiz, returned to condemn the modern age for its social oppressions. His dangerous magical abilities instigate unrest in the streets of Cairo that threaten to spill over onto the global stage.

Alongside her Ministry colleagues and her clever girlfriend Siti, Agent Fatma must unravel the mystery behind this imposter to restore peace to the city—or face the possibility he could be exactly who he seems...

Machinehood

S.B. Divya

Welga Ramirez, executive bodyguard and ex-special forces, is about to retire early when her client is killed in front of her. It's 2095 and people don't usually die from violence. Humanity is entirely dependent on pills that not only help them stay alive, but allow them to compete with artificial intelligence in an increasingly competitive gig economy. Daily doses protect against designer diseases, flow enhances focus, zips and buffs enhance physical strength and speed, and juvers speed the healing process.

All that changes when Welga's client is killed by The Machinehood, a new and mysterious terrorist group that has simultaneously attacked several major pill funders. The Machinehood operatives seem to be part human, part machine, something the world has never seen. They issue an ultimatum: stop all pill production in one week.

Global panic ensues as pill production slows and many become ill. Thousands destroy their bots in fear of a strong AI takeover. But the US government believes the Machinehood is a cover for an old enemy. One that Welga is uniquely qualified to fight.

Welga, determined to take down the Machinehood, is pulled back into intelligence work by the government that betrayed her. But who are the Machinehood and what do they really want?

A thought-provoking novel that asks: if we won't see machines as human, will we instead see humans as machines?

Plague Birds

Jason Sanford

Glowing red lines split their faces. Shock-red hair and clothes warn people to flee their approach. They are plague birds, the powerful merging of humans and artificial intelligences who serve as judges and executioners after the collapse of civilization.

And the plague birds' judgement is swift and deadly, as Crista discovered as a child when she watched one kill her mother.

In a world of gene-modded humans constantly watched over by benevolent AIs, everyone hates and fears the plague birds. But to save her father and home village, Crista becomes the very creature she fears the most. And her first task as a plague bird is hunting down an ancient group of murderers wielding magic-like powers.

As Crista and her AI symbiote travel farther from home than she ever imagined, they are plunged into a strange world where she judges wrongdoers, befriends other outcasts, and uncovers an extremely personal conspiracy that threatens the lives of millions.

Plague Birds is a genre-bending mix of science fiction and dark fantasy and the epic story of a young woman who becomes one of the future's most hated creatures, with a killer AI bonded to her very blood.

The Unbroken
C. L. Clark

Touraine is a soldier. Stolen as a child and raised to kill and die for the empire, her only loyalty is to her fellow conscripts. But now, her company has been sent back to her homeland to stop a rebellion, and the ties of blood may be stronger than she thought.

Luca needs a turncoat. Someone desperate enough to tiptoe the bayonet's edge between treason and orders. Someone who can sway the rebels toward peace, while Luca focuses on what really matters: getting her uncle off her throne.

Through assassinations and massacres, in bedrooms and war rooms, Touraine and Luca will haggle over the price of a nation. But some things aren't for sale.

A Desolation Called Peace
Arkady Martine

A Desolation Called Peace is the spectacular space opera sequel to Arkady Martine's genre-reinventing, Hugo Award-winning debut, *A Memory Called Empire.*

An alien armada lurks on the edges of Teixcalaanli space. No one can communicate with it, no one can destroy it, and Fleet Captain Nine Hibiscus is running out of options.

In a desperate attempt at diplomacy with the mysterious invaders, the fleet captain has sent for a diplomatic envoy. Now Mahit Dzmare and Three Seagrass—still reeling from the recent upheaval in the Empire—face the impossible task of trying to communicate with a hostile entity.

Their failure will guarantee millions of deaths in an endless war. Their success might prevent Teixcalaan's destruction—and allow the empire to continue its rapacious expansion.

Or it might create something far stranger...

ANDRE NORTON NEBULA AWARD FOR MIDDLE GRADE AND YOUNG ADULT FICTION

A Snake Falls to Earth

Nina is a Lipan girl in our world. She's always felt there was something more out there. She still believes in the old stories.

Oli is a cottonmouth kid, from the land of spirits and monsters. Like all cottonmouths, he's been cast from home. He's found a new one on the banks of the bottomless lake.

Nina and Oli have no idea the other exists. But a catastrophic event on Earth, and a strange sickness that befalls Oli's best friend, will drive their worlds together in ways they haven't been in centuries. And there are some who will kill to keep them apart.

Darcie Little Badger introduced herself to the world with Elatsoe. In *A Snake Falls to Earth*, she draws on traditional Lipan Apache storytelling structure to weave another unforgettable tale of monsters, magic, and family. It is not to be missed.

Victories Greater Than Death

Tina never worries about being 'ordinary'—she doesn't have to, since she's known practically forever that she's not just Tina Mains, average teenager and beloved daughter. She's also the keeper of an interplanetary rescue beacon, and one day soon, it's going to activate, and then her dreams of saving all the worlds and adventuring among the stars will finally be possible. Tina's legacy, after all, is intergalactic—she is the hidden clone of a famed alien hero, left on Earth disguised as a human to give the universe another chance to defeat a terrible evil.

But when the beacon activates, it turns out that Tina's destiny isn't quite what she expected. Things are far more dangerous than she ever assumed. Luckily, Tina is surrounded by a crew she can trust, and her best friend Rachael, and she is still determined to save all the worlds. But first she'll have to save herself.

Thornwood

Leah Cypess

For years, Briony has lived in the shadow of her beautiful older sister, Rosalin, and the curse that has haunted her from birth—that on the day of her sixteenth birthday she would prick her finger on a spindle and cause everyone in the castle to fall into a 100-year sleep. When the day the curse is set to fall over the kingdom finally arrives, nothing—not even Briony—can stop its evil magic.

You know the story.

But here's something you don't know. When Briony finally wakes up, it's up to her to find out what's really going on, and to save her family and friends from the murderous Thornwood. But who is going to listen to her? This is a story of sisterhood, of friendship, and of the ability of even little sisters to forge their own destiny.

Redemptor

Jordan Ifueko

For the first time, an Empress Redemptor sits on Aritsar's throne. To appease the sinister spirits of the dead, Tarisai must now anoint a council of her own, coming into her full power as a Raybearer. She must then descend into the Underworld, a sacrifice to end all future atrocities.

Tarisai is determined to survive. Or at least, that's what she tells her increasingly distant circle of friends. Months into her shaky reign as empress, child spirits haunt her, demanding that she pay for past sins of the empire.

With the lives of her loved ones on the line, assassination attempts from unknown quarters, and a handsome new stranger she can't quite trust... Tarisai fears the pressure may consume her. But in this finale to the Raybearer duology, Tarisai must learn whether to die for justice...or to live for it.

Root Magic

Eden Royce

It's 1963, and things are changing for Jezebel Turner. Her beloved grandmother has just passed away. The local police deputy won't stop harassing her family. With school integration arriving in South Carolina, Jez and her twin brother, Jay, are about to begin the school year with a bunch of new kids. But the biggest change comes when Jez and Jay turn eleven—and their uncle, Doc, tells them he's going to train them in rootwork.

Jez and Jay have always been fascinated by the African American folk magic that has been the legacy of their family for generations—especially the curious potions and powders Doc and Gran would make for the people on their island. But Jez soon finds out that her family's true power goes far beyond small charms and elixirs...and not a moment too soon. Because when evil both natural and supernatural comes to show itself in town, it's going to take every bit of the magic she has inside her to see her through.

Iron Widow

Xiran Jay Zhao

The boys of Huaxia dream of pairing up with girls to pilot Chrysalises, giant transforming robots that can battle the mecha aliens that lurk beyond the Great Wall. It doesn't matter that the girls often die from the mental strain.

When 18-year-old Zetian offers herself up as a concubine-pilot, it's to assassinate the ace male pilot responsible for her sister's death. But she gets her vengeance in a way nobody expected—she kills him through the psychic link between pilots and emerges from the cockpit unscathed. She is labeled an Iron Widow, a much-feared and much-silenced kind of female pilot who can sacrifice boys to power up Chrysalises instead.

To tame her unnerving yet invaluable mental strength, she is paired up with Li Shimin, the strongest and most controversial male pilot in Huaxia. But now that Zetian has had a taste of power, she will not cower so easily. She will miss no opportunity to leverage their combined might and infamy to survive attempt after attempt on her life, until she can figure out exactly why the pilot system works in its misogynist way—and stop more girls from being sacrificed.

MULTIMEDIA AWARD FINALISTS

RAY BRADBURY NEBULA AWARD FOR OUTSTANDING DRAMATIC PRESENTATION

WINNER

WandaVision: Season 1

Peter Cameron, Mackenzie Dohr, Laura Donney, Bobak Esfarjani, Megan McDonnell, Jac Schaeffer, Cameron Squires, Gretchen Enders, and Chuck Hayward

Vision and Wanda live a normal life in Westview and conceal their superpowers. However, as decades pass by, they start doubting that everything is not what it seems. (from *Disney+*)

Loki: Season 1

Bisha K. Ali, Elissa Karasik, Eric Martin, Michael Waldron, Tom Kauffman, and Jess Dweck

The mercurial villain Loki resumes his role as the God of Mischief in a series that takes place after the events of *Avengers: Endgame*. After stealing the Tesseract, Loki comes into contact with a mysterious organization that gives him an ominous ultimatum: either fix the timeline or cease to exist completely. (from *IMDb* and *Disney+*).

What We Do in the Shadows: Season 3

Jake Bender, Zach Dunn, Shana Gohd, Sam Johnson, Chris Marcil, William Meny, Sarah Naftalis, Stefani Robinson, Marika Sawyer, Paul Simms, and Lauren Wells

A look at the lives of four vampires who've lived together for hundreds of years on Staten Island. The self-appointed leader of the group is Nandor the Relentless, a warrior and conqueror from the Ottoman Empire. Then there's the British vampire Laszlo—a bit of a rogue and a dandy and a fop, he might say. He's a lover of mischief and a soirée, but not as much as he loves seeing Nandor fail in every attempt. And then there's Nadja: the seductress, the temptress, the vampiric Bonnie to Laszlo's Clyde. Also cohabiting in the vampire household is Guillermo, Nandor's familiar; Colin Robinson, an energy vampire and day-walker of sorts—he feasts on humans, but not on their blood. (from *Rotten Tomatoes*)

Shang-Chi and the Legend of the Ten Rings

Dave Callaham, Destin Daniel Cretton, and Andrew Lanham

Marvel Studios' *Shang-Chi and The Legend of The Ten Rings* stars Simu Liu as Shang-Chi, who must confront the past he thought he left behind when he is drawn into the web of the mysterious Ten Rings organization. The film also stars Tony Leung as Wenwu, Awkwafina as Shang-Chi's friend Katy and Michelle Yeoh as Jiang Nan, as well as Fala Chen, Meng'er Zhang, Florian Munteanu and Ronny Chieng. (from *Rotten Tomatoes*)

Encanto

Charise Castro Smith, Jared Bush, Byron Howard, Jason Hand, Nancy Kruse, and Lin-Manuel Miranda

Encanto tells the tale of an extraordinary family, the Madrigals, who live hidden in the mountains of Colombia, in a magical house, in a vibrant town, in a wondrous, charmed place called an Encanto. The magic of the Encanto has blessed every child in the family with a unique gift from super strength to the power to heal—every child except one, Mirabel. But when she discovers that the magic surrounding the Encanto is in danger, Mirabel decides that she, the only ordinary Madrigal, might just be her exceptional family's last hope. (from *Disney*)

Space Sweepers

Jo Sung-hee 조성희

Chasing after space debris and faraway dreams in year 2092, four misfits unearth explosive secrets during the attempted trade of a wide-eyed humanoid. *Space Sweepers* is a 2021 South Korean space western film directed by Jo Sung-hee, starring Song Joong-ki, Kim Tae-ri, Jin Seon-kyu and Yoo Hae-jin. (from *Netflix*)

The Green Knight

David Lowery

An epic fantasy adventure based on the timeless Arthurian legend, *The Green Knight* tells the story of Sir Gawain (Dev Patel), King Arthur's reckless and headstrong nephew, who embarks on a daring quest to confront the eponymous Green Knight, a gigantic emerald-skinned stranger and tester of men. Gawain contends with ghosts, giants, thieves, and schemers in what becomes a deeper journey to define his character and prove his worth in the eyes of his family and kingdom by facing the ultimate challenger. (from *IMDb*)

GAME WRITING

Thirsty Sword Lesbians

April Kit Walsh, Dominique Dickey, Jonaya Kemper, Alexis Sara, Rae Nedjadi, and Whitney Delaglio

Thirsty Sword Lesbians battle the Lady of Chains when her enforcers march down from the frosty north. They rocket through the stars to safeguard diplomats ending a generations-old conflict. Even when swords are crossed, they seek peace with their opponent—and sometimes connect more deeply than anyone expects.

A sword duel can end in kissing, a witch can gain her power by helping others find love, and an entire campaign can be built around wandering matchmakers flying from system to system.

Thirsty Sword Lesbians is a roleplaying game for telling queer stories with friends. If you love angsty disaster lesbians with swords, you have come to the right place. (from *Goodreads*)

Coyote & Crow

Connor Alexander, William McKay, Weyodi Oldbear, Derek Pounds, Nico Albert, Riana Elliott, Diogo Nogueira, and William Thompson

Coyote & Crow is a tabletop role playing game set in an alternate future of the Americas where colonization never occurred. Instead, advanced civilizations arose over hundreds of years after a massive climate disaster changed the history of the planet. You'll play as adventurers starting out in the city of Cahokia, a bustling, diverse metropolis along the Mississippi River.

It's a world of science and spirituality where the future of technology and legends of the past will collide. Created by a team of Native Americans, this is a world where players from all backgrounds will find excitement, adventure and something new in the world of role playing. (from *Amazon*)

Granma's Hand

Balogun Ojetade

The Golden Age of Comic Books gave birth to the superhero archetype, and many well-known characters were introduced to the world. But the golden age was not so golden unless you were a white man in tights or in a big fedora with a scarf over the bottom half of your face.

Granma's Hand asks, "What if there were many Black superheroes in the early days of superheroes, but they never received the publicity or accolades they deserved due to the reluctance of the media to tell the stories about heroic Black men, women and children? Due to the oppression of racist police and politicians?

Granma's Hand explores the "Golden Age" of comics, from the 1930s through the 1950s and imagines a world in which Black heroes fight against Nazis, mad scientists, sinister cultists, the mafia, the police that terrorize Black neighborhoods, and even the media that paints a picture of Black people as ignorant, ugly, lazy, criminal and buffoonish.

Superheroes in *Granma's Hand* include hard-boiled detectives, criminals forced to become heroes to fight against an oppressive and brutal system, veterans of war, forced to keep up the fight even when they return home and brilliant gadgeteers rocketing into battle with their jet packs against bloodthirsty vampires in the Ku Klux Klan.

This book contains all you will need for adventuring in a world where your fists and wit may be all that stands between you and certain doom. *Granma's Hand* is a role-playing game of superheroes and science fantasy with a dark, gritty feel.

Wanderhome

Jay Dragon

Wanderhome is a pastoral fantasy role-playing game about traveling animal-folk, the world they inhabit, and the way the seasons change. It is a game filled with grassy fields, mossy shrines, herds of chubby bumblebees, opossums in sundresses, salamanders with suspenders, starry night skies, and the most beautiful sunsets you can imagine.

You might be a tamarin who dances with small and forgotten gods, a leporine mail carrier who relies on moths to get packages where they belong, a little lizard with a big heart and a mysterious past, or a near-endless number of other thrilling possibilities. No matter what, we're always travelers—animal-folk who go from village to village and get to see the length and breadth of all the world of Hæth. The seasons will change as we play, and we will change with them. (from *Steam*)

Wildermyth

Nate Austin, Anne Austin, and Douglas Austin

Wildermyth is a character-driven, procedurally-generated tactical RPG. Like the best tabletop roleplaying experiences, Wildermyth gives you choices and answers your every decision with consequences that drive your characters forward.

Lead a band of heroes as they grow from reluctant farmers into unique, legendary fighters. Combat unexpected threats and strange monsters across interactive battlefields. Unravel mysteries and share pensive moments in an ever-new fantasy setting that blends hard truths and sacrifice with humor and personal storytelling.

Where does your myth lead? Come help us uncover it! (from *Steam*)

ABOUT THE SCIENCE FICTION AND FANTASY WRITERS ASSOCIATION

The Science Fiction and Fantasy Writers Association, Inc. (SFWA) was founded in 1965 by the American science fiction author Damon Knight under the name Science Fiction Writers of America with a charter membership of 78 writers. Today, SFWA is home to over 2,500 authors, artists, and allied professionals worldwide, and is widely recognized as one of the most effective non-profit writers' organizations in existence.

The mission of the Science Fiction and Fantasy Writers Association includes the promotion, writing, and appreciation of science fiction, fantasy and related genres and field; informing, supporting, promoting, defending, and advocating for writers of science fiction, fantasy and related genres; and to promote and defend the interests of writers in these genres within the publishing industry. Each year, SFWA assists members in various legal disputes, administers grants to SFF community organizations and members facing medical or legal expenses, and hosts the prestigious Nebula Awards at our annual SFWA Nebula Conference.

All authors can benefit from our Information Center and well-known Writer Beware® website. Between online discussion boards, private convention suites, and a host of less formal gatherings, SFWA is a source of information, education, support, and fellowship.

SFWA Membership is open to authors, artists, editors, and other industry professionals who meet our eligibility requirements. To learn more about SFWA or to apply for membership, please visit our website, www.sfwa.org.

ABOUT THE NEBULA AWARDS®

The Nebula Awards, presented annually at the SFWA Nebula Conference, recognize the best works of science fiction and fantasy published in the United States as selected by members of the Science Fiction and Fantasy Writers Association. The first Nebula Awards were presented in 1966.

The Nebula Awards are voted on and presented by full, senior, and associate members of the Science Fiction and Fantasy Writers Association. Categories include awards for outstanding novel, novella, novelette, and short stories, as well as for game writing, the Ray Bradbury Nebula Award for Outstanding Dramatic Presentation, and the Andre Norton Nebula Award for Middle Grade and Young Adult Fiction.

SFWA also administers the Kate Wilhelm Solstice Award, the Kevin O'Donnell, Jr. Service to SFWA Award, and the Damon Knight Memorial Grand Master Award, SFWA's highest honor for lifetime achievement in writing science fiction and/or fantasy.

Over the years, the Nebula Awards banquet grew to become the SFWA Nebula Conference, one of the premier professional development conferences for speculative fiction industry professionals and people aspiring to become one. It takes place each spring. For more information on the awards and the Nebula Conference, please visit the Nebula website at nebulas.sfwa.org/nebula-conference.

www.ingramcontent.com/pod-product-compliance
Lightning Source LLC
Chambersburg PA
CBHW031440200726
48289CB00007BB/2050